PRAISE FOR
A GIRL LIKE US

"Readers will have fun... With its fast-paced, intriguing prose, this story filled with complicated family dynamics à la *Saltburn* or *Succession*, coupled with the isolation of a Ruth Ware novel or *Mexican Gothic* by Silvia Moreno-Garcia, will appeal to mystery/ thriller lovers."

—*Library Journal*

"Twisty, glamorous, and prickling with tension from the very first page, *A Girl Like Us* was everything I needed to fill the *Succession*-sized hole in my heart. The ending left me speechless, and I can't wait to see what Anna Sophia McLoughlin does next."

—Sara Ochs, author of *The Resort*

"*A Girl Like Us* is a captivating, suspenseful tale of marriage, murder, and madness. Anna Sophia McLoughlin crafts a layered, atmospheric look at celebrity, wealth, and vulnerability—and what happens when those closest to us take advantage of it. I didn't want it to end, but I desperately needed to keep reading!"

—Clémence Michallon, international
bestselling author of *The Quiet Tenant*

"A deliciously addictive page turner full of billionaires behaving badly, tantalizing secrets, and jaw-dropping reveals. Juicy as hell."

—Nadine Jolie Courtney, author

of *All-American Muslim Girl*

"Fellow elder millennials, prepare to binge *A Girl Like Us* in all its *Succession*-meets-2004 glory. From reality star to billionaire wife, Maya is dropped into her own *Inheritance Games*, and readers will devour the dark secrets and twisted lies that are as big as the bank account at stake."

—Vanessa Lillie, *USA Today*

bestselling author of *Blood Sisters*

"A delicious thriller about family secrets, old money, and the ruthless Wild West of early '00s reality stardom, *A Girl Like Us* is a crackling, perfectly paced delight. Anna Sophia McLoughlin masterfully unspools a nail-biting plot against a backdrop of old money, new fame, and the juicy secrets that undergird both."

—Jessie Gaynor, author of *The Glow*

"This one goes out to the gold diggers! Dripping with snark, jewels, and unrepentant party girls, *A Girl Like Us* is the perfect mashup of *The Inheritance Games* and *Succession*, with a dash of *Stone Cold Fox*. Pitting a scrappy TV star against her old-money in-laws, this fast-paced, sexy, serpentine mystery charts the ways money makes the world go round, pulling off the triumphant achievement of both critiquing and reveling in the pleasures of the one-percent, equal parts take-down and gossipy drama all the way until its jaw-dropping ending. Fans of rich people behaving badly will gobble this up."

—Ashley Winstead, bestselling author
of *Midnight Is the Darkest Hour*

"Smart, sly, and perfectly suited for the cultural moment. Readers will devour this thriller based around the secrets high-profile people keep…for some, to protect their wealth. For others, to survive."

—Megan Shepherd, *New York Times*
bestselling author of *Malice House*

"Anna Sophia McLoughlin's *A Girl Like Us* is the best kind of read, full of beautiful, terrible rich people, criminals and con artists and celebrities, and featuring a heroine we can all get behind. Sharp, clever, juicy, and incredibly fun, this book is one part *Inheritance Games*, one part whodunit, and every page an absolute banger. If you're looking for a great read, here it is."

—Sarah MacLean, *New York Times* bestselling author

"A glittering mix of *Knives Out*; *Girl, Interrupted*; and reality TV in the early aughts, *A Girl Like Us* is filled with secrets, intrigue, backstabbing characters, and a scrappy heroine you can't help but root for. Delicious!"

—Sara Shepard, #1 bestselling author of *Pretty Little Liars*

A GIRL LIKE US

ANNA SOPHIA
McLOUGHLIN

sourcebooks
landmark

Published by Sourcebooks Landmark, an imprint of Sourcebooks
P.O. Box 4410, Naperville, Illinois 60567-4410
(630) 961-3900
sourcebooks.com

Cataloging-in-Publication Data is on file with the Library of Congress.

Printed and bound in the United States of America.
MA 10 9 8 7 6 5 4 3 2 1

For my Maya,
the girl who introduced me to Diesel jeans and The Strokes,
goddess of estate planning,
a baddie for the ages

When consorts, concubines, and heirs
apparent have organized their cliques, they
long for the ruler's death for, unless he dies,
their position will never be really strong.

Prepare as you may against those who hate you,
calamity will come to you from those you love.

~HAN FEI TZU,
"Precautions Within the Palace"

Look at Drew Barrymore bending over
to pick up a penny from the sidewalk!

It's, like, stars, they're just like us.

~BONNIE FULLER,
EIC of *Us Weekly* (attributed)

PROLOGUE

Maya keeps waking from this awful dream, the one with the paparazzi and the kiss. Always the same details, more or less—real memories coated in the oil slick of nightmare. It first came when Maya was pregnant and recurs even now that the baby is four months old. In the dream she is single. She's in the heat flush of early fame, that era when magazines ran listicles on her romantic history and analyzed her daily caloric intake. The dream usually begins in a luxury hotel: white everything, skyscraper views, a sheet wrapped around her nakedness.

She listens while a man she doesn't think she can live without negotiates deals, barks orders at underlings, nestles her foot against his crotch. He's one of those men—when he's with you, you're the most rapturously alive you've ever been; and when he's gone, you're nothing. Desiccated, left for dead. His appetite is huge, almost legend. It scares her, but not as much as the idea of him getting bored and moving on. She lights cigarettes, drinks room service wine out of paper cups, watches every move he makes.

When he's through with calls for the day, he pulls her up, helps her step into the little black Dior dress he brought as a gift. Rips the tag off with his teeth.

In some versions of the dream, the dress is red.

In others, his lips taste like blood.

"Let's go out," he says. She protests—she smells like sex, she can't even find her underwear. He shows her his wolf's grin. "Perfect."

They're making out in the service elevator. They're running down an alley. She hears the paparazzi before she sees them. She and the man she doesn't think she can live without grab each other for a last compulsive kiss before taking off in opposite directions. They both know it's her the paps want.

In a few minutes, she's on the sidewalk and they've swarmed her.

They're asking all the questions they always ask.

They want to know who she slept with to get cast on *The Springs*. They want to know if her father is still living in a trailer, even now that she's rich and famous. Is her father a criminal, like they say; is it true he might go to prison? Who is Maya, really—that's what they're asking. A liar, a mercenary, a social climbing fake?

Or is she just a girl who wants what we all want?

Yellow cabs are honking. The sidewalk is mobbed. She darts into the slice shop on the corner. The pizza men of New York have always been kind to her. But there's no pizza man now. Behind the counter is her husband's aunt, the doyenne of a great family, the indomitable Helen Sterling. She's wearing a spangly silver evening gown and a little white paper cap, leaning over the display case to show off her taut cleavage. She has the unreal eyes of a husky, pale irises rimmed in black. "What'll you have, dear? It's on the house if you show us your new tattoo."

What tattoo? Memories are surfacing—a wild impulse, that hole in the wall parlor on Rivington, the buzz of the tattoo gun. Was she drunk, high? Was she stupid enough to ink the name of a married man on her hip?

Horrified and desperate to know, she lifts her dress, forgetting she isn't wearing anything underneath. Just black lettering, Old English script, over the skin where one day she'll have a C-section scar. The tattoo is always the same: *GOLD DIGGER.*

And that's when the flashbulbs become blinding.

PART I

1

New York City from above, with its neon neural pathways pulsing in the dark, always thrills Maya with a shiver of possibility. Through the window of the Sterling family's private jet, the city looks abstract and alive. Her shoulders are rigid from hours of travel, her skin sticky with the sheen of week-old spray tan and sea salt, but the flurry of energy below gives her a bolt of electricity. She's glad to be coming home. Manhattan, that worthy stage. Home of the great and grandiose. It's where she recovered from the lowest period of her life, where she's begun to reestablish herself.

Now she's returning, not as Maya Miller of the reality show *The Springs*, but as Maya Sterling, the wife of Colin Sterling. The mother of his child. She's made what a Victorian novel might term an *advantageous match*.

The plane's descent stirs her new husband but doesn't wake him. He's still slouched against the soft leather of the opposite seat, long limbs sprawled, extra-large Persols pushed to the bridge of his nose, his mouth hanging slightly open. Though he's six years older than Maya, Colin still has the boyishness of his Cambridge years. He's classically handsome; all the magazines think so, with his sculptural nose and easy dimples, and Maya does too. Even with those puffy semicircles under his eyes. He looks bad—but just comparatively, just bad for him.

She guesses they're both in pretty rough shape after last night.

Maya should rest too. Once they land, there will be a lot to do; she'll need her energy. But she's wide awake now, thinking about what's to come. It's 2004, the start of a new year. The year she shows the world she's capable of more than anyone's ever given her credit for.

This new role—wife of Colin Sterling of the powerful Sterling media family—comes with a higher public profile. It requires more polish, more control of her personal narrative. More secret keeping. She doesn't mind that; Maya always does well with a goal.

The family Maya just married into controls SterlingCo, one of the first global media companies. Operations in dozens of countries, a massive portfolio of cable channels, publishing houses, newspapers, magazines. A family business with extensive reach. But it isn't just their economic and political clout that inspires obeisance. Their every move is captured, analyzed, obsessed over, reproduced by cameras and journalists for the great masses of people who aspire to be just like them.

They possess an aura of royalty, and their lineage does go way back.

Or so they say. But even the Rockefellers were only a generation or two removed from hardscrabble farmers and snake oil salesmen. Maya's been around long enough to know that gentility is mostly a smoke screen for power grabs and treasure hoarding—which doesn't mean she's not susceptible to getting swept up in the spectacle.

On Maya's third date with Colin Sterling, after a late dinner at Masa, he took her to Sterling Tower. A security guard nodded them into the empty building. They tipsily roamed the dim halls, making out in the glow of museum lamps illuminating the wall displays that told SterlingCo's storied history. Black and white photos of brimmed-hat-wearing men in three-piece suits. Full-color shots of this generation of Sterlings, grinning to reveal whitened teeth, as they bring the company into the digital age. The legendary Sir Richard Sterling, Colin's grandfather, lording over one of his newsrooms. Maya knew all about Colin's legacy even before they started dating. But she didn't really understand until she was in the building. *This is real power*, Maya thought as Colin made love to her against his office window, the whole city a feast spread out below them.

It looks that way to her now too. The glittery bridges, the big dark rectangle of the park. Maya snuggles into her capacious seat, draws the cashmere blanket around her body, watches the silent glide of the landscape. She thinks about the rest of their honeymoon party, still in Mexico sweating out their tequila and lime hangovers, waiting to fly home via the more pedestrian first-class. The wedding was understated, and their trip to Puerto

Vallarta was more of a corporate retreat than a romantic getaway. A big deal was about to close, SterlingCo gobbling up a smaller Mexico-based media company, and Colin nearly had to cancel the trip until one of the PR people suggested he invite the key players along. They could spin the whole thing—the Sterlings as the kind of people who seamlessly blend family and business.

And Maya saw an opportunity to shift the media narrative on her, recast herself as one of those hypersupportive corporate wives who understands how to be flexible in service to her husband's ambitions. It was a part she was born to play. Or, anyway, there's an advantage in making it *seem* that way.

The "working honeymoon" in Mexico was carefully orchestrated by the Sterling PR team, and Maya suggested that it was a good opportunity to "reintroduce" her to the public as well. Wholesome photos of Maya, Colin, and baby Becca looking low-key and relaxed on the *Agyros*, one of the Sterlings' more "modest" yachts, will soon appear in *People*, with quotes from Maya about her nursery decorating scheme and postbaby diet and her admiration for her husband's business prowess. A dominant new narrative to distract from Maya's reputation as the sharp-tongued party girl of tabloid fame, not to mention the moneyless origin story the Sterlings, and Maya herself, want very much forgotten.

Yesterday was, in fact, spent mostly at sea, although Maya hardly felt free of her old public image. She spent a lot of it isolated on an inflatable swan raft in the *Agyros*'s infinity pool while the other women—none of them actual friends of Maya's, all of them wives of SterlingCo executives—circled like a flock of prying, highly aerobicized gulls.

The wives wore Gucci sunglasses and white bikinis and commented on how fast Maya lost the baby weight. *Just in time for the honeymoon!* they exclaimed, trying to hide their not entirely kind fascination. These were the same women who speculated on her pregnancy—on how soon after Maya and Colin started dating her bump became visible—and took bets on how long the marriage would last. They seemed to think she was doomed, or dangerous, that they'd better drag their own men away by the lapels of their Brioni suits. Stella, Linds, Cece—Maya has trouble telling them apart. They've all had the same work done with the same Park Avenue doctor. They all have that Madonna circa *Ray of Light* face: heart shaped, with tigress cheekbones.

To Maya, they seem useless. Her father taught her how to change a tire, roll a joint, and pick a lock. Skills to make sure she was never left out in the cold. Without big bank accounts and multiple assistants, these women wouldn't make it through a single day.

They turned their flashing doll eyes on Maya, asking the same invasive questions as everyone else. At once voyeuristic and condescending.

What's it like to be followed by photographers? I'd be so embarrassed *if a magazine ran a picture of* me *in my gym clothes...*

How are sales of your makeup line—that's with Kohl's, right?

Becca is such a doll—you aren't giving her formula, are you?

Maya tried to answer with sweet evasion. She reminded

herself that they're just jealous, and a part of her finds that thrilling. Her childhood was spent with her nose pressed against the glass of the haves, fueled by a consuming envy. She doesn't miss being on the other side, but she still has the drive of those early years. The want. Whether that want is a liability or an asset, she's still not sure.

What these wives were dying to figure out is how Maya Miller—a low-rent reality TV star—married into one of the wealthiest and most powerful families in the world.

How could a girl like her become a girl like *them*? Except, more famous and way richer.

It seemed to really haunt them.

They started with catty little questions—did she always *dream* of being famous? Was getting cast on a show about young people spending summers in the Hamptons—bikinis, mojitos, surfing, scheming—always meant to be a stepping stone to a lucrative public profile? Those questions evolved to: Who was better in bed—Joey or Tripp? Did she really love Tripp, or was she just using him to punish Joey? How did it feel to go from being nowhere, to being *everywhere*? Did Maya like having the cameras on her at all moments of the day?

"All moments" was a prudish euphemism, of course.

Even though it aired in 2001, her outdoor shower scene with Tripp from season three of *The Springs* was still one of the top Google hits on Maya's name until nine months ago, when she got engaged to Colin Sterling and the powers that be buried that for good.

These women wanted to know if it was all for the ratings or if it was *real*. Which is just an indirect way of suggesting that Maya's marriage isn't real, either.

As if *their* lives are real, and not curated down to their matching faces.

It's a funny thing about reality shows, though. Joey and Tripp—they *are* real people, and Maya's relationship with them did mean something. Even though much of the drama was engineered, Maya and her castmates were all using aspects of their true personalities. On *The Springs*, she was cast as the local nice girl, all legs and long dark hair. The friendly ear, the confessor. And that was fine. Until Maya realized it wasn't going to get her anywhere, and she brought out another, equally real, part of herself.

In the beginning, she'd based her persona on some advice of her father's. He grew up close with his big sister and her friends and always joked that he knew women (ignoring his romantic failures and fractured relationship with his teenaged daughter). Most women, he'd tell Maya, describe themselves as good listeners, faithful friends, generous to a fault. But in their hidden hearts, all women believe themselves born to take charge and kick ass. Tell it like it is. Transform at any moment into angels of vengeance. You could never go wrong, her dad told her, holding up that mirror to a woman—telling her you see her goodness *and* her secret, take-no-shit ambition.

For Maya, playing up those likeable, girl-next-door qualities worked, in a way. It kept her on the show. But Maya soon realized it also meant fewer lines in the final edit and thus smaller royalty checks. And that just would not do. So, she brought out that other part of herself. The girl who would voice the thing everyone was thinking but was too afraid to say. The sort of thing that might get your ponytail pulled or a drink thrown in your face. When it comes to throwing drinks in faces, though, Maya is a quick draw. Her castmates learned not to try. Eventually they started calling her "Miss Mayhem."

She's different now, of course. More evolved than she was at nineteen. At any rate, the mayhem is in check. She's an adult, a successful makeup mogul in her own right, and worthy of the attention of a man as prominent and pursued as Colin Sterling. This seems to be what riled those women the most, as if the girl who appeared on their TVs was the true Maya, and the woman she's become is the fake.

What could explain the presence of a girl like her on a yacht, in the company of her betters, except that she's a really, really good liar?

They couldn't bring themselves to ask her if she really loved Colin, though Maya wishes they had. She fantasized that, just once, they'd drop their niceness and bare their teeth.

Maya would answer truthfully, if they were brave enough to come out and ask.

Yes, she loves Colin. Who wouldn't? He's gorgeous. But it's more than that. She loves him for his quick understanding, his sense of the absurd, his ability to show her with a glance that he gets it, that they're thinking the same thing. They have that easy rapport, always did. The steady, handsome man who swats away aggressive photogs when they get too close and whose body fits so perfectly against hers when they sleep and who made every financial worry she ever had evaporate.

And sure, so what, she loves that too. If they asked, she'd tell them. Because Maya's not a fake. Shrewd, definitely. Calculating, maybe. When the producers on *The Springs* asked her if she could bring a little drama to a scene, she understood what they wanted, and delivered. She always knew what her dad meant about the secret angel of vengeance. She has chaos in her soul. The little girl with her nose against the glass and the pulsing in her throat always understood that a sure way to get on the other side was to take a crowbar and smash her way through. Shock those people on the inside eating their hundred-dollar steaks in thousand-dollar dresses. Make them see her.

Now that she's become one of them, that part of her has chilled out. She can keep the chaos down, like a coiled spring.

But sometimes she senses Miss Mayhem is still with her, prowling, a tiger in a cage.

Last night, for instance. When Colin went to party onshore with the other executives and their wives, and she begged off with a little lie. Claimed she had a headache and would rather stay behind. Once he was gone, she left the yacht on her own, heart hammering but facial expression smooth. Careful not to be followed.

The plane is descending now. Maya straightens up, tells herself not to think about last night. They've passed over the city and the suburban airfield is coming into view. In the opposite seat, her gorgeous husband smiles in his sleep. She's glad the wedding is over, the honeymoon, that they can return home and start their life together. Over the last year, she's sometimes feared the insinuations the press makes about her past will turn Colin against her. But his reaction has been the opposite. Every attack on Maya's credibility has only drawn them closer. Especially since Becca was born, the tiny person they both adore.

Of course, he doesn't know everything about Maya's past. He doesn't know about that little girl she used to be—he understands her grit, maybe, but he doesn't know all the things she did to get by.

But without her or Miss Mayhem, Maya would never have gotten here.

That little girl always found a way. She was smart. Even when she was just a kid working alongside her father's sister, cleaning houses. Those huge mansions behind hedgerows, with their long gravel drives and immense ocean views and multiple refrigerators—glowing, immaculate, stocked with neat rows of artichokes, blood oranges, burrata, caviar. She'd dust shelves and scrub toilets for her aunt, and for her father, she'd slip a necklace into her pocket, an absurdly expensive handbag into her beaten JanSport. She had a gift for sensing which of these tokens of wealth had been forgotten among too many similar items and would not be noticed missing. Her father knew how to turn these into rent, a Chinese takeout feast for the whole family, a weekend in Atlantic City. And not even the worst years—those years he gambled all his money and got sent away—could dim for Maya the thrilling memory of his proud face when she'd open her pockets, her old backpack, so he could see what she'd smuggled out. His eyes would go starry and he'd show her his cigarette-stained smile and say, "Smart girl." And she'd beam right back.

If only her father could see her now, arriving home by private jet with a million-dollar ring on her finger and a billion-dollar surname on her passport.

Daddy's little angel of vengeance.

2

The private airfield comes into view, one control tower surrounded by a vast field of deep emerald. Tonight, there appear to be an excessive number of vehicles surrounding the runway. The usual refueling truck and town cars, but other, unmarked vans too.

What's with the parade of clown cars? Maya thinks, turning to voice the question to Colin. But then a flight attendant appears with a gracious offer of Perrier and a double espresso—Maya's usual—along with a boiling hot washcloth. She cleanses her hands and downs the espresso, then pulls her cashmere throw around her body for the final descent.

As they sink earthward, Maya rests her hand on Colin's knee, watches the illuminated gray strip of the tarmac rise to meet their jet. The closer they come, the more it appears those vans are surrounding the landing strip. Waiting. Her heart rate ticks up. For a few irrational seconds, she remembers the helpless feeling in her chest the night her father was arrested. But she blinks that away. That part of her life is dead now. Maybe the jet's due for an engine repair or something.

The landing jolts Colin back to consciousness. "Christ," he mutters as they taxi. When his eyes focus on Maya, he smiles. "Was I snoring?"

Maya relaxes now that he's awake. It feels good having his watchful gaze focused upon her. Before they moved in together, she'd been afraid that the quotidian sights of domestic love would bore her, but they don't. He's usually well put together, her husband, but she likes him in his unkempt morning state too, snores and all. She likes getting to call him her *husband*. "Only a little."

The attendant appears with a chipper, "Welcome to New York, Mr. Sterling," that makes Colin wince.

He asks for a double flat white. To Maya: "I'm a pile." He pushes his head into the seat back and gives Maya his signature sheepish grin. Women all over the world swoon for that smile. Maya too. "You're good to tolerate me."

She smiles back. "I love you, baby. Doesn't mean I tolerate you, though."

He laughs. She relishes this, the ringing proof of their closeness.

Sometimes it really does amaze her that they are here, together. That everything seems to be working out. Even though she knows it's all bullshit, she's sensitive to the tabloids' salacious handwringing. The suggestion that they married too quickly, it can't last.

And it's true that they were on and off for a couple years. Since so much of their relationship was in the public eye, it thrived on the exciting surface of things. They were young when they first met, she especially so; it wasn't like either expected a long-term commitment. But when they got back together this most recent time, it felt immediately serious. So many things came naturally—he knew her drink order, her favorite songs; there was no awkwardness when they walked down the sidewalk side by side, his arm around her waist. They spent a long weekend together, and at the end of it, he said, "I want you to know you're my girl. If that's all right with you, of course." And she was surprised by the ease of her reaction—*yes, of course*, as if everything had already been agreed upon.

In those happy days, when everything felt new again, she was surprised by the thought that despite their very different backgrounds, they had a lot in common. They're both more than they seem, more than anyone gives them credit for.

And then things were moving fast. The pregnancy happened quick, a joyous surprise. Once they realized, there was so much to figure out, and they didn't even move in together until a few months before the birth. The last year had been an adrenalized rush.

But now they're here, coming down to earth, going home. Together.

The jet is slowly turning itself around and the view through her airplane window is a swirl of red and blue emergency lights. In the next cabin, baby Becca begins to cry. This makes a perverse kind of sense—Becca's wails always set off an alarm inside Maya.

Her heart rate picks up as three official-looking vans surround the landing pad.

"What's this?" Colin calls to the attendant, who hurries over with Colin's coffee. She glances through the window, sees the ominous lights. There's some delay, the attendant says, probably to do with another plane; she'll get more details. Meanwhile, on the tarmac, a woman in a navy windbreaker steps from a black Suburban and takes a long disappointed look at the airplane. The orange lights of the tarmac make her face appear stark, shadowed. Her hair is in a no-nonsense bun. She waves to the drivers of the vans, the unmarked car with the swirling light. After a few words, she walks toward the nose of the plane and disappears from Maya's view.

The baby's wails take on a skull-penetrating pitch. Maya's exhausted; she wants her own bed. Scenes from last night surface in her mind. Where she went and what she did while Colin was onshore. Even though it was convenient for him to be off partying—it allowed her to do what she had to do—she can't help a little surge of resentment now. That he should go off so easily into the world, leaving the baby with her. But maybe she's just thinking that to justify the lies she's told so soon after their vows.

It's just her past that's making her feel trapped and squirrelly, she rationalizes. Cops always remind of her dad, make her feel like they're both in trouble. But the presence of law enforcement here can't possibly have anything to do with her dad, those years she'd rather forget.

Coming off *The Springs*, she was a mess. Fame had come to her so young. She was nineteen and just out of high school when she was cast on the show. Still just a helpless ball of infantile need. The cycles of filming, publicity obligations, the paid night-club gigs, everything that came with the show, had focused her attention. Kept her in line most of the time. After all that ended, she still had access to clothes and money and parties, but nothing to sublimate her despair, to quell her appetite for more and more and more. Her life grew small: the partying and drinking, the pills. It was like she had to, in the manner of a snake, shed a layer of skin and burn it on a pyre of high-end vodka to emerge as a new grown-up person.

All the while, the little girl she used to be was on her shoulder, whispering, *You come from losers, and to losers you shall return.*

Having more of everything didn't satisfy the frightened girl Maya used to be. The one versed in coming up with a new story to tell the landlord, a more convincing promise that she'd be able to pay the rent tomorrow—Friday at the latest. Having *more* just made her vertiginously conscious of how much she could lose, how much farther she now had to fall.

But all that messiness is behind her now. She's Maya Sterling, and Maya Sterling is protected in every way possible.

A discussion up front grows noisy. The attendant and the captain are talking to someone from the ground crew. Is there an issue with the plane, with their car? Maya rarely waits for anything these days. She has lost the ability. Her therapist tells her this is a problem, and in an abstract way, Maya can see her point. But it does nothing to contain her anxiety now.

Maya moves to relieve the nanny. She wants to hold Becca, soothe her. But just as she unbuckles, a man in a black suit, mirrored aviators, with a black cord curling from behind his ear, appears in the aisle. Security—he's straight out of central casting.

He bends to Colin's ear, whispers something.

None of this settles Maya's nerves, and she moves away as quickly as she can toward the rear of the plane. Takes Becca from the nanny, cradles her, relieved to have Becca's warm body in her arms, smell her baby skin.

By the time she's returned to the front, the security guy has multiplied. Now there are five black-suit-clad men with wires in their ears. Colin glances up at Maya. His face has lost color. His hazel eyes have a strange and unfocused quality. He's usually so in control, so cognizant of those around him—of Maya and her safety and comfort. Seeing him like this, Maya can do nothing to quell a creeping sense of dread.

"Colin, what's wrong?" she asks.

But he just blinks at her, confusion in his eyes.

One of the lesser security guys comes forward, pointing to the nanny trailing behind Maya, then grabbing her bag, taking her arm, and leading her off the plane.

"Hey, what are you doing? What the hell is going on?" Maya asks, her voice rising, a vein throbbing at her temple. An image of her father, hands cuffed behind his back, flashes once again in her mind. Maya, only nine years old, frozen at the window, helpless to change the outcome.

"Ma'am," Security Guy Number One says. Then he corrects himself. "Mrs. Sterling. I apologize, but you're going to have to take a seat."

Colin glances at the guy, which infuriates Maya. He's a fucking Sterling. He should be giving the orders. The plane's engine is whirring, they're taxiing again. Maya's heart bucks. "Colin, I want to go home."

"Travis?" Colin says, asking for permission. Apparently, to Colin, this security guy is not generic. They are on a first-name basis.

Travis shakes his head. "Sir, a protocol 202 requires immediate action."

Colin nods, stands, gently pushes Maya back into her seat. He's never done anything like that before, touched her that way, not explained himself. Her mouth opens and closes, trying to form one of the thousand questions roiling in her brain. *Is the nanny being arrested? Or is it Maya the authorities are curious about?* Maya's so confused she just watches as Colin puts her seat belt on, kisses Becca's head, then sits down himself, his eyes still far away, his mouth a hard line.

When she glances out the window, she sees the fuel truck moving out of the way.

"What's a protocol 202?" Maya's pulse pounds in her ears. "Where are we going?"

"England," he replies brusquely. "When there's a death in the family everyone convenes at home in England."

"Death? Home?" The plane is accelerating again, but she still believes that if she can figure out what's happening, she can go home. To *her* home. The high-rise apartment with the big open spaces and neutral palette, with its expansive views of the city.

A GIRL LIKE US

"Colin, please tell me what is happening. Right now. Are we going to a funeral? I'll need clothes."

Travis has buckled himself into the jump seat by the entrance to their cabin.

"Don't worry about that. We'll figure it out when we get to Silver House."

Silver House. The grand Sterling estate.

The situation is absurd—the ordinary girl she used to be can see that. Properties with names, the fleet of personnel who've appeared at the first sign of trouble, as though Sterling is a realm unto itself, a kingdom with a private army that rises to meet any peril.

But the Sterlings *are* a kind of kingdom, Maya knows—and the bulldozing efficiency of their retinue is unassailable.

She murmurs, "All I have is strappy sandals and resort wear..."

"There's no time," Colin tells Maya, forehead creasing, as the plane lifts off. He glances from her to Travis, as though calculating what he needs to tell her, and what he'd better not. "Protocol 202, Maya—it means there's been a murder."

Her stomach lifts and they're in the air again. Not just a death. *A murder.* The word tightens her chest, though her mind can't quite hold it. This time, she has no view of the city as the plane ascends eastward over the Atlantic.

———

As the plane levels out, Maya, her expression insistent, wills Colin to lift his gaze and meet hers.

"Colin, who—"

But before Maya can get the question out, Travis supplies the answer from across the cabin: "Arianna Sterling." He pronounces the name like a courtier, lowering his head. "The heiress is dead."

Maya knows most of the Sterling family names by heart, knew them even before she met Colin. Then, during wedding preparations, she saw endless lists of Sterling associates and relatives. In the end, they only invited a handful, and only Gigi, Colin's sister, came.

In all the wedding drama, a cousin Arianna was surely mentioned, but Maya can't remember. Neither her presence, nor the reason for her absence, had seemed important. Yet hers was clearly a name Maya should have memorized.

She's *the* Sterling heiress.

A new fear rips through Maya. *What does that even mean? And why didn't she know about* the *heiress sooner?*

Maya's understanding had been that the whole Sterling family shared in the essentially limitless fortune amassed by their forefathers. The business, the multiple estates, including the crown jewel they're now apparently hurtling toward, the wealth, everything. And yet Colin and Travis are speaking of this Arianna as if she's somehow above the rest.

Travis goes on: "A team is assembling at Sterling Park to work out the strategy."

Maya squeezes her eyes closed at the absurdity. Maybe it's the impending agony of a mezcal hangover, maybe it's the whole "protocol 202" thing, but she suddenly feels on the brink of laughter. She manages to tamp it down but can't control a small smirk from twisting her lips.

Colins sees it. He gives an imperceptible shake of the head—this is serious.

Maya nods, recalibrates. "I'm sorry, but… Who is Arianna? Why do I know nothing about her?"

"Arianna is—was—my cousin." When Colin meets Maya's eye, she can see that despite his shock, he's not entirely surprised. "Uncle Harry's daughter. We haven't seen each other in years. Harry is—odd. My father's younger brother. There's been some acrimony about—well—money. Harry was Grandfather's favorite, and the way the Sterling trust is set up, the lion's share of the control goes to one heir, the theory being that too many would dilute the empire. That one is the most powerful. When Grandfather died, his controlling shares of the company passed to Harry—bypassing Daddy and Aunt Helen. Harry, in turn, set it up so Arianna would be the one to inherit." Colin runs a hand through his hair. "Things were…complicated between our families. I really didn't have any kind of relationship with Arianna until after my parents died. And even then, even when she was around, she was hard to really know. For a time, we only saw her at Christmas—and then we stopped seeing her entirely. She was struggling, that much was obvious. Then she sort of disappeared—I don't know where she lived or how she spent her time. And now…" He shakes his head in sorrowful confusion, turning his attention toward Travis. "What happened?"

The flight attendant appears, bearing a tray of tea and coffee.

Travis waits for her to retreat, then answers at a businesslike clip. "Arianna was found this morning, in an apartment in Mexico.."

At this, Maya's stomach twists. Below them is a black ocean, roughed by night wind. Her mind flashes back to last night, that trip in the water taxi, leaving the safety of the *Agyros* behind.

"We were just in Mexico," Colin says unnecessarily.

Travis places a cough into his fist. "It happened in Puerto Vallarta. She was found in a high-rise called the Mismaloya."

"Did she live there, in Mexico?" Maya sounds strange to herself—her voice small.

Colin doesn't seem to have heard her. "Are we in danger?"

"We don't know who killed her, or why. At present, all Sterling family members are considered at-risk targets."

Colin's brows tense. "Not a suicide?"

"No. Obvious forced entry to the premises. Signs of struggle and strangulation, though she died from a head wound. She fought back. We've initiated a dragnet to find Arianna's attacker. The FBI and Mexico's intelligence agencies are putting every resource behind the search, with our team and Interpol contacts coordinating."

"What was Arianna doing in Mexico—so close to where we were?" Maya presses again.

"That's what we're trying to figure out," Travis says. "It's possible it's just a coincidence. But we can't be sure. Maybe she knew about your wedding celebrations."

"And wanted to make a surprise appearance?" Colin glances off, exhales derisively though his nostrils. "Not very likely."

Travis continues, not registering Colin's tone. "We have to do a thorough investigation, make sure this isn't part of something bigger. Colin, have you received any threatening messages? Anything happen lately that we should be looking into?"

Colin takes a sip of his coffee, puts the cup back down on the tray disgustedly, as if the beautiful silver coffee service is gas station decaf. "Take that away," he says, waving at the attendant hovering. "Get me a real drink." Maya flinches. It's one of her husband's few unattractive characteristics—stress brings out his entitlement. Makes it obvious he grew up never thinking about the people who served him, their inner lives. To Travis, he says: "To answer your question, no. No threats, no strange communications."

"And you, Mrs. Sterling?"

Maya swallows effortfully. She draws her eyebrows together, trying to appear only confused, concerned, and hoping the vein she feels pulsing at her temple—the one that often emerges when she lies—isn't visible. She shakes her head.

Travis moves on. "The fact that you were in Mexico, in the same city when it happened—it's a complication."

"Christ," Colin mutters.

"Of course you were with a large group of Sterling people who will vouch for you. And I'm told paparazzi followed you throughout the night, during the window in which the murder occurred, so there should be no problem establishing that this is nothing but a terrible coincidence. However—"

Maya closes her eyes. Travis hasn't said anything accusatory, and she knows she doesn't have anything to do with this Arianna person. Or a murder. Yet she can't help feeling she's under suspicion. Is everything going to be scrutinized now? Are they going to find out where she went last night?

When she opens her eyes, Colin is staring at her. Is he thinking about last night too, wondering what she was up to while he and his friends were carousing through the streets of Puerto Vallarta?

Travis's eyes follow Colin's gaze, fall on Maya.

"However *what*?" she asks, drawing herself up, issuing every word clipped, forceful, the voice of a woman not to be fucked with. Is he going to point out that Maya isn't in any of those paparazzi shots last night, because she wasn't at her husband's side?

Travis's Adam's apple moves under his collar. "We can't rule out that the killer had intentions toward you three as well."

So she's not an object of suspicion, just one of concern. A queasy relief floods Maya at this objectively terrible news. She pulls her cashmere protectively over Becca, still asleep in her arms. She really wants all of this not to be happening. "Now *I* need a drink before I have to deal with all this Sterling family bullshit."

Travis's brow lifts in surprise. Colin flinches. In their normal life, he can acknowledge that the vast, self-serious family operation is a bit much. In fact, he's always found her honesty refreshing. They've even sometimes laughed at Sterling pretensions. Does he find it offensive now?

"Okay," Colin says, obviously sensing that Maya's at her

limit. He signals to the attendant to fetch Maya a drink as well and says to Travis: "Let's take a beat, okay? We have plenty of time. It's a long flight."

Not long enough, Maya thinks. Though she doesn't particularly want to be in this plane any longer, nor is she in any hurry to get to their destination. Sterling Park. Where the entire family will be waiting.

————

While Maya enjoys the advantages of being a member of the Sterling family, there are aspects of the role she simply has no interest in. She obviously loves having next season's clothes sent over by the best designers, automatically receiving invitations to the most prestigious galas, not to mention the widening gulf between her present reality and her past life. But she's never relished the hothouse of their London operation, being part of that whole show. Until this moment, she thought she'd have the best of both worlds. She'd live in New York, with a new, fancy name on all her credit cards, a doting, ambitious husband on her arm—a player in the family firm but far from the intensity of the *actual* family, all the pomp and circumstance of Sterlingland.

Now Maya will have to perform for them. The Sterling family, with their exquisite taste and worldly knowledge and sky-high expectations. All this time in the air has made her hands swell, and she's conscious of her new wedding ring tightening around her fluid-filled finger.

It's wrong to think this way, she knows. Right now, she should feel only sorrow over this Arianna, Colin's murdered cousin. She should be supportive, ready to play the dutiful wife in the family pageant, ready to do whatever Colin needs. But Travis unnerves her, and now he and Colin are huddling over by the jump seats, carrying on the discussion of the crisis privately, and what Maya mostly feels is watched.

Maybe this really is just a "terrible coincidence," that a murder occurred in the same city, around the same time Maya slipped away, telling no one when she left. Or what happened when she returned.

No one noticed her last night as she stood on the *Agyros*'s deck watching the speedboat full of SterlingCo executives and their wives travel out of sight, she's sure of that. Once they were gone, Maya pulled her RAZR phone from the back pocket of her cutoffs and flipped it open to check the address one more time before she herself went ashore.

The message, from a blocked number: *6pm, Iguana Bar, 21 Calle Obredor.*

Sneaking around had made her anxious, but it thrilled her a little too. Miss Mayhem stepping out in the world, relishing the humid heat, the bustling, anonymous streets. Just to be out in the world alone, no one knowing where she'd gone. It reminded her of times with her dad, driving away from the pawn shop with fat wallets, high on the latest grift.

But she hasn't gotten away with anything this time, Maya reminds herself as she adjusts Becca on her lap, as she sips her drink and watches Colin confer with Travis, wonders what they're saying.

Still. Secrets beget lies, and lies beget more lies—her little venture last night is forcing more dissembling now.

Even in the supreme comfort and carefully maintained climate of the private jet, Maya's palms have begun to sweat.

She tries to think—did anyone see her, walking through Puerto Vallarta at dusk, asking for directions? She'd worn a large hat and plain denim cutoffs. Did the bartender take any special note of her? She doesn't think so—Spanish was Maya's mother's first language, and Maya speaks it without an accent.

No. Nobody knows where she went.

On the far side of the cabin, Colin and Travis lean toward each other. Maya watches them, trying to read Colin's body language. She should have played it cooler, learned everything Travis knew—heard everything he's telling Colin now.

Colin glances her way. His expression is hard to read. Is he annoyed that she cut off Travis's inquiry with her rude comment about the Sterling family or just tired and worried and not really thinking about her at all?

She kisses Becca's head, strokes her back. She considers going over to him, asking how it's going, if she can help him talk anything through. That's how they are in New York—they work out their crises together—everything from a misremembered reservation time to a big inventory fuckup at her company. But she's rooted to her seat, afraid to close the distance between them. Last night stirred up old feelings. Fears and longings she believed long buried. She worries she might betray herself somehow, that her insides are too volatile. Not just because she feels guilty about lying, she realizes.

There was a death in the family. A murder. When there's a murder, everyone needs an alibi, and Maya doesn't have one.

3

When she was a little girl, Maya saw images of Sterling Park in a months-old issue of *Vanity Fair* that she found in one of the homes her aunt Rebecca cleaned. She loved those fairy-tale photo spreads of great houses, but the one about the Sterling property had a special allure. The English gardens and regal receiving rooms stirred her romantic imagination, and she couldn't help but fantasize about her own entry into the epic ballroom, with a sweep of skirts and on the arm of someone tall, handsome, and titled. Such fantasies seem silly, now. During the plane's descent, she caught a glimpse of the grounds from above, immaculately kept, even in winter. Hedges demarcating gardens, paths that connect two-story stone buildings to the great crenellated colossus at the center of the property. A greenhouse, a hedge labyrinth, stables, tennis courts, guard towers. The property projects the kind of wealth and power that requires countless generations to amass. The magazine spread could never have captured the spectacular size of the place, nor its ancient guardedness.

Maya holds tight to Becca, wrapping them both in a thick tartan blanket as the convoy of Land Rovers traverses the icy, rutted road. Austere afternoon light falls on rocky hills, cut by a glistening river at their sides.

Beyond that: a forest, misty and dark.

Maya nestles closer to Colin in the back seat.

In New York, Maya and Colin present as a media power couple. If not equals, their status is now close enough. Even before they married, they already went to the same restaurants— the Odeon, Blue Ribbon, Lupa. Together they summered in Shelter Island, skied in Park City. But the reassuring thoughts of their luxurious normal evaporate as the Land Rover carrying them to Sterling Park accelerates over a rise and the *castle* that is Colin's ancestral home comes into view.

"You okay, babe?" Colin asks, cutting into her ruminations. He was tense and quiet for much of the flight, and he's been struggling with his BlackBerry since they landed. But he softens now, sensing her unease.

Maya nuzzles Becca's tiny nose, presses her more closely to her chest. She answers truthfully. "Not really."

Colin gives up on finding a signal and puts his device away. "What's wrong?"

Maya can't exactly tell him, *I snuck off the yacht in Mexico and met up with someone who could destroy our marriage on the same night your cousin was fucking murdered.* Instead she gestures toward the massive estate they're approaching. He must understand how intimidating that part is, anyway.

36

"Don't worry, they'll like you," Colin says, giving her knee a squeeze. "Just be yourself."

She manages not to roll her eyes. Maya's life experience has told her that *just be yourself* is rarely good advice. "You act like this is your normal trip home to meet the in-laws…"

Colin smiles ruefully and pulls Maya into the nook of his arm. "Pretty wild circumstances for your first visit to the family pile. It's nervy-making, I know. But it'll be fine, I promise, I'll take care of you."

"I just don't know why we had to rush here—I mean, you never even mentioned Arianna until now."

"Yes, I get how it seems that way." Colin sighs, kisses Maya's forehead. "You have to understand, Arianna—her father, Harry— that's a part of the family none of us were close to. Harry has lived like a recluse for years, and Arianna… Where do I begin? She was a troubled girl. Kept alone at Sterling Park for years, just her and Harry."

"Like in a fairy tale," Maya says, as the convoy enters Sterling Park through a massive modern steel gate inserted in the old stone ramparts. Maya notices that, way up on the medieval walkway that surrounds the property, there's a security guard in a black jacket and black balaclava, rifle slung over his shoulder. She can make out several more in the distance, lining the wall like toy soldiers along a child's castle.

"A pretty dark fairy tale if you ask me," Colin says. "Harry is… How do I explain? He was actually the *youngest* of Grandfather's children. They say Harry was very charming as a young man, that he had the golden touch, though I can't remember that version of him. The rules of inheritance were still quite Victorian in Richard's generation—control of the family fortune and businesses was to pass to the oldest son. That would have been my father, except Grandfather favored Harry, and made him heir. A lot of bad blood over that, as you can imagine."

"I can," Maya says. The youngest, chosen child granted all the power and control. The older siblings driven mad with jealousy. It's like something out of a Shakespeare play. She's read them all—the tragedies, anyway. Pilfered them one by one from the well-stocked library of a mansion Aunt Rebecca cleaned every Sunday. They were beautiful, with gold leaf–edged pages and marbled covers, but her father said they weren't worth anything; she might as well keep them.

"Anyway," Colin goes on, "Harry only made the tensions worse with Dad and Aunt Helen. He began to act paranoid, thought everyone was against him in the family, which they probably were, in a way. Then the attack happened—"

Maya glances at Colin, thinking of the helicopter that took his parents' lives when he was a teenager (a story he told her when they first got serious). Of the heiress now dead in Mexico. Of the threats growing around her and her little family. "What attack?"

"Oh, it was a—nobody knows. An accident, or a targeted thing. This horrible fire that killed one of Harry's best friends in the '80s. Harry always thought it might have been meant for him—a case of mistaken identity—because it happened at one of his favorite places, a Sterling family property in Seychelles where he spent a great deal of time. Arson *was* suspected, at some point anyway, but the authorities concluded it was an accident."

"Why haven't I heard about any of this before?" she asks as the Land Rover follows the private road through a copse of trees toward Silver House, the property's crown jewel, its wings forming a goalpost shape around a paved courtyard.

"I don't know if the attack really *was* meant to kill Harry, kill anybody for that matter—that was just his theory. My uncle is, you have to understand, extremely paranoid. I mean, it was a time of unrest, in a very poor country. If there *was* arson, and that's a very big if, the arsonist might not've even known his target or planned his attack. What's important is that it was the beginning of Harry's first reclusive period. He holed up at Sterling Park with Arianna, who was still quite young at the time. He ran the business on his own; almost no one was allowed here, not even us. It was eight years or so of that. Just the two of them, isolated."

Maya nods, thinking of her father—the years after her mother left and it felt like it was the two of them against the world.

"What about Arianna's mom?"

"Died in childbirth," Colin answers, as the Land Rover goes over another bump. "Poor thing. After Mum and Dad died in '93, Helen insisted we all spend more time as a family. We were so shattered, Gigi and I, and Gigi was still in school then. We started having holidays here again. But..."

"But what?" The Land Rover is slowing. A light rain is

starting to fall, the sky gone moody, making it impossible to tell whether it's still day or evening.

Colin shrugs. "Just…the damage had been done—Arianna was so strange, after all those years with no friends, no contact with the outside world. Needy, erratic. Then she discovered partying, and it was downhill fast. The tabloids became interested in her, and she was in and out of addiction treatment for years. Then there was a terrible row with Harry. And after that she just—disappeared."

There's something disquietingly familiar in this story, something that stirs memories of Maya's own downhill slide, and Maya hears herself ask, in a faraway voice, "What do you mean disappeared?"

"Well, she stopped getting into newsworthy trouble. But also, we stopped hearing from her. I confess it was a relief—she was always causing problems, making scenes. It was becoming a liability for the company; we were all on high alert about that. Personally, it was exhausting. So, I suppose I didn't question why she wasn't around anymore. Inasmuch as I thought about it, I thought she probably was in a facility… That she went to dry out and decided it was just easier to stay." A sigh travels the whole length of Colin's body, and Maya, tucked against him, feels it too.

"And now she's gone for good. It's terrible. I have to warn you, though, the family is going to be talking about the business implications—how it affects the brand." Despite the heaviness of the story, Maya feels calmer now that Colin is really talking, giving her the background. It reminds her of their life together in New York—the private moments before a big event, when they hold hands and strategize. Who they need to connect with, who to steer clear of, the politics of their evening.

"That's just the way it is."

Maya reaches her free hand to Colin's, holds it tight as the car crunches to a halt. She watches out the window as the vehicles pull up in formation around an empty fountain at the front entrance. Numerous servants, almost all in mourning black, jolt into action.

As they prepare to exit the car, Maya takes a deep breath, ready to play her role. To be the sympathetic wife in this hour of need. By the time they leave Sterling Park, she'll seem as much a part of the family as any of them—an essential partner, an accepted new member of the club. Maya Sterling, the girl with nothing to hide.

Various staff members in black livery swarm to the luggage as Maya and Colin exit the car, and a woman in a brown cloth coat and white gloves takes Becca from Maya's arms as though she were another piece of baggage. Maya glances back at Colin with concern and he nods reassuringly. "Don't worry, any nanny employed at Sterling Park is top-notch," he murmurs.

They continue forward, through the two columns of servants. Colin tips his head in recognition at the staff members he must know from long ago and deftly negotiates the paving stones, holding Maya by the elbow as they enter the front doors. A massive entry hall greets them, illuminated by a series of chandeliers, tiers and tiers of dangling gilt and cut glass. On either end of the long hall, two marble stairways curve upward to higher floors, to fineries unknown. Maya realizes she's holding her breath, reminds herself to exhale.

A butler addresses Colin as soon as they've stepped into the grand foyer. "My deepest condolences, Mr. Sterling."

"Thank you, Barrow." For a moment, Colin looks like he might go in for a hug, American style, but Barrow takes a step backward and solemnly lowers his head. Colin follows suit, effecting a formality that is unusual for him. To Maya, Colin says, "Barrow has run Sterling Park for as long as I can remember."

Maya moves to introduce herself, but seizes up at the sound of a heavy door hitting a well-built wall. The staid ambience is broken. A young woman prances forward loudly, caroling, "Hello, you gorgeous bitch!"

Maya puts on a smile, thinking: *Ready or not.*

———

Regina Sterling, known to her friends and the tabloids as Gigi, is a shocking contrast to the elegant surroundings. She's wearing a mandarin Hervé Léger bandage dress, an olive Barbour jacket, and indifferently laced Timbs. Her dark roots are showing, and her long dirty-blond hair is baroquely augmented with extensions. Maya retracts. Gigi's familiar manner is at once reassuring and unnerving—Maya is relieved to be welcomed, but unsure if Gigi is the right element to be associated with. Something about her kohl-smeared eyes and bony limbs feels off here in the *castle*, and Colin's younger sister has a bit of a reputation as the messy one in the family. In any case, before Maya can decide on the best course of action, Gigi's on her, kissing either cheek and forcing a gin and tonic into Maya's hand.

"Just in time for family cocktails! Sorry I didn't fix you one, Colin; you'll have to fend for yourself."

"That's to be expected," he says with weary affection. He puts a warm grip on his sister's shoulder and for a moment the somberness of the whole scene lifts.

"Don't be like that, I've been *dying* for your arrival. I literally yelped when they said your plane was down. Everyone is so hideously serious right now. They're all assembled, waiting in the salon. But of course *you're* used to us. It's dear Maya who's going to need a little boost before the show."

Gigi's only a year younger than Maya, so it's assumed they get along. Which, in fact, they do, more or less. Gigi has, unlike the rest of the Sterlings, "made the effort," according to the celebrity weekly *On Dit*. Although Maya suspects that Gigi was the source for that quote, she also knows it's true. Gigi is the only member of Colin's family who hasn't avoided Maya like some untouchable arriviste throughout her and Colin's courtship.

"Gigi," Maya says. It's the best greeting she can manage. She sniffs the gin and tonic. "What time is it?"

"I just told you. It's cocktail hour, dear. Everyone's in the salon. We'd better go in." Gigi tenses her mouth around her charming underbite and gestures vaguely to the grand set of doors through which she emerged. "In case you couldn't tell, I only arrived a little ahead of you. They dragged me away from the most fabulous party in Ibiza. Haven't slept much."

"Me neither," Maya admits. "I feel like shit."

"You are a little heroin chic around the eyes, doll." She collects Maya's lustrous black mane in her hands, pets it. "But this hair! *Such* pretty hair. I would kill for hair this thick. Anyway, I'm *so* glad you're here." She drops the hair, drops her voice, leans in conspiratorially. "What a nightmare. Honestly the whole lot is flapping about like chickens in a foxhole. And I mean, poor Ari, obviously. Helen is beside herself."

Maya glances around, wondering if Helen is close by. Watching, judging. Though Maya's only met Helen, Colin's aunt, once, she's still a little traumatized by the cool appraisal of her steely eyes, the unease of being in her presence. But Helen is currently nowhere to be seen as Maya turns over Gigi's words. *Poor Ari* as though Arianna has suffered a humiliating public wardrobe malfunction. Not *died*.

Maya feels on display and unable to summon the right response. She shoots a look at Colin, but he's deep in conversation with Barrow, ignoring his sister and unavailable to guide his wife through the unpredictable currents of the Sterling psyche. She's beginning to see the complexity of his responsibilities here. Colin is acting more formal, more remote already. "It's terrible," Maya says to Gigi, which seems safely inarguable.

The sympathetic note doesn't register with Gigi, who seems

distracted, pulling at her manicure. "Drink up, gorgeous. Trust me. You'll want a pick-me-up before you meet the in-laws."

Maya does as told. The quinine-lime combo has a reassuringly medicinal quality. Gigi's right, she needs to take the edge off. Get her game face on. Get ready to perform bereavement over someone she didn't know existed until yesterday. Her gaze flicks to the high buttressed ceilings as she thinks about what Colin told her on the way over. Arianna grew up in this palatial home, a luxurious and isolated childhood. Like Versailles— gilded, reflective, thoroughly disorienting. As a child, Maya dreamed of living in a place like this, but now that she's here, it seems sort of crushing.

She takes another sip to push away that thought. "Colin, where—" She cuts off when she notices that Colin is gone, slipped away without her notice. She glances up and down the hallway, still populated by quite a few members of the staff. Did he break away to direct their luggage? Check on Becca? A brown-hatted servant is following a pile of Becca-related baggage down the hall toward the swerving marble stairway on that end.

Gigi places a hand on Maya's shoulder. "Don't worry, Becca's in good hands." Maya hadn't realized she was making a worried face, but Gigi finds it necessary to add, "O'Brien is a Norland nanny. Lance and Ian each have their own, and Lance is eight now. It's plain stupid to have Mary Poppins following an eight-year-old around all the time, trying to get him to hand over his Game Boy, but there you have it." Maya hasn't met Lance, but she knows he's the older son of Marcus, Colin's eldest cousin, who runs the Sterling empire from London.

Gigi pauses for a word with Barrow before turning back to Maya. "You were the last to arrive, so we had to put you in the old nursery."

"The nursery?"

"That's just what we call it. It hasn't been a place for children since Dad and Aunt Helen were kids. When our generation was in school, and visiting a lot, it was the room we'd request if we were bringing someone *special* home for a night—it's the farthest from the other guest rooms. So, it has a bit of history, if you know what I mean." Gigi gives Maya a lurid wink and begins to lead her down the hall. Maya can smell woodsmoke, hear murmurs. "Those were the days when Harry started opening up the house to us again, and we were all here a lot more. Now we only convene once or twice a year. For Christmas, special anniversaries, when someone gets murdered."

Maya experiences a rising inner heat as she realizes where she's being led. When she sees the rest of the Sterlings, she wants to be arm in arm with her husband, to present a united front. "Right, of course," Maya says, unable to laugh at Gigi's joke. "Sorry, but did you see where Colin—"

"I'm really blathering, aren't I? Come on, love, let's say hello to the family." Gigi wraps an arm around Maya's waist and pilots her in the opposite direction the nanny took, toward the low chatter, the fireplace.

"But I really ought to find Colin first," Maya protests.

"Oh, he's gone in already, surely." Gigi still sounds spirited, but there's a note of warning now too, as she abandons Maya and goes on ahead. "Come along, gorgeous. We Sterlings don't like to be kept waiting."

4

Last night they moved me to a new room. Spare, white. Nicer than the other, I guess. The bed is a normal bed—no wrist or ankle restraints, hallelujah. There's a window too. The window is a very big deal, to hear the orderlies tell it. A privilege I've been granted for good behavior. I'm so bored and zombified I actually *am* a little excited about it.

If I'm very, very, very good, they promise a little TV time, a few magazines.

OOOooo goodie!

Outside the window: A lush garden. Big trees that block most of the view. Impossible to tell where I am. Somewhere warm, though the climate is perfectly controlled inside. The greenery reminds me of some faraway and long-ago place. The bright tropical flowers on vines winding their way 'round the bigger tree's branches.

The window doesn't open, of course. I tried.

All in good time, the doctor said, when she came to check on me just now.

A new doctor, I haven't met this one before. She isn't as brusque as the others, the ones on the higher floor whose domain is a warren of padded, windowless rooms. She asked questions, feigning friendliness: How was I doing, was I still having the bad dreams? She even joked about the quality of the food. She's very pretty. I like that about her. Always have been a sucker for beauty. Not sure I can trust her though. They all have the same goal— subdue and control—they just use different tactics. I've seen this before, the old *I'm on your side* act. I watched her as she went over the chart, took notes, doled out my meds. Then she gave me this sly smile, like she knows I'm watching her, knows everything I've been through.

She doesn't, though.

No one knows what it is to grow up with the curse of a last name like mine.

I don't want it, I told her. Whatever you're giving me. Told her I feel like I'm floating in the upper atmosphere. Toes numb. Can't remember what I ate for breakfast. Or even really who I am.

The doctor goes: No? You don't know who you are, your name, where you came from?

I rolled my eyes and said: Arianna Sterling, born in England, 1981, to a narrow-hipped woman who didn't survive the night.

Dr.: Would you like to talk about her, your mother?

Me: No. (Really, that I never knew my mother is the least of my problems.)

Dr.: That's fine. Take your time. Right now, you need to concentrate on getting better. Isn't that what you want? It's certainly what your family wants. They sent you all sorts of things: a silk nightie, shortbread, the special Ceylon tea they serve at Sterling Park.

I watched the doctor for signs of trustworthiness, but she's hard to figure. I suppose that's part of her training, to seem assiduously neutral. Love that word. *Assiduously.* Dad used to use that word a lot, made me think of acid rain.

Dad.

No, no, can't think about that bastard right now. That's how a girl gets the wrist and ankle cuffs put back on.

I don't want any of that stuff, I told her, even though I kind of did. They have the best of everything at Sterling Park (as they like to remind you every ten minutes). But no, I don't need all that; I'm not getting comfy here.

The doctor nodded and said she understood. Said: I hate my family too. You get better for yourself, then. But take your meds. I promise, it's lighter stuff now, but you need it. You don't want to start hallucinating again, do you?

No, I don't. I put the little plastic cup to my lip, tipped my head back.

Good girl, the doctor said, as though I were a trained dog. I thought about that a moment, how they all believe they can bring me to heel. Then the doctor gave me this journal, and told me it might help me sort out what's real, what's a hallucination. Get my feet on the ground, that's how she phrased it.

I stared at her. This was a genuine kindness. I knew because I've experienced such gestures very rarely, and they always create an unbearable pressure in my chest. You know, where the heart's supposed to be. I thanked her, drew my fingers across the soft black leather of the cover, told her it was nice. It was. Is.

Maybe this doctor and I were going to fall in love with each other, I thought.

I don't usually like the females, but beggars can't be choosers and she does have one of those full mouths that seem invented for kissing. Before leaving, she told me to keep getting better, and maybe I'd get a room on the first floor, where the windows actually open.

I wasn't sure what to say to that, so I just listened for the click of the door shutting behind her, opened to the first page, and began to write out our interaction, which is really all I know for sure. Everything before that is hazy, anyway, mixed up with ugly nightmares, my family gathered around my bed—I know it's them, though they are wearing animal masks—and with them are multitudes of staff in-home therapists. Saying, *We know what's best for you, we only want what's best for you, this place you're going, it is what's best for you.*

Well, *fuck* that.

This place is best for no one.

You know what I do here? I wait and wait and wait and wait. That's the worst part. Not the wrist restraints or the feeding tube or the padded walls. It's that I'm a prisoner. I'm as trapped as I ever was at Silver House.

I know what they're doing. Cleaning up their problems. Taking me out with the trash.

There's really only one thing to write. I could write it a thousand times, fill these pages with it. All there really is to say is this:

Fuck you, Sterlings.

5

In the photos of the family Maya saw at SterlingCo headquarters, there was only one image of the family at Silver House. The Sterling family was posed in a gold silk–paneled parlor, surrounded by splendor like a royal family's portrait done in oil on canvas, all jewel tones over a dark ground. Will it be like that now? Colin a little off to the side, standing wide-legged and with arms folded behind his back, ready to prove himself to his idol, Marcus. Marcus, sitting in a throne-like armchair, impervious to those around him, how hungry they are for his attention. Eva, his rail-thin wife, perched at his shoulder like a strange decorative bird. Julian, Helen's husband, with his elbow on the mantel, jauntily posing with hunting dogs at his feet, the man who assumed a paternal role with the passing of Colin and Gigi's parents. Or so the magazines say.

And then there's the woman so magisterial she haunts Maya's dreams, her eyebrow perpetually cocked in judgment, her mouth downturned in permanent distaste. Helen Sterling. She has another surname, her husband's, but no one ever bothers with that. Every inch of her is Sterling.

Maya still feels stung by her first and only meeting with Helen.

A month before Becca was born, Helen flew across the ocean to formally vet Maya. Told Colin they needed some time, "just us girls," to get to know each other. Colin had urged Maya to go ahead with the meeting, explaining that Helen had taken a maternal interest in all her motherless nieces and nephews. Maya had been irritated at the time. He seemed so eager to obey Helen, and so uncharacteristically oblivious to Maya's wish for him to come along.

Once they were alone in a corner banquette at Bemelmans's Bar, Helen stopped pretending their meeting was anything but business. She put the prenuptial agreement next to the little tasseled table lamp and handed Maya a pen.

Maya balked. She'd have to have her lawyer read it first, surely that was understandable. But Helen just waved her concern away, smoothly explaining that this was all standard. *Sterling boilerplate, all very generous.* Maya would be well taken care of, should the marriage fail. And, if Maya didn't sign, Colin would have to relinquish his position in the family trust. The bullying was all very smiling and tactful. As Maya bent, eyes scanning, pen moving along the dotted line, Helen began a seemingly unrelated story about Marion Davies, the film star companion of William Randolph Hearst, who had been left a controlling share of the Hearst Corporation upon the great man's death. "What a time of it his family had, wrestling control of all they'd built back from that gold digger," Helen concluded, taking the signed document from Maya's hand.

When Maya later showed the document to Bob Feld, her own lawyer, he dropped his head into the bowl of his hands. Bob was an old-school New Yorker. Head-high stacks of paper blocked the views of his downtown office. If clients asked for Evian, he'd offer tap water served in chipped CUNY School of Law mugs. He hated pretention, hated nepotism, hated the trust fund kids who were his bread and butter. Maya adored him.

"Just call me next time, okay?" he told Maya, as though Maya were a child.

And maybe it was childish, signing the papers in the hope that it would make Helen like her. What Maya hadn't told Bob was that after she signed, in that brief moment of hope that this would endear her to the Sterlings, Helen tipped her head to one side and asked a variation of the question Maya hears all the time. From tabloid writers, fans, so-called friends. *Did she marry Colin for his money?* Or, in Helen's rather more arch formulation: "You've played a mediocre hand rather well, haven't you, dear?"

Maya's throat closed. She was furious with herself for being so naïve, for not seeing this bait and switch coming. While she sat there trying to contain her anger, move through her shock, Helen slipped a black velvet box across the table. Maya's engagement present, she said. Helen insisted she open the box, put the present around her neck. Maya's fingers fumbled with the clasp, she felt the cold metal fall against the skin of her chest. It was a slender gold chain with a tiny gold charm.

A pickaxe.

For digging gold.

Later that night, Colin dismissed this as "just taking the piss," but Maya was relieved when Helen replied with regrets to the wedding invitation, and doubly grateful that she and Colin were going to stay in New York, far away from the Sterlings.

She promised herself she wouldn't let Helen bully her that way again, make her feel that small.

We Sterlings don't like to be kept waiting.

Gigi's warning hangs above her as Maya hovers at the open door, afraid to step in alone. What kind of reception should she expect—friendly, mocking, hostile?

With a fortifying breath, Maya follows her sister-in-law into a wood-paneled salon with burgundy velvet settees arranged across expansive, overlapping, threadbare Persian rugs. The Sterlings are not posed monumentally for an official portrait but rather huddled together, close to the fire. To Maya's surprise, and immense relief, Helen actually isn't among them—it's just what Gigi referred to as *her* generation, and younger.

Now Maya sees where Colin disappeared to. He's pulled an ottoman up to his cousin Marcus, semireclined on a stuffed leather chair by the blazing fire, and is talking animatedly. Sensing Maya's presence, Colin pauses his conversation long enough to give her a secret smile, before returning to what must be a discussion of SterlingCo's latest acquisition.

She hovers a moment, wondering if she should join him, just

as Marcus Lambert-Sterling—the obvious gravitational pull of the room—frowns in her direction. He's CEO, Colin's boss, and she takes him in for a moment, his standard black button-down rolled to the elbows revealing muscled forearms. There's a resemblance between him and Colin, but his good looks are rougher, more weathered—gray patches at the temples, a boxer's nose and hands. He's thicker than the last time Maya saw him, she thinks, before taking the hint of his steely gaze, and glancing away.

Nor does Maya want to look directly at Eva, positioned close to Marcus on a velvet settee just as she had imagined, wearing a blue oxford shirt and beige Tod's kitten heels. She looks much thinner in person, immaculately thin, and her hair is that classic Fairfield County shade of ash blond. (Her father was an American businessman and sent Eva to be educated at Miss Porter's like her maternal grandmother; Maya knows that from a Google search.) Currently, Eva's mouth is doing a thing that would, in some circles, be called a smile. She's rubbing the shoulders of her eldest child, tucked beside her on the settee, as he furiously works the controls of a boxy handheld game. Ian, the younger boy, is sprawled on the floor, examining a sepia-colored globe that appears to depict the world as the British understood it in the time of Sir Francis Drake.

They don't even acknowledge Maya until Gigi swaggers over to Eva's settee, gives Lance a little pinch of the chin, announces, "Hey, chaps, look who's here!"

And suddenly all eyes are on Maya.

"You've arrived," Eva says, with effortful cheer. "Boys, say hello to Colin's wife."

The boys glance up, mumble their greetings.

What happens now? Are they all supposed to hug? Maya raises her arms halfheartedly and is met by blank glazes and slightly tilted heads.

Guess not, she thinks, unsure what else to do. Maya takes a further step into the room. Her palm is sweating as she holds tight to her highball, afraid it might slip from her damp hand. She gestures at the coffered ceilings, the oversized oil paintings, and reverts to the sweet all-American persona that she used on *The Springs*. The one she brings out when she goes on morning shows to talk about the miracle of her rosewater cleansing set. "This place is like—*wow*."

"Yes," Eva says with supreme neutrality. "It is indeed very wow."

Eva leans forward, tosses the magazine she was reading on a pile strewn over a low walnut table. It's one of the celebrity weeklies, the most recent issue. The cover image is Maya crossing the private airfield outside Puerto Vallarta in big black shades and a little black dress. Behind her stands Colin, burdened with numerous bags. Maya looks regal, her long hair floating behind her, lips twisted in triumph, her face pure determination. Gigi leans forward, picks up the magazine. The headline: *Maya Gets the Guy...Again. And Lots of Sterling Treasure Too.*

Maya's pride burns, her shoulders square at the...what? Accusation? Maybe this is Eva's way of getting to know the newest family member, but Maya doubts it. Colin raises an eyebrow at

Maya—a subtle acknowledgment that Eva is the worst, perhaps. Or is he wondering why Maya can't get it together? Usually, she knows what he's thinking at a glance, but here she's lost. She wishes she'd made him tell her everything about Sterling Park, how to carry herself. Is there a secret handshake? Was she not supposed to speak until spoken to, as if in audience with the Queen? Colin's usually so good at giving her a primer on ridiculous social situations—but today he seems distracted. Which makes sense. Still, she wishes he'd stop playing the good Sterling boy, and remember that along with everything else, he's presenting his new wife to his extended family.

Maybe he's in shock.

Oh fuck this, she thinks, before disregarding her nerves and taking a few more strides toward the others, eyes scanning the space as if smitten by the décor. A table is laid with heaping bowls of ice and citrus, bouquets of mint and rosemary, and a rainbow assortment of liquor in cut crystal decanters. The logs in the massive hearth give off a homey smell. It might be cozy, except for the harsh energy of the inhabitants.

Meanwhile, the men converse obliviously. Marcus leans back in his chair to listen to Colin once more, newspaper still open before him as though he might go back to reading it at any moment. In addition to holding the top job at the family firm, Marcus also has the extra clout of having worked his way up through the ranks at a rival newspaper, *The London Standard*, reporting from Kosovo and Sierra Leone and the Vatican. She has wondered if beneath Colin's hero worship there's something sharper. Jealousy, fear? That Marcus has the clout of a self-made man, and Colin is pampered by comparison? Maya has to admit that it is impressive how Marcus went out and made a name beyond the family firm.

Maya is finding Helen's absence more unnerving than reassuring.

Simply to do something other than loiter pointlessly, Maya heads to the table with the cocktail fixings, thinking she'll get rid of her glass, which has gone slippery in her hand.

But Gigi rises and is swiftly at Maya's side, replenishing her ice, topping her off with gin.

"Good girl," Gigi murmurs, as she fixes her own beverage.

Maya is rankled by this persistent, not entirely sincere-seeming attention from her sister-in-law. But, what with the overall chill in the room, Maya could really use a drink. She raises her glass to Gigi's, utters a moronic "Bottoms up!" before taking a hearty gulp.

"I'd say that you should be more concerned with *tops*," Eva says pointedly from her seat. She does a little eye flick in the general direction of Maya's chest.

Maya glances down and cringes inwardly at the visible outline of her nipples showing through her thin tee. Her cheeks burn at this fresh attention to how absurdly underdressed she is. With the pace of things, the plane to the car to Silver House, Maya never found the right moment to change out of her travel clothes. Which left her still in the bikini top, white tee, and Adidas track pants from the day before—streetwear chic in New

York, wholly inadequate for the current setting. Maya feels the bite of her comment, humiliating as a ruler across the knuckles. *Cover yourself.*

Maya gestures to her casual attire. "Sorry, I meant to change, but—"

Colin, finally picking up on Maya's distress, raises his head. "Oh, don't worry about that, love. This is family, you should feel at home." Eva lowers her lashes slowly and shrugs.

Gigi's eyes are very bright, darting from one family member to another, enjoying the awkwardness. It's a game for her. "Well, it's not *her* home, though, is it? It's *our* home." Gigi says innocently, playing with a split end. "Or is it Harry's now—"

"*Harry*," exclaims a man bursting through a door. Maya gasps in surprise, jolting her glass and splashing drink down her arm. No one else seems alarmed by this sudden entrance—a raised eye from Marcus, a sigh from Eva, a smile from Gigi. His hair is chin length, streaked with gray, his skin tan, cheeks ruddy. He has the washed-out handsomeness and springy bowlegged gait of an aging athlete, though he's wide with good living around the middle. "Did someone say Harry?"

Maya turns to greet him, shaking the gin off her skin. This must be the father of the deceased heiress, summoned by his own name. "Oh, hello. I'm Maya, Colin's wife. I'm so, *so* sorry," she says.

As he approaches Maya, trailed by two heavy-breathing dogs, he turns down the corners of his mouth.

"Whatever for?"

"Oh." Maya tries to recalibrate. This man is not Harry. Of

course, she should have realized. The energy he's giving off is far too jovial for him to be Arianna's father, the recluse. The bereaved. Harry Sterling is probably off somewhere with Helen, dealing with the grim realities of his daughter's death. "Sorry, I thought you were—"

"*Harry?* Heavens no." The man reaches Maya with arms outstretched. "Julian Lambert-Sterling, Helen's husband." Maya sees the resemblance to Marcus now, the broad shoulders and pronounced brow, the full mouth and shrewd eyes. Julian engulfs her in a hug that lasts slightly too long and allows him ample time to smell her hair.

"It's a pleasure to meet you," Maya says mechanically. "I'm so sorry for your loss."

"Ah yes, dreadful. Poor Arianna." Julian studies her, assessing. She's used to that, certain people reacting to her because of how she looks. When she was about thirteen, her aunt lit a cigarette, grimaced at Maya, and said, *I was afraid of this. You're the kind of beautiful where people won't take you seriously. But that doesn't mean that you can't take* yourself *seriously. When people are distracted by the pretty, they can miss what you're capable of.* Maya doesn't love Julian's proximity right now, but who knows? Maybe she can find an advantage there—maybe he'll help her navigate this Sterling world.

Julian goes on. "And poor old Harry, I'm sure he's coping in his way, wherever he is."

"He's not here?" Maya asks. This is a surprise. Doesn't the protocol 202 thing apply to him too? Surely he, of all people, would be the most eager to gather up with family and determine what happened to his daughter.

There follows a humid silence.

Julian breaks the quiet. "The truth is we have no idea where Harry is. Which is not as odd as it might seem, because we rarely do." He wilts slightly, but his hand remains on Maya's hip. Colin doesn't seem to notice, but his cousin does. Marcus's eyes go from his father's hand to Maya's face. His noticing makes her feel twitchy, like she's the one doing something wrong. She narrows her eyes slightly at Marcus, urging him to look away. But he holds her gaze, his mouth hitching to one side, a hint of a grin.

"What a tragedy that girl's life was." Julian releases a plaintive breath. "Always with that father of hers, always hiding."

"Hiding from whom?" Maya asks.

"Everything." Julian sighs. "Spies, thieves, the press. Goblins, ghosts. His own worst instincts. He was paranoid, really."

"I told you about all that," Colin says to Maya softly. "After his friend was killed in his villa, he became convinced that *he* might have been the real target. For a while, he was always on the move. And more recently, he's gotten like that again. He's lived in…how many countries is it now?"

"The real question," Julian says with a smirk, "is how many countries is he *banned* from living in."

"Come on, Uncle Jul, it's only Morocco he's been asked not to return to." Gigi, bless her, takes Maya's other arm, parts her from Julian's overly familiar grasp, and guides her closer to the fire. "Oh, and Singapore, but who among us has not been told to leave Singapore and never come back?"

"Is he all right?" Maya asks.

"It was nothing, really, a silly brouhaha over—what was it that time?" Julian flicks his hand through the air. "His antique firearms collection? Or was it a conspicuous drinking spree in an illegal gambling den?"

"I meant, like, emotionally. Because he's the father of the... of Arianna?"

There's a long silence in which Maya tries to figure out what she's said wrong. Hadn't Colin said Harry and Arianna were close, the two of them against the world? Or was Maya projecting her own father-daughter story on Colin's cousin—the unpredictable, charismatic father and his accomplice of a daughter? Her brain is fizzing like cheap champagne, the drink and the jet lag going to her head. Everyone is staring, and she suddenly feels stupid and very much out of place.

Finally, Colin stands with a sigh, leaving the tight circle of his family. When he reaches Maya, he puts his arm around her shoulders. "Let's go get washed up before dinner, shall we?"

"Yes," Julian says, backing toward the door, the dogs panting along close behind. "I have to get back to my little novel-writing project. Anyhow, I just wanted to stop in and say hello. Terrible circumstances but might as well take advantage of being confined to Sterling Park and do some research. We have the archive here—you'll have to see it, Maya, once you're settled. It goes quite far back, and it's more personal, cheekier, than the archive corporate maintains in London. The novel is based on Richard's exploits during World War II. I plan to have a manuscript for everyone to critique by Christmas."

Maya, overwhelmed, nods at Julian as he bounces away through the door, trailed by the border collies.

This feels like a trap, being rushed here, presented in rough shape—underdressed, ill-informed, three steps behind everyone else, and with her husband, the man who usually helps her through every challenge, consumed by the crisis and no help at all. She needs to shower, collect herself, sharpen up.

"Excuse me," Maya says, retreating toward the door. "It was really nice to meet you all."

There are a few barely perceptible nods. No one says a word as Maya and Colin leave the room. When Maya glances back, hoping for a smile or something, she does catch a lurid wink from Gigi. And beyond Gigi is Marcus, eyes still on Maya, grinning like he knows all the secret contents of her mind.

Most especially the secret that could get Maya expelled from Colin's life for good.

6

"Did I say something wrong in there?"

Maya and Colin are following Barrow down the hallways of the second floor. Or third? How this massive house fits together is mystifying, with all the corridors and wings, stairwells and halls. But she's relieved to be away from the rest of the family. And, mostly, to have avoided Helen in her pitiful posttravel state. She needs to shower, get sharp.

"What makes you think that?"

"When I asked if Harry was all right—*after the death of his only child*—everyone looked at me like I was insane."

Colin's eyes go to the ceiling, his brow creases. He looks pained and thoughtful. After a moment, he replies, carefully placing one word after another. "They were very close for a long time, Harry and Arianna. Then she grew up, realized she'd been a princess locked in a castle, and became rebellious. They had some fight, I don't know what about—and then you couldn't mention her name to him. And she must've felt the same."

"I get that." Maya actually does. She's heard it said that rich and poor have more in common than the middle class. Whatever the gulf in security and comfort, rich and poor are both in their own way free from bourgeois conventions. They understand that life is cheap, don't cling to sentimental connections. Instead, they mythologize their family. Or destroy them.

This has been true in Maya's family, and it seems to be true in Colin's as well.

Maya's mother fell in love with her father when she was young, younger than Maya is now. When his roguish charm stopped working on her, she went off to find something better, leaving little Maya in the care of an underemployed gambler living in a trailer on his sister's property. Mostly her aunt looked after her—a salty fisherman's daughter who could praise and curse her feckless brother in the same breath.

"But, what about protocol? Shouldn't he be here with his family?"

"That's true, but trust me, it's better he's not," Colin replies with unexpected force.

Maya flinches at his tone, searches his eyes.

In a calmer voice, Colin continues, "He's not so bad, really. Just a bit of a wild man. I mean, it's true what Gigi said. If he couldn't pay his way out of his scrapes, he'd be rotting in a jail in Havana or Tangier or who knows..." Colin shakes his head. "From a certain angle, I suppose you could say he has everything. But from another, Arianna was all he had."

They've slowed, let Barrow advance out of earshot. Colin looks tired, and very sad, even if he's been pretending otherwise. "I'm so sorry," she whispers, and grabs his hand.

Colin squeezes back, nodding for them to catch up to Barrow, who is holding open a carved mahogany door. As they enter their quarters, his manner shifts. He puts on an affected breeziness—a performance for the staff, Maya thinks. Apparently, that is the way to be here.

"Ah! The old nursery," he says. "Same as it ever was."

Maya follows Colin into the room, which doesn't resemble any nursery she's ever seen. If she were a child, she'd be uneasy with the stale atmosphere and ominous décor. The room has mahogany wainscoting, above which a rich wallpaper stretches to the crown molding, dark with jewel-tone green and gold accents. The ceilings are maybe twenty feet, with a dimmed chandelier hanging at the center. Amber velvet drapes are drawn over the windows. As her eyes adjust, she sees the nanny who took Becca in a little alcove of the main room, situated in a rocking chair, finger pressed to her lips. The nanny rises and lays the sleeping Becca into a canopied crib. Maya experiences a burst of angry longing—her tiny child is far from anything familiar, and brand-new in the world; she deserves to be put down by her own mother. Why did Maya let herself be bullied; why didn't she just keep the Sterlings waiting? It's not like they seemed all that thrilled to see her anyway.

"Little love just went down," the nanny tells Maya as she passes into the hallway. "And the staff has unpacked your bags and taken your laundry to the wash." Maya's mouth tenses in irritation at this invasion of her privacy. Like any keeper of secrets, she possesses a hair-trigger paranoia.

But, mindful of Colin at her side, Barrow not far off, Maya murmurs thank you.

The nanny bows her head, then gives Maya and Colin a parting look of appraisal, their unkempt hair and disheveled clothes. "You ought to get some sleep too, both of you."

"Thanks, O'Brien," Colin replies.

As the nanny departs, it occurs to Maya that perhaps it isn't family members alone who are watching her, judging her missteps. The staff is a small army, every one of them with a watchful eye.

Colin begins to unbutton his rumpled shirt, and Barrow immediately fetches a hanger for him. They begin to discuss the evening's itinerary. Already Colin is giving orders—telling Barrow when he wants to be awakened, when he'd like his morning coffee service—with more ease and entitlement than she could have imagined. Maya realizes that she's still holding the highball glass from downstairs. It's smudged with lipstick and her greasy fingerprints, and she has a sudden horror that the butler will be taking this item, this evidence that she does not belong, and bringing it back to the kitchen, judging her the whole way for being so sloppy and plebeian. When her aunt cleaned houses, she kept up a constant commentary of the disgustingness of her employers— the red wine rings on the bedside tables, the tampons rotting in the wastebasket. Maya quickly places the glass on the nearest surface, a side table, and steps away. But she must have placed it too close to the sloping edge of the tabletop.

In the next moment, she hears it smash against the floor.

"Shit," Maya mutters as she turns, crouches, begins to collect the larger pieces, careful not to catch the sharpest edges.

"Madame, please." With a swiftness that surprises Maya, Barrow removes the shards from her hand. "Allow me to—"

"No, no, I mean it was *my* fault," Maya says in a rush, cheeks flushing scarlet. "And trust me, I've cleaned up *way* worse."

Barrow graciously tilts his head. "But it is my responsibility."

"No, really, that was very clumsy, I can do it, I'll—" Maya breaks off when she feels the hand grip her forearm.

"Forgive my wife; she doesn't understand how things run in Silver House yet." Colin lifts her from the floor by the elbow, smiles indulgently as though she's a silly child. It's a different side of him, a side extremely comfortable being attended to like a dauphin. "Maya, you don't clean up messes here." She raises an eyebrow, as if to say, *Come on, I know the real you.* To which he only grins. "Don't worry, Barrow—we'll get this one trained in no time."

Maya winces at the word.

And strangely, in the moment that follows, Barrow seems to wince too. He touches Maya's hand, saying with supreme gentleness, "You must allow me, Mrs. Sterling."

"Thank you," Maya replies. In an instant, he's produced a small broom and copper dustpan, and shortly thereafter the whole mess disappears.

Barrow lowers his gaze in deference, then informs them that dinner will be served at eight before sweeping from the room. There's something about the whole scene that tenses her jaw.

Barrow's self-denying professionalism, that astonishing ability to make oneself invisible, it reminds her of her aunt, how weary and drained she always was. How, after a day of cleaning houses, all she could do was lie out on the couch on her back porch, swatting at mosquitoes, asking Maya to be a good girl and bring her a Merit and a glass of red Zin.

But at least Rebecca never had to pretend she wasn't who she was. Her employers expected her to present like a gruff local. The way the solemn, sagacious-seeming Barrow is standing at attention, knees and ankles pressed together, breaks Maya's heart.

Maya turns away, her finger tracing the pattern of the wallpaper: a stylized jungle, tigers watching from between the trees, looped by words done in fanciful gold script. "What's this?" she asks, once Colin's closed the door and they're alone again. She can't quite keep the bitterness out of her voice. "A secret Sterling family code?"

"It's a Blake poem," Colin says, glancing at Becca to make sure she's still asleep. He comes away from the bed, where clothes have been laid out for dinner, and stands beside Maya. "My father used to recite it to us at bedtime, same as his mother did for him and Helen and Harry. 'Tyger, Tyger burning bright/ In the forests of the nights/ What immortal hand or eye/ Could frame thy fearful symmetry?/ In what distant deeps or skies/ Burnt the fire of thine eyes...'" There's something hypnotic in his recitation. The rhythm seems to have borne him back into some painful past, and Maya regrets her irritation with him.

Maya rests her hand on her husband's shoulder. "What's up?"

"I was just thinking about staying here when I was little. When Mum and Dad were still alive, and it really was a nursery. I was afraid of the wallpaper—the tigers, the poem. Seems silly now. But Richard—Dad's dad—he barked at me, said maybe I wasn't a Sterling at all, if I was exhibiting that kind of timidity. He said maybe I was a changeling."

"That's awful. I mean, no wonder you moved across the ocean."

Colin smiles wanly. "He was just taking the piss. I think it was really something he thought about Dad, not me, but kids don't understand that sort of thing, you know?"

She pauses, studying her husband. He's relaxing his façade, now that he's away from his family again. "Babe, are you okay?"

He glances at her warily. "I'm just…worried. About everything. But also about you. This is the worst end to our wedding imaginable. None of this is what I hoped for." He shakes his head. This is the man she glimpsed behind the sparkling public image of Colin Sterling back when they first met, the one she knew would make a good partner. A young man who lost his parents in a tragic accident, who is hyperconcerned with the well-being of those closest to him, who idealizes family and will go to great lengths to prevent his own history of loss from repeating itself. "We should've had a proper honeymoon and made our first visit to Sterling Park together under happier circumstances."

"I mean, how long do we have to stay here?"

The line of Colin's mouth hardens. "Until the murderer is found, I reckon. Or at least until we can confirm the safety of the family." He releases a breath from deep in his core. "I know you don't want to be here."

A wave of guilt moves through Maya. She really doesn't want to be here, it's true, but maybe she *could* try a little harder, given the circumstances. "Oh, honey. I'm fine."

"Really?"

"Really. It's family." That sounds ridiculous—like this is a sitcom, like the Sterlings are some normal midwestern clan crowding around a Formica tabletop. She knows she's lying. And yet, it's also true in a way—she's here to support Colin. He's her family now. It doesn't matter if anyone else likes her. She and Colin just need to get through this together. And probably what's best for both of them is that he plays his role in the family right now—Colin, the one who keeps everyone happy, the dutiful second-in-command. She needs to put away her uncertainty, her scorn. "You want to go talk to Marcus again, don't you? Check in on the business?"

Colin glances at Maya, gives a sheepish smile as though he's been caught. "Yes."

"You should go, babe. Do what you need to do."

"I'll find out what the plan is. The lawyer is coming tomorrow—that should illuminate some things. Maybe we won't have to be here all that long."

In the dim corner of the room, the baby softly wails. Maya tenses at the possibility that she will wake, that Maya won't get the nap she needs if she's going to survive dinner with the Sterlings. She and Colin tiptoe toward the crib, Maya smoothing the baby's fine, wisping hair as she settles, turns back into sleep.

"Go ahead," Maya whispers to Colin. "I got this."

She feels some tension between them dissipating. "Thank you for understanding. For being my partner. I had the right idea, marrying you."

She laughs. "Same here."

"Plus, you're hot." Colin grins, teasing.

Maya grins back, takes Colin's face in her hands. "I know."

Colin puts a kiss on her mouth, then reluctantly pulls away. She fights the urge to keep him close, draw him into bed beside her. She wants to be naked with him, to hear him say, "I love you." But he's already giving her a quick primer on how to call the butler if she needs anything, warning her about the old plumbing, and then he's gone, and she knows this is for the best. She'll have time to clean up, get her head on straight—just after she rests her tired eyes. Then she can prepare to be the Maya Colin needs, the one with no secrets and nothing to hide...

———

The baby is screaming. Maya's mouth is a dead riverbed. The room is dark. It's late; she slept much longer than she meant to. She must have missed dinner entirely. So much for putting on a show for the family. Colin is beside her, face stuck to the pillow. She wills him to wake up, deal with Becca, but of course he doesn't. Even the most progressive and attentive husband doesn't *really* hear a baby crying, feel compelled by the little wails to rouse himself and take care of the problem.

Maya tosses back the bedding, swings herself off the bed's high platform, plucks the baby from the crib. After a few moments swaying back and forth, cooing and shushing, it's obvious Becca isn't going to be easily put down again. Maya sighs, decides she might as well spare Colin, and goes into the hall to walk the baby back to sleep. Her body is slow, heavy with sleep, but she's at least thankful for Silver House's expansive corridors as she moves down one labyrinthine hall, then another.

As Maya walks, Becca quiets in a light, temporary way. Maya keeps on, padding along the thick runners. As she rounds a corner, she's met with a ghostly sight, rows of painted portraits hovering on the walls, faces shadowy and stern. Dead Sterlings, watching Maya as she does an awkward baby bounce. She's distracted by those ancient ermine collars and silver scepters, and then surprised by the creak of a floorboard sighing under her weight, the eerie echo of the sound against the far wall. A few portraits are more recent—the great man, Richard, with his translucent blue eyes beside his narrow-nosed wife. Harry, the prodigal uncle, in his youth—golden, glowing, a little Colin-like.

And there, at the end of the hallway, Maya can just make out a portrait unlike the others. For one thing, the subject is not situated in a dark room or upon heaping yards of velvet. The background is green and bountiful—an overgrown field, from which a huge trunk grows. A yew tree, perhaps? Maya feels compelled forward toward this unusual painting. Against the trunk is a little girl in a white pinafore, and though her clothing, her babyish arms, and short stature suggest a child of no more

75

than four, she has the shadowy, heavy-lidded look of someone much older. She looks unlike any Sterling Maya has encountered yet.

Arianna? Her eyes trace the hang of golden plaits, the sad dark gaze, the little features done in smudgy brushstrokes.

Not far from the portrait, a simple door stands open. Through it, Maya sees a narrow stairway. She approaches, trying to remember if she's seen any other open doors as she's walked on. *Was this her room, the heiress, whose portrait hangs nearby?* Maya takes the stairs, compelled upward, hand protectively cupping Becca's little head. The steps are narrow; they groan underfoot, making Maya feel like an intruder. Like she's still that little thief with her nose pressed up against the glass, staring in at the beautiful people, lurking in the night. Maya steels herself, remembers Colin's words from before. She's a Sterling; she's on the inside now.

In the garret room, the drapes are parted, allowing a faint gray dawn to peek through the windows. The light is spectral. It plays tricks on Maya's vision. She blinks against the gloom, trying to make sense of the shadowy corners and the bright silver slice of early morning. Much of the furniture is faded pink and the decorations are cloyingly girly. She must've been right— this had to be Arianna's bedroom years ago. She steps in farther, compelled by a strong curiosity about this mysterious and tragic girl whose death has summoned the Sterling family home.

There's a (nonfunctioning, Maya assumes) London telephone booth in one corner and the bed is a polished wooden canopy, sheer pink curtains rippling down to the floor. But it's the wallpaper she notices most, the same print as in the nursery—golden tigers and emerald green leaves stretching up to the high moldings.

Tyger, Tyger burning bright.

Becca has finally settled back into sleep, sucking on her knuckle, but the calm hasn't yet spread to Maya. Heart thudding, Maya walks through the room, feeling haunted by this child, this forgotten room.

That's when she catches her reflection in a mirror hung above a white vanity. She steps closer, noting the surface below, still messy with plushies and dusty perfume bottles. She peers at her reflection—for all the poor sleep and travel, she doesn't look so bad. She has that same uncommonly beautiful face that has propelled her so far in the world, and the baby appears comfortable and safe in her arms.

A fleeting sense of relief settles her shoulders. Then she hears the faint press of footsteps, sees the hazy, ghostlike face over her shoulder. The frightened face of a lonely child—the one in the white pinafore, leaning against the yew tree? Maya has this startling conviction that she's staring into Arianna Sterling's eyes. Except, in the painting the eyes were brown—and these are pale greenish blue, and the face in which they sit is ghostly, aged.

The voice jolts Maya from her hallucination: "You missed dinner."

Maya's grip on Becca tightens as she revolves to face the

woman in the white silk robe, her hair a silvery mess. Helen Sterling. She does look much younger without makeup.

"I didn't see you there," Maya says, too quickly.

Her eyes dart around the room. She notices the stuffed mauve chair, a few feet behind Helen. Has Helen been sitting all this time, watching? She must have been. Was Maya that oblivious? She's never seen Helen like this, with a bare face, hair wild and witchy. *You missed dinner* reverberates in the room like an accusation.

Maya tries to justify her presence. "I didn't think anybody would be here."

Helen's eyes narrow. "Nor did I."

Maya feels that she's being asked to explain herself and hurries to comply. "I just came in to find something to soothe Becca." She thoughtlessly reaches for the pile of toys on the vanity, grabbing the first object her hand finds—a doll with a fabric body and a slim porcelain head.

Helen stares at the doll, then her lips part and a breath lifts her chest. "That was Arianna's favorite, curiously enough." She turns away, lowers herself into the chair again, rests her fine chin on a balled fist. She seems so different here. Wraithlike, otherworldly. Helen observes Maya as though from a great distance. That gaze is so penetrating, and Maya squeezes the doll just to keep from squirming.

"You must be curious about her." Helen eyes flick from Maya's face to her grip on the doll.

It's so late—disorienting, the jet lag dragging her down. But is Helen out of sorts too? Sitting in this dark room alone while the rest of the house sleeps. "Her?"

"Arianna. My *niece*."

Maya wants to reply hotly that no, she isn't. She's here for Colin and Colin alone. But that's not entirely true. Maya *is* curious about Arianna. Cares about what happened to her. And if Helen is here in what must be Arianna's room in the middle of the night, it's because *she* cares too. Cares a lot more than any of the people in the drawing room seemed to.

"Well, she's the reason we're all here, right?" Maya replies tentatively. "Makes sense I'd wonder about her, right? Her life at Silver House."

Helen tilts her head, regards Maya. With resignation, with respect? Maya isn't sure.

"It was such a sad life here." Helen sighs. "Always under her father's thumb. Once she began to grow up, become a woman, their relationship was so...volatile. I respected that about her, you know, that she didn't just accept everything he told her to do, as I did with my father. She had a spirit about her."

This wistful, loving description is so unlike anything Maya's heard Helen say before, and Maya feels the sweetness of it expand in her own chest. "I wish I'd known her." After Maya says this, she realizes that it's true.

Helen nods, accepting this kindness before closing her eyes against what Maya imagines to be an inner twist of pain. "When she was a teenager, I convinced Harry to let me redo this room with her. Make it a bit more appealing to a teenager. She wouldn't let me get rid of this wallpaper, though. She said that Harry used to recite the poem to her." Helen's lip curls as she gestures toward the closest tiger. "I told her anytime she wanted, I'd come, and we'd have long walks and take tea and buy her a whole new wardrobe. It's not easy to lose one's mother, you know."

Maya *does* actually know. She wonders if Helen is aware of that piece of Maya's biography, and decides she probably is. All that vetting. Maybe she sent a private detective to Texas to check out Maya's mother's new life, make sure there was nothing tabloid-worthy going on there.

"After my mother left," Maya says carefully, "it was my aunt who saved me. I don't know if I ever told her that, though."

Helen considers this before drawing herself up straight in the chair. "I was *more* than an aunt."

That first time Maya met Helen, she was immaculately made up, just as she always appeared in magazines, at public events. But seeing Helen in her current state reminds Maya of an image she came across down some deep Google search. The three children of Richard Sterling in an old black-and-white photo, hair wind-whipped, sitting in a row on a stone wall in a green field. The seriousness of the middle child, Dickie; the radiant, puckish smile of young Harry; and in the middle, Helen, the big sister, her hair short as a boy's, physique long and athletic, and in her eyes a look of pure determination. When Maya saw that photo, she thought, *This is Helen Sterling*. The glamorous and fearsome matriarch, that's just a character Helen made up somewhere along the way.

In that moment, Maya had never understood Helen more. Until maybe now.

Gently Maya whispers, "You must have loved her a lot."

"I did. Then, as a teenager, she became so hard to reach, so rebellious."

"That's how I was. You couldn't tell me anything."

"Exactly, Arianna wouldn't listen. She was out of control. No matter what I did." Helen swallows. Shakes her head as if to cast off something unwanted. As though she's revealed too much. Once again, she fixes Maya in her gaze, a new hardness setting in her features. If there was a moment of connection, Maya senses it's over now.

"She made enemies," Helen goes on pointedly. "Unfortunately, that's very easy to do in this world."

Maya may only have met Helen once before, but she recognizes this tone. She feels the whiplash, just as she had when Helen made her fasten that pickaxe around her throat. This is a threat. She holds Becca tight against her, digs her fingernails into the doll for ballast. "I'm sorry," she whispers, trying to get back that moment of understanding. "I didn't mean to..."

"It's good you want to know about her. If you want to be a part of this family, you should know our history. But right now, you should go to your room. Go to bed, Maya."

Did Maya fantasize those moments of softness and sorrow, when Helen spoke to Maya with what felt like respect and vulnerability?

Not until Maya is back in the nursery suite, lowering Becca's little body, heavy and warm with sleep, into the crib, does she realize she still has the stupid doll. She tosses it on the night-stand and climbs into bed beside the sleeping Colin. But the doll has fallen in an awkward position—slumped, facing Maya, one eyelid shut, the other stuck open. Another creature of the Sterling realm, haunted, ancient, and bizarre, one eye trained on Maya.

As she drifts into sleep, she can't shake her sense of the surveilling intensity of the porcelain doll's single yellowed eye.

7

Pretty sorry lot here. Now that I've been skipping my meds, I see it. I'm surrounded by slouching, stumbling, hollow-cheeked lunatics. We sit in our "group therapy," a real pack of simple-tons, vacant-eyed, stringy-haired, mumbling and muttering. I'm considering going back on the meds just so that I can shut out the noise. They must all come from money, though—there's not a callus in sight. Plus, Harry's such a snob, I'm sure he told Travis: *Only the finest loony bin for my little wacko!*

Not that I can judge. I mean, it's not like I'm such an impressive specimen.

My eyes have the lovely murkiness of a murdered trout, and my daily uniform is very cult member chic: white scrub pants, a sort of loose-fitting shift on top. And I'm a complete sloth. It's quite the effort to get from bed to window.

All I have energy for is the television, and only the stupidest television will do.

Thankfully, there's a channel that plays nothing but reality shows. They're doing a marathon right now of this show about a lot of teenagers living in a beach town. It's delightful in a soul-curdling way, watching all these spray-tanned Americans shred each other, just for a little attention. They're odious. They open their mouths, and idiocy flows. Great stuff. Except for the dark-haired one—the one who is fucking the main girl's ex-boyfriend. She's always *slightly* above the fray—watching, plush lips pursed in disgust. She'll roll her eyes—

The girl is a <u>maestro</u> of eye-rolling!—

and then she'll point out the hypocrisy of one of the other girls on the show, and it's like a Molotov cocktail tossed. *Boom. BOOM. BOOM!!*

I remember a little more, now—yesterday is fairly solid, and if I try *very* hard, I can recall a few things from the previous morning—

If I told them about the nightmares, they'd say I did it to myself, by being such a degenerate and putting all that poison in myself and scrambling my little brains for breakfast with booze and pills. That the meds really are the best choice now. My only hope (boo hoo).

But every time I look at that little plastic cup, I think of what *they're* trying to do—erase me. Whatever treatment they did when I arrived has erased a lot, and the meds will do the rest. I watch the doctors come and go. They *act* nice; they pretend they care. But they don't. They know who pays the bills, and the people who pay the bills are the Sterlings, the ones who want me gone.

Not taking the meds is rather complicated and disgusting—I tuck them between my gums and my cheek, and when no one is looking, I mix them in with the food I don't eat, an old trick, but somehow it works on these idiots.

Aunt Helen would reprimand me—such poor table manners!

But on the other hand, maybe she would approve. She always did odd things with her food too. *Only ever eat a quarter of what's on your plate* or *Make a forkful, but don't put it in your mouth.* She had rules like that, and it's true, she never gained an inch.

But she had control, and I never did.

I could've stuffed a whole breakfast buffet in my mouth. I could swallow the ocean.

Thank god for cocaine. I remember, my sweet sixteen—just after Gi and I had discovered snow—Helen was so approving.

She said: My *dear* you're a *wraith;* you're down a *stone.*

Actually, Aunt Helen, it was a stone and a half.

I guess I *am* remembering some things.

I remember going down to the kitchen of Silver House, the night before a big formal party, and stuffing my gullet with tiny cakes till it all came right back up.

I remember when I flung a piece of firewood at mean old Harry, gave him a black eye and a mild concussion.

I remember when I stole a case of Harry's champagne, and invited the gardener's son to skinny-dip in the fountain in front of Silver House. It was January, and they say I nearly lost a toe.

After that, they only filled the fountain from June to September.

I remember Harry's place on La Digue, in the Seychelles, the smell of the tropics and the sea, the jungle plants that exploded all around the house, and the feeling of being cared for.

The girl who used to play with me. My best friend—my only friend, skipping through my memories of little girlhood, climbing trees, setting a tea party for our dolls, holding hands, promising we'd be best friends forever and ever.

Another motherless girl. That's what Harry used to say—my daughter needs a friend; these motherless girls need each other.

Until then, I had not known I was motherless.

Is that why the memory fills me with an old, bad sinkingness, a great winch turning in my stomach? Because she's my motherless shadow? Maybe she is just made up, as they say; maybe she represents me, at that very moment, when I realized Mother was gone.

I have this guilt, this sense of a stern presence, that I'm about to be reprimanded. A voice saying, *Don't make up stories!*

And then she and I are alone, and I'm whispering to her that she needn't worry; *I* know she's real. And she smiles at me with her big eyes flashing, and that pale skin and oval face, telling me, *Don't worry, I know you're real too.*

The reprimanding voice: *You must not think of sad things that can't be helped.*

I want to scream back, *What couldn't be helped?*

Me and my friend, hiding in cupboards in Silver House, running between the big rocks on the beach near the villa at La Digue...

It's coming to me now. I'm shaking; my hand's just wobbling across the page.

What couldn't be helped?

The smoke, the flames?

Now, I know what that is. What I'm thinking of is the fire in Seychelles, in Harry's villa on La Digue. The fire that killed his best friend, the fire Harry thought might've been meant for him—to end him.

From the speedboat, we saw the fire, the blaze reflected on the still black sea.

It was later that Harry said, *It was me they wanted; we can't be too careful now; they'll be lying in wait for us, wherever we go.*

Who was they? I never asked...

After that, we went back to Sterling Park, and Harry raised the ramparts, so to speak.

By then I understood it was one of those tragedies that suck other tragedies into it, same as a magnet draws iron filaments. That was what made Harry bitter with the world, turned us into prisoners. *They were after us*, he'd tell me. *We must never let our guard down again.*

And later, whenever I brought it up, then everyone would get *very* gloomy, and I'd have to talk to the doctors again. All the specialists to examine me and ask me questions, ask me over and over, *Was I sure about that? How could I be really sure? Maybe I was just remembering wrong?*

They told me it was dangerous to remember, and perhaps it is. Perhaps it's better to take my meds like a good little girl and watch this daffy television show. These bleach-blond morons, drinking till they say the worst, meanest thoughts they've ever had.

They remind me of Gigi a bit, not giving a fuck, making

the most of a night, wearing a dress that's basically nothing, letting the men buy us drinks—saying to each other, *Come on you gorgeous slut, nothing to see here, nothing good to remember, either; here's to tomorrow; may it be a fog; may we be as beautiful and broken as the tabloids say we are.*

Except, I'd rather not. If I had a choice about it, I'd rather not be broken.

I'd like to be like the girl on the television, the one who waits until the right moment and then speaks a word like a struck match.

Sets a fire that somehow makes it all go *her* way…

8

The morning sun is so bright in the room, Maya senses it even with her eyes closed. For a moment she's suspended in semiconsciousness, aware of nothing but the clean sheets against her skin. She's really here, inside the luxurious haven of Silver House, its richly floral atmosphere, this place she saw pictured in a magazine spread as a child and dreamed of visiting. Then she remembers last night, her encounter with Helen, the sense of claustrophobia, the uncanny doll's eye.

After her predawn ramble, Maya placed Becca in the crib and lay down beside Colin. But now the other half of the bed has been smoothed and the canopied crib in the alcove emptied. Colin must be awake, must've taken Becca with him. Maya showers in a hurry and dresses in what she can rummage from the closet: old trousers and a Fair Isle sweater. Gigi's, Maya presumes, from her days bringing boyfriends home from college for Sterling Christmases, the great family gathered for stag hunts and grog by the massive hearth, a holiday worthy of immortalization in *Vanity Fair*.

In the photos Maya has seen of young Colin and Gigi, they're always dressed in unfashionable, outdoorsy clothes. Always pink cheeked. So unlike their current city chic. She wonders what it must have been like, then. Did they always talk about the markets, the latest profit and loss reports, even when they were still in school? Or was that a simpler, chummier time?

The Sterlings may have been cool and closed about the whole tragedy yesterday, but Maya suspects they're just keeping her out. Arianna's death has surely presented the family with a public relations nightmare. Not to mention the money. Shares of the business, the family trust, the power balance. What does it mean to have one less heir?

The heiress, as everyone keeps saying.

It's still early, but Maya knows she's overslept. Distressed that she is once again making a poor introduction, she ties her hair back in a bun, hurries to put on a little mascara and gloss, and leaves the nursery. Colin mentioned the family lawyer was coming today. Has he arrived already? Probably it's all preamble, she reassures herself. There must be enormous amounts of red tape around anything to do with shifting Sterling holdings. But they'll all have their angles, and her priority is Colin. She needs to help her husband keep his head, argue for what's best for him. Him, and *his* family.

Lost in her inner pep talk, Maya has arrived on the first floor disoriented.

There are so many gilded curlicues and so little sign of Colin.

"Everyone's at breakfast, ma'am."

Maya turns and sees that a maid has come up behind her. Or been there all along? She wears livery of dove gray and white. No makeup. Probably around Aunt Rebecca's age, though they're such different types, it's hard to tell. Her posture is subservient, but there's something insistent at the same time. "Breakfast?" Maya prompts, trying to appear not the sort who would stoop to clean their own shattered glass. For a moment Maya is sure this woman can see through her to the little girl she used to be.

"In the yellow dining room."

Maya turns and rolls her eyes—as if she knows where the fucking yellow dining room is—before the maid takes pity on her and leads the way through a series of corridors. Maya has been inside some of the most extravagant homes in New York City, slept in architectural masterpieces all over the world, but she's never been in a home so labyrinthine it requires color designations to differentiate dining rooms.

When they arrive, the maid gestures Maya toward the threshold of the dining room. The door's ajar, and Maya glimpses the sun-warmed tranquility inside. Fresh-cut flowers adorn a table in the center of the floor, and a breakfast buffet has been laid out on a sideboard: glass carafes of orange juice atop a delicate lace runner, stacks of toast, scrambled eggs in silver serving dishes. It's cozier than Maya expected, less formal.

Maybe this is what it was like when they were college kids home for the holidays, Maya thinks. Everyone helping themselves to homey meals presented on communal platters. Then she remembers what Colin said in the car, how they were exiled from

Silver House for the better part of a decade, during the years it was just Harry and Arianna, and a flash of little Arianna at one end of the table blinks through her mind. How frightful and lonely it must have been.

Maya hangs back, trying to gauge the mood. Through the sliver of the doorframe, she sees the Sterlings sitting around the expansive table with full plates of food before them. Helen doesn't appear to have arrived. Of course Maya should make her presence known, but she's not eager to blunder into the group dynamic again, open herself to another indifferent reception.

"I think the numbers will hold," Colin is saying to Marcus. He's talking about the merger that was the focus of their Mexico trip. Marcus's eyes don't lift from his newspaper. "I spoke to Santos and he said—"

"Can you two stop talking business for five fucking seconds?" Gigi cuts in. She looks a bit rough, kohl-smudged eyes, rumpled shirt, as though she were up late and didn't have much energy to get herself together this morning. Maya can picture her, waving a cosmo late last night, giggling over Maya's see-through shirt. "This meeting is about *Arianna*, and her *tragic death*, not your shit acquisition."

Marcus folds his newspaper and addresses his cousin. "I didn't realize you were so sentimental, Geeg. When was the last time you even talked to Arianna?"

"You're fucking joking. It was me who held that girl's hair back while she vomited; for years it was like that between us; she did the same for me. When Dad and Mum died, she was the only one who cared. I mean, she really understood. *You* certainly didn't. Marcus, the only Sterling with a full set of parents. I cared more about that tragic little slapper than you ever could."

Now Marcus does lay down his newspaper, crossing his arms over his chest. "Right. And that's why you were checking the stock price on your BlackBerry every five minutes during dinner last night. Because you were so broken up about cousin Ari's death, and her sad, sad motherless childhood."

Gigi's complexion goes violet. "You know as well as I do that Arianna's death has a massive impact on each of us, and on the company."

Maya creeps forward. She's curious about this too. If Arianna stood to inherit so much of the family company, does that mean it reverts back to the board? To the people in this room? Or was none of it hers yet; was she only the richest of them in theory?

"Please, let's not," Colin says in his peacemaker tone.

A tense pause follows. Then Gigi asks, in a smaller voice, the voice of a woman who can't help herself, "Any idea what they're going to tell us about the redistribution?"

"No." Marcus shoves back his chair, strides to the buffet, aggressively refills his coffee cup.

"Rory should be here soon," Colin offers. "Travis said he was taking the seven forty-five up from London."

"*Rory.*" Gigi emits a petulant little huff and casts her gaze at the grand window behind her framing elegant, leafless gardens. "I thought we shuffled him downstairs. What happened to what's her name—the one with the flappy ears."

Eva supplies the name: "Silvia." Maya hadn't noticed Eva was in the room, still can't make her out from her current vantage point—but now she realizes that Marcus's wife has been following every detail, just as Maya should.

"Right, Silvia," Gigi says. "She was sharper than old Rory, I thought."

Colin gives his little sister an *are you serious* face. "Only because she was willing to support your little coup d'état—"

"Fuck you, Col, it wasn't a *coup*. It was the right thing to do. Excuse me for wanting to bring us into the new century. You *know* Granddad's will was a dodgy piece of work, leaving everything to Harry like he did."

This is precisely what Maya wants to know more about, but that's when she feels a crawling sensation on the back of her neck.

"Lurking again?"

Maya revolves toward Helen. Last night, in the predawn gloom of Arianna's old bedroom, she appeared broken and haunted. Now she's immaculate. Hair swept back into a chic low bun, and dressed in an exquisitely tailored pantsuit. Not a trace of vulnerability. Helen assesses Maya, one nostril gently quivering, as if she smells something distasteful and is trying to place it.

Did Maya imagine that conversation last night, or is Helen trying to keep her off-balance?

Before Maya can reply, Helen breezes past her into the breakfast room. "Rory's arrived," Helen announces to the others. "He has the paperwork from Arianna's lawyer, so please stop acting like children. We have decisions to make."

Maya sheepishly enters in Helen's wake.

Helen puts a few buffet items on her plate, takes the seat at the head of the table, and draws her butter knife over her toast with ominous purpose. Maya remembers Colin telling her about this oddity of Sterling family mealtimes. Everyone must be served and take a bite before Helen will eat. When Colin told Maya about this ritual awhile back—over steak tartare at 2:00 a.m. at Café Florent—family meals at Sterling Park seemed like the stuff of ancient history. Stiff and absurd and very far away. Colin explained that this custom went back to more cutthroat times, a safety measure to make sure none of the lesser heirs had poisoned the head of house. Or so it was said. Really, the point was that Grandfather set this rule, so Helen did too. And of course, Colin added with a laugh, there was the bonus pleasure of exerting arbitrary control over everyone at the table.

Colin's eyes meet Maya's, then roll toward the buffet. She nods, tamping down the eye roll that threatens at all the unnecessary pomp, before crossing over and hurriedly placing a croissant on a plate.

"Know how many calories those have?" Eva asks as Maya settles into a chair across from her, beside Colin.

Anger sparks low in Maya's chest, but her voice is weightless with innocence when she answers, "Millions?"

Gigi snorts. "Yes, well, Maya likes millions of everything."

"Sure do," Maya shoots back—a plain fact, no shame about it. Colin's awkwardly smiling at the room, and she can tell he doesn't like the hazing. But Maya can take it. She turns her hand up so that the pale-pink emerald-cut diamond on her left finger catches the light. It's actually worth a million and a half. As Gigi probably knows, since the readers of *On Dit* do too.

Maya glances from Gigi to Eva to make sure they're still watching, pulls the end of her croissant, and slowly, purposefully, puts it in her mouth with her left hand, ring finger prominent.

There's a silence, then knives and forks graze porcelain, then chewing, swallowing, and finally, Helen's teeth cracking through the crust of her toast. Maya feels it, that fiery part of herself wanting to keep pushing. Show them who Maya fucking Miller really is. But then Colin taps her knee and Maya calms, remembers her mission, the pep talk she gave herself in the hall. Be there for Colin, be the supportive wife. She readjusts, summons poise.

A man Maya hasn't met before enters the room, takes the seat opposite Helen.

"Hello, pardon my tardiness." He's in a rumpled oxford shirt, hair thinning. Not notably anything—not especially tall or short, heavy or thin. His eyes are a middling brown, but they do have a keen light.

The family murmurs a tepid greeting in his direction. *This must be the lawyer*, Maya thinks, as Colin leans close. "Rory Atkinson, SterlingCo General Counsel," he whispers in Maya's ear. She nods and smiles blandly, though inwardly anxiety tightens her stomach. Even though she expected it, the presence of SterlingCo's top lawyer puts her on edge.

Rory searches the files from his briefcase, removing a few,

before gesturing at one of the black-clad security guards. Maya recognizes this one—Travis from the airplane. He's holding something. A folder, which he places in Rory's hand.

It reminds her of another folder, plain manila, lying open on a humble wooden table in the Iguana Bar, that night in Mexico. The night Arianna died. Her stomach drops.

Why would the security guard have one of the lawyer's folders in the first place?

This is all very normal, Maya tells herself. But she can't quell the screaming fear that her secret is about to be exposed. Could the evidence be there, right now, in Rory's little folder?

"Right, well," Rory begins. "General news first. The Arianna story hasn't broken in the wider press yet, although we believe a journalist at the *Times* has it—probably not with enough to back up her anonymous source. We'll have our strategy sorted by the time it gets out." As he continues with the progress report, Maya begins to relax—this isn't about *her* whereabouts in Mexico; this is about messaging around Arianna's death and the fate of her inheritance. Maya needs to stop darting into these paranoid alleyways of her mind, stay focused.

"The Mexican authorities are close to releasing Arianna's body," he continues. "We're making preparations for that. The murder investigation is as yet inconclusive. We haven't identified any known enemies of Arianna's. Of course, as the person who stood to inherit a majority of Sterling assets, her security threats were always more serious."

"But what was she *doing* there?" Marcus gestures impatiently, fixing Rory in a dissatisfied glare. Maya hopes he doesn't push too much on the details of that night—she doesn't want to be asked about her own whereabouts again.

"Surely she had some plan, someone she emailed her itinerary to, communicated with at the hotel?" Colin asks.

"She wasn't staying in a hotel," Rory says, glancing down at to his file. "In fact, there is no electronic record of the accommodations she made for herself in Puerto Vallarta at all. The building she was staying in, it wasn't a dump, but it wasn't particularly luxurious, either. A few cartel people own apartments in the building, but that appears to be a coincidence. It's a bit of a black box, I'm afraid."

"Have you found any of her little diaries?" Everyone turns toward Julian, who looks back innocently over the rim of his teacup.

Maya would like to know why a grown man is asking about a young woman's diaries—was this poor girl permitted no life of her own?—but she controls herself, imitates Eva's alert and impartial expression. Helen shoots Julian a the grown-ups are talking glare, but Julian smiles blithely, apparently impervious to his wife's disdain.

Julian goes on with a shrug. "She was always scribbling away in some notebook or other, don't you remember, Helen? Could prove useful to find such a thing. Maybe she was in some trouble..." He turns to face Maya. "Did you know I'm writing a book about the fam—"

"No," Rory interrupts, attempting to take back the reins

of the conversation. Apparently Rory, while deferential to the other members of the family, has no trouble talking over Julian, shutting down his book pitch. "I don't believe anything like that was recovered from the crime scene. Our working theory is that it was a botched kidnapping with the intention of demanding ransom. Perhaps the kidnappers guessed she would be in that area, what with the family wedding." Rory's eyes flick toward Colin and Maya.

Maya hopes it only *feels* like she's blushing, that none of the people now staring at her notice.

Rory continues. "There are signs she resisted—that there was a fight."

Marcus makes a grunt of disgust and gets up again. Pouring more coffee, he asks, "Isn't the boyfriend always the prime suspect?"

"Yes, well, we don't know much about Arianna's activities since—" Rory cuts off.

"Since what?" Gigi presses. Maya is surprised to see Gigi's unguarded expression, her eyes suddenly wide and yearning.

Rory clears his throat. "We don't have information on what relationships she was engaged in, how she came to Mexico, or—"

"I'm sorry," Helen interrupts. "What *do* you know?"

Rory nods and tents his fingers. His brows drag upward and together, a little peak of concern. "Ms. Sterling, I completely understand—"

"Like hell you do."

"Told you we should have gone with Silvia," Gigi murmurs.

"It's a frustrating situation," Rory says, running a hand through his hair. "I sympathize. If anyone has any information—anything at all that you think might be relevant—please do let me know so I can loop in the authorities."

Suddenly, everyone seems allergic to eye contact. Maya is glad not to be looked at, glad no one can read the secret on her face, observe the squirminess that overcomes her when she remembers where she was that night. But as the silence extends, she glances around, notices the defensive postures in the room, and begins to wonder, *What might they all have to hide?*

After several tense moments, the silence is broken by Helen. "Well then." She sets her cup down on its saucer with a little clink of finality. "Thank you, Rory, for the update. I believe there are now other matters we need to discuss?"

Maya senses everyone leaning in. Ready to get down to business, what Arianna's death means for SterlingCo, what it means for them.

"Eva, dear—"

Eva plasters a smile on her face. "Yes, Mum?"

"Maya ought to see the grounds. Would you show her around?"

A directive, not a suggestion.

Helen touches Julian's hand, the corners of her mouth twitching in an upward direction. "Why don't you go too? You can give Maya a proper tour of our little home. She should learn all that family history if she's going to be a be a Sterling."

What do you mean if? Maya thinks. But this room is stifling and she finds she's having a hard time sitting still. Moving a bit doesn't sound like the worst idea. She stands, puts her left hand on Colin's shoulder, once more displaying her ring finger; and he takes her hand, pulls her close for a kiss. She draws it out, enjoys his mouth soft against hers, lets everyone in the room see it—that what they have is real.

"Of course, duckie," Julian is saying to his wife, drawing everyone's gaze back to the head of the table. He, too, is on his feet. "Off we go."

As Maya, Julian, and Eva leave the table, the servants begin clearing their dishes. Colin gives Maya an apologetic smile, and Gigi stage-whispers, "As soon as this is over, I'm headed straight to the hammam. You should meet me for some girl time." With a meaningful glance at Rory, she says, "Noon, this should all be over by noon. Right?"

Maya, who hadn't realized there *was* a hammam, can only nod and allow herself to be funneled toward the hall. She knows why she's being so unceremoniously shoved off with Eva and Julian. A discussion about the inheritance is to be had. No interlopers.

Only Sterlings by blood allowed.

Maya is annoyed, but she reminds herself that sometimes outsiders know more—or at least, are willing to share more— than those in the inner circle. She can still be useful to Colin in all this, even while banished from the table, just by listening, poking in the right places. Maya learned that from Deb, a producer she was friendly with on *The Springs*. Early in her time on the show, Deb pulled Maya into her office for a preseason strategy talk.

Look out for the person with a chip on their shoulder, Maya. If they find a sympathetic ear, they'll tell you everything they know.

Maya feels emboldened by this mission, a little excited even. But as she's ushered through the door, she notices that Rory Atkinson is staring at her. His hand still on that folder. What's he got in there? A spider of agitation crawls up Maya's throat. Maybe he already knows everything that happened in Puerto Vallarta, the threat that compelled her out into a strange city by herself, maybe he has photographic evidence of the secret that could detonate Maya's life.

Maybe he already knows everything.

And if so the Sterlings are about to discover the worst of Maya too.

9

A clutch of servants awaits them in the grand foyer, ready with oilskin coats and wellies. Were they summoned that quickly, or had Helen set this plan in motion before the family gathered for breakfast?

As Maya is helped into the coat, she has a sudden desperate need to be back in that room. *Is* everything about to be taken away from her? If Rory is going to blow up her life, she at least wants to be there to witness the wreckage, tell Colin she's sorry; she was only trying to protect them...

But Julian and Eva are leading the way, the dogs loping alongside eagerly, and there's no easy way to change course. They're crossing the massive foyer, moving through the grand front doors, passing the empty fountain. Is Eva perturbed by this banishment from the family meeting? Her blank face—handsome more so than beautiful—is rigid. Julian, on the other hand, appears jovial about the whole thing, striding toward the gardens, taking in big mouthfuls of air while humming appreciatively.

"A little trek with the *out*laws!" he proclaims as he leads the way over the paved courtyard, the pair of border collies keeping pace with him.

Eva, by contrast, drops her façade. "Cute little names don't make our dismissal any less galling," she says, flipping up her collar to cover her throat. "I'd say they make it more so. But go ahead, lie to yourself, Mr. *Lambert-Sterling*." Maya hides her smile at this obvious dig, Julian blatantly pinning his wife's name on his own.

Julian casts a pitying glance at his daughter-in-law—who of course also benefits from their surname—and gives Maya an apologetic smile. "There is no shame in our position in the firmament, my dear. It is their family *business*, but our *family*, and we contribute in our own way. I'm the historian; that's my little niche. I know all the Sterling nooks and crannies. You'll find yours—the thing that makes you indispensable. Great families don't need new money so much as they need constant infusions of fresh blood," Julian goes on, rambling and associative, his voice swelling with imagined significance as he sets off up the hill. After the coldness in the drawing room, the icky false intimacy of Gigi's welcome, the friction over the breakfast table, Maya's grateful for Julian's affability, his willingness to acknowledge what others won't. Her, mainly. "You must not feel, dear Maya, that you are the first commoner brought into the Sterling fold."

"Oh, yeah, that's been made very clear," Maya replies with a laugh, hoping to cover the slight sting. "The part about me being common, anyway."

Eva's lips draw back in displeasure. "I wouldn't be so proud of that," she says.

In a different life, Maya realizes that she and Eva would make good TV—trading barbs back and forth. The audience would love it. At least, Julian seems to, a grin now playing on his face.

"I myself," Julian goes on, pace brisk, dogs swimming between his legs and leading the way, "am a direct descendent of the main Hapsburg line, albeit through a mistress, and could claim a Danish title on my mother's side, though I was working as a ski instructor when Helen and I fell in love. She was nearly ten years older than I, and glorious to behold. I wanted to give her ten children immediately, but alas, we were only to have the one. Perhaps there could be but one Marcus. Where are your people, Maya?"

Maya can feel Eva's smirk at her back. "Yes, Maya, do tell."

Maya's lips press hard together. Maybe she was too quick to warm to Julian. Is he really going to make her describe the sort of hovel she crawled out of?

Or, more likely, he already knows, and is poking her, wanting to see how she'll react. A heat rises in her chest. But then Maya notices the spark in Julian's eye and realizes he's not condemning her. It's all playful, at most a test of her mettle.

"I myself," she says, lightly imitating his tone, "am descended from a distinguished line of gamblers, fishwives, and thieves."

"Ah," Julian says, barking out a laugh, "the flinty humor that made you such a success on television! Don't tell any of my literary friends, but I loved *The Springs*. Absolutely lapped it up!"

"Oh yeah, brilliant stuff," Eva comments with savage sarcasm. "The trouble with people like you," she says, looking Maya plainly in the face, "is that when you come around, suddenly all of our dirty laundry gets pawed through."

Before Maya can reply, a figure calls to them from the base of the hill. It's a nanny—white-faced, huffing her way up the rise.

"Madame!" The nanny is trying to keep her voice even. She's definitely a little panicked, and that stirs Maya's anxiety too.

"Yes?" Eva lifts an imperious brow. The stricken face of a nanny does not, apparently, make her fear for her children's safety.

"It's Lance. And Ian. Lance was going to do some target practice with the air rifle, but he got the Mauser and—"

"Right." Eva adjusts her gloves, squints at the nanny. "So, what's the issue?"

"Lance shot—killed—a squirrel."

"Oh." Eva's posture relaxes. Maybe she is human, after all? "A squirrel. Is that all?"

"Well, you see, it seems that Ian had given the squirrel a name. Bubbles the squirrel. It was his *favorite* squirrel, he says. And now he's inconsolable. He wants Mama."

Eva turns toward Maya, who once again has the unpleasant experience of being the object of Eva's full attention. "Can you believe this? You know they train for four years to wear that uniform—but if the young master wants *Mama*..." She brightens up her features, calls back to the nanny with mocking cheer. "In that case! I mean, it's not every day you get to explain squirrel heaven to your little angel..."

Maya and Julian exchange a glance as Eva charges down the hill. Could that be laughter behind his eyes at his daughter-in-law's expense? Maya, for one, feels a weight lifted now that she's gone.

"Come on." Julian takes Maya's arm. Over his shoulder, the wind cries against the old wall. "Helen told me to give you the tour—shall we?"

As they move away from the grand house, ascending through a series of tiered gardens, Maya senses the adjustments of the security team in her peripheral vision. A wind is up, and Julian keeps sucking in deep lungfuls of country air, making those gratified pips and hums.

"Magnificent, isn't she?" he says. They've reached what may be the high point of the walled portion of the property—below them, the land slopes toward assorted outbuildings, vegetable plots, a greenhouse. It's the backstage of the estate and Julian narrates it all for her, pointing out interesting features, its limits, its historical significance.

He gestures at the battlements, listing the wars during which they saw action. ("Long ago, of course, dear Maya; now there's really nothing out there, just some stray hunting lodges deep in the woods and a few old villages.")

The spa ("the hammam, as the family likes to say,") nestled between the tennis courts and the greenhouse. ("We're a rather outdoorsy lot; we need a good steam now and then.")

The hedge maze, planted in the 1800s. ("The kids used to go in there with *crates* of booze, thinking we wouldn't notice them trying to stumble their way out at midnight, the drunkards.")

Maya listens, soaking it all in, nodding with dutiful interest. Julian wraps up with a chummy, "Should we drink to it, then?"

"To what?" Maya asks, eyes still roaming the kingdom before her.

"Our inclusion in the Sterling ranks, of course," Julian says. From the breast pocket of his waxed jacket, he pulls a flask and two stainless steel shot glasses, and pours them each a few fingers of brown liquid. "Eva has a reasonable claim to being of the manor born; her people were very prominent before her father lost it all, and she was obligated to work for a living. She gets by pretending there is not a scrap of ignominy in her past, though. But you and I, we understand our place." Maya feels her eyes narrow, but Julian brushes off her defensiveness with a quick laugh. "Don't misunderstand me, dear girl. I don't mean to diminish you. Or me. In fact, you and I may have more to celebrate than most in this house. We know what the Sterling name really *means*, because we know what it's like to live without it. There's power in that, Maya. In remembering what it's like out there, knowing how much it would mean to lose the name, and all that comes with it."

Maya considers this. She was born the opposite of a Sterling; she knows what it is to want and strive. Besides Colin, Julian's the first person in the Sterling family to make that sound like an asset. She touches her glass to his, and the tightness over what's going on back in the house loosens slightly.

"If you ever need a confidant, please know you can trust me. I understand how bristly the Sterlings can be at first." He tips his chin and Maya nods in return. For a moment, she's reminded of her dad—the best part of him, the part that really knew how to enjoy his spoils. "*Argentum semper vincit!*" Julian toasts.

The Sterling family motto—*Silver always wins.*

Maya is wary of drinking on an almost empty stomach, but it's freezing out here, and the whiskey warms her going down. "Argentum semper vincit."

She's seen the motto engraved on various frames and trophies and commemorative platters around the SterlingCo office. But she's only heard it out loud once before, from Colin, after she agreed to put his ring on. He was grinning broadly, and she told him *yes, she would marry him*, and that he could now get off his tennis-battered knees. Then he said the motto, translating the Latin for her, and there was something in the way it came out, a gravelly sincerity that made her believe he needed her as much as she needed him. That maybe he was the real winner.

Maybe Helen needed her ski instructor, and maybe Marcus— who, after all, is a bit of a rogue—needs his fearsome wife. Maybe the Sterlings need Maya too. And maybe, just maybe, she'll need Julian in her corner.

At the very least, a friend in Silver House could make the social rituals less opaque, could help her untangle the family tree.

As Julian refills the glasses, she once again notices the resemblance between Marcus and his father, that powerful brow and easy, charming grin.

"Julian." Maya speaks slowly. "How long do you think we'll be here?"

"That's for them to know and us to find out, I suppose." Julian shrugs, gestures grandly at the surrounding landscape. "In the meantime, there's all this to enjoy."

"Well." Maya releases a white cloud of breath. "Yeah, I guess."

"You aren't satisfied? Isn't this all you ever dreamed of?"

She thinks back to those glossy photos in *Vanity Fair*. "It's gorgeous. But New York is home, you know?"

Julian smiles kindly and takes her by the arm. "It *is* all a bit of a nuisance. This whole protocol 202 thing! I'd never heard of it. If it were me, or even Gigi—someone a bit further down the ladder—there wouldn't be so much to-do. Arianna, on the other hand... Well, there'll be a lot more to sort."

"There's no protocol for the father of the CEO?" Maya asks teasingly. "I think you should protest, Julian. You're a big deal—Hapsburg royalty, I've heard!"

Julian laughs, but halfheartedly, like he knows it's the proper reaction. "Bless you, but—no. I signed, just like you." Maya stomach tightens at this reference to the prenup, how easily she succumbed.

"Did she give *you* a pickaxe necklace?" The words slip from Maya's lips before she can stifle them.

Julian takes a breath. She wonders if she's miscalculated, talking about Helen like this. "Oh, that," he says. "I told her not to do that. But you can't take it personally. Don't let her think she can cow you. And, frankly, I expected more from Miss Mayhem! A little more fight."

"She doesn't think I'm in it for the money though, does she?"

"Oh, probably, but what does that matter? I never had any either, before Helen. It feels good, doesn't it? And then, once you have it, you'll do anything not to lose it."

Maya wants to protest in the usual way—she makes her own money; she has a job. But that seems silly in this moment. Of course marrying Colin has brought her into a new stratosphere of wealth, and of course she doesn't want to lose that. She smiles sheepishly, and Julian gives her a little nod of understanding.

This is feeling friendly, Maya thinks as they amble on—friendly enough to push a little. "But I mean, if Arianna was the *heiress*—and her father is still alive—is there really anything to be surprised about in her will?"

Julian blinks at Maya. "Curious creature, aren't you? Well, it's true, she would've inherited more if she had not predeceased her father. But it's a bit tricky, I believe. Seems he transferred much of what she was to inherit into her name during his lifetime. For tax purposes, I believe. Inveterate cheat that he is. With Harry, there's often an ulterior motive too—perhaps he worried that Arianna wouldn't have the wherewithal to defend what was hers once he was gone, wanted it all squared away while he was alive." Then he smiles big and says, in an avuncular manner, "I suppose you're fascinated by her? Hungry to know about the little lost Sterling girl?"

"Not really." *Did that sound harsh?* The opposite admission to Helen hadn't gotten her very far. "I mean, I didn't even know she existed until we were on our way here..."

Julian pauses, taking her in again. "Really? You never read about her?"

Maya shrugs. "No."

"Never tried to look her up?"

"Maybe I would have, if I'd known she was so important."

"Then I wonder why you're so curious now?" Julian clicks his tongue, not seeming quite as merrily unaware as a moment before. A pause opens inside Maya—has she been too candid? Has Helen, or Marcus, asked him to prod Maya, get her to lower her guard so she'll share her secrets? She puts on a carefree smile.

"You already know the answer, Julian." Maya winks and rubs her thumb and forefinger together like a greedy pickpocket. She laughs, and he laughs in return. "But truly, I'm not really curious. For Colin's sake, of course. He's so dedicated to his work."

Julian chuckles, seemingly amused by Maya. "Clever girl!"

"Not because of the money. Just because he cares, and what my husband cares about, I make it my business to understand."

"Well, you're right, as it happens. She *did* have a seat on the board, and a majority stake in the company, because of how Harry had structured her inheritance, transferring holdings to her early. But that was always theoretical, because she wasn't very interested—Harry was still in charge." Julian continues talking, about the other members of the board, what's on the agenda for the board meeting—explaining that Helen has long been concerned that the SterlingCo media assets are behind the times, that when Marcus came on as CEO he made moves to set that right. Maya nods along, glad she's gotten Julian gabbing, moved the attention away from her, her intentions.

"Anyway, commoners like you and me don't have to worry about that—we'll leave those corporate maneuvers to my son. It's not like *we* have a seat on the board or anything." Julian pauses to pour out another nip of whiskey for them both. "The only thing *you* need to worry about is how they reorganize the family trust now that Harry has no heir. It will put all the Sterlings in your generation into competition with each other, I'm afraid. I'd start dead-bolting my door at night, if I were you." He lifts his glass again, letting out a loud bark of a laugh. "Just kidding! Kidding, *of course*." He tips his head back, draining the cup. "But, in all seriousness, *do* watch out for Gigi. I know you two are pals, but she's a sneaky one. And cleverer than she looks."

"But not cleverer than me." Maya smiles.

"No dear, not cleverer than you." Julian's voice has gone down an octave. "I like you, Maya. I'm a gambler myself, you know. I never was good at the card table—Helen made me quit that. But I know how to bet on myself, and I suspect you do too. Don't let them make you feel ashamed of that."

The awkwardness Maya had been experiencing over her first day in Sterling Park lifts for a moment, and she's trying to think of a way to express her gratitude, when she's jolted by the sudden ecstatic barking of the dogs. She revolves, then notices that Travis is standing a little way down the hill. "Mrs. Sterling!" he bellows. "Your presence is requested in the dining room!"

"Me?" Maya turns to Julian, confused.

Julian's gaze fixes on Maya with sudden lucidity, as if he's just understood something crucial about her. "That's very unexpected," he says, and Maya senses that the intimacy of the previous moment has been squashed by this surprise turn.

"Yes," Maya agrees, furious at herself for wandering around the grounds and relaxing her vigilance. *Rory knows; he told them; he told Colin that I lied, that I met with someone the night Arianna died…* She can't manage even a smile for Julian as she turns away.

"Good luck," Julian calls after Maya as she trots down the hill. "Argentum semper vincit!"

Silver always wins.

There's a silent part, Maya thinks as she strides back toward the house: *No one else ever has a chance.*

———

A storm seems to have passed through the yellow dining room. No one greets Maya—they just stare at her, a row of hard and inscrutable faces. Even Colin seems to be trying to read her—what she's doing there or who she really is. His lips part and his gaze drifts down from her eyes to the mud she's tracked in. On *The Springs*, she always knew in advance if a big showdown was coming and made sure she was put together. She hates how underdressed she is now, still in the wellies and waxed jacket. She hates not knowing what's coming for her. *I'm sorry for lying; I'm sorry for everything.* And all the while her pulse is hammering: *they know, they know, they know.*

"Rory, fill her in," Helen says, in the same tone one says, *Clean that up,* to a child who's made a mess.

No one invites Maya to sit down, so she hovers near the edge of the table, trying to figure out something to do with her hands. Colin's face is pale and he's pulling at his ear; Marcus is slouched, eyes burning in Maya's direction—assessing her like a naughty pupil who's just said something interesting and inappropriate. Gigi is openly glaring.

"Unlike Richard's predecessors," Rory begins, "who left the majority of their wealth to their eldest son, Richard named his youngest, Harry, as the primary beneficiary of his estate, skipping over Dickie and Helen." Colin said something like this already, but Maya nods for Rory to continue, relieved that this at least doesn't seem to be about her whereabouts in Mexico. But then, why is she being given this lesson in Sterling family estate planning? Rory smothers a cough in a hankie and continues. "This inheritance meant a controlling percentage of the company, as well as a controlling number of votes in the family trust. Plus the crown jewel in which we all sit, Sterling Park..."

Maya would like a glass of water. Her mouth is bone-dry. She tries to stop herself from shifting from foot to foot.

As if his mouth is dry too, Rory clears his throat before continuing where he left off. "Some years ago, Harry transferred half of his individual shares in SterlingCo, all of his shares in the family trust, and his ownership of Sterling Park to his only child, Arianna Sterling."

Maya bobs her head, desperate for him to get to the point.

"The trustees have been nervous about this for some time," Rory continues, "especially given the increasingly erratic behavior of the heiress herself. When Harry began transferring his assets into her name, he did so with the assumption that she was his protégé, that they'd make all decisions together."

Gigi rolls her eyes at the mention of Arianna's special status, splashes champagne into a glass, and gulps as through trying to wash a rotten flavor from her tongue.

"But," says Rory, "when Arianna's will was faxed over from London this morning, it came as a bit of a shock."

"*Quite*," says Helen, those glacial blue eyes sliding up to meet Maya's.

"It seems Arianna made some last-minute changes. Instead of her estate being transferred back to her father upon her death, she named her own heir."

The way Helen, Colin, Marcus, and Gigi are staring at Maya makes her want to shrink. She wishes she hadn't taken that second shot of whiskey. Her lungs are on fire with a horrible realization. *Colin,* she thinks, *Arianna left everything to Colin, and they're worried that the prenup doesn't cover his new holdings...*

"An heir*ess*, you mean," Helen corrects.

Rory nods in regretful agreement. "*You,* Maya. You've been named the new heiress."

"Me?" she says idiotically. Her mind goes blank. All she can think is: *These assholes are punking me.* She turns to Colin, her expression begging for clarification. But he simply lowers his chin.

It's true. She's the new Sterling heiress. Maya feels unsteady, as if on a steep tilt. Her fingers feel numb. Toes too. A gust of wind rattles the windowpanes, shaking her already ragged nerves.

She waits for what Rory said to form some kind of logic in her mind. But before she can truly make sense of it, think of her strategy, Miss Mayhem peeks her head, snakelike, licking the air, sizing up this situation. Sizing up this stranger who's fucking with Maya from beyond the grave. Maya is scared and confused, and not a little pissed off. But there's something else too—a cold ripple of glee shivering through her at this wild turn of fortune. She closes her eyes, swallows.

"But I didn't know anything about Arianna until yesterday, and I can only assume she didn't know anything about me, either."

Helen is smiling ferociously. "Agreed, it is *very* strange."

"Not to mention legally questionable," Marcus puts in.

"Obviously it was some imbecile at the law firm who allowed this travesty." Helen taps the tabletop with her fingernails and gives Maya a withering look. "To be clear, that imbecile is no longer with the firm."

"I knew Arianna best," Gigi adds with a scowl. "I mean, if she were going to blow up the rules and leave it all to a girl, it would have been *me*. So obviously this will be handled."

Marcus scoffs at his cousin. "Arianna wasn't often in her right mind. For all we know, her will was made out to Gigi the week before it was made out to Maya, and made out to me the week before that. The point is," he goes on, ignoring Gigi's snort of disbelief, "no judge would give this new will any credence. Right, Colin?"

At Marcus's prompting, Colin finally speaks. "Maya, love," he begins, tone gentler than the others. But there's distance in his eyes, as though he can't risk their usual closeness. "The simplest thing is if you just sign it all back to the company, and our lawyers and financial advisors can redistribute Arianna's assets to the family according to their own metric."

Maya fights the rage rising through her body. This morning she was so ready, *so ready*, to fight alongside him for his share. And now here he is, doing the exact opposite because—she feels certain—his auntie told him to. If Colin hadn't just said *to the family*—as though she weren't one of them—if Helen weren't glowering so intensely—if Marcus hadn't just steamrolled over Arianna's wishes—if Gigi didn't seem on the verge of laughing at Maya's muddy wellies—maybe Maya might have reacted differently. But as Rory rises from his seat, puts a pen in her hand, she has a humiliating sense that this is how they deal with people like her. To them, it's not even that big a deal. It's happened before and it will go on happening again and again, and they'll just bully their way through.

The paperwork has already been drawn.

They expect her to sign without asking a single question, just like last time.

But things have changed, she realizes, the thought slicing through her confusion.

She is now the most powerful Sterling in the room.

Maya glances at the documents, arranged on the dining room table. With a gentlemanly hand at the elbow, Rory guides her arm toward the bottom line.

Maya thinks of Julian's parting words: *Argentum semper vincit.*

Was that just an insignificant remark, or did he mean it as a warning?

Colin nods again from his seat at the table, urging her on. "Maya, Arianna was unwell. We are your family. We'll take care of you."

All Maya can think of is Bob Feld, with his CUNY School of Law mugs and his endearing comb-over, and how proud of her he was when she signed her first really big contract, even as he fought like hell to protect her in the deal. *Just call me next time.*

"No," Maya says, dropping the pen.

"No?" Helen echoes.

"Obviously I can't sign any of this until it's been vetted by my lawyer."

"I am your lawyer," Rory says.

"No." Maya feels lightheaded, but she holds herself together. "You're not my lawyer. You're *their* lawyer." She gestures at her husband—his eyes dark with surprise—and his closest relatives, elbows pressed against their fine table. Their faces are pure contempt. There's a heat in the way they watch her leave the room, but she's interested to discover that she doesn't entirely care. Not anymore.

In the hall, the madness of her new situation finally crashes over her, a nauseating wave. She spots Barrow, waiting.

"I need to make a private phone call," she says, managing to keep her voice steady.

"This way." He gestures for her to follow, guiding her to his office and into an upholstered sitting chair. Seated, she begins to finally experience the heavy exhaustion of these past two days. Maybe Barrow senses the chaos growing inside her, the confusion, because he places a bottle of mineral water on the table and, glancing over his shoulder, murmurs, "I must warn you, this line isn't all that private. But you should have a few moments while they're all still in the meeting."

Maya lowers her head in understanding, mouths "thank you." Then she dials Bob Feld's office. But after a few rings, she realizes that in New York, it's still early; no one's in the office yet. Though she knows it's pointless, she hangs up and dials again. And again.

As she sits there, the weight of Arianna's final act drags Maya down below, to some scalding, molten place, alien and dangerous. For a while she just waits, too stunned to move. Too worried. Too...*ecstatic*. She can't begin to think about the implications, of what her so-called *family* out there might do in retaliation. What they might dig up. So instead she sinks down, listening to the dial tone, wondering why Arianna would leave everything to someone she had never met...

What kind of girl would *do* that?

PART II

10

DECEMBER

Signs of Christmas in the psych ward:

- CDs shuffle between Mariah Carey and Frank Sinatra; it's Carey/Sinatra roulette over here
- A horrid plastic tree has appeared in the common room (sad tinsel, rope of cranberries, popped corn)
- Some of the more catatonic patients are now wearing Santa hats (I wish Gigi were here; we'd have a good laugh about that, though I can't find the humor in it just me by lonesome).

Signs that it's all one endless day:

Not a *dot* of snow. Outside, it's rainy season. Wild torrents from the sky travel across my window. When it clears up in the afternoon, sometimes I'm allowed outside for a walk, which I am supposed to be slavishly grateful for. But then I had that déjà vu thing again—some familiar odor in the atmosphere—and I stopped enjoying it.

The air smells like our place on La Digue—

Which has this lovely hallucinatory association with the smell of burning flesh.

Now that I think about it, this fucking Mariah Carey album was what we listened to the first Christmas that actually felt like *Christmas*. When the cousins came back to Sterling Park—Harry let them in and said, let's try being a family again. I hadn't seen them since we were very small; I couldn't even remember them. And then suddenly they appeared before me, fully grown. Colin brought this absolute *drip* of a girlfriend with him from Cambridge, and she loved that Mariah Carey album—it had just come out that year—and she made us listen to it over and over.

She was very pretty, that girl, and I remember seeing her emerge from the nursery suite, which she and Colin were sharing, and her face was all pink and her hair was all undone and even though I was only twelve, I had this very deep and unnerving sense of what they had been doing, and it made me hungry in a way I had never been hungry before.

What was her name? Something ghastly like Victoire or Leopoldina.

Now there's a memory I wouldn't mind having zapped away.

And it's irrelevant anyway, because then Marcus, who had just come back from reporting in some war-ravaged hellhole, was merciless about the sappy sentimentality of the music—

not to mention the crass commercialization—

and then Gigi piled on, and Colin too, until this poor girl was driven from Sterling Park in tears. Colin was a bit irritated, but he agreed with the others. The girl was vile—it was better she was gone.

And I was glad because I wanted my cousins all to myself.

They were fascinating and terrifying. They seemed to *know* so much—not just about each other and what it meant to be a *Sterling*, but also about music and movies and world leaders and the right way to speak and talk about all of it. I followed them, worshipful as a dog.

I remember thinking how handsome Marcus was, a swash-buckler like in the books that Harry *did* allow me to read (that is, published no later than 1801), all those years I was locked up in Sterling Park with nothing but tutors and servants and nurses. And then I was afraid he might say something as cruel and dismissive about me as he did about Colin's girlfriend.

At first it was fun. We played cards and Gigi taught me how to smoke cigarettes.

She was fifteen, I think—she told me all about her boyfriends, this one and that one, what she'd done with them, what they'd do for her. I was so impressed, I just nodded along. She must have liked the audience. It didn't occur to me that all her bravado might have been on account of losing her parents.

Having never had a mother, really, it all seemed normal to me.

Glamorous early death, orphanhood. *That* old story.

Christmas Day that year was brilliant. Bracing, blue. For me this will always be what Christmas should be. It was very cold at night, and Marcus and Colin and Gigi and I got very bundled, and we snuck out from the house with a bottle of whiskey and one of Grandfather's hunting rifles and shot at the nocturnal things. The sky was pitch dark and alive with stars. In the morning the ground was frozen. Coldest day in years. And when us cousins came down—dreadfully hungover, sick with shame—Helen and Harry were sitting by the fire reminiscing. They looked very cozy, petting these border collie puppies, a brother and a sister, that Harry had given Helen for Christmas, and they were pouring sambuca in their coffee and laughing. It was such a strange look on Harry's face; I'd never seen my father like that—

and I thought, *So that's what he looks like happy.*

I suppose they were reminiscing about their bonny childhood at old Sterling Park. Barrow came in to see if the breakfast buffet needed replenishing and reported that the pond had frozen solid.

Then Helen smiled radiantly and said to Harry, "Shall we?"

Another tradition I was in the dark about. When grandfather Richard was in charge, apparently, whenever the temp dropped sufficiently for the pond to freeze, the locals were invited for a day of fun. Refreshments served, the store of fur coats brought out and handed around so that the pig farmers could be king for a day. I got to see it that day. They opened the gates, and the peasants (as Harry called them) came and donned these magnificent furs and drank Sterling Ceylon with rum, and the sun was pure and bright.

At first, I hung back with the cousins. We spiked our tea, and Gigi made jokes about the locals, how much they were enjoying their borrowed coats. There was this one boy—he was tall, whip thin; he had a very sculptural nose and pretty dark eyes. I couldn't stop staring at him. Whenever he glanced my way, I felt this mad heat between my legs.

The cousins noticed and began razzing me. *Young Arianna fancies a boy.*

126

It was partially because they were teasing me, and partially because I wanted to be closer to the boy, that I skated onto the pond...

Skating was one thing I *did* know—one of the things Harry permitted that I enjoyed. Maybe I was having too much fun. Maybe I was showing off.

Anyway, everything was wonderful until everything was horrible. I did a little jump, and the crowd applauded me, and then Gigi skated alongside and began to tease me, saying she was a Tonya and I was a Nancy, which I didn't understand at all, at the time.

Later of course, when Gigi and I were like sisters, I learned how to operate with her—reflecting her meanness right back. But at the time, I let her go on with it, saying I was the big-dog heiress, and maybe she should kneecap me.

I was very confused. But I understood that Gigi was being cruel. Then the boy was coming toward me, him with the deep brown eyes. He must've seen me staring at him—and came to introduce himself. His name was Lyman, and later we fucked in many outdoor locations, all over Sterling Park and everywhere else we could think of too. Just to prove to Gigi that I could, if I wanted to.

And I did. Want to, that is. Until Lyman got spooked by Gigi interrupting, Marcus close behind. Their words cruel and teasing.

Afterward, I went inside. I went up to my room. I felt all alone. I felt that too much time had passed, just me by myself, and that loneliness had created a chasm between me and the world that I would never, ever bridge.

In the bathroom, I stared at the mirror, trying to believe in myself, that I was real.

I feared that there was no one else like me—that they were real, and I was not; or I was real, and no one else was. I stared at my reflection, and my reflection stared back, and then I saw her again. Jessica.

And I spoke to her in the mirror, saying, "Hello, Jessica, I've missed you."

And in a slightly different voice, I said, "I've missed you too, Arianna. I've missed your letters. I read them, and I kept them all. Why don't you write to me anymore, Arianna?"

And then I said, "Jessica, you're not real! Everyone says so!"

"But, *Arianna*," I replied, "that hurts my feelings. You *know* I'm real. Who will remember me if you don't? Just write my name now and then, so that I'm not completely forgotten. Don't be afraid of them."

I was about to say it wasn't true, I wasn't afraid of them, but that would've been a lie. And I couldn't lie to Jessica.

That's when I heard the door open, and my body seized in fear.

I'm afraid now, remembering the trouble that always came when I saw her, mentioned her.

If Harry had been the one to find me...

If Helen...

But it wasn't any of *them* entering the room just then, it was Barrow—and Barrow was always kind. He didn't interfere with the doctors' work, but he didn't participate, either.

That day, after skating, when he caught me talking to myself, he just asked as he always did if I needed anything.

And I told him, *No, just catching my breath!! Down in a minute!*

I couldn't look at my reflection again, couldn't risk seeing her there instead of me.

Then I turned to the great silvered expanse of windows on the east wing of the house. Those windows that were created with a special mercury glass treatment, the effect being a sheer cliff of metallic gleam.

Through my childhood window: the façade burnished by the setting sun. Red as flames.

That old window, this window here in the dreadful facility, it's all one window.

I see it now, though.

It's all I see. Not her, no, but the house out my window when I finally turned away from the mirror. Maybe it's the only real thing, and this hospital, and this book, are all delusion. Through the Silver House window:

Silver House on fire.

Or is it the villa on La Digue? Flames punching through the glass, a little girl screaming within.

Maybe they're right, after all—memory is dangerous; better to take my pills and forget.

Memory is a house on fire, one I shall never leave.

11

There's a gentle rap on the door, and then Colin enters Barrow's office, removes the receiver from Maya's hand, and returns it to the cradle. She leans back in the chair, crosses her arms over her chest. He's the man she married: hair cut close behind the ears and a little floppy on top, that searching green-brown gaze. But different too. The sweater he's wearing is moth-eaten and patched at the elbows. In New York, he'd never wear anything moth-eaten. It's something the Sterlings do, here in Sterlingland, in this ancient, expensive, beautiful, moldering monument to their family's globe-spanning, bulldozing power.

"I'm sorry," he says, perching on the edge of the desk. "They shouldn't have tried to railroad you."

Maya's throat feels tight. *"They?"*

"We." Colin releases a heavy sigh. "I don't want to *take* anything from you Maya, and neither do they. It's a burden more than anything, that inheritance—certainly it was for Arianna. Returning it to the family trust is the right thing to do; it will benefit you more in the long run. We're a team, you and I—"

"Are we?"

"*Yes.*"

"But I mean, if you're married to *me*, then everything I have is yours. You didn't sign anything that says *you're* not entitled to half of what's *mine*. So then why isn't this a good thing, for *us*?"

He pauses a moment, studying her. "I suppose one could look at it that way."

"Yes, one *could*." Maya's words have a lancing sarcasm. She sees Colin wince, but she can't prevent herself from continuing. "You're not looking at it that way though, are you? Because *we're* not a team, you and the *Sterling family* are a team, which is why you let your aunt bully me into signing a prenup my lawyer hadn't laid eyes on, when I was a month away from giving birth. That's why you excused her casual cruelty toward me, why you let me be brought here when I just wanted to go home—"

"Maya, I'm sorry, that's not—"

"Not *what*? Not true?"

For a long while Colin doesn't say anything. He can't quite meet her gaze, and Maya's eyes burn into him. She takes a long breath, stopping herself from filling the quiet.

It's some relief to be here, in this simple room, with its few pieces of heavy wooden furniture, its small window onto an orchard bare of fruit, its chipped off-white walls. She has no desire to go back out there into those opulent auditorium-sized salons and parlors and libraries. It all feels like a bait and switch—*Come in and see our Louis Quatorze; it won't cost much, just your future, your past, your good name, and your soul.*

Much like Arianna's final act—leaving Maya an otherworldly inheritance without telling her why. Enough for Maya, and not just *Maya*, but also Maya's children, and their children, and the generations after she'll never even get to meet. Yet it seems foolish to believe in the gift; it's a couture gown with a bull's-eye on the back.

Even now, every Sterling will be scheming to bring Maya down. And Maya has secrets. Like that night in Mexico, the night Arianna died, and that other indiscretion, the one that forced her there in the first place.

Suddenly her lack of alibi feels guillotine sharp. No one can know that Maya was at the Iguana Bar that night—or why.

"You know I'm right," she says, when she can't bear the silence anymore.

"I know. You are right." He sounds very tired. "I'll go talk to them—tell them to send the paperwork to your lawyer. It's your decision, and you need to figure out what you want to do. But it's not just *me* that you have to reckon with, Maya. You know I'm in your corner. But they get to decide how they'll all respond too. This isn't the sort of thing they'll just accept and walk away from. And it's true, you know—Arianna wasn't in her right mind, but even so, it's really odd. I mean, I just can't imagine why she'd have done this. Singled you out. Can you?"

She shakes her head. He nods. The space between them crackles with static. When he stands up, she reaches for his hand, and she's relieved when he takes it, presses his mouth to the center of her palm.

"We are a team," he says. "You and I."

The tension in her throat relaxes a bit. She feels his sincerity, and she wants to throw herself into his arms, say, *Forget it; it's all yours; I'll sign anything you want.*

After all, he's the prize, isn't he? And what he said may be true—perhaps the inheritance is a burden as much as anything. Maybe it was the thing that ruined Arianna, made her withdraw from life. Partially at first, and now absolutely. But Maya only has the Sterlings' word for that. She's not sure she trusts what they say. She trusts Colin, but does *he* ever really question his family?

Meanwhile, a whole other part of her is thrumming. She hasn't felt like this, at the gravitational center of controversy, since those dark days after *The Springs* wrapped. She recognizes the headiness of leaving Butter at 3:00 a.m., the crush of eyes, the fuck-it attitude that made her known by millions. She's forgotten that girl. She's forgotten that on some level, she always *liked* that girl.

But that girl doesn't belong in Sterling Park. Or at least, she hasn't before now.

"Okay" is all Maya says.

"Right. Now I'm going to go talk to Marcus, calm everyone down." Colin nods and releases her hand. "Love you."

The words hang in the air as he moves through the doorway.

Love you. She knows if she says it back, says it out loud, she'll lose her nerve. Give in.

And maybe that's what she should do. Give in. Defer to the Sterlings, make things easy for Colin. Be the good little in-law, just grateful to be included. Would Helen respect her then, view her as a vital member of the team? Would Marcus stop sniffing around; would Travis ask no more questions? Maybe. But then she can taste some other, larger prize lying in the other direction. If she went for it—this inheritance Arianna marked for her—she'd be truly secure, untouchable. At the mercy of no one. Not like those wives on the yacht—compulsively snobbish, competitive, brittle, terrified of losing their status. Isn't that what the little thief she used to be dreamed of? To have everything and answer to no one?

Is this yet one more wild turn of fortune that Maya need only step forward and receive?

Or is it a curse?

The answer seems to lie with Arianna herself, that puzzle of a dead girl. It's true what Julian suggested on their walk despite Maya's answer. Maya *is* curious about Arianna. She needs to figure her out, why she named someone she never even met as her heir. Maybe Maya should go finesse Julian for more information. He seemed to like talking, having an audience for his vast knowledge of the Sterling family. A *historian*, he called himself.

But no, she needs someone who knew the real Arianna. Someone who once held Arianna's hair back when she drank to the point of oblivion. That's who Maya needs to talk to—Gigi.

Who, before all this, had invited Maya for a steam in the hammam.

———

134

The hammam is part of a whole wellness complex, located a short walk away from the main house. Barrow escorts Maya from the office, pointing out different features of the house. The ballroom, the formal dining room, the library, the archives. This tour guide routine evolves into a gentle listing of the hammam's amenities. There's a solarium for sunbathing, Barrow says, a yoga studio, a Turkish bath. Maya can't help but wonder if he notes a trace of panic on her face as she struggles not to be overwhelmed by the grandeur. He slows so they can continue on equal footing.

"There's also a greenhouse, and as the old rumor goes, it's where Sterlings past once grew their hemlock and nightshade. Foxglove, delphinium, lily of the valley." His tone is gravelly and serious, and Maya glances at him, wondering why he's telling her this. His lips part—is this the first time she's seen him smile?— and he continues lightly, "You know, for their bacchic rituals. Orgies, human sacrifice, that sort of thing."

Maya smiles too. She thinks Barrow must understand how difficult it is to be hazed and hated by her family-in-law, and this is the only way he can acknowledge it. "What's next, secret tunnels and dungeons? Wardrobes that lead into fantasy kingdoms?"

Barrow's smile fades away. "I haven't seen any dungeons or magic wardrobes."

Maya lifts an eyebrow—but there *are* secret tunnels?

"This is an old estate. There are passages for staff to get around, while not being in the family's way. But of course, if you need them to get around, Madame—"

"Please, Mr. Barrow, you can just call me Maya."

Barrow shakes his head. "You are the lady of the house. As I was saying, if you want to move about more privately, you can always use the tunnels."

She takes a breath, nods. *The lady of the house.* Is Barrow just hedging his bets? Confirming his allegiance to a potential top Sterling heir?

She doesn't speak again until they've arrived at the hammam entrance and Barrow turns away. For a moment, she wonders if she's imagining things—Barrow's joking about poisonous plants and secret tunnels, the sheer ridiculousness of the past twenty-four hours. If her sleeplessness, a murdered woman's will, and this grand oppressive house are distorting reality with some sort of gothic lens.

"If you need anything," Barrow says, formal again, retreating, "call the house line. We are always here."

She doesn't doubt that—always here, always watching.

But maybe they are, at least a little bit, on her side.

———

Maya advances through the impressive antechambers into the shower room, illuminated by a domed skylight. Steam rises over one of the marbled stalls. She takes a breath, beginning to strip off the clothes she put on so hastily this morning and then wore to tramp through the muddy grounds with Julian.

"Who's there?" Gigi calls, her voice carrying over the shower's falling water and echoing against the marbled walls.

Maya sucks in breath. "Me. Maya."

"Oh," says Gigi. "*Maya.*"

Maya steps into the stall next to Gigi's. "You angry?"

"Angry? At you? No. None of this has anything to do with you; don't go thinking it does." Gigi's trying to sound careless, but Maya can hear the bite beneath the words. "Arianna's been scheming for years to get back at the family. I mean, it's terribly inventive of her really, to bring *you* into it."

Maya might be stung by this, except that she knows it isn't true. This obviously has everything to do with her. Rory's words from earlier mix with Barrow's, a drumbeat in her mind: *You're the new heiress. The lady of the house.* She's pulsing with it—this new possibility.

Maya exits the rinse and waits while Gigi takes her time, a petty power move on her part, Maya's sure, before finally emerging from the stall, Turkish towel knotted around her chest, ready to enter the hammam. Maya smiles at her sister-in-law, but the smile is not reciprocated. Maya follows her down the low-lit hall toward an underground cavern. Within is a turquoise pool under a domed ceiling, all filigree and honeycomb patterns lacing the top. It's like a cathedral, a sanctuary, and Maya is struck with a calming awe. Gigi, however, crosses the space as if it were a locker room.

Just as they reach the fogged door to the steam room, the lean, aristocratic figure of Helen Sterling emerges, entirely nude. Maya freezes.

Helen's hair is wet, pushed back from her forehead and

wound into a low bun. Her skin is naturally tanned and taut. She doesn't have the figure of socialites in New York—nipped, tucked, stuffed with silicone. She has a ropey, hard-won physique that tells of a lifetime spent aggressively striding down city streets, over windblown fields, across well-appointed rooms to take the podium at blue-chip charity balls.

Go ahead and look, says her icy hard gaze.

Helen certainly doesn't hesitate to look Maya up and down, the corners of her mouth sinking. "Ah," she observes. "The body that launched a thousand ships. Getting familiar with our new house, are we?"

"As you said, it's important I know this place, it's history. Now that I *am* a part of the family."

Maya holds Helen's gaze, allows a grin to flicker on her lips, lets Helen imagine her bite, the snake she carries deep inside. There's no point in playing small now.

Helen makes an impatient hand gesture. "What's done is done, but the outcome is—I'm sure you understand—far from certain. In the meantime, *do* enjoy."

Already Helen is sweeping onward, shoulders back, tits up, ass gloriously on display. Then she's gone, footsteps echoing until the heavy front door to the hammam slams shut.

When Maya turns back, she sees Gigi smirking again, an opening for Maya at last. "So I guess it's safe to assume Helen is furious with me?" Maya asks as they continue into the heat of the steam room, lower themselves upon the tiered marble bench seats.

"Furious? No. That's not furious. If she were *truly* furious, you wouldn't have to ask. She's annoyed, of course. But mostly she's devastated by Ari's death—and this is just salt in the wound."

Sweat springs from Maya's pores. She thinks of Helen last night in Arianna's childhood room. So strikingly different from her formidable presence today. "Was she close with Arianna?"

"Depends on how you define *close*." Gigi's head is thrown back, elbows rested on the marble tier behind her. "She always wanted a daughter, a daughter *just* like Arianna. She said that in front of me, once. Can you believe it? I'm no less her niece, near the same age. And prettier, nine out of ten would agree. But I suppose Helen felt bad for her, and in the early years, before Harry opened up the house to the rest of the family, she was the only one who really tried with Arianna. She wanted her to know she had a place in the family, no matter what. And then Arianna began to ice Helen out, around the same time she started partying with *me*, frankly. She was always trying to get us to behave like perfect little symbols of Sterlingdom, to no avail. We would laugh and laugh and go for a cigarette with the groundskeeper. So, for Helen it's complicated."

"And for you?"

Gigi gives Maya a face that says, *Nice try*. But in the next moment she becomes voluble again. Maybe she needs the attention. "At first, she was just a story. You know, like in a Victorian novel, the phantom in the grand house who no one sees. Then, after Mum and Dad died, Colin and Marcus and I were invited back in. It was all part of Helen's plan to make the family whole again." Gigi pauses and Maya watches as she shifts in the heat. "And we *were* friends. Fast friends. She was a little younger than I, but very hungry for the world. So off we went! *You* get it. Me and Ari, tabloid superstars. We loved that game—keeping the paps running all over town. The archives have all our best covers; some of them are even framed. So, I guess that's something Arianna had in common with you." Gigi's smile suddenly becomes a frown. "But then of course she and I have that in common, too. *Had.*"

"She sounds fun."

"She was. But she was a nightmare too." Gigi looks at Maya pointedly, but Maya has no desire to talk about her very public trainwreck years. She can't. If she does, she'll fall apart, and she can't risk that here.

"You think that's why Arianna took an interest in me? She related to all that, another victim of the bloodsucking tabloids? I mean, why *do* you think she picked me?"

Gigi barks out a laugh. It has a mirthless, angry echo. "I don't know; because she was *insane*?" Gigi gives a bitter shake of the head. "It is *funny*," she says, not sounding amused at all. "If she was trying to get back at Helen, then she chose well. Helen *hated* that you were on that reality show. That you of all people reeled in Colin. But, of course, Arianna had disappeared before that, before you came round, before you were even a glimmer in a paparazzo's eye…" Gigi adjusts her towel over crossed legs, jerks her shoulders with violent indifference.

"But okay, say Arianna was just being spiteful, trying to get

140

back at her family... How was it even hers to give away in the first place? Your and Colin's father was the eldest sibling. Helen's the chair of the board. Marcus is the CEO. What am I missing?"

"Let's get some things straight." Gigi's eyes are wide-open now. Shining with old hurt and fury. This is a different anger— deeper and blunter than what she showed Maya earlier. "Those fuckers—the ones who made the rules of succession for this family? They let my father get screwed. It should have been primogeniture—firstborn sons of firstborn sons, and all that bullshit, since the days of Aethelred. But somehow Grandfather Richard got to do it his way and leave everything to the baby of the family. It's been gone over a thousand times, we've spent millions on lawyers looking for loopholes. The part about Harry inheriting the controlling stake in the company and the family trust, I mean. Oh, all of us are well taken care of—big allowances, the use of every luxury SterlingCo can buy. Never have to work a day in our lives if we don't want. But the real money, the real power—*that* can only go to one. I guess Harry thought he was being clever, moving things into his one heir's name—but he didn't anticipate Arianna. No one could. She was always impossible to understand. And certainly, none of us could have anticipated Arianna taking a very expensive interest in you. Putting the crown, as it were, on *your* head. And now here we are, rivals in this mess."

Maybe the steam is getting to Maya. She's feeling a little lightheaded. "Are we rivals?"

"Jesus, you don't listen. All my life, I've been told I'm a

Sterling first. Before anything else. It's the most important thing about me. I am an understudy for a role I will likely never get. And then there's you. You just waltz in, no Sterling about you, and somehow that all changes? It's not *me* you should worry about, it's the whole cavalry about to come down on you." She sighs, like she's suddenly exhaustingly bored. "Anyway, it all makes for some good drama, doesn't it? And you know me, I love a rival. So yes, maybe you should watch your back."

Gigi grins, the low light of the hammam glinting off her teeth.

So, that confirms things. Maya is struck silent with the impossibility of it, being trapped here under one roof with so many people who'd rather she never existed at all. The best she can do is tip her head against the stone wall and smile back.

12

After their steam, Gigi leaves Maya to shower off alone, saying she has to redo her extensions before dinner. Maya lingers in the shower awhile longer, trying to wash off the sticky foreboding of their conversation. It was friendly...ish. For all of Gigi's faults, at least she isn't boring. But she didn't really help Maya understand Arianna any better. Could it really be that Arianna simply saw images of Maya chased by paps and imagined some deep connection? There must be more to it.

Maya takes her time in the hammam, mentally cataloging how she's going to present tonight at dinner while facing the Sterlings again. Gigi can get away with a high-low aesthetic, augmenting her horsehair extensions, smudging kohl liner on her eyes, letting her bra straps show. But Maya is under a different kind of scrutiny. She needs war paint.

Julian told her to watch out for Gigi, and maybe he was right. In the steam room, their conversation veered from cloyingly intimate to sharp elbowed, and Maya had believed herself to be pressing Gigi for information, but maybe it was the other way around—maybe Gigi was trying to learn how Maya was handling the news, how to dismantle her.

What did Gigi tell her, really? Arianna was a troubled party girl. She was a captive of this house, of her father, and then she disappeared. Maya can't help but take the story personally, vibrate with its resonance to her own history of wild, lonely, desperate nights.

There's one thing that she couldn't bring herself to voice with Gigi, something she was just starting to register. Gigi—and everyone else, for that matter—seems to think that Arianna writing over her will to Maya was some sort of diabolical "fuck you" to the family. And perhaps they're right. The thing that keeps bothering Maya, though, is that in order for this "fuck you" to make sense, Arianna had to have *known* they'd be reading her new will. Which would mean...

Arianna expected to die young.

Even under the warm waterfall of the shower, Maya shivers at the thought. If she's right, it means the botched-ransom story Rory spun this morning is probably wrong, because Arianna must've suspected that someone wanted her dead long enough to go ahead and make that change to her will.

And why would she think that, unless the person who killed her was someone she knew?

———

At first the underground passage that connects the hammam and the main house is nicely plastered with floors of solid wood. But once she's closer to the kitchen, she finds the passages are less well-kept. As Barrow said, it's not really for the masters of the house—it's a thoroughfare for the servants. She sees the office where earlier she tried to call Bob, then takes a flight of stairs back to the ground floor. As she ascends, she experiences the house's disorienting force, those corridors onto corridors, rooms onto rooms.

Maya keeps steady, makes her way. Anyone who came across her would think she was just a little lost. But she knows exactly where she's going. Gigi mentioned it, and so did Julian—the Sterling family archives. The Sterlings have their own agenda when it comes to Arianna—who she was, why she did what she did. They're probably spinning all that to write the narrative that flatters them the most. But perhaps the key to understanding Arianna, the truth of the title she's passed on to Maya, will be in plain sight in the archives.

Maybe it'll be right there within the lurid folds of a tabloid piece. Maya knows how to read those magazines—and there's always a little truth mixed in with the speculation and the lies.

———

The room that holds the Sterling family archive is as country luxurious as the rest of the house. The chairs are large stuffed leather topped with plaid wool blankets. The rug is bearskin. The walls windowless. Maya remembers that early date with Colin, when he took her to headquarters in New York, her sense that

145

whatever the Sterlings do is deemed worthy of immortalization, preserved for future generations to study. Or worship.

Museum-style fixtures cast yellow cones of light over magazine covers, hung salon-style on the wall, mixed in with framed papers—medieval contracts, Dickens-era wills. Glass cases display old medals, regalia, and weapons—ancient knives, trowels, pistols, brass knuckles. Little plaques state the long-dead owners. She lifts the glass cover, turns over a small leather-bound copy of *Hamlet*, with a note dated Christmas '94 that reads: *To Julian, the Polonius of our family—this was my friend Mikey's in university, he was an expert on the Bard, and he gave it to me, but I've never had a head for it! Yours, Harry Sterling.*

Maya's fingers move onto a leather ankle holster for a knife, and reads the inscription:

To Harry. "He was too good to be"—Cymbeline.

When I grow up, I want to be just like you. Mikey.

There's a small note: Gift of Michael Blackburne to Harry Sterling, 1967—Blade lost.

It's all very impressive and serious. Except when it's not.

Among the oil paintings of stately women posed in oceans of silk skirt are smaller frames. Not the swerving ormolu rectangles that encase the paintings—these are more modern, steel finish or clear glass panel. Instead of the proud, upturned chins of the portrait subjects, there are mouths hung open in outrage, lopsided drunk smiles, peace-sign fingers, palms thrust forward to block the camera's glare. These are adorned with over-the-top magazine headlines, silly nicknames, an excess of exclamation points.

Many of them are black-and-white—Colin's parents in sandals and straw hats on Capri, Helen and Julian wearing sweaters over turtlenecks in Gstaad, making the combination appear somehow chic. But others are brightly colored. Marcus and Eva, emerging from the cathedral in their formal wedding wear. Colin grinning in graduation regalia, mortarboard pushed back at a cocky angle, a cigar between his teeth. Among these, Maya is surprised to see herself—on the cover of the *New York Post*, holding hands with Colin as they stride past their doorman, her trench coat flapping to reveal the curve of her pregnant belly.

Bumped Up to First Class says the headline.

Maya's cheeks flame, but then she notices she's not the only one singled out on the wall. There's a cheeky humor to the choices. In one, Julian and another man (Harry Sterling, the caption says), both young and whip thin, are caught in what appears to be a fistfight outside a pub. Colin's parents leaving a party in the Côte d'Azur by speedboat, middle fingers extended. Gigi in a spangled minidress, ready to launch herself out of a cab, legs spread to reveal a hot pink lace thong. Maya remembers Julian saying that this collection was more personal—it's not like the archives in London. Here, the Sterling family can own their less flattering depictions, turn them into a private joke.

Even so, there's no Arianna, not that Maya sees.

The room has such a stained-wood-and-cracked-leather tranquility that she almost feels like she's in a forgotten world. But she's not. She must remember that—people are waiting for her, anticipating her next stumble. She's never unobserved in

Sterling Park, not for long, anyway. She strides to the far wall, reaching for a promising shelf.

On the low built-ins that line the room are bound leather volumes, each labeled with a year and a season. Maya pulls an old one—spring 1922—and turns the pages of preserved press clippings. It's a time before paparazzi—these pages are just long lists detailing the movements of the sporty set, names of the luminaries arriving to London by a certain ocean liner, an account of polo field heroics, the attendees of such and such a ball. Maya replaces that book, tightens her robe, jumps ahead to the '90s.

Here she finds volumes full of what Gigi alluded to in the hammam: the two Sterling girls out on the town in London, straps slipping from shoulders, mascara running, drinking with young lords and footballers and boy band members. They look like babies, the two of them, and Maya guesses they were—fifteen and seventeen, something like that, faces round, limbs slender as saplings. Though these are the first photos Maya has seen of the heiress, there's something almost familiar about teenage Arianna. Her pointy chin is not unlike Colin's, and her delicate mouth and slight overbite are similar to Gigi's.

The teenybopper coverage gives way to more ominous stories. *Another Drying Out for Ari*. Shadowy pictures of Arianna smoking on the street at night with dodgy-looking men. Arianna, hair dyed bleach-blond, open-mouth kissing what appears to be an ambulance driver. Even in the photographic evidence, Arianna has begun to recede—the paps can't get as close to her; their shots are all through reflective windows, blurry, far away.

Then there's one of Arianna being restrained by security guards, her face a study in violent intent. Eyes screwed tight, a mess of tangled hair sticking to her mouth. Even in two dimensions, even with the gulf of time, Maya feels a little frightened by that face. What that young woman is capable of is terrifying, and so is what she must be feeling inside. Maya knows because she's been capable of the same things, she's been roiled by that same mania.

After that, the tabloids recycle the same images. Mostly they use a shot of Arianna smoking out a hospital window, her posture slumped and sad, her hair stringy, obscuring her face. The headlines are all some variation on *What Happened to the Lost Sterling Heiress?*

When Maya came in here, she thought she might learn about the heiress, what motivated her. But all these pictures of Arianna breaking down in public have done is remind Maya of the nights she was chased, photographed when she was out of her mind, subdued, forced into gowns made of paper...

Maya puts the volume back, stung, not wanting to touch it anymore. She tries to walk away from the photos, the feelings that accompany them, to move toward her rooms with an air of imperturbability. But that's bullshit. There's an inner tremble she can do nothing at all to still.

Mind focused on her past, that old bruise, Maya travels down one hall, up another, until finally she arrives at a door that looks familiar. Has she been here before? The knob is white iron. It's familiar, but no, this part of the hall is new. Still the desire to move as far from the archives compels her, she turns the knob and steps into open air, warm and fragrant with chlorophyll. Another realm contained within the universe of Sterling Park.

This must be the greenhouse Barrow mentioned. The fatal herbarium. Maya's gotten badly turned around; the greenhouse, Barrow said, is off the east façade of the house, to catch the morning sun. At least, she thinks he said that. She advances along a brick path, through dense jungle plants. Vines grow up the walls and intertwine, overhanging the walkway. Smell of earth and leaf. Little flowers dangle from branches, vivid orange and fuchsia blossoms. Maya walks farther down the path, entranced—this feels so different from the staid air of the rest of Silver House, and even from the gardens she glimpsed with Julian. It's uncultivated, messy, alive.

In this tropical atmosphere, vegetation laced with rot, so near the archive's bitter, dirty truths, she's reminded of a night in Miami when she was at her worst.

Those sleepless days. She lived in bars, drank vodka with breakfast. It seemed that overnight her life, which had been a series of practical decisions, had become a conspicuous wreck. The decision to tend bar back on Long Island had been a practical one—it was fast money, double what she made cleaning houses—and the decision to join the cast of *The Springs* was also practical—it paid more than tending bar alone. But she found that it wasn't so easy to keep her head around drink and fame. They—her patrons, her fellow cast members, the paparazzi who followed her, the tabloids who ran stories about her—called her a party girl, portrayed her as a kind of insatiable monster.

The practical thing at the time was to play along with the tabloid narrative, have some fun with it, turn it to her advantage. Or so she reasoned.

Then Miss Mayhem became more than a handy sliver of her personality, convenient for stirring the cast of *The Springs* into viewer-friendly drama. Something inside broke, the reins loosened, and she could no longer contain the virulent anger, ancient and venomous. She had everything, but what did that do? It couldn't stop the law from catching up to her dad, couldn't make her unsee his face in the back of the cop car when they took him away. That's when Miss Mayhem became the driving part of Maya's *real* personality, her real life. The life that was captured by paparazzi late at night, rather than TV producers. Those people at least knew her, and in some ways had her best interests at heart.

At the very least, they got the lighting right.

But there's a key difference between Maya Sterling now, and Maya Miller the party girl of the past. Back then, she had nothing to lose. She had no one left. No one but herself.

Except, of course, the married man she thought she couldn't live without.

The swarm of memory, the heat, is fogging Maya's mind. Her sleep has been inconsistent after the days at sea, the flying across time zones, Becca waking late at night. And now this isolation, deep in the country, surrounded by hostile in-laws. This place is all poisonous plants and heady atmosphere. She has a sudden need to find Colin, to make sure they're good, that they really do have the same vision for their family.

She'll tell him she doesn't care about the inheritance—she'll sign the papers if that makes him happy, if that's what it takes for them to hold together through this.

She walks faster now, through the ferns, long tendrils catching in her wet hair, brushing her face. Her heart is slamming against her chest. No matter how vociferously she tells them to go away, the damning memories persist. She comes up against a glass wall, not unlike the glass wall in the place where they locked her away after that night in Miami.

Think nothing of it, she warns herself. *Just a coincidence.*

But it doesn't feel like a coincidence. What it feels like is every bad thing that's ever happened to her returning. All of it one moment. This moment, a moment she'll never escape.

What's true is the heat, the tropical air. The trapped, helpless, mad-with-rage feeling of Miami, more real than the here and now.

The police approaching her at 4:00 a.m., waist-deep in the ocean, asking her name.

Her *name?*

She'd laughed, thinking her inability to remember her own name was temporary. But nothing came. The police were kind, gave her a blanket, escorted her to the street. A photographer jumped out of a bush, got the shot. *He* knew her name. Shouted: "She's Maya fucking Miller, from *The Springs*!" Maya struggled out of the arms of the police, screaming, smashing the camera, bloodying the photographer. She kept hitting him and hitting him until they subdued her. Tranquilized her, she found out later. She woke in a glass room. A danger to herself, they said.

"That's ridiculous," Maya told them. She gave them the name of the man, that man, the only name she could remember, said he was going to come get her, and they'd regret treating her this way. They didn't seem to believe her, even though she kept calm, tried him again. Told them he'd be here in any minute, told them all this in her most calm manner.

But her most calm manner didn't mean shit.

So, she threw her body against the glass, bruising herself, until they restrained her again. Subdued her like a nuisance, like a threat. Like her dad, who'd finally gotten himself locked up in a permanent way.

I'm Maya Fucking Sterling, Maya reminds herself now. But the glass walls of the Sterling greenhouse seem to constrict around her.

Then she spots the front door, and she lets out a breath of relief.

She's okay, she knows where she is, she can get out.

The doorknob is cold to the touch. She grabs and turns, but it doesn't give. Her fingers are trembling, struggling to grip. She needs to be out of here. Right now. She twists again, pulls the door harder. The glass shudders and groans, but the door refuses to open. Did someone lock it from the outside? She can see now that this is not the door she came in through—it's a door out to the park. The winter sun has already begun to set, shadows fall across the lawn. She's alone here, in a terrifying jungle, in a brain-melting heat, in a swiftly disintegrating sense of reality.

Her eyes rove, fall on a spade leaned up against the wall. She picks it up, turns it over in her hands, wondering if it would be enough to shatter the glass. Then she hears footsteps. Swift, decisive, behind her.

"Trouble with the door?" a man asks.

13

For a second, she thinks it's Colin come to rescue her. But no.

This man is broader than Colin and taller by several inches.

"Marcus." It's as if the memories have somehow conjured him. His salt-and-pepper stubble, his thick outgrown hair. He's always been a rougher presence than Colin. As he emerges from the shadows, Maya gets the impression of a wolf in expertly tailored clothes.

Even though Marcus makes her feel preyed upon, she also has this odd, contradictory, possibly insane feeling that he's the one person she could be completely truthful with.

Once upon a time, she thought of him as the man she could not live without.

His hand shoots out. Her heart rate spikes. He seems about to touch her.

Then he gently removes the garden spade she forgot she was holding. "This old door's been stubborn since the beginning of time. No need to go damaging Sterling property," he says, half grinning. He steps between her and the door, finesses it open, then gently closes it again to block the cold current from outside. "Or is it *your* property now?"

"What are you doing here?" A moment ago, she'd felt alone in a world made entirely of her own bad memories. To be with Marcus is a cold slap, shocking and vital.

"Came to fetch you for cocktail time." His gaze passes over her robe, and Maya feels the uncovered skin of her chest go hot. "But you don't appear cocktail hour ready."

"Gigi and I came from a steam. I—got lost," Maya says, trying to recover her wits. Not wanting the family to know where she has been. "How did you even find me all the way out here?"

"Followed your scent." This phrase, his slight sneer, skewer her. For a moment, it's the same as it used to be, and he's gazing at her like there's nothing in the world that could pull his attention away. Offering his elbow, he says, "Shall I escort you?"

She's afraid to touch him.

He marks her hesitation, drops his arm. "Maya *Sterling*." The lancing irony of the pronunciation seems to indict her for every mercenary act she's ever committed. It's as though he's submitted the little girl she once was as evidence to a court of law. Called up the child who saw the inside of a Sterling mansion in *Vanity Fair* and wished for one of her own.

"I can't help but feel," he says, holding her in his gaze, "that you've been avoiding me."

She tugs tight her robe. "And why would I do that?"

"You tell me." That lopsided grin again. He disappears his hands in his pockets. Waits.

There is a version of Maya that brushes past him, sails above his taunt. The version that's been to therapy, that knows what's good for her and what isn't. But that version of Maya seems remote right now. Instead, she sees a lost Maya, a hunted Maya. Naked, or close to it, alone, in the heat, swarmed by memories. "I have good reasons to avoid you, Marcus. You know that."

"Inconvenient choice of husband, in that case."

An old anger pulses in her throat. "Colin saved me, Marcus. After you...you..."

"How's that now? What are you trying to say?"

"I'm not *trying* to say anything, Marcus. You know what happened in Miami."

"Yes. Miami." There is a hint of a smile on his face, but in his eyes there's the same old blunt hunger.

"I mean, why would I ever want to speak to you again, after you ran the story about my dad going to prison on the front page of your newspaper?" Even years later, Maya winces at the pain of it—the image of her dad in handcuffs next to an image of her, similarly restrained. The realization that she herself had exposed that secret history, given it to someone she'd trusted, and that he'd betrayed her by sharing it with the world. "Did you write the headline yourself, Marcus? 'Like Father, Like Daughter—Maya Miller Always Wanted a Big House'?"

"I don't put anything on the front page of my newspapers. The editors do that. I certainly don't write the headlines."

"Come on," Maya scoffs. "Everyone knows they'd never run

a headline without your approval. That wherever you are in the world, they get you the first proofs."

"Editorial independence is a core value of SterlingCo." Marcus's tone is one he might use with a reporter from a college newspaper. The fact that Marcus meddles in his newsroom is one of the worst-kept secrets in the business.

"You let them come for me. Let them *ruin* me."

"Ruin you? After Miami, you were on the cover of six magazines. The whole world wanted a piece of you. All that press, all that attention, and you at the center of it. Isn't that exactly what you wanted?"

"If you believe that—that getting committed was a fair trade for some publicity—then you really don't understand me at all."

Marcus forces the corners of his mouth down. "Don't I?"

Maya's breath is long and deep. "Marcus." She could just move past him, go outside and make a run for the main house. It's cold out there, but she'd survive.

"You're the damsel in distress on all the magazine covers," he says. "The girl who knows how to get the attention, spin it just right. Somehow you turn that into millions in makeup sales. And then you show up at my family home, two years later, married to my cousin." He waves his forearm, rattling his thick platinum watch. "*Then*—and here's the real zinger—turns out you've somehow managed to get yourself in line to inherit more of the Sterling treasure than I will. Seems you've worked *all* the Sterling cousins…even the old guard, if my father has anything to say about it."

"Oh, and how's that?"

"Going on the little tour with that shit-eating grin on your face, getting him talking, which of course he'll *always* do, given the chance. Collecting family secrets. I clocked it the minute you arrived, Maya. I mean, how long have you been planning this?"

Maya spits out a disdainful laugh, but this characterization stings. "As if I could have *planned* any of this. How dare you, Marcus? I mean really, all you've done is stand against me. And meanwhile all I've done is protect you."

"Protect *me*?"

"Yes, Marcus. Protect you. Protect *us*." Inside she's at war with herself. One part, still wounded and furious over this old betrayal, insists she shouldn't reveal a single thing to Marcus. But the stronger part still believes Marcus is the only person who can really see her, look at all the parts of herself and solve the riddle between them. That part is insistent. Says: *Tell him.* "I—there's something you need to know."

"Now you're starting to worry me." His gaze has a blistering focus.

"Good. That means you'll actually fucking listen." Maya takes a breath. "A few nights ago, in Mexico. The night your cousin died. I...I left the boat. No one knows. I snuck away while Colin was out."

Marcus's jaw shifts. "What exactly are you telling me, Maya?"

"Just listen," she snaps. She's trying to steady herself, keep hold of the most important details from that night. "I snuck out to a bar to meet someone."

His brow spreads in angry surprise.

"Relax, it wasn't an affair. It was a journalist. She—"

"Wait, Maya—you were talking to a journalist in Puerto Vallarta on the night Arianna died? And you didn't disclose that to Rory?"

"How could I tell him without revealing what she had on me? She had evidence, Marcus. A photo."

Marcus exhales. Puts his arms firmly across his chest. "Of?"

"What the fuck do you think?"

———

In a rush, Maya tells Marcus everything.

How she met the woman in the Iguana Bar in Puerto Vallarta. The woman seemed to have taken precautions not to be seen. But she was also quite concerned about being followed, that was the first thing she asked Maya, when Maya sat down.

Had Maya noticed anyone on her trail?

Maya had been pretty sure that *she* was the only one who should be worried about being spotted, but restrained herself from saying so with a roll of the eyes.

When the first email hit Maya's AOL account, from the unfamiliar handle *j_oncemoore*, Maya's instinct had been to ignore it. But the emails kept coming, the threats growing more specific. This woman barraged her with messages, saying she could destroy Maya's "situation" if Maya didn't agree to meet. At first, Maya rationalized it all as a limp attempt at extortion from a tabloid writer.

How could this *j_oncemoore*, Jessie as she later introduced herself, prove anything about Maya's past?

Still, Jessie's emails were full of alarming details. She seemed to know about Maya's life, the secret she most wanted to keep. And Maya told herself she had to be thorough. Smart. She hadn't gotten this far with a laissez-faire attitude around her own public image. It was true what Jessie said. She had a good thing to protect.

So, Maya lied to her husband and went onshore that night, hoping that would take care of things—that she could meet this reporter, figure out what she wanted, and make the emails stop.

The woman—Jessie—had been dressed like Maya—sunglasses, with a baseball cap, T-shirt, and cutoff jeans—and she couldn't have been much older than Maya, if that. Late twenties at the most. There was something shaky about her, as if she'd skipped a few too many meals. Her manner was furtive and urgent, as though she was afraid of more than being overheard. Then she gripped Maya's arm with surprising force and drew her across the empty room to a rustic wood table by a window.

"Jesus," Maya muttered, reluctantly allowing herself to be pulled. "If you're so paranoid," Maya said, rubbing the place where Jessie's fingertips had dug in, "why meet in person?"

"I just had to get a look at you," Jessie whispered. Her tone was strange, personal—different from the tabloid journalists Maya had met in the past. More like a stalker, eager to appear intimate. Maya felt her guard rise, her doubt surge as Jessie fixed her in an unblinking stare. "I need to make sure we can trust each other."

Maya couldn't help but heave a sigh, refusing to succumb to the slight prickle of fear. She'd handled paps before. Trust was never a part of the equation.

"This is a bit much, no? All this cloak-and-dagger?" She sipped her drink, ice clicking softly in the glass. "And following me to Mexico? Was that really necessary?"

Jessie assessed Maya with pale-green eyes. And Maya assessed her back. She was pretty in a jolie laide sort of way, eyes a touch too close together, mouth delicate. When she put her elbows on the table, leaned toward Maya, she seethed with eerie intensity. "If you think it's unnecessary, you don't understand the family you've married into."

Maya took another sip of mezcal, annoyed at being told once again that she was beneath her husband's family, out of her depth. As though she were some idiot who'd wandered off a farm and bumped into one of the most eligible bachelors in the world, never having heard of SterlingCo before. "I can handle the Sterlings. The only person harassing me is *you*, Jessie. So. What do you want?"

"I want you to understand. You *need* to understand." Jessie's eyes had the high emotional sheen of an actress playing her part with a bit too much verve. "The Sterlings are capable of anything. *Anything*. You notice how the world seems to pelt them with tragedies? Don't believe it. Anything that befalls them, in some way or another, it's self-inflicted. An inside job. Sterlings like to watch things burn, but only if they're the ones to light the match."

Jessie was leaning forward, rapidly tapping her fingers on the table. Maya wondered if she was an addict. She had that air of desperation. Maya was beginning to feel a little desperate herself. This woman was obviously unhinged. And already time was slipping. Colin might miss her, might already be heading back to the *Agyros*. He was capable of a sentimental turn—leaving his friends because he missed her and the baby. Maya needed to extricate herself from this situation as soon as possible.

"Enough fucking around. You say you have a photo of me. What do I have to do to make sure it never gets out? Staged paparazzi shots? An exclusive interview with your outlet?"

Jessie held Maya in a blinkless gaze and declared: "I need you on my side. On the *inside*."

"I'm sorry, *what*?"

It suddenly occurred to Maya that this wasn't a journalist at all. Why had Maya been so shortsighted as to assume she was horse-trading with a rational actor? Maya had almost walked right back out of the bar, and would have, if Jessie hadn't at that moment produced an eight-by-ten glossy of Maya and Marcus in the alleyway off The Mercer.

"Okay." Maya's mouth went dry as sawdust. "I'm listening. What do you want from me?"

"I need you to help me get my hands on something. Call it an insurance policy. It will protect both of us. I can't talk about it here." Jessie's eyes darted again, as if scanning for danger. "But I *can* tell you what it will get us. Freedom. And...control. I'll be in touch with more instructions."

Then she left in a hurry. And Maya has refreshed her emails dozens of times since landing in England yesterday, but those "instructions" have yet to come. She still doesn't know what Jessie wants from her—but whatever it is, Maya is still theoretically at her mercy. Either Maya does what she wants, whatever that turns out to be, or Jessie leaks that photo, the photo that would instantly destroy Maya's marriage and everything she's built.

———

The grimace Marcus wore, listening to Maya's confession, begins to fade. Maya recognizes the way he wipes a hand across his face, leaving a mask of calm where concern or fury had been before. She's seen him do that during business calls, in the backs of cars with tinted windows after they've narrowly escaped being caught.

"You've got terrible timing," he says now. "But she was manipulating you, Maya." He waves his hand as though it's all a minor irritation. "We'll get her off your back. What did she want, money?"

"She didn't say. But if anyone finds out—"

"No one will. We'll take care of it." He says it with such brisk confidence, she feels silly for caring, at ease, like when she first met him. Turned on as much as intimidated by his adeptness, his handle on things. The two feelings indistinguishable. This is the Marcus she remembers best. The man who can bend a room to his will, make any problem disappear. Or blow it up, if that's what he wants.

The man who could do anything to her—and she'd let him. *Has.*

"How?" she asks him now.

He shakes his head. "This is a real mess you've gotten yourself into, Maya."

"Oh, you think it's *my* mess? *My* problem?" Maya gives a low, derisive whistle. "You have just as much to lose."

"Perhaps you've forgotten, but as of this morning, you've acquired quite a bit more power. You're practically my boss."

"Oh, come on. Your family won't let me keep it. They're already pushing me to sign papers I haven't even read."

"Not me. *I* don't agree with that."

"You don't?"

It's Marcus's turn to bark out a laugh. "Well, I mean, I don't think you should just go along with what we're telling you to do. It would be completely against your own interests. That's not the Maya I know."

"I had nothing to do with Arianna's plans. I didn't *ask* for this fucking inheritance."

"But it is what you want now, isn't it?" His stance is tough, slightly interrogative, but she has the sense that he's genuinely curious. "Or isn't it?"

Maya's lips part. She wants so many things.

At this very moment, in the hot floral-scented greenhouse, she's surprised to find herself almost levitating with want. It scares her how easy it is to slip back to that place. But she holds her ground, lifts her chin, pushes her hair off her shoulders so that it falls down her back. "What do *you* want?"

"I want you," he says, "to tell me one thing."

Maya's lungs fill. "Okay."

"When you went into that tattoo parlor. Near The Mercer." He pauses, as though remembering. Eyes glinting. "After we... fought. What did you get?"

The question hits like a slap. "The tattoo? That's what you want to ask me? Fuck you, Marcus."

"I just want to know." He shrugs, and there's a sincerity, almost like pleading, in his voice.

"Was it your name, you mean?" Before she can think better of it, she moves her robe to the side, reveals a little sliver of skin high on her hip. "Go ahead. See for yourself."

A bolt of surprise goes through her as he crouches down to examine the little wolf walking the ridgeline of her hip bone. His eyes tick up to meet hers. "Is that supposed to represent—"

"You? No. It's not you. It's me."

He whispers, "My lone wolf," so close she feels his breath on her hip. He brushes his lips over the tattoo, and all the blood in her body goes to the skin where his mouth touched.

Then it's the same old carnal vortex. She's back to that night when they were caught in the alley outside The Mercer. Coming down in the service elevator, wearing the four-thousand-dollar dress he'd bought her on a whim and no underwear. Impossible to keep their hands off each other. His mouth, it was an obsession; she just wanted to feel it. If only she'd been able to resist him for a few minutes, they wouldn't have been exposed like that—the photographer, having a cigarette in the alley, wouldn't have had time to lift his camera and get the shot.

That was almost the end of whatever it was between Maya and Marcus. But the photo never appeared, never graced the cover of tabloid rags or popped up on celebrity gossip websites, though it would have been worth the down payment on a house. A really nice house. She always figured Marcus found the photographer, made the problem go away.

Apparently not. Instead, Jessie has it. And it seems possible he didn't even know...

A clear inner voice says: *What the actual fuck are you doing, Maya?*

His kiss moves upward, his fingers yank at the knot that holds tight her robe, letting it fall open. He shudders a breath against her naked skin, and she sucks in air, grabbing his head to pull him closer. *This, this. His teeth on her skin, his tongue in her mouth, his force of will subduing her, alchemizing her mania into pleasure.* How she's missed this. It feels so good and it's all too much; she might burst with the too-muchness, it could disintegrate her into a thousand points of ecstatic light.

"Marcus." She touches his shoulders, pushes him away. "No."

He stands, puts his hands on both sides of her face. "What? Please, Maya, I—"

And her mouth opens to his; they're kissing with that familiar hunger, the rich weave of his fine clothes against her bare skin, and like that, all she wants is him.

But that's madness. She knows it, if dimly. This could cost

her everything. "I have to go," Maya whispers, pulling away from him, closing her robe. Mastering her trembling fingers to get the damn thing retied. This is why she sighed in relief when he RSVPed no to their wedding. Why she balked at his gaze from beside that salon's fireplace.

He does the swipe of his face again. Back to calm. Though there's still something, a little lingering pain in his eyes. "Yes, I've learned to expect that from you," Marcus says. "Maya fuck-and-run Miller."

Her rage kicks. Why is it so impossible to dismiss a man who says shit like that?

She forces herself to look away from him, from the strong creases of his face, his broad chest expanding. She begins to stride away, hoping he doesn't see how much she's shaking.

If she did look back, she'd be beset with the old malignant pining—the creeping belief that what he makes her feel, she can't live without.

That Marcus is the only one she really believes in, who really knows her, even when all the evidence suggests she can trust him less now that she's been handed something he surely thinks of as his.

Knowing Marcus, he probably feels entitled to do whatever he wants to get that thing back.

14

By the time Maya's back in the nursery suite, she's very nearly calmed herself. But as soon as she's through the door, she encounters another surprise: towers of beautifully wrapped clothes boxes arranged in the middle of the room. A note from Colin rests atop an enormous white bow:

> *Darling—I'm so sorry. I haven't been great, I know.*
> *It's just the shock of it all. We'll figure it out together, I*
> *promise. Here are some things from Paris to make you*
> *feel more at home in Sterling Park.*

Shame whips through her, stinging her eyes with guilty tears.

But she holds herself upright. Refuses to crumble. Then slowly and intentionally, as if to punish herself, she opens each of the boxes.

Inside, amid candy-pink tissue paper, she finds countless pieces of clothing from her favorite designers. Marc Jacobs high-heeled boots and flip-flops. Buttery soft Seven jeans and a structured Balenciaga pants suit. Miu Miu pumps and a Prada dress. She's overwhelmed by his thoughtfulness. She knows it's not just a gift, though—he wants her to look the part, feel at home so she'll appear at home.

The heady emotions of those minutes with Marcus in the greenhouse seem like a dream, and she's thankful, at least, to be alone right now, in this room that smells like Colin's aftershave and Becca's baby-smooth skin. Adrenaline is charging through her system, but just thinking about her husband's sheepish smile, his warm brown eyes, and shiny, flopping hair, gradually begins to settle her. Colin, her protector. Colin who loves and trusts her. And has no idea about Marcus.

And never will.

This relief, the wildness of just a moment ago—it's like Maya's whole story in miniature: the stability and comfort of Colin, the crazy jolt of Marcus. Her warring parts competing for control. The irony strikes her, not for the first time, that neither one of them would have this incredible power over her, if it weren't for the other.

As she processes the spin-cycle intensity of it all, this seems briefly like the order of things. Marcus winds her up and Colin brings her down. Colin has always known what she really needed. He did everything properly—got down on one knee, gave her a credit card to set up the house for their little family to grow in. He would have asked for her dad's permission, but Dad was back in prison after a series of parole violations, and she had decided, after much careful coaching from her therapist, to stop bailing him out.

She swallows back the memory—freshly stirred—of Marcus's touch, his mouth at her neck, his hands cupping her face, tilting her head back, exposing her throat... *Those days are over.* The truth of that cracks her heart, but it's a truth she has to learn to live with.

Even though she's freshly clean from the hammam, she steps into the shower. And as she rinses Marcus's smell off, she tells herself what she will do next, as though she's her own coach, sending herself out for the big game: *You will get dressed; you will go to dinner; you will show these people that you're Colin's wife and a member of the Sterling family, whether they fucking like it or not.*

You will act like the kind of girl who deserves it all.

———

That was the kind of talk she gave herself before going out to meet Colin. *You're Maya Miller; you get what you want because you know what you want...*

She met Colin first, on purpose. Marcus came later, by accident. That's how being with Marcus felt after a while too. A big accident. A real ten-car pileup.

Maya's always been good with a goal. With Colin, she had one. He was single, she was single, and he was exactly who she wanted. Handsome, kind, sexy as hell, and, especially when they were together, a total publicity magnet.

Later, with Marcus, it was always understood that she could

never have him; there was nothing to achieve. All she had was the insanity and pleasure of every secret stolen moment together.

Colin she met at a party in the Hamptons, when she was still on *The Springs*. Someone had told her he would be there. "The eminently eligible bachelor, Colin Sterling," as the gossip pages called him. Maya had read that article and thought that seemed like a good logical next step for her. Something to shift her profile, keep her relevant. Her dad was coming around more often, asking for more money, asking her for more everything— Maya didn't want to be associated with the tawdriness of it all, not publicly, anyway. She wanted to keep earning so she had enough if anything really bad ever befell him. Or her.

Money came easier now, but it went easier too.

It was summer and she wore a red bodycon dress. Aunt Rebecca always said red was a power color. She planned exactly how she'd accidentally-on-purpose bump into Colin and make it seem natural. Start a conversation, hold his gaze with her warm honey eyes. By that point, she'd dated the guys from the show, a pro baseball player, an indie rock star. A billionaire bachelor didn't seem like such a reach. Maya didn't pretend she wasn't doing whatever it was she was doing, or that she didn't want whatever it was she wanted.

In that sense, you never could accuse her of being fake.

Colin had met a lot of fakes, but he'd never met anybody like her.

He'd wandered away from the sprawling gray-shingled house, toward the beach chairs, looking out at the waves, at the surfboards someone had left on the sand. She said, "Want to learn?"

He glanced at the red dress. "*You're* going to teach me?" he asked in a tone of friendly challenge. "In that?"

"Colin Sterling, hold on to your hat." She winked, slow and long. "I'm about to tell you the secret to life."

He was amused. "Okay."

"Can you handle it, though?"

"What's your name again?"

"Maya. Maya Miller."

"I can handle it, Maya Miller."

She turned, put his hand on the zipper of her dress, waited for him to pull. After a moment, he loosened the zipper, pulled it a chaste halfway down her back. She stepped out of the dress, showed him the bikini she'd been wearing underneath. Tasteful, athletic, very flattering. "The secret to life?" she said, heart beating madly. She had no idea if this was too much, if he would be turned off by her boldness. "Always be ready."

"For a swim?"

"For anything." She smiled, a little afraid that the moment was about to end, and he'd walk away, but glad anyway that she'd taken her shot.

He didn't seem to think she was too much, though. "I'm always ready," he said with a smile.

"Then come on. I grew up around here; I'll show you where to paddle out so you steer clear of the rocks..."

And the next thing she knew, they were an item. It only took a couple months for the press to discover this new couple and to start calling her a gold digger. The weekly tabloids made deals with shop owners, did two-page spreads about the lavish gifts Colin bought her in exchange for press about their businesses. It wasn't like she was asking him to buy her things. But she wasn't about to turn them down either. She's no martyr. They could call her whatever they wanted.

But the tabloids liked her too. She knew because they ran pictures of Colin smiling, doing fun things he never would have done before. She took him to Belmont, where her dad used to take her. They rode roller coasters at Coney Island and ate dim sum in Chinatown and went dancing at Lit Lounge. And it *was* fun. Real fun.

Even so, Maya guessed Colin probably had lots of girlfriends and she didn't think anything of dating other people herself. But around the six-month mark, it began to occur to her that Colin wasn't what she'd expected him to be. He called when he said he would call. If he was going out of town, he told her when he'd be back. If she stayed the night at his, he made her coffee in the morning, and they would go out for breakfast with a stack of SterlingCo newspapers. It became her first real, respectable, grown-up relationship. Safe. Pleasant. A teeny tiny bit stifling. The show was ending, and Miss Mayhem's streak was just beginning—she was restless for reasons that had nothing to do with him.

Then Colin took her to a party on Fishers Island, and she met Marcus. She could see how much Colin longed for Marcus's approval, and it made her want to take Marcus down a peg. She challenged him to a tequila drinking competition; he scoffed but agreed. And when Maya won it had the opposite of the intended effect—it was as though he'd recognized some recklessness of his own, seen something in her he wanted for himself.

The next thing she knew, Marcus—he had just assumed the top spot at SterlingCo—had given Colin a big job on the West Coast. It was the dot-com crash; Colin was supposed to see what could be salvaged there and keep an eye on the SterlingCo movie studio. Maya knew she had her out. "You're going to date real actresses; that's part of the assignment," she'd told him, and he had agreed, good-naturedly if a little sadly, that long distance never worked.

Marcus came to New York often in the following months. She was flattered by his interest in her, and it seemed like she and Colin were probably over. Now and then he'd send an email, ask how she was faring. But he was on the other coast, out of sight and mind. The newspapers said he'd taken up surfing, been seen around town with an entertainment lawyer. Marcus was acquiring the Cox Dunn Company and its suite of newspapers and financial magazines. He seemed high on the enormous amounts of money he was moving. He was solidifying his own persona, fucking with the market's perception of him—was he a corporate raider or a truth vigilante, building on his journalism bona fides? His uniform was all black, always YSL. He was never without premium cocaine. He knew everyone; he could tell you a secret about almost any prominent person, knew everybody's Achilles' heel. He didn't care about restaurants, unlike most of the people Maya knew in New York. The places they went did not appear in the press—they were dark rooms, unmarked and beautiful, where an idle comment might move billions.

They were the kind of privileged places where enormously privileged men did what they wanted, knowing their secrets would be kept. Maya always expected to sit off to the side like the other women, who were more or less accessories. But then Marcus, in the heat of discussion, would turn away from whatever geriatric power broker sat near him, and say, "Maya, what do you think?"

And she, radiant with his attention, would reply boldly. Because she was always listening. Always ready. He would grin, as though she were the brightest heavenly body in the sky, return his gaze to the man, and say, "That's my answer, then."

When they were alone, it was like there was no one else in the world.

Still, he never lied—he was married. He wasn't leaving his wife.

Maya would look at photos of Eva back then, would read interviews about her garden, her pet charities, her children. These obsessions filled Maya with misery and loathing, but she couldn't stop herself.

For a while, she just accepted it. A maelstrom of her own making: lonely days, endless partying, tabloids reporting every instance of bad behavior. Miss Mayhem, they called her. Meanwhile, he never called when he said he would call. She'd decide for herself that things had ended, that it was time to get over him, and then he'd show up at her door, and she couldn't turn him away. Just being in his presence would seem like the most exciting thing she'd ever experienced. And then he'd be gone. But then she came disastrously close to a public declaration of her feelings for him, he freaked out, and that precipitated the shit show trip to Miami. Her final spiral. The big dismissal. After Miami, he seemed gone for good.

And then Colin came home.

Maya was invited to the launch party of a web magazine she didn't realize Colin owned, on the Tribeca Grand roof, and they picked up again, just like they were before.

And then she was pregnant. There was that.

———

As Maya selects a dress from the many Colin chose for her, as she tries on the different shoes, her jewelry, she has that same shivering feeling as when she arrived yesterday, that the house has eyes. In fact, this room *does* have eyes—the fading sunset flashes on the gold foil of the tigers stalking through the jungle wallpaper. And then there's that damn doll she swiped from Arianna's room.

Maya reaches over and turns the doll face down on the side table, before swiping it off the surface for good. *Get lost, weirdo.*

What she just did—and her past with Marcus—it could destroy the goodness between her and Colin. He'd be devastated. Here, on Sterling turf, she doesn't doubt that any slight against him will prompt the others to close ranks. Turn her out in the most humiliating way possible. In fact, it's exactly the kind of fuckup they'd love to uncover, the better to declare Maya expendable.

It will be all of them against her, and whatever power Arianna granted her, they'll figure out how to take it away.

But Maya is pretty good at figuring too. Always has been. As she smooths her hair, her skin, she commits to that. This house is full of secrets, about Arianna and everyone else. That was what Marcus accused her of already—teasing out the family secrets for some shrewd use. As long as he thinks that anyway, why not commit? If she learns the deepest Sterling secrets, she can run the table.

Whatever the Sterlings are planning next, Maya will be ready for them. She's not the kind of girl who just goes down without a fight.

Once more before she goes to join the others, Maya checks her appearance in the mirror. Gleaming black lashes. Scarlet red lip. And dangling over her breastbone, on a delicate chain, is a shiny, sharp gold pickaxe.

15

There's a new nurse on my floor. I *loathe* her.

I know why too. She reminds me of Helen—tall, imperious, nasty bark.

She keeps asking me what I'm thinking about, and I know what she really means is [creaking evil witch's voice]: *Are you trying to remember upsetting things again?*

And yes, I am, and no, I'm not going to tell her what. I remember more all the time.

The trouble is that some of my memories are relevant, and some are not. Some come pounding into my brains, madly heralding their significance. And some are just, you know, the taste of the coconut tea with milk that Barrow used to make me when I was sad.

I have this *feeling* about this nurse, that she's watching me, that she wants to take away my "rewards"—the privileges I've earned by being "good"—

I can smell it on her.

The pack of cigarettes a week, a felt-tip pen, a television in my room.

Not to mention the things I've collected—one of the doctor's nicer pens, a pack of pastilles, an empty Altoids box, a business card from a taxi service.

Not sure how I'd use that one, but a girl can dream.

I've made a compartment in the mattress—that took some very slow and patient work undoing seams with my fingernails, which the doctors' secret police have now cut again. They called it a "manicure," but I wore quite elegant French tips for a good two years; I know the score. They don't want me going full Greek tragedy on my eyeballs or anything. *That* would be bad for business *Hahahaaaaa*.

I'm considering wedging off one of the drop ceiling tiles overhead—an even better place to keep contraband, not to mention this diary, YOU, my dearest darlingest onliest friend, whom the spies may well be onto—they'd *love* to get their hands on you, no doubt there.

The staff here are from all over. They all speak nearly accent-less English. I try to ask them questions, get some hints about the facility, its location. They just smile their placid smiles, and say, "Where do *you* think you are?"

They remind me of the sort of questions Harry's little team of headshrinkers used to pose, back in the solitary years at Sterling Park, when I first started having the hallucinations.

Here in the facility, it's been explained to me that one of the symptoms of advanced alcoholism—which apparently I have, though in that case, why doesn't Gigi?—is hallucinations. Especially during withdrawal. And it's true, when I first got here,

I saw awful things behind my eyes, and the veil between this realm and the next was thin—between the realm of spotless white walls and soft baby blue booties, and the realm of pain and suffering and thieves and little girls with hair going up, up, up in flame.

As far as I know, I was not withdrawing from gin back in 1985, back when I saw walls on fire and a girl going full Joan of Arc in the window of the house in La Digue, and then returning to me, her little charred ghost whispering from the next bed pillow over, calling to me from the eaves, leaving me tiny treats and things all over the house. I heard her, I know I did, saying, *I'm still here; I'm still Jessica; don't forget me!*

But they all said I was seeing things.

I mean, listen, I'm not *that* mad.

I knew there was no Jessica anymore; she was gone. I couldn't *see* her, not with my eyes anyhow. She was gone, but she was with me too, in some profound sense—

I don't know how to explain that, but I know it's true.

Jessica used to leave little presents around Silver House, for instance.

I'd find them without even looking. They'd just appear. In the library. Harry's bedroom. The back seat of the car. A coin from Japan, a little stationery pad from a hotel in Argentina— she used to spend time in those places, because her father was sort of a wanderer. A gambler, a crook, a man who lived in the seamy underbelly of the world. He was an aristocrat too—that was the sense I got—Harry was vague about the father, his old friend. Mikey was the name. Said he felt guilty, didn't like to think about him. Once I found a watch etched with the name *Blackburne*. Somehow I just knew that she left it there, where she knew I would find it. In Sterling Park. How did she get there, to leave me that message, I do not know. The message was clear, though—she was saying, *I am real, no matter what Harry's doctors and nurses say, no matter what Harry says. Or Helen.*

When I said Jessica's name, Helen's face would be absolute murder.

What was I talking about, though?

Ah yes, the watch!

I found it one day in Harry's study, which was a place I liked to hide. There was a closet in his office, and I put a lot of pillows in there, and cupped my treasures right under his nose (often he didn't know I was there), and tried to listen for the voice of Jessica saying, *I'm here, I'm here, I'm here.*

Later, when Harry decided I was better, when the nurses went away and I was allowed to roam free, he found me in that closet, and he wasn't even upset. It's like he suspected I was there all along.

He gave me a little toy Dictaphone, like his, and said—

Now you can make your own business calls and record them, just like me. That way, when you take my place, you'll know what to do. Practice giving orders; practice telling your underlings what to do.

That's what I'm doing, he said, *making sure my voice doesn't falter.*

So that no one dreams of lying to me. Then he'd laugh. *You'd never lie to me, would you, Arianna?*

We're in it together, you and me. The heir and heiress of the Sterling empire.

Harry had so many tapes—now that I'm older, I suppose he was paranoid. But as a little girl, I believed him, believed that he was practicing how to sound indomitable. I would have liked to be that way too. That's why I collected them, whenever he left them out.

A cassette tape here, a cassette tape there.

I'd tuck them away in my secret compartments—in Harry's office, in the lesser used hallways, in my own bedroom, the hidden crannies of which were rather stocked by then.

I suppose they've found all those now.

I suppose back at Sterling Park, they've raided my secret places.

But maybe not. There were quite a few, and some of them were very cleverly placed...

They *always* underestimated me.

God, I've had this fucking song in my head... I can't remember the lyrics... Something about taking to the streets for the kill.

I can see the shadow of the Helenish nurse outside the door, and I just turned the TV on so she'll think I'm watching.

It's that *Springs* show again, so of course now I do want to watch. Here's old dumb-as-dirt Kendra saying: *You can never have too many pairs of shoes—or boy toys!*

This show should have a laugh track.

Ooh, and there's the one I like. The bartender with the long dark hair. Maya. Giving an epic eye roll—I mean it's an operatic performance of exasperated disdain, truly one for the ages.

I just love her.

Shit. Must hide you away now—the nurse doth approach.

I know they won't permit it, won't like it.

How much I've written.

How much I've remembered.

16

"Ah, at long last," Helen says, spiking a high, shaped eyebrow. More to the room than anyone in particular, she adds, "Do you know how much I loathe waiting?"

Maya, having just entered the Red Gallery for this evening's cocktail hour, smiles blandly, says, "Oh yes, me too," and takes in the room. It's different from the room they had drinks in yesterday. In this one, the windows face southwest, where the sun is setting spectacularly over frozen gardens, making the icy stretches brilliant with reflected light. A stark contrast to the inside, the space warmed by a large hearth, casting shadows on the rose-flocked wallpaper. The Sterling clan is gathered by the fire, drinks in hand, dressed once again as though they're expecting company: Colin, Marcus, and Julian in sweater vests and jackets, all well-made and well-worn, Helen in a slim black dress with a square neckline, and Gigi in a peach Dolce & Gabbana bodycon dress, a shade off from her skin tone. If Maya squinted, it would be as though Gigi were wearing nothing at all.

The children are a little way off, assembled on a velvet couch on the other side of the pool table, the boys playing a dice game with their nannies while a third attends to Becca, strapped into a bouncy chair. The nanny waves old wooden toys through Becca's field of vision. Liveried servants hover in the corner, ready to leap at the first sign of any Sterling want. The scene has a timeless wash, it could be the 1970s, the 1870s.

All rather quaint—to the untrained eye, anyway.

Helen's still assessing Maya, apparently. "That's a very pretty dress. New?"

The dress Helen is referring to is next season Lanvin, drapey mauve silk with a fitted waist and full skirt. It's ladylike but still insanely flattering. Maya looks expensive and elegant. Not an outsider, but already one of them. And she can hear it in Helen's tone, a grudging acknowledgment of this. *You could never have afforded a dress like that before—you thief.*

She can sense Marcus's gaze, too, knows from prior experience how he likes to watch her enter a room. But it's Colin she needs. Not the pulse of electricity she feels from across the space, that sparking of old desire, but her worried, patient husband.

Colin, who she has been lying to. But no—she has to put that thought away now.

As if he's heard her think his name, Colin comes away from the others, kisses Maya's forehead, whispers, "You look beautiful."

Beyond him, Marcus's eyes travel slowly over her dress, taking in the length of her. She remembers that look. It requires the full force of Maya's will not to return it, not to succumb to the sensation of his breath on her skin only hours ago in the greenhouse. She could really use a drink.

"Thank you for the gifts," she whispers to her husband.

Colin nods. "Of course, my love. You all right? You look a little pale."

"It's just jet lag. I'm fine."

He's so good, her Colin. At his side, in the warmth of his attention, she wishes she could just tell him everything: about Jessie, the Mexico meeting. Even the photo. For a moment, she believes she could. They'd huddle together, figure out a fix, the way she and her dad would conspire when she was a kid to scrounge up rent, get his car out of the impound lot.

At least, until the problem was too big to solve, and she had to accept that her dad was beyond saving. Is *she* beyond saving now too? The thought comes out of nowhere and sours her stomach.

No, she can't tell Colin. The truth would break him. Not only did she sleep with the older *married* cousin Colin worships, she fell madly, ill-advisedly in love with him. If she told Colin, it would be obvious that some part of her isn't over it, and maybe never will be. The fallout would be chaotic, it would go on and on, one disaster begetting another. Joey and Tripp on a catastrophic scale. He'd be wide-open to Helen's influence, her opinions of Maya. Would he try to take Becca away?

That's a fate Maya can't begin to contemplate.

Colin's still looking at her, a question in his eyes. Maya smiles softly, lips sealed shut. He seems to take this as a cue that she needs a cocktail—which she definitely does—and heads to the bar.

That's when Maya really feels the weight of the room's silence. When Colin steps away, no one says a thing—they just look at her like a pack of dogs assessing an unfamiliar creature. Threat or prey? *Don't let them guess you're afraid*, she tells herself. *Find an ally.*

"Julian!" she exclaims as soon as she spots him. Julian rises from the chair nearest her, surprised and intrigued by her attention. "Thank you again for the tour this morning. It really was the perfect welcome to Sterling Park."

The fact that Maya has started a friendly conversation seems to please Colin, now returning with her usual drink—vodka over ice, squeeze of lemon. He looks relieved as she leans forward to place a kiss on his cheek and nods her okay for him to move off toward Marcus, toward business talk, no doubt.

"It was my pleasure, dear," Julian replies, taking the opportunity to give her waist a squeeze. "Seems a long time ago, doesn't it? The whole world has changed since then. Very exciting, in my humble opinion. Congratulations on creating such a stir," he adds, lifting his glass to her with a wink.

She smoothly replies, "Wish I could take credit for the stir, but really, it was Arianna we have to thank for that," and clinks glasses with Julian. As she drinks, she accidentally catches Marcus's eye, which makes the room go sideways. She turns away quickly, refocusing on a regal painting that occupies a great deal of wall space.

"Handsome portrait, isn't it?" Maya says, trying to ignore the heat of Marcus's gaze on her neck.

"Ah, yes. Another masterful depiction of young Richard Sterling. It was a gift from one of his fellow airmen. Lord Blackburne. Jago Blackburne."

Maya doesn't really have an interest in Julian's little history lesson, but she takes a ladylike sip of the crisp vodka, nods for Julian to go on.

"The story goes that they were in Paris together, after D-Day—in which they both valiantly participated—and Richard bested Jago in billiards at some hole-in-the-wall in Pigalle. Richard waved off the money he was owed from their bet, telling Jago it would be better he survived the rest of the war and repaid a rather more substantial debt, a loan the Sterlings had given the Blackburnes so they could expand their parachute manufacturing operation. Of course, Jago took that for the insult it was. When they returned from the war, Jago sent the portrait to Richard as a gift—but with a bit of a *fuck you* thrown in. See there?" Julian indicates a section of the painting in the manner of a museum docent who's been waiting all day to tell his favorite anecdote. "Jago had the artist paint in a fifty-pound note. You can see it sticking out of the breast pocket."

"Did he ever repay the loan?" Maya asks.

Julian makes a face. "Tsk tsk, Maya. Sterlings may be all about business, but they don't talk finance over cocktail hour." He gives her a wink, showing his jest. "I believe they made an arrangement. The Sterlings are always cleaning up the Blackburne messes, you see..."

"Oh?" Maya prompts, but her attention is pulled by Rory

Atkinson entering the room, his face the same mask of officious preoccupation as earlier in the day. Except, on second glance, more officious, more preoccupied. His eyes linger on Maya and Julian, who waves a hand in cheery greeting. Rory replies with a curt nod and—is Maya imagining it?—a hard look Maya's way.

Anxious to appear unaffected, Maya asks, "Is that still the case, the Sterlings cleaning up after the Blackburnes?"

"The Blackburnes always were—I don't want to say *pirates*, but they had a taste for plunder, no other way to say it, and they knew how to walk right up to the line of legality."

Maya nods, still watching Rory as he leans over and whispers to Helen, her stomach turning over.

"Their business was ever the unseemly kind—war profiteering, dodgy mines. But Michael was bad even for a Blackburne. Always in trouble, always on the wrong side of the law. And yet he and Harry were particular friends, schoolboy friends, in fact—carrying on the camaraderie and rivalry of their fathers. At university, they traded girlfriends, competed in rowing. But Harry favored maths; he was smart about systems. Mikey read Shakespeare, the tragedies, and he seemed to take them literally. When things got especially dicey for Mikey, Harry let him hide out at the Sterling villa in Seychelles, on the island of La Digue…"

Maya is brought back to Julian's story. "Wait, the house that burned down?"

"Indeed. Harry never forgave himself for Mikey's death— though Mikey had plenty of enemies. He was almost destined for an early grave. But Harry always wondered if it wasn't somehow his fault, a case of mistaken identity. Not that there was any evidence. Just because it happened on Sterling property, and that it had tragically taken Mikey's daughter, Jessica…"

Maya nods, but the story has lost its hold on her. She's consumed with her own precarious situation.

Does Rory know about the kiss in the greenhouse; is that the news he's pouring in Helen's ear?

"Sorry Julian, I'm just going to…" Maya steps away from Julian midsentence, raising her glass in the air in apology. She turns in the direction of the bar and finds herself against Marcus's chest.

"Oh!" she gasps. "Sorry, I was just—drink."

The corner of Marcus's mouth twists up. She inhales that familiar mix of pepper and flint. "Can't stay away?" he says, meaning—she's pretty sure—from him and the bar cart, both.

"Is this *not* cocktail hour?" Maya replies aridly.

Before Marcus can reply, Becca begins to wail over in the corner. Maya's temples throb. She's about to cross the room to her, but Marcus lightly touches her arm to stop her, just as one of the nannies lifts Becca from the bouncy seat and tries to soothe the baby herself. "Let them," Marcus says—kindly? Commandingly? She has no idea. All she can think about is his hand on her thigh.

"Cetin?" Helen asks Rory, loud enough that everyone can hear. Marcus turns sharply at the name. A moment ago they were embroiled in a grave and silent communication. Now Helen shouts: "Will somebody. Shut. That. Baby. *Up.*"

Rage reddens Maya's face. She doesn't want some stranger wearing a stupid costume consoling her child anymore. Maya gulps her drink, slams it on the bar cart.

Helen turns her head toward Maya a fraction of an inch. "Not *you*."

Rory steps away. "Maya, you're going to have to come with me."

Her blood goes cold. "What? Why?"

"Our investigation has turned up some new information. Agent Cetin, a special friend of ours at Interpol, wants to talk to you. About Mexico."

Maya's thoughts stall. Then Colin is at her side, face flexed with worry.

Early in their rekindling, when she was still dealing with legal issues stemming from her Miami spree, he joked they should just get married—the Sterlings have private security, a team of lawyers, a whole apparatus that serves as a buffer from legal irritations. Once you had the last name Sterling, you were taken care of. The assault charges the photographer was threatening— the one who jumped at Maya as she came off the beach—that wouldn't even be a thing if she were a Sterling.

But here she is, Maya Sterling, and that whole team is coming down on *her*.

Colin puts a soothing hand on Maya's shoulder. "Rory, come on—we don't need to talk to the authorities right *now*. Surely it can wait; we can meet with Cetin tomorrow."

Helen's tone is striking. "Not *we*. Maya, and Maya alone, needs to talk to Agent Cetin. *Now*."

Colin sighs, turning to Maya and resting his forehead against hers. "It's okay. Agent Cetin is a friend of ours," he says. "I'm sure it's just background information. If it's longer than fifteen minutes, I'll come for you, all right?"

Maya nods, steps away from him. She has an absurd instinct to grab Becca and flee.

But she doesn't. She's promised herself not to be impulsive. With all the fuck-you dignity she can summon, she follows Rory through the door.

———

As soon as they exit the gallery, she regrets following orders. Travis, the omnipresent security guard, is there hustling them through windowless halls and Maya's heart races with each step. She takes deep breaths of musty air, trying to calm herself. Has Agent Cetin seen the photo of her and Marcus?

Would she even care about that?

An *agent* wouldn't be interested in an old photo of her with her husband's cousin, wouldn't make a house visit on account of some illicit kiss. What they care about is Arianna. Maya's alibi.

Or Maya's lack of alibi—why she lied about where she was that night in Mexico.

They're descending a staircase. Maya can smell cooking oil—they must be near the kitchen. That's good. That's something to hang on to. From the bottom of the stairs, she's brought into a plain office—big desk, ancient ledgers—and placed in a wooden armchair.

Travis and Rory stand like twin sentinels on either side of the door. Across the desk is a woman Maya recognizes, though she's only seen her once from a distance. At the time she was wearing a windbreaker, giving orders. Now she dons a sensible black suit, her hair slicked back in a neat bun. The woman on the tarmac when the touched down briefly in New York.

"Hello, Maya." Maya's pulse quickens. *You've done nothing wrong*, she reminds herself. But that's not entirely true. "Agent Cetin, Interpol. I'm coordinating the investigation of the murder of Arianna Sterling."

"Yes, okay, how can I help?" Maya is relieved she doesn't look like a jet-lagged mess anymore, that she took the time to put on makeup and blow-dry her hair, that she's wearing a new dress.

"We're just chatting."

Maya glances at Travis. He's blocking the door. Would it be wrong to ask this woman for her credentials? Demand Maya's personal lawyer be flown over from New York before they continue?

Agent Cetin fixes Maya in her unblinking stare. "Congratulations on your marriage. And the baby."

"Thanks," Maya replies carefully.

"You have a beautiful family."

Maya levels her gaze. "That's not what we're chatting about though, right?"

"No, I suppose not." Agent Cetin seems amused. "Tell me about your last night in Mexico."

"You mean the night Arianna died."

"Yes. The night Arianna Sterling died."

"Colin's already gone over this with Travis. There were some festivities onshore, but she didn't try to contact us."

"What did you do that night?"

"I was on the *Agyros*. Spent a lot of time in the pool. We had oysters; I must have had a bad one, because I felt sick suddenly and couldn't go onshore with the others."

"Rapid onset food poisoning?" Agent Cetin glances at Travis. "So, you're saying you *didn't* go ashore."

Maya's tongue feels thick. "I didn't say that. What I said was, I didn't go *with them*. But then I started to feel better. I guess it wasn't food poisoning. So, I left the *Agyros* to find them, but couldn't. And then I came back."

"Maya, who is this?" Agent Cetin begins to turn over a piece of paper.

Maya's skull seems to constrict around her brain. There's a pounding at her temples.

Fuck. An eight-by-eleven glossy. So they know—they all know about her and Marcus.

The vodka Maya just drank rises in her throat.

But no. It's not the photo Jessie showed her.

It's a picture *of* Jessie, of Maya and the journalist, inside the Iguana Bar in Puerto Vallarta. It's security footage, grainy, not great. But the journalist and Maya had removed their sunglasses in the dim bar, so Maya's face is clear and recognizable.

Her mind goes to Colin. What has he been told? Does he

think she's working with a tabloid, that their whole relationship is a sham? Or does he know about the photo behind this one, of her with his cousin, the man he worships? Her heart makes a fist.

"Maya?"

Maya's gaze flicks up. "I had a drink with her, that woman, in a bar, while I was trying to text the others," she says. "Colin and the other Sterling executives."

"Did you *plan* to meet her?"

Maya holds Agent Cetin's gaze. She's been interviewed before—by celebrity journalists, mostly, but she knows the art of the subtle sidestep. "I'd never met her before in my life."

"Who was she?"

"She's a journalist. That's what she told me. It was all a bit... confused. She could have been something else, I suppose. I wondered, for a moment, if she wasn't just a fan."

"And what did she want?"

"Oh, you know. Everyone is fascinated by the Sterlings."

"Why didn't you alert your security team that a journalist—or whatever she was—was harassing a member of the Sterling family?"

"The press was interested in me before I married Colin. I'm used to handling these irritations on my own."

"Does it seem like an irritation to you now?"

The questions are coming rapid-fire. Maya wishes she could slow it down. "No, but—"

"What was her name?"

"Jessie. That's what she told me."

"And did you believe her?"

Maya tries to make a careless gesture. "Sometimes those people use aliases. I took it with a grain of salt."

"What's her *real* name, Maya?"

"I have no idea."

"Take a guess."

"I need a break," Maya says with as much force as possible.

Rory is hovering behind her. She can smell his gin and olive breath. With regretful finality, he says, "We should really keep going."

"But I feel sick," Maya protests. She does, kind of. It's occurring to her that the fact that the Sterling family have strong connections with law enforcement is only reassuring if you're in the family's good graces. Maya stands, sidesteps Rory.

Travis comes away from the door, looming. "What were you doing with Arianna Sterling the night she died?"

What? The room tilts.

She glances at the others, thinking she's heard wrong. Rory doesn't blink. He stares at Maya, waits for an answer. Agent Cetin's eyes narrow in irritation—not at her, but at Travis. She coughs pointedly and holds up the photograph—Maya in Mexico with the woman who called herself Jessie. "That is you, Maya Miller Sterling, correct?"

When Maya says nothing, the agent nods. There's no denying it.

Then Agent Cetin confirms what Travis just implied: "And

the woman you were talking to is Arianna Sterling, in Puerto Vallarta, the night she died."

Maya's lips part in shock. Jessie…was Arianna. So different from the Arianna she saw in the archives earlier. But there, yes, now that it's in front of her, she sees it, the resemblance between Jessie and the girl in the magazines, face softened with baby fat, the hair not yet stringy, still full and lustrous enough to fall into her eyes.

She has the strong urge to laugh, even as the possibility of laughing, ever, at anything, seems suddenly impossible. Her lungs are dry, her toes feel dangled above an open flame.

"As far as we know, Maya, you're the last person who saw the heiress alive."

PART III

17

1994,

MY GIRLHOOD (IN MY MIND)

Here's what I can figure out: I was a very bad girl.

How, exactly?

In new and interesting ways, or the old terrifying ones? Is there any difference? These days have been a blur. For all I know, what seem like days are in fact years.

My jaw aches—as though I've been working it hard in the night. I feel turned upside down again, like they've strung me from the ceiling by my ankles to shake my troublesome thoughts out and let them fall fall fall a long way down and far away.

They must've zapped me again, given me a shot to shut me up and calm me down.

But here's what else I'm guessing, from the absolute mess that is my mind: the less I take these pills they want me to take, the longer I'm here on my own—away from Sterling Park—the closer I am to the Truth. Not that it's so great here, but it's different. How long have I been here, in total? No idea, but I was full-grown when I came—that I know. At the same time, it's as though I was learning to breathe, and eat, and stand,

and speak, and put three facts together to make a pattern, and make a guess from that pattern about what might be coming next. I think I remember all the different parts of who I have been—

When I was little girl with my imaginary friend, Jessica.

When I was a slightly bigger girl, telling fairy stories, to explain myself and construct a Self, or something like it.

When I was rebelling, smashing whatever I could—

fucking around with handsome Lyman from the farm, with whatever boy I could find—

so that I could become my own person.

Though of course, they wouldn't let me. Harry didn't want that.

He said it was because he loved me so, I was his only daughter, he wouldn't want to lose me to the grown-up world—

And for all I know, that's true.

But I also remember times he told me I was nothing, I was unworthy of what I had been given, I had better not cross him.

I remember once when I vommed on the medieval tapestry in the Red Gallery, and Harry was so angry he kicked one of the collies, and then they didn't like him anymore; they growled whenever he came, and he told Barrow to get rid of them—said: Give them to Julian, *that lackey*, that's all he's good for—

Last night, I bit someone. I'm remembering it now. I was in a rage with her—

It was the Helenish nurse, of course. I was so *angry* at her. Why?

Angry for threatening to take away my TV, my cigarettes, if I wasn't a good girl, if I didn't eat all my food. Angry for her part in the whole wide world, and all its unfairness, and for my lot—alone, always alone.

The strange thing is, the past and present, it all bends into one continuous loop.

I *know* that I am here, in this facility, wherever this facility is.

But very recently, I also knew that I was in Sterling Park, following Gigi through the tunnels, smelling that earthy smell down there.

And we're on our way to the real world, the wide world of pulsing music and swirling lights. I could drink the whole world, I swear I could, and if Harry doesn't catch me, I will...

There, you see? For a minute, I was *there*.

But then there's here: this journal, these notes I've written to myself so I don't forget, these puffy blue booties on my feet, the bruises on my arms.

These really are hideous pulpy bruises. From being restrained? Yes, I think so. But then what are these cuts and bandages about?

I know sneaking around with Gigi was long ago and far away.

That time when a normal life seemed possible.

I was only fourteen. Gigi needed a friend. Her parents had died. Their helicopter trying to get away from the paparazzi went smashing into some Italian cliff. She was an adult, practically. She was proud of that, her adultness. And very sad. And very determined not to *seem* sad, even for a moment. In some ways, I must have still been four years old, still terrified that the slightest breeze of the outside world could harm me. But in another way, I was far older, because till then Harry had been my only friend.

Then one morning in the office, Harry said, "All right, my dear, you've had your fun."

Why was I there?

Someone fetched me, I suppose.

Harry said, "You're a Sterling, it's time to get serious, we have to prepare you for what's ahead."

I started laughing my head off.

I was halfway across his office, that office we used to spend *ages* in.

Later, tied down to the bed, they insisted that I was a danger to myself. And I kept saying, no no no *no*! I just want to be free, and what's freer than a window? It was a nice summer day, the world was full of pollen, bees, boys taking their shirts off to wipe the sweat from brows upon which nothing had been written.

I was hungry, and I wanted to feel free, I wasn't at all trying to harm myself.

But no one believed me.

Like no one believes me here.

I wasn't trying to hurt myself; I just wanted to open the window.

18

Maya wakes to the sound of screaming. Icy panic spreads from her belly upward toward her throat. In her mind she sees the woman from the Iguana Bar, observes a sudden nervous constriction of that delicate mouth, as though she's seen a ghost. Hears her parting words: *I'll be in touch.*

But now she'll never be in touch.

Because she wasn't a journalist named Jessie, she was Arianna Sterling, and Arianna Sterling is dead.

As Maya's wakes up fully to the present reality—she's in the nursery suite of Sterling Park, in the dark hours of the morning. The screaming is Becca. Becca, she reassures herself, just Becca's baby wails—getting stronger all the time as she grows and grows. Becca, close by in the crib, fussy over being so far from home. Something in the water at Sterling Park has been making Becca miserable. Maybe it's the British formula. Maybe it's an old rot in the walls. Maybe, Maya thinks, it's the Sterlings.

As she lifts Becca from the crib, swaying from one foot to another to soothe her, Maya watches Colin turn over in the sheets and not quite wake. Even asleep, there's tension in his jaw. He feels divided, she knows—loyalty to his family, loyalty to her.

They promised to have each other's backs, but that was before Agent Cetin came, showed the Sterling family the photo of Maya and Arianna together in Mexico, right before Arianna died.

The photo changes everything.

Last night, getting ready for bed, their suite felt airless.

"You really expect me to believe that you met with Arianna, not knowing it was her, and then she decided to leave you everything?" Colin strode across the room in frustration, raking his fingers through his hair.

"Yes." Her voice was low, emphatic. "Come on, you know me. Do you think I could've known that was Arianna, kept the secret all this time? You've got to believe me."

"You did lie to me, though," he said, relenting. "About being sick—the reason you didn't come with the rest of us."

She grabbed his hand, pulling him to face her. "Colin, please, I didn't ask for any of this."

Colin closed his eyes, exhaled long and low, from some deep place of pain.

"And now they're going to try to turn you against me, you know that."

Colin grunted. "You're exhausted" was his curt reply, dismissing Maya's fears.

She *is* tired, and she wishes she could sleep the way Colin is sleeping now.

As Becca's eyes flutter shut, and her body grows heavy in

Maya's arms, Maya tries to recall the details of that night in Mexico, the meeting in the Iguana Bar that she had so completely misunderstood. Some things seem obvious now. "Jessie Moore's" mouth was delicate, formed around a slight overbite, like Gigi's. Those darting pale eyes, somewhat shadowed by the low baseball hat, were a striking green, striking as Helen's. Maya's been ransacking her mind for some telling detail from that brief, coerced exchange. But everything has shifted so dramatically, it's hard to get her bearings, to know what's real and what's her imagination.

Maya's been assured numerous times that Agent Cetin is a *friend*, and no one has flat out accused her of anything. But their conversation was unsettling; it felt like both an interrogation and a warning. Maya knows what everyone's thinking. Or at least, she knows what the media would make of these facts. *Doesn't it seem strange that Maya should come out of nowhere and insinuate herself into one of the most powerful families on earth? It can't be a coincidence that shortly thereafter, the heiress dies, leaving her everything.* Before this latest bombshell, Maya faxed Bob Feld the agreement that Rory asked her to sign, and he immediately faxed her back a one-word reply: *No.* Maya has since asked for the will to be sent to him, but Rory and his team are evasive. The machine is broken; they'll do it tomorrow. No one says so, but Maya suspects that the purpose of the slow rolling is to search out new reasons to question the validity of Arianna's will. Probably also to buy time to strategize, assess whether—if a scandal should break out—the family will keep Maya close or throw her away.

Maybe they think Maya's more likely to cave, now that she's been caught in a lie.

During her years on *The Springs*, she was so accustomed to her life being on display that the camera's gaze started feeling like a second skin. Here, the constant observation is more personal, harder to shake off. The steely, suspicious eye of Helen, the arch, puckish appraisal of Julian, the brooding glances from Marcus. She feels not just exposed but studied, dissected. They don't seem protective of Maya, so much as concerned that she's a pirate here to loot their gold.

How long has she been pacing the floor, her thoughts cycling through her weary brain? How many nights will she have to stay here—awakening to Becca's screams, locked away in Silver House? It's still dark outside. In her arms, Becca has fallen into deep sleep. Maya lays her baby carefully down in the crib. But she doesn't think she'll be able to fall back asleep herself—she's twitchy and restless, harassed by fragments of the conversation she had with the heiress in Mexico, on her last night alive.

She might as well make the best of her insomnia and go down to the kitchen to prep Becca's morning bottle. The baby will probably be awake again soon, and Maya would rather not have to talk to any more nannies, servants, or other potential spies, than necessary.

Is it just paranoia, this feeling of being surveilled? As she makes her way, Maya keeps noting little disturbances in the atmosphere. A creak in the hallway, just as she's turned a corner. A sudden hush when she enters a room. The lingering smell of another person in her bedroom, a new, unfamiliar order to her clothes or makeup, as though they've been rearranged. The most reassuring explanation is that the old house might in fact be haunted, which is obviously not reassuring at all.

As Maya descends the various hallways and passages to the basement kitchen, her mind circles the meeting in the Iguana Bar.

I just had to get a look at you. That's what "Jessie" had said when Maya demanded to know why she'd summoned her there. *I need you on my side. On the inside.*

Now it's clear she wanted Maya to report back on Maya's new family members, become a mole.

But she wasn't a journalist; she was Arianna. So what did she *actually* mean? The Sterling family heiress was already as "inside" as it got.

When Maya tried to pin Jessie down, ask what exactly she was looking for, Jessie had been vague. Mentioned an insurance policy. But why do you need insurance against your own family unless you see them as a threat?

Which means Arianna wanted Maya "inside," because she couldn't return to Sterling Park herself. Not if she wanted to walk out again... The floor ripples; the walls are liquid. Then a new thought arrives. The leverage Arianna had on Maya was proof of her affair with Marcus. Which means Maya isn't the only one who would want Jessie/Arianna to disappear.

Marcus's reaction to Arianna's will was unlike the rest of his family's—he seemed to think Maya should go ahead and cash the check.

An arctic current moves through Maya's nervous system. It all seems so insane, and she doesn't really think Marcus could have meant his cousin harm.

But on the other hand, *someone* killed Arianna.

And Maya has been a fool for Marcus before.

At the Iguana Bar, Arianna had ranted about how dangerous the Sterlings were. Maya had thought it was just the warning of a journalist with a chip on her shoulder, or a slightly obsessive fan. But no. She was talking about her own family.

Maya's eyes are adjusting—she thinks the room where Travis and Rory took her was somewhere down here, in this warren of plain, subterranean hallways.

A commanding voice breaks Maya's ruminations: "Mrs. Sterling."

Out of the shadows emerges the square steady figure of Barrow, nicely dressed in a suit and tie, even at this early hour. She's suddenly embarrassed by her unbrushed hair, her sleep-rumpled robe.

"Oh, I—I'm sorry, I didn't think anybody else would be awake at this hour."

He smiles wanly. "What can I get for you? You really shouldn't be in the kitchen; they wouldn't like that. It's not how Sterlings do."

He says this lightly—so that she can hear that it's both real and a fiction—just a rule everyone has agreed to follow—and she almost laughs out loud.

"Oh, well, I don't feel like much of a Sterling anyway," Maya admits.

After all, Maya was the only *Sterling* Agent Cetin interviewed last night. As though she were the prime suspect, and the others simply her victims. Even though they all have just as much motive as Maya. They were licking their lips to carve up Arianna's holdings until they learned she'd changed her will that morning. Why should they be above suspicion?

Barrow smiles faintly and gestures for Maya to follow him out of the dark hallway and into the somewhat less dark kitchen. "It's funny," he says, as they arrive in a large room, ancient walls and modern appliances all immaculately clean and ready for the day. "Miss Sterling—Arianna—she used to say the same thing. That she didn't feel like a Sterling. Harry was strict with her, as parents were then. But when she came down here for a warm milk in the middle of the night, I let it be our little secret. Is that what you want, Mrs. Sterling? Some warm milk to help you rest?"

"Oh, no, not for me—" Maya awkwardly waves the canister of formula at him. "I was just going to boil some water to heat a bottle for Becca."

"Let me help you with that."

Barrow removes a pot from a hook on the ceiling, lights the stove.

"Barrow," Maya asks, watching Barrow's efficient movements. "You knew her? Arianna."

"Of course. I have been with the Sterling family all my life."

"Did you hear? About the, uh…" Maya gestures helplessly at herself, at the house above, unable to put words to all that's transpired over the last twenty-four hours.

"Yes, I heard." Perhaps sensing her embarrassment, he goes on. "Don't worry, the staff is discreet."

There's a quality in his voice that seems to say he's seen more, and worse, than this. "Colin said there were years when it was really only Harry and Arianna who lived here. That they were holed up."

When Barrow hesitates, she adds: "I want to understand her. Why she picked me when I didn't even know she existed."

Barrow nods, and Maya glimpses, beyond his professional demeanor, how much he cares. "Yes, there were hard years. We tried to make them tolerable for her, be a comfort when we could. She was such a strong-willed child. A survivor."

"Was Harry...abusive?"

"Oh no, I just meant the isolation. Being without a mother. That sort of thing."

"I do know. She was like me, I guess—in that way, anyway. My mother didn't stick around long. She's still alive, but—after a certain point, I stopped hoping she'd come back. And with my dad, it was complicated."

"Yes, it was a complicated relationship between her and Harry, as it would be for any two people trying to make a family between them, depending on each other for everything as they did. They did fight, but they loved each other too. She really was the light of his life. Even when they were isolated. They had fun together." He stirs the boiling water, deep in thought. "They used to spend hours in his office—he even moved his office, so that it would be closer to her bedroom in

212

the west wing. They had little games, private jokes. They were each other's world, I suppose. I'd bring them lunch up there, and they'd gape at me with these strange expressions—it was as though, for a moment, they forgot that they weren't the only two people on this earth."

Maya struggles to swallow, images of her own father rising unbidden in her mind. "Sounds like a hard way to live—but kind of nice too."

"I think he felt that they had escaped death once, and he was determined not to allow it to come close again."

"After the accident that killed the Blackburnes, you mean?" Maya prompts.

Barrow glances up from the bottle, which he's finished preparing. She senses that he's retreating from the conversation, that he's avoiding saying more.

In a rush, she says, "I had a father like that, you know. I mean, he was dirt poor, but it was just us a lot of the time, and we fought, but I loved him more than anyone. Understood him better. It was hard to know where he ended, and I began. It still is."

Barrow nods deferentially. Maya feels sure now that he's regretting his openness, yet she continues, hoping for more.

"Colin said something happened—some break. That Arianna became difficult, and that she was sent off to treatment or disappeared on her own. Were you aware of that? Did she run away from Harry; did she…?"

"Mrs. Sterling," Barrow interrupts, and the formality of his tone makes clear that the conversation is indeed over. "It's all a long time ago. Really—you shouldn't think about such things, and I should certainly not speak of the family."

Maya can see that he's reached his limit. But she keeps on, allowing her true desperation to be visible on her face. "I'm so confused, you must see that. How did all this happen, and what should I do now that I am in the middle of it? I just want to understand her, that's all. What she was thinking, why she named me—"

The grooves of Barrow's face are deep, exaggerated by the shadows in the dimly lit room. His eyes are deep set, shrouded, yet they shine with warning. Is he just alerting Maya that she's transgressing the boundaries of their roles, or is it something else? He puts the warm bottle in Maya's hand and, with a firm and gentle touch, moves her out of the kitchen.

"Unfortunately, she was a mystery to me too. They both were, really. When Harry was young, he was so charismatic, so proficient at everything he did."

Maya is surprised—she hasn't heard of Harry spoken of in this way. "You admired him?" she says wonderingly.

"Yes, of course."

Maya thinks of that portrait of him, in the hall near the nursery suite. "Is that why he was named heir, even though he was the youngest?"

Barrow opens his palms, as though to say, Who am I to know? "Some do say that Sir Richard favored Harry."

"Why?"

"Mrs. Sterling, it's really none of my—"

"You don't think it's your place to tell me?"

Barrow regards Maya.

She shifts her weight, fixes him in a piercing gaze. "But I am the lady of the house." And when he does not immediately reply, she assumes a more imperious tone, lengthening her neck. "You know. I can see you know. Tell me. Why did Richard name Harry?" Barrow eyes her, considering his words.

"Helen was the eldest, the most impressive in some ways. But it was a man's world, and Sir Richard was a man of his generation."

Does he not want to say anything about Dickie, the father-in-law Maya will never meet? "And?"

"I admire you too, you know," Barrow says, smiling faintly.

"Thank you." Maya declines her chin. Lets him picture her commanding a house like this—shows him, with the steel in her eyes and the forcefulness of her words that she could. Voice clipped, she says, "Tell me. I insist that you tell me."

With a sigh, Barrow begins, "One night, when the children were home from school for a visit, Sir Richard proposed a game. He was always proposing little games. He said the winner would be named his heir. The children, knowing the spirit he most wanted to see, agreed with bravado. And then he had me serve them their dinners, and declared a race to see who could clear their plate first—but without utensils, without even their hands."

"You mean, eat like dogs?"

"Well—"

"And Harry finished his dinner first?"

"No—I can't, to be honest, remember whether it was Helen or Dickie who finished first. But Harry saw them going at it—like pigs more so than dogs, I would say—and refused. He had that inborn nobility about him, you know. And he was named the winner—Sir Richard had not said that the winner of the race was the winner of the game. One of his classic tricks. He had not said what the aim of the game was at all. And Harry certainly was the most dignified, the one who thought for himself. That was the real test."

"That's why you admire him."

"It was how he was."

"That's such a different picture of Harry then I've gotten so far."

"You don't understand, Mrs. Sterling. When he came back to live full-time at Sterling Park, after that accident in La Digue, there was a shadow over him."

"What do you mean, *a shadow?*"

Barrow has a faraway look; he almost seems to have forgotten for a moment that Maya is there at all. "He was—changed."

Maya—thinking of her dad, so flashy in his youth, now at the beginning of another year in another prison—pauses for a long moment at the base of the stairs. Almost to herself, she muses, "What do you mean, *changed?*"

"He was different," Barrow says. "He was just a different man."

She turns, opens her mouth to thank Barrow, but he's already retreated back into the kitchen, leaving Maya to face the family alone.

19

Hours go by at the chaotic pace of the Sterling family in full crisis management mode.

After a day of back-to-back meetings, conference calls, and Sterling strategy sessions organized around assorted beverage services, Maya feels more on the outside than ever. Between Rory burying her in legalese and the Sterling PR faction peppering her with possible NDAs and media plans, Maya grasps the family line toward her. And even if the countless assurances of *We'll take care of everything* and *We're just trying to protect you* have placated Colin, on Maya they've had the opposite of the intended effect.

Maya follows Colin up the wide stairs at the west end of the entryway. He's carrying Becca, humming to her softly. Maya wants to feel warmed by this blissful domestic image, but she's too knocked flat by eight guarded hours of standing her ground to really absorb the sweetness. She's prevailed upon Colin that they need to skip the sacred cocktail hour to regroup, just the three of them. Go over the advice from her own legal team—after a lot of tough love from Bob Feld, who's begun to wade through the complicated documents the Sterlings are slowly faxing over—and talk through their next steps. Thankfully, after a bit of haranguing from Bob himself, Colin agreed.

The avuncular exasperation of her New York lawyer is loving and protective, she knows, but it also reminds her of the years when the situation with her dad got truly ugly, when she needed Bob to guide her through the worst of her father's crimes. Protect herself. At that point in her career, she was finally able to give her dad more money to help him out of his various scrapes, but that just meant he kept getting in bigger scrapes, until he was selling his own daughter's location to tabloid photographers, making himself available for interviews about Maya's early life at a price. She was trapped in a cycle of trying to escape him and trying to prove that she was still his partner in crime.

Not unlike the picture she got of Arianna from her conversation with Barrow that morning. The two of them—Harry and Arianna—locked up in his office together. In each other's confidence, sharing secrets. Accomplices.

An idea strikes Maya. Maybe the secret to Arianna is with the man that molded her.

As they arrive at the top of the stairs, at the hallway that runs the length of the west wing's second floor, she glimpses the portrait of Arianna. It's in the opposite direction of her and Colin's quarters. Just beyond the portrait is the unobtrusive set of stairs that leads up to Arianna's room. Arianna, who is seeming either like a trickster spirit who has bestowed a dangerous fortune upon Maya or like a lost twin Maya never knew she had. Maya's been worrying the question—who was this Arianna person?—and always the answer seems to recede in the direction of the absent father.

The man who hid himself away in this palace with his daughter, ran his kingdom from his home office, created a world for the two of them where even their attendants felt like interlopers. *Who is Harry Sterling? And what did he have to hide?*

Maya turns toward Arianna's old room at the end of the long hall. "Colin," she calls softly, so as not to disturb the baby in his arms. "I forgot my notes from Bob downstairs, I'll be right there."

Without turning he waves a hand, calls back, "Take your time."

As Maya moves away from her and Colin's room, toward the portrait of Arianna and the room she knows is waiting beyond, the floorboards sink and wail, adjusting to her movements as though issuing a warning ahead. The way animals alert each other, cawing to those deeper in the woods: *Something's here that does not belong, it is coming your way.* She hears a slow thumping ahead, long and rhythmic. *You're alone up here, Maya.*

She turns the corner, reaching the hall that runs along the north side of the house, toward the east wing where the other bedrooms are located. She knows the Sterlings are all downstairs, sipping gin and making jokes at her expense. Harry's office must be nearby. Barrow said so this morning—that the office and Arianna's room were close. Maya slows her pace, listening.

A bang cuts through the silence. Maya seizes up, as if grabbed by the throat. *Just the house settling,* she tells herself, and quickly identifies the source—an old door, warped and popping in its frame. Maybe they've heated this hallway for the first time in a while, since Maya and Colin are sleeping not far from here, and the changes in temperature are making the wood expand.

Yet when that door bangs open, strikes the wall again, she almost screams, turns back.

But no. She needs to toughen up. She certainly can't let a fucking *door* scare her. A voice—her intuition, the guiding spirits of the house?—tell her that this is it; she's found the entrance to what she's been looking for.

As she pauses on the threshold, she glimpses a magnificent study. Book-lined, the atmosphere stale, even though a window is cracked open—that must be what created the air current, made the door to the hall open and swing wildly.

When she goes to close the window, she sees a long drop down to the backside of the house. There is, of course, no one out there, lurking in the darkness below. Why would there be? Sterlings aren't climbing in and out of their windows, scaling the ancient walls...

And yet it seems odd for a window to have been left open in the dead of winter.

She moves around the room, skirting the massive oak desk. Surely this is Harry's—the monumental furniture of a great man's study. The bookshelves are built-in, gray with dust. Her fingers glide over the marble desktop and old fountain pens. The look is masculine, that very 1980s master-of-the-universe aesthetic. It's the kind of space a young Tom Cruise character might ascend through the ranks to occupy, then lean back in the boss's chair, arms folded behind his head as he roguishly flings his feet upon the desk.

But this isn't a movie—this is Maya's life, the one where she's become an object of suspicion to her powerful in-laws, where she was unwittingly present for the last hours of a murder victim's life.

A tremble moves through her shoulders as she considers it, that this room can only be the private lair of that murder victim's father, Harry Sterling. He's out in the world right now—away in some bolt-hole, far from the intrusions of the authorities or the press. Yet everything in this room suggests a man who pulls the strings, or at least wants people to believe he does.

There's a map of the world, framed behind the desk. A dozen or so Montblancs, jammed in an old coffee cup initialed *HS* in silver scrawl. A pile of newspapers, off to the side of the desk— the Sterling papers and the rival publications, such as they were in the early 1980s. The dates stamped on those yellowed pages are twenty years old. A big black Dictaphone, placed at the center of the desk, with its little microphone on a cord laid beside the hulky black box, as though awaiting its next missive.

And why isn't he here, the elusive Harry Sterling? Is he hiding from them, the family, or are they hiding something from him?

Here in his study, she has this feeling of what it's like to be in his company, and she doesn't like it. He's left a ruthless energy. Yet she can't help but run her hands over the desk, jerking open its drawers. A mess of old black cords—hopelessly tangled; a pile of mimeographs, yellowing paper with bleeding lavender lines. On the mantel, there are old-fashioned books, leather bound and crumbling. Under the carpet, it's all dust. Motes rise from the floor, making Maya cough.

That's when she notices it. The half-sized door, maybe four feet high. It's plain wood, tucked away in the bookshelves, easy to miss. Maya crawls over, pushes it open. Particles rise and she coughs again, peering inside. A bare bulb, a pull chain. Maya pulls, illuminating a child's nook complete with piles of velvet, tasseled pillows, illustrated storybooks, a few dolls, handmade stars covered in glue and glitter hanging from the ceiling. Along the walls are stacks of ochre-colored shoeboxes. It's kind of sweet, almost a relief.

Maya opens one of the boxes and sees a stack of crayon drawings on faded printer paper and old Sterling stationery. There's one of two little girls holding hands, one green-eyed, one brown. One of a yew tree, with tigers in the branches. And a drawing of a tall woman in a pantsuit, her face exuberantly x'd out by an angry hand with a black crayon. Helen, obviously. Maya almost smiles, puts that box back.

The next is packed with cassette tapes. Harry's Dictaphone musings? On whatever would've been a big business coup in 1987? Maya checks a few more of the boxes—more tapes, some unspooling, some in plastic cases, cryptically labeled with initials and inconclusive numbers that might indicate dates or might be some long-forgotten secret code.

Or might indicate nothing—a shorthand, the meaning of which is lost to time.

Maya sits for a moment, legs pulled against her chest, suddenly feeling very small in Arianna's domain. What did Arianna hear when she hid out in this cubbyhole? What conversations of her father's—about the business, about her own fragmented mind? After a moment, it occurs to Maya that even if she could somehow hear the spirit of Arianna, calling to her from the interior walls of the old house, it still wouldn't do her any good, either. Arianna obviously didn't know how to make it through.

This connection to Arianna, this crazy notion that Maya's going to find something in some secret corner of the house that's going to tell Maya what Arianna wanted with her, why she tracked her down, why she named her—it's reminding Maya of the years she was at her worst, desperate, driven by fury and illogic, that time when they locked her up.

Maybe Maya just needs a minute to hide out, as Arianna surely did. Maya holds herself in a tight ball and tries to think of nothing.

She's not sure how long she stays like that. The whole history of her life, its echoes with that of the tragic heiress, the mercurial father, the loneliness, the being locked up—those memories come pounding over her like wave after wave of a turbulent sea. After a while, she knows it's been too long; she should get back. On hands and knees, she maneuvers toward the little door, toward the main space of the office.

Under her knee, she feels it—a shifting of the board. She sits back, runs her finger over the rough floor. There's a piece that's been cut out, is unattached to the rest of the flooring. She lifts it, not sure what she'll find, and sees a small collection, different than the childish objects elsewhere. Here is a man's watch, a wallet. Antique brass knuckles. An old blade, sharp, with a pewter handle, wrapped in a scrap of leather. All nestled among white papers, elaborately folded. The watch is maybe the most 1980s object Maya has seen outside of Long Island. In fact, her dad had one, of which he was very proud. It's a Seiko, like the one Ripley wore in *Aliens*.

She turns the watch over in her hand and finds a name etched on the inside of the band. *Michael Blackburne*.

Maya reads the engraving on the brass knuckles—*MB*.

The friend of Harry's, the one who died in the Seychelles fire.

What kind of child magpie would collect a dead man's things, hide them under a floorboard? Did Arianna sit here, years ago, as Maya sits now, feeling apart from the other Sterlings, wishing she were somewhere else? Or did she still have a chance—the little girl who hoarded these objects? Was it only later that it all went wrong?

It occurs to Maya that someone is calling her name. Maybe they have been for a while. Shouting, drawing out the first syllable: "Maya? Maaaaaa-yah?"

The sound is ghostly, but that's just the effect of the tunnel-like halls. Maya replaces the watch, the brass knuckles, the piece of floorboard. Steps back into the study, then into the hall.

"Yes?" she shouts.

Maya turns and sees Eva, wearing a structured charcoal

dress, her hair swept into a French twist, her lips pickled with irritation. "What are you doing here?"

"Looking for you," she says accusatorily. "Everyone's been looking. Colin called down to Barrow, wondering if anyone had seen you, and now it's a search party."

"Oh."

"What are you doing here?"

"I—" Maya shrugs hopelessly, shoving away the involuntary flash of fear—the years she and Marcus worried Eva might walk in on them and ask just that question. "Got lost."

"In *here*? Bad idea. If Harry hears you're snooping in his things, he'll kill you."

"But Harry isn't—"

"Present? Are you a little dim? Just because he isn't here doesn't mean he isn't entirely aware exactly what's happening in his home. Everyone keeps tabs here. Tips the servants, listens from behind the drapes. Get a little leverage on a Sterling and you might just win some negotiation down the line." She pauses, eyes flashing, smile feline. "For instance, now I know that you told your husband you went to fetch some notes, but then I find you here. Perhaps that little deception will prove useful when I need it. Perhaps it's not the first lie I've caught you in. Get it?"

Maya tries to swallow the fear that Eva *does* have more on her. That she knows about the affair. The truth is, Maya used to think very little of Eva, dismiss her, even. The cold wife of the man she needed so bad, who needed her. But standing face-to-face, Maya feels the wrong she's done. She can't help but think that Eva, of all the players, might have the most reason to ruin her. Does Eva long for her husband to notice her, love her, the man who only yesterday kissed Maya in the greenhouse?

Eva turns, dismissing the conversation with a swish of her skirt. "They'll be paranoid you've run out on us if you disappear like that again. So, be on time for dinner, why don't you?" Eva strides off, caroling, "You're welcome for the tip, Maya Miller."

20

After dinner, Julian proposes games in the Red Gallery, and Maya reluctantly follows the others through the corridors. The family, having exhausted each other wrangling over the family business, apparently must now seek out new modes of competition. Marcus and Colin are soon circling the snooker table, Eva and Helen become involved in a game of cribbage at the little table by the fireplace. Gigi turns enthusiastically to the bar cart—she's lapping everyone else in that category, at the very least. Julian smiles broadly, gestures toward a small tabletop inlaid with a chessboard, and Maya decides she could do worse than follow his lead.

Julian assumes the seat on the white side of the board and begins to methodically polish a set of carved stone chess pieces. He looks pleased with himself; he's apparently luxuriating in the sumptuous atmosphere around him. As Maya sits opposite, she feels the late Richard Sterling frowning down at her.

The day was long, and Maya wishes she could retreat to her room. Through dinner, she couldn't help but marvel to herself that this is only her third night in Sterling Park. In so many ways it seems she's been trapped here forever. New York, her old life, her freedom, that's all very far away. What remains is this grand house, this smothering family. Taking a sip of vodka, she lets her eyes slide back to Helen's husband.

"Have you played before?" he asks.

"A little."

Julian hums in response, ducking his chin, and Maya feels eyes from over her shoulder. Marcus, staring at her as he leans across the green felt of the table to make his shot.

"Everyone is fascinated by you, my dear," Julian observes. He begins placing the pieces for a game as Maya flushes, attempting an airy ambivalence.

"And does that include you?"

"Well, *yes*," Julian replies drolly. "I am a man."

Maya laughs, spins her queen idly in place.

Julian removes the queen from Maya's palm, places it back on its starting square. "But Arianna—what made *her* so interested in you, that's the billion-dollar question."

"I'd love to know, to be honest. What do you think?"

"It's a true riddle. For all of us, I suspect." There's a merriness in Julian's eyes now. Maya has the sense that Julian likes her, that her coup amuses him. Maybe he shares his son's view—he'd be disappointed if Maya just went along with the Sterling mandate. "What did she say to you when you met? Any *clues*?"

"Honestly…" Maya's glances around the room, stalling. She likes him, thinks he could help her, but what Eva said earlier, about everyone snooping for a leg up, has put her in a distrusting mood. And the way Jessie—Arianna—ranted about the Sterlings being dangerous... Sterlings *like to watch things burn*. Maya isn't sure if that's something she should share, even with Julian. Overhead, the fearsome Richard Sterling glares down from his portrait. Watching. Maya thinks about the history of this portrait, which Julian had mentioned in passing, and of the relics of Mikey Blackburne she found under a floorboard upstairs, and thinks maybe she should stay quiet for now. Especially with a gift from the Blackburne patriarch hovering over her. Did he know his only son went out like a match on Sterling land?

"It was more like she was checking me out," Maya demurs. "She told me she was curious about me, that she wanted to 'have a look.' But she didn't say *why*."

"Between you and me, I'd be mum about the details of that meeting as much as possible. With the authorities, I mean. Helen really likes the family's business kept quiet." Julian emits a thoughtful hum, frowns at the chessboard. "Though you can confide in me, of course. I understand the Sterlings, the way they like things done. And I think I understand you, the way you operate, as well." He grins, and Maya feels that he really might. "Ready?" he says.

Maya nods, smiles. Julian advances an ivory pawn two squares, and Maya mirrors his move with seeming thoughtlessness, so that her own pawn faces his down. Perhaps Julian does understand her, but he can't possibly know that her father taught her strategy for every game a bookie would take money on. When she was little, she and her dad played a lot. But she figures Julian will probably share more, be friendlier, if she lets him win.

Of course, trying to win is an old habit, hard to break.

As Julian considers his next move, Maya's eyes slide again toward the portrait. Maya is thinking of the watch she found in Harry's office, the name etched on its band. "Julian, you said the Sterlings and the Blackburnes were very entwined, didn't you?" she asks offhandedly.

Julian makes a fluid, evasive gesture of the hand.

"Did you know him well?"

"Jago? No. Before my time, really."

Maya pretends to be absorbed in the board, considering her next move. "And the son? The one who died…"

Julian shifts in his seat, eyes rising to meet hers. Maya senses that he's holding something back. That he's strategizing. She wonders if he knows less about the Sterlings and their secrets that he claims, if it's all bluster. "Mikey was Harry's friend," Julian says casually. "Not mine."

"Come on, have pity on a fellow 'outlaw,'" Maya presses. "I'm still pretty hopeless when it comes to the family lore. But you—you're an expert!" Lest this flattery be insufficient, Maya moves a knight farther into Julian's territory. "I went to the archives, like you suggested. I noticed a blade that Mikey gifted to Harry… You must have seen it?"

"Oh yes, that. The story goes that Harry had gotten Mikey out of some jam or other, and Mikey gave it to him as thanks. It was a little joke, that he'd want to grow up and be like Harry. But

I think another part of him meant it—he was jealous of Harry, that was the ugly truth of their friendship." Julian captures her sacrificial knight, settles back into his chair. "Jealousy is a horrible emotion, don't you think? Mikey and Harry, they were born the same year. Roommates at Gordonstoun. That's a boarding school," Julian adds, when Maya gives him a blank face. "Anyway, Harry and Mikey had parallel lives—youngest sons of powerful fathers. But Harry was *his* father's favorite. Was, you might say, anointed. Even better than being a firstborn, in some ways. With Mikey it was the opposite—he was always trying to win his father's approval, without success, I must say. It's said they got into some trouble at boarding school, but it was always Mikey who took the fall, one way or other. Harry had charisma, you see." Julian shrugs and castles. "He could have sold a snake a baseball bat."

Maya sacrifices a pawn, asks: "And then he never got over his friend dying?"

Harry laughs mirthlessly. "You could say that."

"Was it horrible?"

"The attack was brutal, yes. Housefire, total destruction, had to identify their bodies with dental records…"

"*Their* bodies?"

Julian appears to be very absorbed in figuring out his next play. Despite Maya's best efforts, he's gotten himself in a bad situation. She can feel his irritation as he stamps another move on the board and continues a distracted recitation of the family lore. "Yes, yes, as I told you yesterday. Mikey had a daughter—a little girl, similar in age to Arianna. And like Arianna, Jessica's mother also died shortly after childbirth. You see what I mean about parallel lives? It's like that Blake poem, the one the Sterlings are so fond of—a 'fearful symmetry.' That was part of what set Harry off down a bad path. Either he thought it was his fault about Mikey or that the attack was meant for him. I mean, he said both, at different times."

"And Arianna? Did *she* think the attack was meant for her?"

Julian jerks a shoulder toward his ear. "I really couldn't say."

"But you knew her. Didn't you? And Helen of course, they were close."

Julian looks pained. "Maybe Arianna was destroyed by guilt. Hard to know with that girl. Mad, bad, dangerous creature. She was unhinged, really she was. Reckless."

"I wonder why they even told her about the tragedy? She was very young, they could've just kept it from her..."

"Kept it from her? She was there." Maya looks Julian in the face as her stomach sinks. After all the horrible ways Arianna has been described to her, why leave this piece out? It seems such a crucial piece of the tragic saga.

"She was *there*?"

"Oh, well, yes—she was there with Harry. It was one of their favorite places. The Sterling Compound at La Digue. Helen used to go there all the time too—she loved it. It was her place to get a break from it all. They rebuilt the villa after the fire, but she won't go back now."

"So, Harry and Arianna were there when the fire began? How

did they escape and not...?" Maya is thinking of that engraved watch hidden in the child's nook. How did Arianna come by it? Surely from her father, but how did *he* get it? And why keep it hidden? Unless he was too pained by the memory of it, the sight? Something about the way it was squirreled away under those dusty floorboards reminds Maya of how she swiped items from fancy homes as a child. Some she gave to her father; some she kept. The way Arianna kept the watch, it seemed almost like a trophy, the kind of souvenir a soldier might snatch off a confirmed kill.

Sterlings like to watch things burn, but only if they're the ones to light the match, Arianna had said when she was posing as a journalist.

Was she implying that her father set that fire?

"I mean," Maya says to Julian, moving her queen's side castle up a square. "Harry was at the scene of the crime but came out unscathed; isn't that *odd*?"

"I see what you're getting at, Maya."

Maya must be looking a little wild-eyed, because Julian finds it necessary to give her hand a double pat. But her palms are sweating and her brain is buzzing, reconfiguring the puzzle pieces. She has that ecstatic, half-mad feeling as though she's on the verge of finally being able to explain the whole history of everything.

While he considers his words, Julian takes one of her obsidian pawns, replacing it on the chessboard square with his own ivory one. "You think maybe he killed Mikey and that means we should look into the possibility he was the one who killed Arianna?"

In fact, that is *exactly* what Maya was starting to think, but she doesn't betray it, and he goes right on talking.

"You're thinking—why is Harry exempt from this family lockdown; what sort of rogue is he? But you have to understand, his whole life was arranged to protect Arianna. And Mikey was his *friend*. No, in this case I think the simplest explanation is the one that makes the most sense. Have you heard of Occam's razor?"

Maya suppresses the instinct to roll her eyes. "Yes."

"Well. The likeliest thing is that this was an old house in a developing country with lax building codes. Harry had to go back and forth to the main island of Seychelles frequently on Sterling business; Arianna was his only child; she had already lost her mother—so she came with him always. Mikey was a drunk—if a fire spread, he was not the most reliable man to put it out. And, that's it, a tragedy."

"But—" Maya exhales sharply, sits back in her chair. She still doesn't get why Harry doesn't have to be here too. Why he isn't being questioned and interviewed by the investigators and family alike. What if he found out about Arianna's new will, that she was leaving everything to an outsider, and wanted to force her into changing her mind? What if that bullying escalated into another tragic accident?

In her mind's eye, she sees Arianna in the Iguana Bar in Mexico. A woman on the run. Afraid. A woman with an hour or so to live. "Do you think Harry knew she changed her will?"

Maybe Julian feels Maya's horrible foreboding, the ickiness of death, so inexplicable and permanent, because he can't look at her suddenly. "Excuse me." He coughs, shakes it off. "Who knows, with him! But the night is young, and so are we—he may show his unwanted face yet, and then you can ask him yourself. But I don't think he'd hurt his daughter. No, no, that would ruin everything. After all, he kept her here in this fortress for years precisely because he wanted to *protect* her. Keep her safe."

An old sadness wells in Maya—that unrealized fantasy of a father who keeps his daughter safe—and she can't help but feel that Arianna might have shared and been let down by the same dream.

The elegance of the gallery, the surrounding rooms, the colossal edifice that holds them all together, it's all a front. Maya sees that suddenly. The museum-quality furniture, the generous velvet seating, it's just a mask for the driving acquisitive mania of the Sterling family. Across the room, Maya's in-laws have become absorbed in their competitive pursuits. Helen is losing—Maya can see that her little silver pegs trail Eva's gold ones on the cribbage board—and her mouth is tight with agitated concentration. ("Card playing is one of her few gifts," Helen has apparently said of Eva—Colin repeated that line to Maya once after he'd had a few drinks, much to Maya's secret delight.) Colin must have beat Marcus at snooker, because he's playing Gigi now, while Marcus stands aside, obviously jonesing to get back into the game. Maya looks at them, amazed, and thinks, *This isn't a family; it's a pack of adversaries.* "You think she felt safe? Here, I mean."

"Of course, nothing can be completely secure," Julian continues, oblivious to Maya's ruminations. "There are the old tunnels for getting to the different outbuildings in bad weather, for instance—I've heard the phrase *Swiss cheese* used to describe them."

In a hollow voice, Maya replies, "Yes, I used those tunnels to get back from the hammam."

"Ah, yes, well. They were extended during wartime; one or two may go as far as the nearest farm. I know back then the staff, and Harry himself, made an effort to ensure they were properly fortified. But Arianna was tricky. She must've discovered the tunnels as a teenager, or maybe before. And if she could get out..."

Wait, what are they talking about? Maya had drifted into her own past and lost the thread of the conversation. "So—this place *wasn't* safe for Arianna?"

Julian speaks in a blustery rush. "The security here is world-class. She was safe *here*. She just wasn't safe from herself, the chaos she could cause out *there*. That's why they put her in Portas. For her own good. If she'd just stayed there—well, anyway, I'm rambling on now, aren't I?"

The ambient sounds of the gallery recede. There's a fierce ringing in Maya's ears. "Portas? Do you mean...Portas Brancas?"

Julian eyes her; she can see him trying to pull himself back from his emotional ramble. "Excuse me," Julian replies, pushing away from the board. "I've upset myself."

He stands and walks across the room, leaving Maya alone before the chessboard, unsure if Julian knew his defense was weak, that she was only two moves from checkmate. Probably he did not—he's a sloppy player, impulsive. Even at a distance, he appears consumed with emotion. That's a little stroke of luck. Because Maya is too thrown by this revelation to mask the shock on her face.

Arianna Sterling, before she died, was in the Portas Brancas facility.

The same place Maya—after Marcus, when she at her very worst—was locked up.

21

Here's something to remember. I mean, here's a *super* hot tip—for
the future me who's forgotten everything again, or the unknown
captive who finds these pages and is strategizing how to survive
here in Portas Brancas:

> *Dear [future me/stranger captive]—I have no words
> of hope for you;*
>   *the world is devoid of goodness or sense. I can only
> say this—*
>   *avoid if you can stabbing out a cigarette in the fat
> arm of a nurse.*
>   *Love, [past me/long-gone compatriot]*

Tempting as it may be—to sear their skin-deep happy jolly
act and get right to the blackened core of their intentions—the
result will be *(listen to this!!!)* that your <u>cigarettes</u> are confis-
cated, and your window privileges are rescinded, and if you are
unremorseful—which, unfortunately, <u>yup yup</u>, *guilty*—you will

be put in a room in the basement with the absolutely worst shade of pink walls, padded, naturally, and a mattress on the floor—a foam one, no springs for *you*, you naughty melancholic—and you will be taken out for twice-daily zap zap zaps, and force-fed, under observation, blended, healthful meals, full of pulp and seeds and the like—

until you forget what a ravaged nasty glorious beasty you have lately become, and they let you out, back to your room with the highly lauded low-to-the-ground window, and what will you need? What will you need, my dear? A motherfucking cancer stick, *obviously*, but you *shall not have one*—

even as the worst memories and most vivid delusions surge over you like tsunamis.

But none of those compare to the *real* thing that happened today in group. I'm still shaking over the whole thing, still trying to nail down what was real.

So picture it—there I am in the big bland room sitting on the plastic armchair with the blankie on it, listening to these self-pitying, monosyllabic girls I've been forced to live with— listening to them hollowly reciting the various stock positivity mantras that they force upon us here—saying that they're grateful for *air* and *water* and the most pathetic things—

And then it's my turn, and I'm so out of sorts from my time in solitary, from my nicotine deprivation and then my nicotine fix—and the hallucinations that feel as real as anything here, anything in Portas Brancas—and I just start talking—

saying I don't know what—

239

I only know from the face of the therapist that it's *bad* what I'm saying, that I'm saying entirely too much, that I'm being too honest.

Saying (I think): I hate hate *hate* my family; they're evil; they're criminals; they really—

And then the therapist interrupts, smiling idiotically, and says, "Thank you, Ari, that's your time…"

And then we go around the circle a bit.

And then I see her, HER! She's sitting in one of the plastic chairs, even more gorgeous in person. The sleek hair and pillow lips and this very *sharp* look in the eyes. The baby blue matching sweatsuit, the lashes that are so long they look false but must be real—because none of us are allowed makeup here, much less false eyelash glue.

Of course, I think I'm hallucinating, even when it's her turn and she speaks.

When she gestures in my direction and says, "I agree with that one. This is bullshit. You don't want us to be better, you just have an insurance scam going, and the insurance companies have a scam with the government. The powerful men who run everything and pull the strings and think women are disposable. *I'm* not crazy; *she's* not crazy—none of us is crazy. It's the *system* that's crazy—"

The therapist is frowning vigorously. "Maya—"

"Do you know what Portas Brancas means?" Maya, the newcomer, has walked off my television screen and into the asylum; she has made her big eyes extra wide as she scans the circle. "I mean it's like they're *telling* us, Here you are, girls, at the Pearly Gates. Last port of call. Life is over for you. Move along, now, move along—"

"Thank you for that, Maya," says the therapist with finality. "But we're not here to editorialize. We're here to feel. How do you *feel*?"

Maya Miller, the girl from *The Springs*, my immaculate delusion, folds her arms over her world-class tits and slouches into the chair. She raises an eyebrow in my direction. "I *feel*," she says, "like shit."

The therapist sounds really impatient now. "Care to elaborate?"

"Sure. I worked my ass off, okay? I made a lot of money. I thought, *What is money for, if not to help your family*, you know? I gave my dad an allowance; I gave him the keys to the kingdom. And then I ended up in jail, and I call him—which let me tell you, I have received plenty of those calls from him. But the one time I call him for help, he says, *Oh sorry, I spent all the money you gave me, can't bail you out honey, wish I could*. And you know what? That's it. That's the last time. I'm cutting him off. I'm calling my lawyer and telling him—take my dad off my payroll, take him out of my will, he doesn't get another dime."

At this point it still felt like I was watching some bonus episode of the show—I suppose I've watched a lot of *The Springs*; it's as embedded in my brain folds as the rest of my little trage-dies. This was a monologue I could have written for her myself.

Later, when I was passing through the common room on

the way to lunch, I heard her talking loudly on the pay phone—talking with her press agent, sounded like, of all things—in a very even manner, none of that frantic energy from before, just calm determination. And even *then* I still thought Maya Miller here in the facility was my mind playing tricks. It was when the nurse—Sarah-Jane, the one who is always smiling, the one with the fresh cigarette burn—crossed my path, and said with a sweet face and venomous tone, "Looks like your idol came for a visit!" that I believed she was real.

Sarah-Jane is real, unfortunately.

And if she said—pretending it was a good thing, but really just to make fun of me—that Maya Miller was here, in the facility, then it must be true. Objectively, observably, in the world outside my head—whatever. In *reality*.

I turned away from Sarah-Jane and walked toward Maya on the pay phone.

I smiled at her, waved my hand.

She glanced at me—a flinch of irritation, then recognition. She covered the mouthpiece of the phone with her palm. "Hey. I really appreciate what you said earlier. You're the only real one here."

I was kind of struck dumb—but I think I nodded at her that I agreed.

"Listen, I gotta finish this up before I run out of quarters—see you later?"

I hope I smiled, or in some other way conveyed that I hoped I did see her later.

As I was walking away, I heard her very nearly shouting into the receiver:

"The *New York Star* says what? Fuck the Sterlings—fucking *fuck them*, I don't care——if they think I'm going to just disappear, they have no clue who I am."

PART IV

22

Two years ago, New York. Everyone in the city was still fucked up over the towers falling, their country careening toward war. Maya went on one of the morning shows, fresh from a night of partying. She'd thrown on a cropped motorcycle jacket over the leather McQueen dress she'd worn to Marquee the night before, added a little charcoal to yesterday's smokey eye, and told the on-set makeup girl that this look was her "brand." After all, her latest "edgy" makeup collection had just launched and sold out instantly.

But she couldn't fool the morning show host, who actually asked her—on live television—if she was doing all right, face contorted with pity. Maya couldn't stand that.

"Yeah," Maya had said. "I'm great. Actually? I'm in love."

The audience gasped, leaned forward.

The host struck a canny just-us-girls tone. "Who's the lucky guy?"

"We-ell, he's tall, handsome, and his name is..." Maya cupped her hand over the host's ear and whispered, "*None of your fucking business.*"

The host was a pro. She dropped her bottom lip like she'd just heard the most delicious secret.

But as far as Marcus knew—when he watched the tape later that day in SterlingCo's New York office—what she told the host was the name Marcus Sterling.

In his suite at The Mercer, he berated her. "How stupid could you possibly be?" he asked over and over. Then they had make-up sex. Made out in the elevator. The paparazzi caught them in the alleyway. She thought: *Marcus gets me; he likes that I know how to provoke.*

The next day he said, "I have to go to Miami." She thought: *Not without me you're not.*

She found him, in his favorite hotel in South Beach. The concierge knew her and sent her up. "What are you doing here?" he said. "You can't be here."

Later, she wondered if he had any business in Miami at all, or if that wasn't part of his plan to get rid of her. If Portas Brancas wasn't his endgame the entire time. He kept worrying that his wife knew about them—maybe he was trying to fix things, for Eva. After he called Maya an idiot, a trainwreck, a liability, she ran away, into a dark leafy street she didn't recognize. She didn't know Miami, had not a single friend in that town. When she looked at her feet, she realized she didn't even have shoes. But there was no way she was going back and asking that monster Marcus Sterling for footwear.

She waved down the first car she saw—two nice-seeming women, dressed for the club. Maya clambered into the back seat and off they went. She must have closed her eyes for a minute, and when she opened them, she saw the man in the front—a paparazzo she recognized; he'd stalked her in LA and New York—leaning over the front seat with his camera.

The next morning, that photo was on the cover of the *New York Star*, SterlingCo's daily tabloid. Maya's dress hiked up, her black lace underwear exposed, the red lipstick still smudged all over her mouth from when she and Marcus started making out, midfight.

Headline: *Maya-mi Vice.*

Everyone knew Marcus got the first proofs before it went to print every morning, and a courtesy call from the editor telling him what they were running on the front page. The only thing Maya was unsure of was whether Marcus planted the photographers and created the story to finally get rid of her, or if he merely approved it after the fact.

Even so, when she woke up—head pounding, desperate for water, afraid she'd throw up all over her room at the W—her biggest fear was that she'd really lost Marcus this time.

She did the sensible thing—went down to the pool and ordered a Bloody Mary. Some nice millionaires from Colombia began chatting her up, and they had a fabulous lunch at Café Versailles, and after that Maya's brain stopped recording. The next thing she remembered, she was dancing on the roof of some South Beach hotel, distressed that the view of the ocean was obscured by high plexiglass walls.

Those walls were *in her way*! They were fucking *killjoys*!

She became fixated on the idea of seeing how far she could swim into the Atlantic.

She probably should have considered that someone slipped her a mickey. She was fucked up plenty in those days, but she'd never blacked out.

How she got to the beach is lost to time. The next thing Maya knew was the policeman, asking for her name. At the police station, she asked for her phone call, and learned, not for the first time, who her father really was. Eventually someone came and told her don't worry—SterlingCo's lawyer had taken care of her paperwork. The SterlingCo lawyer was professional, understanding, sympathetic. He told her that there would be no record of any of this. Then he put her on the private jet, which she assumed was charted back to New York. But it wasn't. When they landed in Bermuda, she figured Marcus was planning to make it up to her. A few days on a private beach. She didn't totally get it until she was in the lobby of Portas Brancas, and then she was so furious—screaming and fighting—that she had to spend another five hours in the glass-walled observation tank, begging her captors to believe that she was sane.

If Marcus felt bad about her stay in the psych ward, she never knew. She didn't see or hear from him again until she arrived at Sterling Park in the wake of Arianna's death, and he told her that it had all been a lucky PR break for her.

That's why she married Colin. Because he would never let her be locked up like that; he'd never think being humiliated and exposed was *lucky*. Because Colin likes to save.

Maya must have overlapped with Arianna at the facility. Was it a coincidence, or is it the Sterlings' preferred facility for getting rid of their half-mad girls?

Perhaps it's like Julian said—the simplest explanation is usually correct.

———

Maya rises slowly from her seat at the chessboard. Across the gallery, the Sterlings are still embroiled in their games. Between her ears is a deafening roar. But on the outside, she must still appear cool, quiet. The others don't seem to have noticed the change in Maya.

Colin stands up from taking his shot, glances at his wife making for the door.

Bathroom, she mouths, and he nods in understanding.

She's amazed to see her feet moving so steadily as she leaves the room. Her mind howls over what Julian said. Both she and Arianna were at Portas Brancas.

Has she been a puppet all along, her strings yanked by an invisible hand?

The thing that's really getting to her is that all this time she's been hearing about how unstable Arianna was—and believing that version of the story. But somehow, learning that Arianna was, in fact, holed up in a mental facility for years before she died has made Maya begin to question whether that's a fair depiction of Arianna. Maya was sent to Portas not because she was insane, except maybe in the most temporary, heartbroken way, but because the Sterlings wanted to make their little problem go away—wanted to make sure she didn't leak the affair. What if that's true for Arianna too? What if she was sent away so the Sterlings could bury a secret she threatened to reveal?

What did you know, Arianna? What secrets got you sent away?

In the nursery suite, Maya grabs her RAZR, flings open the large window onto the courtyard. There isn't much signal out here, but the Sterlings have some sort of booster that works at the right hour, in the right position, so long as there aren't too many stone bricks in the way. Or so Maya discovered, trying to get Bob Feld on the phone for a few moments of private conversation earlier that afternoon.

She clicks through her phone, trying to remember the name of that nurse. She was sweet—almost *too* sweet—but she identified herself as a fan, and at the time Maya was committed to Portas Brancas, she didn't think she was in a position to lose any fans.

So, they exchanged numbers in parting. The nurse—Sandra? No, Sally. No, Sarah-Jane!—seemed to think that she and Maya had something in common. And Maya had cultivated that, at least a little, playing into her father's theory. Sarah-Jane was definitely one of those generous-to-a-fault types. But what with her dramatic tutting at Maya's predicament, the way she allowed Maya extra phone privileges over those few days, Maya knew that inside she possessed angel of vengeance potential too.

As the phone rings, Maya tries to think through all the

excuses for why she hasn't been in touch till now, or even some natural way to open the conversation. The nurse was genuinely kind to her in the facility, helped her secure special privileges. She was celebrity crazy, but she was also just genuinely nice. Maya thought so, anyway. And as soon as Maya was free, she ignored her.

On the fourth ring, Maya's insides sink. Why would Sarah-Jane pick up the phone?

But then she does, opening with a giddy and confused, "Maya?"

"Hey, girl!" Maya replies, trying to sound natural, like they're old friends playing phone tag.

"Wow, I thought I was hallucinating there for a minute!"

"That's not you, hun; that's the patients," Maya says, and then winces, worrying she's said something offensive.

But Sarah-Jane chuckles gamely. "It's good to hear from you, anyway. I just wasn't..."

"Expecting it? Well, yeah, I should have called earlier. I... You were kind to me at a really dark moment, and I wanted to tell you how much that meant to me. I mean, who knows, it could have gone another way for me. But it turned out okay! I just got married and—"

"Maya, I know." She snorts. "Everyone knows you're a Sterling now."

"Right, well—" Suddenly, Maya feels foolish. Why would Sarah-Jane be anything but wary of Maya, checking in after all this time?

But apparently Maya is misinterpreting Sarah-Jane's interruption. Maybe she's just been trying to contain herself, because the next thing she says is, "I mean really, good for you! When I saw the announcement in *People*, I was so happy for you. And girl, your hubby is cute!"

"I know, *right?*" Maya replies, trying to match the enthusiasm. She squeezes her eyes shut and hopes she's remembering right when she says, "How's that guy...the one who managed the restaurant?"

"I did just what you said—always waited at least twenty-four hours to call him back, always had somewhere else to be, and you know what? I'm engaged!"

"Oh my god!"

"Right?"

"Yeah. Wow. Congratulations—that's huge!" Maya takes a deep breath and tries to make a natural transition. "Sarah-Jane, listen, I've been meaning to ask you something... It's a bit awkward, and I don't want to put you in a difficult position, professionally..."

"Yeah?"

"I mean, it *would* obviously, but you're really the only person I can ask. Who I trust, anyway. You see, I've learned that my husband's cousin Arianna was at Portas at the same time as me..."

"You don't remember?" Sarah-Jane says carefully.

"Of course, of course I do." Maya bites her lip, tries to sound like they're just reminiscing. "I just didn't know who she was at that point, so I'm trying to put my memories of it together, make some sense of it, you know?"

"Well, it was so soon after you left that you and Colin got engaged, so it did seem like a really giant coincidence... I figured you were probably already dating him; it just wasn't public yet, so once I put it together I assumed it was as simple as the same people who helped her get treatment helped you."

"Oh? What made you think that?"

"Well, it was the same lawyer guy who came after you were discharged that showed up when Arianna went missing."

"Oh, yes, that'd be Rory." She wants Sarah-Jane to keep talking, like they're friends, simply reminiscing. But her mind has stuck on that last word—*missing*? So Arianna wasn't released from Portas Brancas prior to her death—she *escaped*? "Was he helpful with that? With Arianna...leaving."

"He was furious!"

"Well, that's not fair. Surely."

"No. I mean, we aren't a prison. But it is bad for business, patient going on the run—and now all our procedures are tightened. It's really made everything difficult. Maddening, really."

"That doesn't seem fair. I mean, why do you think she...left?"

Sarah-Jane sighs heavily, then continues in that regretful yet excited tone people use when they detail the sins of their workplace enemies. "It was all the new therapist's fault, Dr. Caro, though it turned out she wasn't a therapist at all. More of a phantom if she was anything, just disappeared into the mist on the same day Arianna went missing. I should have known there was something up with her. Not very friendly. *Too much* eye contact, you know? Dyed her hair too dark, sort of emo. Bad skin—all scarred and splotchy. I used to think to myself, *She should get herself some of Maya Miller's X Marks the Spot Concealer to cover that—*"

"Sarah-Jane?" Maya interrupts. "Do you think she...remembered me?"

"Oh, Dr. Caro was long after your time."

"I mean Arianna."

Sarah-Jane laughs. "If she remembered anyone, she remembered you. I mean, poor thing couldn't remember her name half the time, but she *loved* you, or anyway she watched your show all the time—*loved it* when you put those other girls in their place."

"This is embarrassing, but I was pretty fucked up when I got there. And then I was so angry... I don't know, it's all a little fuzzy. Did we...hang out a lot? Me and Arianna?"

"I mean, yes. Briefly. You were kind to her. She wasn't doing well when you were there. Some days she'd say I was Satan himself. She came when she was nineteen, a wreck of a thing, and I honestly thought she'd stay here forever..."

"Do you think she really was just delusional?" Maya knows she's pushing. A professional wouldn't divulge the circumstances of a patient's admission. But she's hoping Sarah-Jane's urge to connect with Maya will override her professionalism. Was Arianna just a fucked-up rich girl with a tragic past? Or was she someone who simply knew too much?

"Well," Sarah-Jane replies in a halting, haunted voice, "when she first came, they said it was on account of her drinking, but her hallucinations seemed like more than withdrawal to me, always.

256

It was spooky, really. She kept saying all these things about her family—about *your* family, I guess. Sorry I shouldn't—"

"That's all right." Maya tries to keep the desperation out of her voice. "Go on."

"You know," Sarah-Jane says in a tense whisper, "she'd say that they're all murderers, that kind of thing."

"Poor dear, she really was seeing things. That must be hard to watch. For you, I mean."

"Half the time she was screaming murder; half the time she was singing eighties rock songs at the top of her lungs. She used to—" Suddenly, Sarah-Jane's voice is very different: "You got it, Mom, we'll talk tomorrow!" A supervisor or somebody must be passing by her station. There's a pause, and for a moment all Maya can hear is a woman breathing far away. Then Sarah-Jane returns with a hushed, "Sorry, I have to go. But thanks so much for calling. I miss you, girl!"

"Wait, could you—"

"Bye, Mom, bye!" Sarah-Jane says in the cheery theatrical tone, and then the call ends.

Maya listens to the dead air. She's standing in the folds of the heavy velvet drapes, gazing at the façade of the south wing of Silver House, imagining the unhinged, tormented Arianna, heaping the Sterling fortune onto Maya's shoulders in an attempt to get free of its curse.

Because she suspected—and at least on this point, Maya admits, she was seeing clearly—that curse wasn't finished with her yet.

Did she see Maya as someone who would understand—see, somehow, a glimmer of herself in Maya?

Did Maya haunt Arianna's dreams long after she left the facility?

The strange thing is that Maya almost feels that way about Arianna—as if she's still alive in this house, trapped inside its walls.

23

ANOTHER DAY,
PORTAS BRANCAS—SURPRISE, SURPRISE

I'm sick with some heinous flu that's going around the ward. Instead of my usual schedule of therapeutic activities, I got to stay in bed and watched TV.

Well, you'll never guess.

The OMG! Channel has a new "news" program. And the news was all about the marriage of Maya Miller to—wait for it—*my cousin.*

At first, I have to say, I experienced this as more proof of the conspiracy against me and wasn't even really surprised. It's been, what? Six months since Maya was here? A year? I've got no way to measure these things, and it all felt like a fever dream in the first place. If my dream-memory can be trusted, she was only here a few days and then *poof*—she was out. And here she turns up on the tube, and I'm watching her kiss Colin, doing a fake shy smile and wave for the photographers.

Colin *is* nice, but he is such a Sterling true believer when it really comes down to it.

Here's what I figure: Colin started dating Maya—and then

the powers that be had to scramble to get her more presentable. Take care of her little drinking or shoplifting or bingeing-and-purging problem or whatever it was. Throw in a little brainwashing at the loony bin while you're at it. *Et voilà.*

The thing is though, I don't think they succeeded. In the brainwashing bit, I mean.

The OMG! Channel keeps playing a clip of Helen coming out of headquarters in London, the paps yelling questions at her about Maya. "Any words of wisdom for the newlyweds?" that sort of thing. Helen is wearing massive shades and a bitter twist of the lips. She says, "Won't last," as she strides toward her town car.

It's such a tiny moment, to anyone else. A slip.

But I know that Helen means it. She doesn't want this marriage. It's killing her that this walking tabloid cover is marrying into her formidable family.

Somehow, Maya got them.

So that got me laughing hysterically, laughing so hard it kind of hurt. And laughing made me remember Maya saying she was going to cut her dad out of her will, and I'm realizing that I have a will too, and a father to cut out, if I want.

I had to control my laughing at the pay phone, using the ten-minute allotment of call time I've earned by being a very good girl.

Roiling inside *moi*: the *blackest* humor.

If they kill me, I want them to have the rudest surprise. So: I dial up my lawyer, a junior solicitor in the firm of Posh Fuckers, Esq., that the family has used since the dawn of time.

"This is Edward Civil-Holmes," Edward says, very professional-like.

"This is Arianna Sterling," I reply, mimicking his tone.

"Oh—"

"Edward, I need to make a tiny tweak to my will. I'll be naming a new beneficiary." I try to sound firm. Confident. Like Maya did talking to her people.

"Arianna, I don't think—" He's going to say I don't have the authority to make such big changes while I'm in here. Because of course, he and all the Sterling puppets must know that the heiress was very naughty and has been sent away.

"Eddy," I cut him off. "It's just for a joke, all right? We can always change it back later."

"Respectfully, madame—"

"When you came to Sterling Park with that mountain of paperwork—do you remember?"

"Yes."

"Did we...?"

Long pause. "Yes."

I had a feeling. I remember him coming to set up my will when I turned eighteen. He was baby-faced and muscular. In those days, I fucked whatever I could get my legs around. I can't honestly remember most of the dicks I've caught. But opportune I caught his.

"Good. I'm glad to have made your intimate acquaintance, Eddy. But you know... That was a *bit* unprofessional of you, wasn't it?"

Yet a longer pause.

"Indeed. Don't worry, though, I'm not going to tell anyone. Here's the thing though; I need you to do me a favor..."

After that call, I slept like a baby. Dreamed of walking out of here. Invincible now.

Oh, they can still come and get me, I know.

They can even kill me if they want.

Good laugh that would be. I'll be rolling in my grave.

Ha ha ha!!

PORTAS BRANCAS

I can't stop laughing about it, but *they* seem to think it's a sign of my increasing madness.

They're saying I'm a hopeless case. The therapists are afraid to work with me. One that was assigned to me has supposedly been institutionalized herself. HA!

Now here's a new one. Dr. Caro. Surprisingly young to be a doctor, or anyway she has the *look* of youth. Dr. Caro has dyed her hair an ugly black. Maybe that's the only option with that bad skin of hers—it's a bit punk rock, that choice. Unusual in her profession. Respect.

Still, she started off with a very *suspicious* prompt.

"Tell me about Harry," she said.

"He was my best friend. I used to want to be just like him," I replied. "And now I'd sooner die."

"Why is that?"

I shrugged violently. "He's a capitalist pig."

"That's a very abstract thing to say about one's father. Anything else?"

"No."

"Tell me about your aunt. Tell me about Helen."

Me: "I'm very tired."

And, though I'd meant it to be hostile, to end the conversation (this insidious snooping on behalf of the Sterlings, surely they put her up to it!), I was, suddenly. Tired, I mean.

I thought this Dr. Caro would probe. But she didn't.

She tilted her head in sympathy and said, "I understand. Why don't you get some rest, and we can talk more tomorrow."

TOMORROW

Today, Dr. Caro started off with this:

"Tell me about Lyman, the first boyfriend."

And I was so happy to hear that name (it reminded me of being young and free, and what it was to be touched and to touch and have fun) that I just began babbling.

I told her about the time we rode through the Peak District on his motorbike. And the time we made love standing up in the croft at the edge of Sterling Park. And the time he took me to Manchester, to a disco, and how he got me a fake ID—not like the counterfeit one I'd bought at a dodgy tourist shop, but the license of a real girl.

He showed me how the license shimmered when you turned

it against the light, the little squiggly lines that appeared—that's how you could tell a real license. My tourist shop one didn't have those. He told me that a real girl, who looked passably like me, had procured this license from a real government agency.

I felt uneasy, suddenly.

You don't think I'm real? I asked.

What? he said. *Of course* you're real.

Do you think this other girl, the real one—is she dead now?

No, Lyman replied. Why would you think that? Don't be mental.

I said: *You really think I'm mental??!!*

And he smiled so kindly and took me in his arms and told me it was just a saying, that there was nothing wrong with me. That I was real. He was holding me so tight as he explained that the girl probably lost it—she probably had a new license by now—and I was glad my face was pressed against his jacket, because I was crying by then, it felt so nice to be told I wasn't crazy, that I was real, and there was nothing wrong with me...

Well, I felt very proud, recollecting all this. So many memories! They were just flowing.

And I smiled at Dr. Caro, thinking: *What's next?*

But she just said, "That's very good. That's enough for today. You get some rest, and we'll pick up tomorrow."

It's odd. Usually, I *hate* the doctors and can't wait to get away from them. But I was disappointed to be leaving so soon...

MAYBE TOMORROW, BUT PROBABLY NOT

They fucked with my meds again. They pumped me with I don't know what.

Woke up this morning in my own room, the one with the window (view of: tropical flora, monkeys, blah blah)—and I swear to everything holy, Harry was there, sitting in the plastic armchair, legs crossed, smoking a cigarette, saying: "Would you like one dear? Yes, I know you would. Well—*that* won't be possible, lovie. But if you can just see it our way—if you can just see that you're *mad*, darling—then maybe I can see my way to giving you a few ciggies."

So you see, something's not right with the meds, chaps. Something's not right at all.

Because after Harry, there was Gigi, saying come on, there's going to be a great DJ at Club Verve tonight; there will be cute dumb boys for the picking; *let's goooooo.*

And then it really was as though I'd gone through the tunnels with her, laughing our pretty heads off, screaming laughing so it echoed from Sterling Park to the villages—and that I was there in the club, feeling seasick with vodka and the smell of cheap boy cologne, thinking—

Seasick is the best thing I could possibly feel, isn't it? Isn't it?

So much better than foggy, or frightened, or stabbed with the fear of—

After Gigi, my next visitor was the boy with the rough, singsongy way of talking.

Lyman, for a while there I thought there was nothing better than going to town with *Lyman*. He was sitting in my chair, here in Portas Brancas, his face a bit sheepish. I said, "Where'd you go, Lyman? We spent every day together, and then you were just gone."

And he sighed very heavily and said, "Ah, pet, I thought you knew. Your dad paid me to go away."

And then there was the little girl—quite a relief, for it was very sad after the boyfriend phantom. She was standing over me, whispering: "It's me; Jessica, remember me? Don't forget where you've hidden your things—"

And thank god for that, because there in the little slot I made in the mattress, next to the business card from Winston's Taxi Service [service from the airport to Portas Brancas for Bds$30] were cigarettes! Three slightly stale, perfectly delicious Marlboro Lights.

Now—

Trying to write and smoke and think all at the same time and it's too much because this smoke? Smells like Gigi. I miss that raggedy cunt. I need her now—wish she'd jailbreak me out of here, like she used to back home.

I can't stop crying. I miss the world.

24

Although Maya promised herself she wouldn't drink tonight, she was overwhelmed with thoughts of Arianna, locked up in this place for most of her childhood, then trapped in the bright prison of Portas Brancas. Across the warm expanse of the parlor, Colin kept flashing his eyes at her to slow down, but she couldn't; it was all too much. When she wakes later that night, mouth well-brined from all the vodka, she remembers how he barely spoke to her when they retired to their own suite.

To hell with you, she thought—or said?

Then she just lay down on the bed and let Colin deal with Becca.

Now she sees that her clothes are strewn on the floor. She did manage to get a black silk slip on—one of those nice things he had sent over from Paris, she thinks with a punch of self-flagellating guilt.

It's cold in the nursery suite. The heavy drapes are open to the outside air. Maya shivers, pads across the room to close the window. As Maya pulls on the old leaded-glass pane, she notices a flash of color across the courtyard. A light goes on in another bedroom.

Gigi's.

Maya stands in the darkness, wrapped in the drape, staring at the old edifice of the east wing. The moonlight gives the windows a metallic sheen. There's an illuminated square on the second floor in which Gigi is now vamping in front of her bathroom mirror.

And the media says I'm *desperate for attention*, Maya thinks.

The rows of large windows over on that side are mostly dark. During the day, they're reflective, but at night it's a different story. In her lit square, on the far side of the courtyard, Gigi poses in the mirror, applies lipstick.

She can't be going out, Maya thinks. What time is it, anyway? Maya has no idea how long she slept, or how late game time went, either. But it is late. She's sure of that.

Maya's mind is prickling awake. Angry.

No one is supposed to leave the compound, but Gigi is.

What gives her the right to go where she wants, chase her fun? Because what else could she be doing, stuffed into that skintight dress, while the rest of them are monitored and locked in?

Maya's fury is wide-awake now. Maybe it's the wine sediment in her belly, her vodka-parched brain primed to catch fire. Maybe it's her phone call with Sarah-Jane, and the memories of being locked up in Portas Brancas. Locked up by the *Sterlings*. Maybe it's Eva's smug declaration of the family way—acquire your intimates' secrets for personal gain.

No one is supposed to leave the compound, but Gigi is.

Why? What's her secret?

Maya has to know.

———

Even after three days at Sterling Park, the halls of Silver House still get Maya mixed up. But now, with her mind focused on Gigi, it's easier to navigate. Right. Long hallway. Right. Left.

Is Gigi about to reveal some secret inner workings of the Sterling family to Maya? Or is the fact that Gigi's breaking protocol-whatever-the-fuck, sneaking off property in the middle of the night, the whole secret itself?

She feels this rising irritation with Gigi—the little sneak. Waiting until everyone's in bed, then scampering off. Maya's a little out of breath when she reaches the hall that leads to Gigi's room, and she only just catches a glimpse of her sister-in-law as she disappears through an inconspicuous door onto a servants' staircase.

There's no one to notice as Maya darts across the hall and follows Gigi down the stairs. She descends as silently as she can, listening to the old boards that sigh beneath Gigi's footfalls.

Soon Maya is following Gigi through a warren of servants' corridors that lead past kitchens and staff rooms. The temperature drops as they reach the lower levels of the house, passing pantries and cellars. Stores of onions, potatoes, apples, bags of flour, tea tins, crates of Sterling gin. The tunnels were built out for the staff during the war. They were built to survive a siege, to bring in supplies. Or, to escape the stronghold, if necessary.

What is this bitch up to? Maya is compelled by this question, tracking Gigi through the darkness, that earthy, moldy, underground air.

I've heard the phrase Swiss cheese used to describe them, Julian said.

Maya keeps her bearings by running her hands along the damp plastered walls, following the weak swish of a flashlight up ahead. She thinks about how easily one could get lost forever down here—especially a young girl. She can picture a young Arianna, slipping through inconspicuous doors, exploring these halls during her years of solitude. Maya has this uncomfortable feeling of the dead girl as a teenager—her phantom—nipping at her heels. If the house has Harry energy, the dim subterranean labyrinth seems to be as likely an expression of Arianna's mind as anything else.

Maya keeps having these visions of Ari, stuffed into a van unwillingly, driven to a private helipad, and flown off to the tropics with no idea where she'd be deposited. Shot up with sedatives and subdued, the way Maya was in her first few days coming to within the awful walls of Porta Brancas. She shivers, shakes off her own toxic associations.

She strides faster, away from that ghost and goblin thinking. Yet her mind turns back to the woman who forced her to meet in the Iguana Bar, her frightened expressions and strained voice.

She must have been aware, when they sat there—lightly

sparring over some paparazzi shots—that she and Maya had both been committed to the same psychiatric hospital, sent there with the help of the same Sterling lackies. Sarah-Jane said as much—Arianna saw Maya in the facility, knew who she was.

As they continue on their underground path, Maya loses sight of Gigi a few times—only catching a crunch of gravel up ahead, a glimpse of bouncing light.

At some point, Maya's legs start to feel fatigued—the lack of sleep and first signs of a hangover slowing her down. They've walked a long way. She wonders if they've crossed the property line of Sterling Park. A little while later, she's sure they have. Maya thinks of her warm bedroom, but she can't quite abandon her mission, finding out what Gigi is up to.

The tunnel begins to slope upward, toward what Maya realizes must be a garage: cement floors, smell of gasoline, dimly lit by moonlight through dirty windows. Maya hides in the doorway, watching as Gigi jerks open one of the garage's exterior doors, and moonlight reveals, amid old paint cans and yard equipment, a once red 1980s Jaguar.

Gigi clambers into the front seat, fusses around for a key, turns the ignition.

While the engine warms up, she goes to open the other garage door, leaving the Jaguar wide-open.

Now what? Maya could turn back before Gigi notices her lingering in the shadows... But would she be able to find her way in the darkness alone? Meanwhile, Gigi's frustration with the second, rusted garage door is mounting.

"Fucking shit!" Gigi exclaims, throwing her weight against door, making the whole structure shake. Then her cell phone rings. "What?" Gigi is shouting, but even so, Maya can only barely hear her over the rumble of the motor. "Yes, I'm en route, and hear *this*, fuckwit: if you're not there when I arrive, I will hunt you down and have your scalp."

Maya is accustomed to Gigi's mordant humor, the cruel, ironic, meaningless way she speaks. But there's an edge to her voice now that gives Maya pause. *Who the hell is she meeting at this hour?*

A wild impulse takes hold of Maya, and instead of retreating into the passageway, as she most certainly should, she darts toward the car, slipping through the Jaguar's open door, nimbly arranging herself into the rear, hiding under a stray blanket on the back seat.

When Maya was little, her aunt Rebecca would, in this way, sneak her past the security gate and into a mansion she cleaned on Georgica Pond. On the other side, Maya'd get to play in the swimming pool and sneak snacks from the fridge while her aunt cleaned.

If her aunt had known the way her father had been coaching her to "borrow" from the houses, she never would have brought Maya along. The house on Georgica Pond was the first house Maya helped her father rob. No one ever found out—she'd been careful not to be obvious—but that doesn't mean she wasn't sick with fear as they drove in and out.

The same fear squeezes Maya's stomach now.

Across the garage, Gigi crows in triumph, having finally succeeded with the rusty door. As she clambers into the driver's seat, she says, "Thirty minutes," into her phone. Then: "I'll make it worth your while," before a snap of her phone ends the conversation.

A moment later, Gigi's got the Jaguar racing over rough country roads. Maya holds on to the old leather of the seat, trying not to make a sound.

Now that they're hurtling through the night, Maya's thoughts spiral. Julian told her not to trust Gigi. Even Gigi said they're rivals. *Why the fuck didn't I listen to Julian? He married into this family and learned to survive.*

Gigi is driving fast toward who knows where. If Maya were to disappear, everything she's been left would go to Colin. And if anything were to happen to Colin, it would all go to Gigi, at least temporarily—*their* wills, hastily made up in the whirlwind leading up to their wedding, naming Gigi as the caretaker of Becca, should both her parents pass.

The car flies over a bump, takes a sharp turn, and suddenly these hypotheticals don't seem so improbable, especially thinking of what Gigi would have to gain—she would be next in line to control the Sterling empire.

But does Gigi, the profane party girl, even want it? In the hammam, she sounded so bitter when she declared the inheritance "the thing" in the Sterling family.

When Maya first saw Gigi at Sterling Park, she had a beachy look.

She said she was coming from Ibiza. But could she actually have been in Mexico?

It seems like madness, but Maya can't shake the feeling she's made herself vulnerable, that she could easily be disappeared, just a body in a trunk.

The Jaguar comes to an abrupt stop. Maya grips the old leather to keep from flying off the back seat. She smells Gigi's cigarette, freshly lit. There's the sound of men shouting, not far off.

Maya's heart thuds and her hands tense. What trouble has she gotten herself into now?

Gigi coughs like she's clearing her throat.

Maya peeks out from under the blanket, hazards a glance at the rearview mirror, and sees that Gigi is staring right at her.

Gigi's lips twist in a mean smile. She blows smoke at the mirror and whispers: "Peekaboo."

25

Gigi's eyes rake over Maya. She tilts her chin and chokes out a blunt laugh. "You're wearing *that* with *that?*"

Maya's blood rushes hotly to her face. She's speechless, her tongue thick with fear. It takes her a few moments to process Gigi's words. Then Maya remembers she's wearing Colin's moth-chewed navy cashmere and sneakers, thrown hastily over the black silk slip she'd put on for bed.

"You look sort of...nineties. You know, like..." Gigi turns down the corners of her mouth. "*Eclectic.*" Gigi moves the cigarette from one side of her mouth to the other—no hands necessary—and releases a stream of smoke. Then she's out of the car, yelling at Maya over her shoulder to hurry the fuck up.

Maya follows, mumbling: "I—how long did you know I was in there?" She feels stupid asking, but not as stupid as she'd feel remaining ignorant of the answer.

Gigi twirls around to look at Maya, walking backward now, doing a shimmy shrug. "Believe it or not, babe, you're not my first stowaway." Then she swings around and strides onward, hustling over a cobbled street toward a nondescript windowless building. "Come along."

To Maya, in her current state of mind, it looks like the sort of warehouse where powerful interests hold undesirable persons. She tries to sound merely curious when she calls out, "What is this place?"

Gigi gives Maya a merry over-the-shoulder look. "You think I'm taking you for your enhanced interrogation?"

By then the muted cacophony within is audible. Voices, bass. Some deep muscle memory kicks in as Maya follows Gigi to the unmarked door.

"These hills are studded with the estates of the very posh and very rich." Gigi lights a new cigarette off the old one and bangs on the painted black door. "Their children need somewhere to shake it off. I mean, it's not the Meatpacking. But at least they serve alcohol."

Maya, becoming reasonably confident she's not about to be dismembered and disappeared, gives an airy laugh. "Right, of course."

Gigi grips both Maya's shoulders, leaning in as if to give her a scolding. "You can come with me. I will make a one-time exception. Even in *that*. But only because we're in this backwater. In London, I would not allow you near me in that getup. And you'd better be fun. If you're planning to be unfun, *do* fuck off."

With that, Gigi spins and an oversized, all-black-clad man ushers them inside where the Franz Ferdinand is deafening.

Maya follows, puzzling over Gigi's words, wondering if she

can possibly be serious. *Fun? After everything, she's breaking the rules for fun?* As Gigi orders them drinks, Maya tries to dissipate her panic. She still feels insane for taking that ride. Now she's back in another fishbowl, very much on display. *Your cousin was brutally murdered and we're in a forced lockdown*, Maya thinks. *But sure, let's have* fun.

It's all so absurd she almost laughs.

Maya looks over her shoulder, taking in the room. The dance floor is full of pudgy white people, too far along in their evenings to be very aware of their surroundings. Girls in ill-fitting tube dresses, boys in Members Only jackets that seemed to have been worn unironically since the first era of their popularity. A group of men in their early thirties—ruddy-faced, handsome in a straight-out-of-prep-school way, shirts untucked, circling a bottle service trough—is arrayed in a tatty red velvet banquet on the other side of the dance floor. They all stare slack-jawed at Maya and Gigi.

Especially the one—lean, hair bright as a new penny, with a long swerving nose—who is particularly shameless about the staring.

Maya takes a gulp of her Grey Goose and Red Bull, shouts above the music, "Do you know those guys?" and tips her head in the direction of the banquet. "They seem to want to know us."

With a bored little roll of the eyes, Gigi says, "Him? That's just Wilfred Chancer. *Willy.*" With savage irony, she adds, "The lad who took my *flower.*"

"Oh." Something in Maya settles. Maybe this *is* a harmless, if tawdry, adventure? "The ginger?"

"'Fraid so."

Maya briefly wonders if Willy is the one who called Gigi when she was in the garage. If he has been waiting for her. And if so, where is Gigi hiding that animosity from earlier?

Or—is that just how she talks to her friends? Probably. Maya can't help a little laugh as she sips her drink. "Huh. He's sort of cute. What's wrong with him?"

"You, mean why aren't we together? That was an age ago. I was thirteen."

"Thirteen!"

Gigi snorts. "What, how old were *you* when you bloodied the sheet?"

Maya dodges this question. The tension in her jaw is ebbing. It does feel good to be out, to have escaped the compound. To be in the kind of situation she thrived in once upon a time. It was paranoid to think Gigi could be up to something nefarious. She's just petty and mean and dislikes Maya getting a share of what she views as rightfully hers. Underneath that, maybe she's just...*fun*.

And if Gigi does anything *too* fun tonight, maybe that's good. Maybe, Maya thinks, taking another sip, it's time to bait the hook.

Not that Gigi's wild side really needs baiting.

"I think he still likes you," Maya says, brightening her eyes with mischief. "Interested?"

"God, no, I'd end up like all the Millies and Poppies I went to school with. All those useless girls with double-barrel surnames— Lady Heaping-Banks, and the Duchess Worsted-Babbler. My life would be all polo matches and children stuffed into doll's clothes and idiotic hats. Or like Eva, a total zombie with nothing to do but redecorate the house every other year. You know why she keeps buying houses? Because she doesn't want the dread to catch her. If there's always a new house to decorate, she can keep from knowing the things it would kill her to know..."

"Oh." Maya wishes that she'd had Gigi to tell her that in the days when she was mortally desperate for the attention of Eva's husband. "You don't think that's her dream life? Redecorating houses?"

"Don't think so. Know how they met? She was his editor, at the *Standard*. She comes from fancy people and all that, but her daddy blew it all on mistresses and stupid deals, and she was deathly afraid of sinking lower and lower—as are all people who get bopped down a rung. When Marcus persuaded her to quit and marry him, I suppose it seemed like an offer she couldn't refuse..."

Maya, not wanting to show how personally interested she is in this topic, manages a flat and neutral "Oh." Maya could see Eva as someone very much in need of attention, brightening any time Helen addresses her, always fluttering at Marcus's side.

Gigi plows on: "Those men over there, half of them are in government, half are in finance, and half are in media. The math sounds funny, but I promise you, it's not. They all went to school together; they're all next in line to own some sizable portion of the universe. Being one of their wives is a hideous gig. You're plenty comfortable, of course. But you're always selecting the children's holiday clothes while your dear husband decides who the next PM's going to be. It'll drive a girl with any ambition mad." Gigi pats Maya's hand, twirls her finger at the bartender for more drinks. "Don't worry, I know you have your eyeshadow brand or whatever it is to keep you busy. And now that Arianna waved her wand at you from beyond the grave, you'll get a say just like all the big boys too."

"Not sure that's worth it, either," Maya replies noncommittally as Gigi hands her another glass. Gigi narrows her eyes.

"You've got to learn the players, my dear. That one next to Willy—that's David Aston, deputy editor of *Finance*. He was in school with Colin, best friends with the current PM's daughter, so you'll never see a mean word about them in *that* paper. Pathetic."

"SterlingCo papers don't pick favorites?"

"Of course! But not for sentimental reasons. Nobody gets a free pass because they *went to the same school as one of us*. If we go easy, it's because we're getting something better in return. That was Granddad's great insight—newspapers are only mildly profitable. In a few years, it's likely none of our papers will be profitable at all. But as an information arm of a larger business organization, they're everything."

As Maya listens, she begins to observe another side of Gigi. The glint in her eye. The cunning. *Maybe she does after all want what Maya stands to inherit?* For all her outlandishness, Gigi is sounding a lot more astute than Maya has ever given her credit for. Or Colin, for that matter. To Colin, Gigi is always the fuck-up kid sister—the liability.

"Maybe you should be in charge of SterlingCo," Maya says. "Seems like you know a lot about how things actually work."

A shadow passes over Gigi's face. "Nobody likes a girl who knows too much." She drains her drink and glances around irritably, impatient for the next round.

That phrase sends a trickle of cool water down Maya's spine. *Nobody likes a girl who knows too much.*

New drinks arrive and Gigi takes a vicious sip.

Maya tries to sip slowly but gulps instead. Her thoughts drift and her head buzzes pleasantly as she scans the room. She notes Willy's approach. "I think your deflowerer is getting ready to advance in our general direction."

"Fuck me."

"I'm sure he'd be happy to."

Gigi's eyes glitter. "Duh."

Maya laughs. She actually *is* having fun. Her body feels warm and alive in a way she hasn't experienced in a long while. Even her honeymoon was orchestrated and largely for the cameras. This though, this is simple, like the *Springs* bar after hours, those hot summer nights when she was nineteen and nobody cared what she did.

Is this what it was like back in the day, teenaged Arianna and Gigi sneaking out of the house to party...before everything went so terribly wrong, and Arianna was sent away? Beautiful, young, untethered, still with a chance in the world? When the story still might've had a different ending?

The droning Brit-pop is replaced by the opening synth

strings of Britney's "Toxic." Gigi, smiling mischievously, does an on-beat robotic swing of her arms over her head. "Let's *go*," she says. "This is my song."

Gigi grabs Maya's hand and pulls her into the fray. Maya lets herself be drawn under the strobing green and purple lights. Gigi rhythmically moves through the crowd, tossing her hair, twirling Maya. She looks gorgeous and drunk, and Maya can't help but think back to Miami. *Pre*-Miami. Her lost period after *The Springs*. Did she look like that? In those days, every song was "her song," and she was the one grabbing her unwilling, only moderately intoxicated friends, pulling them up to dance on bars.

It feels good, though. Freeing. For just a moment Maya wants to cast off the heaviness of playing Sterling. Not to mention the pillaging thief role her family-in-law has cast her in.

They bump hips, swing their arms, scream about being too high to come down. Maya was wary of being spotted when they first arrived, but the crowd doesn't seem to recognize them. They're just two girls dropping to their knees, popping back up, whipping their hair around. Not so different from the other girls, in jeans and party tops, shifting away from the heavily sweating boys attempting to sidle close. A college girl doing her best Geri Halliwell impersonation in a Union Jack minidress has pulled Willy onto the dance floor.

When they're close enough, Gigi leans toward the girl, stage-whispers: "Just so you're warned, his wang is like his nose; it goes a bit…" She trails off and hooks her index finger.

Willy grins at Gigi. The girl in the Union Jack grimaces and moves on.

"Hey there," Gigi shouts up at Willy, lifting her horsehair off her sweaty neck. "Long time. How's that big investment in Pets.com turning out?"

"Gi, that was years ago. Isn't your family in the news business?"

"Yes. Heard you're a photo editor at *Parler* now," Gigi says. "You should have let me know you were looking for a new gig. I'd have asked Marcus to set you up at one of our magazines instead of that rag."

"I'd rather not work for publications that stalk the families of murder victims."

Gigi grins. "Yes, we know what *actually* makes money, unlike you pretentious fuckers. You know our motto. Hurt one grieving family, entertain millions."

The exchange is barbed and flirtatious. But there's something off about it. It feels too forced. Too *staged*.

Like a conversation on *The Springs*, when they were shooting it for the fourth time.

Now they're grinning at each other and dancing close. Willy slides his hands into the pockets of Gigi's jacket, gripping her hips as they sway, then sliding the jacket off her shoulders and tossing it onto the banquet. Gigi throws her naked arms around Willy's neck. Maya clocks this, mildly horrified that a white fur coat would be so casually flung aside. She hasn't yet lost that compulsive reverence for very expensive things or the cleaning lady's knowledge of how quickly white objects turn gray.

The DJ plays "Hey Ya!" next and then it's "Survivor," and after that "All These Things That I've Done," and soon Maya's carried away once again, letting the music take her. Next thing she knows, she's soaked in sweat and accepting a shot of tequila from a friendly stranger.

And then another, and another.

She scans the room, looking for Gigi, but is struck by an uncanny sensation of being watched. Like being under the glowing tiger eyes of the nursery suite wallpaper. But this time she's not imagining it. There, across the crowded dance floor, someone *is* watching her. A woman with dark hair. She has a very serious, round-eyed look that puts a stitch in Maya's side. The woman doesn't seem like she belongs in a raging dance club; there's something misplaced about her, like a wraith from a Victorian dream. She doesn't look like the belongs in this *century*, or even the last. The sweat on Maya's neck goes cold.

Someone's trying to grind on her from behind. It's the guy with the tequila. She slips out of his grasp, and when she looks back, the dark-haired woman has disappeared. Maya tells herself she's just being paranoid. These people are more likely to recognize Gigi than Maya—Gigi's the local celebrity—and surely whoever Gigi brought along would be an object of curiosity.

But maybe it's fair warning to switch to water. Since Julian said the words *Portas Brancas*, Maya's felt reckless. As if the name of the place, spoken out loud, were a spell that summoned Miss Mayhem herself.

As she maneuvers through the crowd toward the bar, she's

continually pushed back onto the dance floor. The throng is pressing in. That tequila buzz intensifies to a high, swarming whine. She's shoved aside by intoxicated bodies, moving ecstatically to the beat. Her stomach does a hard turn. Is she about to be sick?

Maya pushes in the other direction, toward the women's room.

In the bathroom stall, she counts four deep breaths, trying to regain balance. Usually she handles her liquor well, but after a year of pregnancy and new motherhood, she's out of practice. How many shots did she take? It didn't seem like that many. Or was she drugged? Like in Miami?

At the sink, she splashes water on her face. Her mascara is running. She looks awful. Except she's seeing double. Maya blinks, sees her again—the dark-haired specter. But no, not a specter. She's real, she's moving, turning her head to check that the bathroom door's shut. In the dirty mirror, Maya can see the woman's left cheek, a rough imperfection in the shape of a crescent moon.

"Maya," the woman whispers.

Is Maya hearing things, seeing things? She wipes the moisture from her eyes, then pivots.

Where the woman was, now there's a gaggle of drunk girls who barely look drinking age.

Maya *must* be seeing things.

She brushes the hair back from her face. Squares her shoulders. Just a hallucination, she tells herself. And who wouldn't be seeing ghosts? After what Julian told her in the gallery, and the phone call with Portas Brancas, and all the hot, ugly Miami memories, and the stories of poor Arianna, the troubled teen, all of it taking permanent residence in Maya's mind. It's all sloshing in there, spiked with tequila. No wonder she's seeing ghosts.

Back out in the thick of the club, Gigi appears and flings a warm arm around Maya's waist. She's pliant, way drunker than before, and Maya is relieved by the touch of a real person (even if it's her slippery sister-in-law), an anchor in the present moment. Maya glances around for Willy. He's back at his banquet, glowering.

"I think you hurt his feelings," Maya says to Gigi, glad of something to joke about.

"Good!" Gigi begins hopping wildly up and down to the music, chanting along with the song as it crescendos, chanting about how she has soul but she's not a soldier.

That's when Maya notices a man in black at the bar, watching them. What remains of her high shrivels. Alarm pounds in her skull. The man is staring at Maya, not blinking, even as he says something into his wrist. Maya takes a breath, tries to make a quick determination. Friend or foe? Real or vision?

"Gi—you see that guy? He's watching us. There was a woman too, but she disappeared."

"A woman? *Who?*"

"I don't know; she had dark hair, and—"

Gigi isn't listening; she's already wheeled back into the crowd. But only for another beat. The man at the bar has multiplied. Now ten men, all wearing black, are descending on Maya and Gigi. An instinct to run rises in Maya.

But before she can act on that impulse, she recognizes Travis emerging from the pack. He takes Maya by the arm and calmly says, "We need to get you out of here."

She's petulant again, chafing under that overwhelming force of the Sterling strong arm. "But *why?*"

Is he suppressing an eye roll? If so, he succeeds. His reply is bland. "This is an unsecure location, and against protocol."

Maya feels her inner fire dwindle. Her head is pounding. She thinks of Kendra, the Southern girl on *The Springs*, saying, "Girl, your slip is showing," which is, at this moment, literally true. Maya *does* feel exposed here; maybe an escort home is a lucky break.

Maya moves with Travis toward the door. Gigi, however, is unpersuaded. One of the other men in a black suit has her around the waist; she kicks the air as he hauls her off the dance floor, the dancers stepping back in shock, eyes big with voyeuristic glee.

"Fuck this, I'm just getting started!" Gigi screams.

Maya, shielded by Travis, hustles toward the black SUV at the curb.

Two security men exit the car, one from either side, surrounding Gigi.

"Time to go home, Miss Sterling," says the driver.

Gigi, still struggling, cries out, "Let me go, you fucking dorks!"

"Come on, Gi," Maya calls, climbing into the shiny black box of the town car.

The security guy deposits Gigi in the back seat a moment

later. She's pummeling the back of the driver's seat with her fists, but she's too drunk to do much damage. "Oh, well." Gigi sighs, throws up her hands, giggles. "Found me again, boys."

Maya snorts, leaning over Gigi, belting her in. She brushes against her bare arms, cold and slick with sweat. "Shit," Maya says. "Your jacket."

"Oh, Maya, you're such a wet blanket," Gigi says. "I thought we were going to have fun!"

"We did have fun," Maya says, sincerely. Now that they're pulling away from the club, from the mayhem and the hallucinations, now that they're in the safety of the armored car, she can admit it—it was fun. Gigi is fun. Maybe Maya misunderstood her harsh words in the hammam, her little tricks. "I'm just worried about the jack—"

Gigi is slurring: "I mean, you're so hopelessly plebeian. 'Your jacket, your jacket.' Listen, I'll just buy another fucking jacket. Here, look." She opens up a compartment in the car, pulls out two cashmere blankets, throws Maya one. "Get used to it, you're a Sterling now."

"So, you admit it? I'm a Sterling." Despite the recent panic, Maya grins.

Gigi arches a plucked brow. A savage clarity flashes in her eyes. "No, Maya. Why don't you ever listen? I know the *real* you, you little operator. You were going to get a piece of Sterling, one way or another, and now look at you, you get more than me, a girl who's been a Sterling her whole life. *That's* how one becomes a Sterling, years and years and years of *suffering*. You seem to think you can skip all that, just vault into a controlling position! *Infuriating.* But it doesn't mean I don't *love* you." Gigi dissolves into giggles and once again appears cross-eyed drunk. "Remember who loves you, when you're suffering and suffering to get what's yours. *I* love you. Even when it might seem like I don't." Gigi pauses, takes a little gasp for air. "Just like I loved Ari, that deranged little nut."

"Gigi, are you…crying?"

"No. No! Don't be stupid." Gigi pushes her palms hard against the sudden swell at the corners of her eyes. "It's just that it's like the old days. The security was always higher when I was with *the* heiress."

"Did you go there with her? To that club?"

"Of course we did. There's nowhere else *to* go."

"And when you said *Nobody likes a girl who knows too much*—did you mean her? Arianna?" They take a sharp turn and Gigi slides around, her body moving fluidly with the vehicle. Then she braces herself against the door, fixes Maya in a fathomless gaze. "Careful, Inspector Maya—sounds like you're saying Arianna died because she 'knew too much,' which means maybe *you* should stop asking questions too."

Gigi's index finger wags *no, no, no.* Then she balls up her cashmere blanket, stuffs it against the door, lays her head down, and closes her eyes.

Maya turns to the window, taking in what Gigi just said, its stark warning.

Don't be the kind of girl who asks too many questions.

Don't be the kind of girl who knows too much.

Don't be the kind of girl who can't shut up, who someone might need silenced.

Outside, the midnight landscape mutates from sleepy village to farmland to wild country, and Maya's reminded how far away and all alone she is.

26

At the door to her bedroom, Maya observes Colin and Becca sleeping peacefully, unaware that Maya ever left her bed. She should go to them.

Her head is still throbbing from the club music and the commingling of vodka and tequila and the grim projections that hounded her as they drove home through the inky country dark. After Travis ushered them inside to safety, Gigi staggered off to bed, but Maya can't bear to do the same. She's vibrating with something she can't explain, a speedball of paranoia and guilt. Miss Mayhem came out ripping tonight, and Maya let it happen. Now a little pack of demons sits on her shoulders, pouring horrible fortunes into her ears. She closes her eyes and sees the woman with the scarred face. Maya isn't even sure she's real. She does *hope* it's just the ill-advised mixing of hard alcohols, a fearful projection. In fact, Maya is coming around to the realization that the car ride didn't sober her, that she's still drunk.

As if in a trance, Maya drops her hand from the doorknob and moves away from the nursery suite, down the halls and up the hidden staircase.

An inner refrain sounds with each step: *Nobody likes a girl who knows too much.*

It's almost like she's levitating, drifting on ghostly currents, back onto the threshold of a garret room, preserved in 1980s girlishness. The night she saw this room for the first time seems a lifetime ago, though it's only been a few days, really.

Besides Helen's absence, the scene is the same.

The mauve chair, the telephone booth, the toys.

The walls inscribed, like the suite where Maya sleeps, with Blake's poem about the tiger and his burning eyes.

Maya advances into the room, no longer merely curious, more like compelled, as if Arianna herself could be waiting for her within, with a table all laid for a dead girl's tea party.

She wanders about the room, touching fabrics, fingertips drawing lines through layers of dust. Tracing the gold lettering along the forested wallpaper—*did he who made the Lamb make thee?*—to a nook bookshelf packed with antique volumes. Leather covers, gold-leaf titles, crumbling, grand.

Among them, some poems by one William Blake. *Of course.*

Moldering old tomes from which the Sterling family took their bedtime lullabies.

Maya pulls the book out. Dust trails it in a smoky plume. She flips the pages, moving to the window where moonlight streams in. On the front endpaper, there's a bookplate with an image of a rose and a serpent and the name *Arianna Sterling* in sweeping script. Maya turns to the title page, reads the words: *William Blake, Songs of Innocence and Experience.*

Inside the poems have been hand-illustrated with haunting paintings. They are beautiful, but they also remind Maya of the watercolors that she saw in the art therapy room at Portas Brancas. Distorted, impressionistic, the hurried lines and images of a feeble hand and disturbed mind. She flips through the pages, trying to find "The Tyger." That's when she sees it. Tucked between the pages is a very thin piece of paper, a little yellowed, with a poem written in looping, girlish script:

The Little Girl with Dark Dark Eyes
after William Blake
by Arianna Sterling

Tyger, tyger, he of towering height
My father who goes off into the night
My best friend who never says goodbye,
Is there anything you cannot buy?

An airplane to take you through the skies
Beautiful women, and their sighs?
While I languish, in a mood so dire—
Can you interpret my dreams of fire?

Did you think you could keep us apart

What I know inside my heart?
And now my heart's begun to beat,
What dread fate must I meet?

Is that the reason for my pain?
The evil that surged within thy brain
That terrible night on La Digue
Watching from upon an ocean so dark, so big!

Tyger Tyger burning bright,
A little girl in the fiery night
Dark brown hair, dark brown eye,
Locked with me in symmetry.

Maya's fingers move fast now, turning the pages. No more Arianna poems, but there are several scraps of lined paper, folded into tight triangles. Maya, breath held, unfolds them. They're all brief, written in the same girlish hand. Younger than the one that wrote the poem.

All addressed to the same person.

Dear Jessica, reads one. *He's not so bad. He says you're not real, but he doesn't mean it, it's just the way he is. He says I shall follow in his footsteps and be big and mighty like him.* Then, *I'll be able to convince him about you, prove that you are real. Don't worry, Jessie. I know you're real.*

A feeling of pity surges in Maya at the heartbreaking naiveté of the note. She feels herself sinking into the past, to herself about age twelve, when she was half a fearful child, half the suave, daddy-trained pickpocket.

Dear Jessica, reads another. *Harry is a monster. He was drunk last night, and smashed up a beautiful supper service. I have to get out of here. He lies. I can't see the truth anymore. If I stay here, it'll kill me.*

Maya's fingers are trembling.

Dear Jessica.

Dear Jessica.

Dear Jessie.

So many notes, all to that one lost girl.

Dear Jessie—I know he lit the flame. I know, I know, I know.

That high floating sensation has drained away, and Maya feels murky and slow with the sorrow of this lonely, troubled child who scribbled her greatest fears on scraps of paper. It's as though she can hear the voice of Arianna, of Jessie—the disturbed woman she met in Mexico—speaking to her across time, from the other side of death, shouting out the things she knew, her worst fears, her nightmares, the horrors she lived with, here, in this very room...

Of course. Of course she used the name "Jessie" as her cover. The name of the girl she was bound to by unspeakable guilt, the friend she lost at a young age. Jessica Blackburne.

Little Jessica Blackburne who burned alive in the same fire in La Digue that killed her father.

And Harry...the man who lit the match all those years ago?

And Arianna, who knew what he'd done and was punished for knowing.

A punishment that ended, with spectacular finality, in her murder.

Maya's fingers are trembling. The idea that Harry Sterling killed his own daughter fills her with terror. The tragedy of it is a blow to her chest.

And not just a tragedy, but a looming threat. *Nobody likes a girl who knows too much.* By naming Maya the new heir to her fortune, did Arianna also bequeath a dangerous curse? Will Harry—the roguish, violent Harry—come for her now too?

She has to learn more, has to find proof of all this, but then—

A cracking sound below. A heavy foot on an old board.

Maya's skin goes cold at the realization that someone's on the stairs...

She stuffs the notes back between the pages, puts the book back. Comes away from the shelves, and hurries toward the open doorway.

The adrenaline rushes through Maya's body as she reaches the hallway. She pauses, unsure which direction to go. Which rooms are safe. She's afraid, and at the same time she can hear the reprimand. What's she doing, wandering around the house in the middle of the night like this? Again.

Her vision is murky, the tequila charging her blood, confusing her path in this rabbit warren of a house. Sound travels strangely, echoes against the high ceilings. The groan of old wood planks.

Her heartbeat is crazy loud, though. So fast it doesn't seem survivable. Was she hallucinating the sound of someone following her?

Just like she hallucinated the dark-haired woman at the club?

She hears footsteps now. Whirls around.

Fuck fuck fuck—where is she, where can she hide?

She turns, collides with another body, and is forced up against the wall. A hand covers her mouth, smothering her scream.

27

It's a Tuesday. Dr. Caro told me so. I asked—a test, to see if she's on my side. Usually, they won't tell me. They just say (patronizingly calm voice): *What day do you* think *it is?*

But Dr. Caro smiled like I was some precocious child asking the big questions, and said, "Today is a Tuesday."

Then she said, "Do you want to tell me about her?"

I was about to be coy and say I didn't know who she was talking about.

But something inside me had already begun cracking open when she asked me that. Everyone else tried to steer around it, avoid her name, for fear of "retriggering my trauma."

But how could I forget, even for all their attempts at brainwashing me? Sometimes I'd wake up in the night sure I *was* her. That's how connected we were. I know it's crazy, we were so little, but it was like she was a part of me, like she *was* me.

Jessica.

For an hour I talked about her.

A jumble of memories, associations, images. It felt, well, the way vomiting up a huge meal feels. Like being scraped out from the inside. But also—a relief.

I told her about those nights, the many dreams. The ones where I woke up crying out my *own* name, convinced that I, Arianna, was consumed in flames. "We have to save her, we have to save Arianna," I'd say, and then the overpaid nurses and doctors and therapists would gather with their knitted brows the next day to tell me that I *was* Arianna, and that I *was* safe, and that it was Jessica who was gone and I needed to let her be gone.

But how could I?

Who else did I have? She and I were one.

I learned eventually to keep it a secret though, our little relationship. Jessica and mine.

The pictures I drew of her, and notes I wrote, things I wished I could tell her.

"Tell me more about what really happened to Jessica," Dr. Caro said.

Which made me angry. I *did* just tell her what happened. But Dr. Caro seemed to want something more.

"What did Harry do?"

"I don't know."

"Are you sure you don't know? Or do you just not *remember*?"

Inside me, it was as though a security gate went up. My exterior felt hard and smooth. Deep within, there was a chaos of memory and sensation coming to a boil. But between that mess of feeling and the world there was the gate, impenetrable. For my own safety, I believed—

But a part of me, yet too weak to speak, doesn't believe that anymore.

"I don't remember anything." My voice sounded dead and automatic. I heard myself say it again: "I don't remember anything about that. Nothing at all."

Dr. Caro put away her pen and paper. "Keep writing in that diary you hide away." She must have seen my face go white because she added, "Don't worry, I'll make sure no one will read it. But I think you know the truth, and if you keep writing, you'll come to it. I won't push you. All right?"

"All right." It was the same dead voice, but inside I felt warm with gratitude.

Frightened too.

And I'm frightened now. Alone. Holding this journal. Trying so hard to get the gate to open. To remember. To be all right with what I'm remembering.

To hold steady as the past comes over me.

Because I *do* know the truth, don't I?

In La Digue, the house on fire, that house I loved visiting, where the air was warm and smelled of salty sea and tropical fruit, where there was that nanny—what was her name? A nanny of Jessica's, who gave us sweets and read us stories and loved us.

It comes at me with a stabbing frenzy.

Harry did something terrible. That was always my conclusion.

He did something so terrible, and no one could ever know. But once I knew, I was as endangered as little dead Jessica.

Because he might do something terrible again, to protect himself, to protect the inheritance. Protect the Sterlings.

The only person I'd ever really felt any kindness from was Helen. She was there, when Harry opened up the house, when there was that period of normalcy. She took me shopping, took me to tea. How many times did she say, "You can tell me anything"?

Not the way Harry or the psychologists did.

She said it in such a way that I believed her.

And I did tell her things—about Lyman, about Gigi, about my dreams—that she advised me on and kept secret. As far as I know, anyway.

But when I told her this, her response was stiff and strange. We were walking through Sterling Park, and she said, "That's enough. You go rest. I'll take care of everything."

And the next thing I knew, I was on my way here.

The fear rushes back over me. Fear of Harry, fear of Helen. The panicky shouting, fighting, struggling I did upon first arriving. How I tried to tell whoever would listen to me about the Sterlings, who they *really* are, what they're capable of.

And then—then they zapped me. And for a long time, the memories were gone.

Or were they just too monstrous to expose to the light of day?

28

Maya swallows her scream, realizing who's pinned her to the wall.

Marcus, whose touch has always had a narcotic effect on her. She softens, her body responding in the old way.

With his big hand covering her mouth, she can barely move, much less make sound. She inhales the skin of the palm pressed to her face—that familiar scent, a mix of bergamot, tobacco, and sweat—and something inside her pulses. She feels she's loudly ticking, like a clock. Marcus relaxes his grip. He was holding his breath, she realizes.

"Marcus," she whispers. Being alone with him—it's like standing at the edge of a cliff. "What are you doing here?"

"Shh," he says. "Not out here, someone might hear us."

He steps back, and she almost can't bear the space opening between them as they part.

Then he takes her hand and he's leading her through the mostly dark hallways. They take one turn and then another, moving away from the parts of the house she's learned to navigate.

His skin, his smell. She has a dizzying impression of time

collapsing. She is once again Maya at the club with Gigi, Maya dancing. Maya crawling out of her skin to be free. The Maya from the years things fell apart.

As she follows him, she's hit by a sense of it, of *them*, happening all over again, same as it ever was. She's loose from the tequila, shaken by the mournful poems in Arianna's room, the dead girl's presence, the ghostly visions. The only thing that feels real is Marcus's hand tight around hers in the dark. Just as she starts to fear they might be getting too close to the wing that houses his shared bedroom with Eva, he instead leads her through a door and closes it quietly behind him.

As she stands there in the darkness, he switches on a small desk lamp and she can see they're in a library. The walls are paneled floor-to-ceiling with books. There are ladders on wheels to get at the high shelves. Ferns with six-foot wingspans droop from high corners.

He's obviously been here before. It has the smell of him. His clothes hang from an old-fashioned wooden drying rack.

His laptop and several hard drives are piled on a desk by the window.

So, this is the lair Marcus has spent so much of his time in these past days, barking orders into his phone and running the SterlingCo international operations remotely.

The room, though she's never been in it, feels familiar. She remembers so many other rooms like it. Rooms vibrant with his aftershave and clothes and moods.

"We can talk," he says. "No one comes in here."

"What were you doing out there?" Maya asks.

Marcus's eyes search hers. "I wanted to be sure you were okay."

"Were you following me?"

"I was up late. In here, working. Travis told me there was a security issue. He said it was taken care of, but once I learned it was you and Gigi having a bit of a spree, I had to see for myself you were okay."

Her first impulse is to whip a bitter remark back at him—*like you care*. But a second thought stops her. *Is* she okay? It does seem like she might maybe be losing her mind.

Or is she just finally understanding what kind of monsters inhabit this place?

Slowly, she nods.

He's hovering. Almost like he's...*nervous?* "Good," he says. "Good. You need to be more careful, though."

"Okay." It feels good, being told what to do by him. She missed that.

"Right." His eyes search hers. "In that case, you should return to your room." He goes toward the door again.

No. She sucks in a breath. A desperate urge keeps her there, not wanting to move from under the sun of Marcus's attention. Maybe it's the mayhem from the club, still churning through her system, the trails of that reckless energy. Maybe it's just an old habit. Or maybe this is the kind of hurt and desire a girl just never gets over.

"You asked about the wolf. In the greenhouse."

He looks back at her, but she can't read him. "Yes," he says.

"I lied about that when you asked me before. That tattoo, it doesn't represent me."

"No?"

"No," she shakes her head. She feels so stupid saying it, but she has this need for him to know. "It was always you, Marcus. The lone wolf who stalked my life but would never stay."

For a while he doesn't move. Did he hear what she said? Then she sees the mechanics of his throat as he swallows. "I've ruined so many things. I'm sorry."

"Not me. You didn't ruin me."

"No." He shakes his head, smirks ruefully. "I couldn't do that if I tried. But it was real between us. I might have ruined *that*."

She really should go now. She takes in as much breath as she can. "Admit it, you were roaming the halls, looking for me."

His eyes glint. He takes a step closer. Waits. Then takes another.

"Maya," he murmurs. He brushes back her hair and kisses her neck. "You're right," he says. "I was. Can I...? Is this all right?"

She doesn't want to shift even a little, for fear he'll stop. "Yes," she whispers. "That."

"That?"

"Yes." One word and they're both in such a hurry to get their clothes off it seems like it might all go too fast. Then they're both trying to control themselves, slow it down.

With Marcus it's always been a storm of fear and excitement and want and dread. But there's something new now—in the way his big boxer's hands cup her jaw, in the way he tugs at her sweater, nudging it off her shoulders, his fingertips almost tentative. Wanting to rush, trying very hard not to.

Was it always there, this gentle intensity that feels so much like love?

"It was always you," he says, fumbling at her slip, the straps coming off easy, the fabric still clingy with sweat from dancing.

She struggles with his belt, his hands are on her waist, pulling at her underwear, sliding it off. Then he's roughly lifting her up, her legs wrapping around his waist. He staggers, lands her against one of the wheeled ladders. They both fumble, get in each other's way, trying to undo his fly.

"Fu-uck," she gasps, as he presses inside her.

It's different, and the same. Being with Marcus feels like a door has been opened onto her deepest core. And then there's all the old bad medicine: desire and fear and guilt and the knowing it will be over too soon and wishing it would last. The wrongness of it, the beating sense that they could at any moment be caught.

And, too, there's the coal of a new mistrust. The knowing that he's always manipulated her, and now he has every reason to manipulate her forever, with her seat on the board and majority stake in his family company.

"Maya," he murmurs, crushing into her. "It always should have been us."

"Yes." She feels riven by pleasure and despair: her life split in half.

"Would you want that?"

306

Right now she just wants this to continue, all its danger and impossibility. The groan of the ladder holding their weight, the rhythm of Marcus bearing into her, the rough skin of his neck against her face, as Maya lets her mind shut off for once, gives herself to the moment, tightens a fist around his hair, whispers, "This is what I want."

"Oh god, Maya," he says. Their breathing is rough and matched. He holds her hips, speaks into her neck. "It could still be us. We could leave; we could…"

They're so close right now, their skin slick and sticky, their movements small and intentional, as though to really let go would be too good, unbearably pleasurable. "Don't say anything you don't mean," she whispers.

"I wouldn't," he says, pressing deeper. "Not to you. Not now, not after everything."

And Maya lets herself be overwhelmed by this promise, the old longing, by his words, by him.

———

Then it's over and they're hurrying to get their clothes back on, Maya racing to smooth her hair, cool her skin, soothe her system back to normal. She smells like him, he smells like her—nothing but a shower could erase the evidence. Maybe not even that.

A line's been crossed. She might not be able to go back. It was bad enough to be on and off with both Colin and Marcus during her single years. But now she's married to one of them. To

Colin, good Colin, the lover who doesn't know about the other. The elation of the previous moment is blown away by the chaos of what they've done.

Wordlessly they advance toward the door. Maya's afraid to look at him.

Just before they cross the threshold back into the hall, he grabs her hand and whispers, "I meant it."

"Me too," she says, as he pulls her against him, takes fistfuls of the cardigan she's thrown over her slip. She grabs his belt, as though they need ballast or they'll be blown off course.

This must be real, she thinks. *This is reality. It feels like the only real and true thing I've ever known.*

She's thinking this, even as she tightens her heart into a fist.

Even as she knows she's felt this way a hundred times before and found out she was wrong to trust him, that it wasn't good for her, that Marcus is her own personal vortex.

Even as her hand slips in his back pocket, nimble like her father taught her, opposite fingernails digging into his forearm to distract his attention.

The kiss lasts. She thinks they'll have to go back into the library, that she won't be able to resist.

But then they do pull away. They walk side by side, breath slowing, neither speaking, tranquility coming over their features, their movements, until she can't really hear him, and without discussing it, when they come to a fork in the hall, they take separate paths.

She doesn't look back. Keeps walking. When she takes

another turn, she scans to make sure she's alone, that no one followed her. That's when she removes the BlackBerry tucked into her waistband, filched from Marcus's back pocket.

Now, why'd she *do* that?

An impulse, she rationalizes. Some old muscle memory.

But she knows the real reason. She took it because some part of her wants to trust him, and another never will.

And also, of course, because she could.

———

As Maya walks alone, she remembers a night toward the end of their first fling. Marcus leaving the hotel room around midnight.

He'd been in New York on business, and he'd taken her with him to a party, a dinner, another party. They were out in the open together, and even if that was only for a few minutes at a time, she allowed herself to imagine a shared future. A whole fantasy life. Pictures of them in magazines—*their* homes, *their* children, all enviable and on display. She'd thought, at the very least, that for that night it was *their* hotel room. Not his room, which he allowed her to visit for a few hours or a night. But it wasn't. It was *her* hotel room—he'd reserved it for her alone.

They fucked, and then he showered, dressed without explanation. At midnight, when she asked him where he was going, he glanced at her like some minor irritation.

"You didn't think I was going to leave my wife, did you?" he said at the time.

She spent days in that hotel room. She'd go down in the morning for a mimosa at the bar. She'd swim naked in the rooftop pool. She'd dare the staff to kick her out, but they never did. They knew who'd paid for the room and had to tolerate her. Those had been deranged days, acute with abandonment. She'd berate herself for thinking he would leave his wife. Eva, the woman she couldn't stop googling. She'd stare at herself in the mirror—drunk, slothful, makeup down her face, a beautiful wreck—spit wine at her reflection, call herself an idiot.

Only now does it occur to her that she wasn't being an idiot. She could have lived in that hotel room for years—could still be living there now, probably, if she'd wanted to. Squirreled away and safe. Even when Marcus had turned away from her, he'd left orders at one of the finest, most discreet hotels in Manhattan that she was to be protected. That she was to be taken care of and could stay as long as she liked.

Maybe that wasn't an act of pity, as she'd concluded at the time.

Maybe that was, in fact, what he most wanted.

Until Maya ruined it all in Miami.

———

Maya sits on the floor in the hallway just outside her bedroom door, curled in a ball, the BlackBerry still tight in her fist.

The thing is, she does love Marcus, and when he said let's run away together, she wanted to believe he meant it. But she's been his fool before.

And now that she's the Sterling heiress, he has many reasons to keep her close, not all of them loving.

She clicks through Marcus's email, unsure what she's looking for.

First she searches for her name, and finds nothing.

Then she searches for Portas Brancas.

Only one email comes up, from *concierge@portasbrancas.org*, and just seeing the address is enough to plunge her into a cold sweat. The subject line reads: *Update on the Patient*, and Maya braces herself for a report of the detox of one Maya Miller, notes on her behavior post-Miami meltdown.

The email is brief and obsequious:

> *Dear Sir: It was a pleasure to talk last week and congratulations on being named CEO of such an important company. I know you said not to discuss the patient with you unless there was something that might affect the company legally. The nurses have reported that the patient has persistent delusions that she speaks about at a high volume. I don't want to go into specifics, but they do seem to possibly fall into that category you mentioned—things that might bear on your company legally. (For example, one delusion involved calling a prominent member of your family a murderer.) Of course, these are no doubt hallucinations, a common occurrence during withdrawal, especially in the case of a patient so physically dependent. However, as there might be legal implications to*

*such an accusation, and the patient says that she has it
all "on tape," I did feel it was my obligation to bring it
to your attention. Please let me know how you would
like to proceed.*

Respectfully, Dr. Garwold

Marcus had responded immediately with one line: *call me.*

Just outside her bedroom, Maya leans her shoulder blades
against the wall.

She should have known by the date. She wasn't the patient
in the subject line. *Arianna* was. Arianna, with her "persistent
delusions." Arianna, who knew what her father did. That he
killed Mikey Blackburne. She threatened him with that knowledge somehow, got locked up in Portas Brancas.

Then she got out of that place—and turned up dead.

And Marcus knew where she was all along.

29

Sterlings like to watch things burn, but only if they're the ones to light the match, says a voice.

That shaky, girlish voice.

It's a dream, Maya knows. But she can't seem to surface, can't wake up. Hands are on her body. Sterling hands, holding her down. Transmitting a malevolent magic.

I just had to get a look at you, first, says the voice.

The voice travels across a distance. Arianna's. She's wearing cutoffs and has a bullet hole in her forehead. A gory, blackened third eye, above her two piercing green ones. Maya wants to ask Arianna for her help, wants to ask her who among the Sterlings she can trust. But already Arianna is receding. The other Sterlings are in between them. One palm print at a time, they are turning Maya's body to ash.

The relief of waking, of feeling the solidity of her body against the silk sheet, is intense but short-lived. Maya is alone in the suite, groggy and hungover. Colin must have gotten up at dawn with the baby. Again.

When she stands, a hard object clatters on the floor. Marcus's BlackBerry. The weight of what she did last night hits her—following Gigi, getting hauled home by security, fucking Marcus. The revelation that he knew Arianna was sent away. Did he already know that Arianna had photos of him and Maya together?

Did he know *that*, even though in the greenhouse he'd acted like he hadn't?

Did *he* kill Arianna himself to keep the affair a secret?

Or was it Harry, who found out his daughter had escaped and believed her when she threatened to tell his secrets?

By breakfast it seems everyone has heard about Maya and Gigi's little outing. When Maya arrives in the room, freshly showered and blow-dried, having washed Marcus, the club, off twice—once late in the night upon finally entering her room, and then again this morning for good measure—she is met by a new level of hostile agitation. A higher grade of side-eye.

A retaliatory fury spikes in Maya. *Careful, girl*, she admonishes herself. She's committed a real sin now. And in the pocket of her full Prada skirt is evidence, the BlackBerry she somehow has to get back to Marcus before it's known she has it and people start asking questions.

Even Colin can't meet her eye, which is a misery. But his anger seems to be less about what Maya did last night than the fallout.

Turns out, it's not just the other Sterlings who know about the unsanctioned field trip.

Rory arrived with an early report on the day's news, much of it stemming from the homepage of *Parler*, the brash celebrity news website. As of 3:00 a.m., anyone visiting Parler.com is met with a huge picture of Maya and Gigi dancing in the club. Arms thrown ecstatically into the air. Teetering in heels across the village street to the waiting vehicles. And the headline: *Sterling's New Heiress Parties On.*

Maya blinks, trying to take this in. *Sterling's New Heiress?*

She skims the page Rory has printed out, and the reality of it comes down over Maya in cascades. The story isn't just about how Gigi and Maya were out getting loose; it's about how Arianna left Maya everything. The story makes it seem like she just found out she won the lottery, and the first thing she did was go to the closest club to celebrate.

Helen waits for everyone to take a bite, daintily spoons some yogurt into her mouth, before asking, with cool command, "Who's the leaker?"

Everyone in the room turns in Maya's direction.

This looks bad. Is bad. "It wasn't me," Maya says, leveling her gaze at Helen. Her mind reels back to the crowded dance floor, the people lining the bar. Anyone could've snapped a pic and cashed in. But her being the heiress? Maya glances at Gigi, who is wearing massive opaque Prada shades, apparently uninterested in explaining how it happened, how Maya ended up at a disco last night. "Gigi, you were there; who do *you* think it was?"

Gigi pushes her glasses down her nose. "No one ever cared about where I spent my evenings," she says. "Back in the old days when I had more shares in my family business than a random girl from Long Island."

"We're not talking about the pictures of your little spree," Helen says aridly. "No one is surprised to see Maya drunk in a club. Or you, Gigi, for that matter. We are talking about the inheritance cockup. This was supposed to stay under wraps until we get it sorted."

Gigi lets one brow stay aloft a good long while. "Oh. *That.*" Gigi smirks at Maya, and in that moment, the obvious truth crashes down on her head. It was Gigi, of course, with a little help from her friend, Willy—the photo editor at *Parler*. Maya was a fool to think Gigi *just* wanted to let off steam and meet an old flame at the club. She remembers the vitriol of Gigi's conversation, the one Maya overheard in the garage. Gigi must have slipped him some evidence, given a firsthand account. Even a reporter for a salacious tabloid like *Parler* still has to do their due diligence. They wouldn't have run a piece of gossip this big without something to back it up. And Gigi wouldn't have risked an email chain that could implicate her. The only thing Maya can't figure out is *why*. Just to fuck things up for Maya?

Maya's hangover surges as she stands from the table and attempts a mask of indifference. She steps over to the coffee carafe, turning her back to pour herself a large mug while deftly slipping Marcus's phone among the breakfast foods.

"It wasn't me, Hels," Gigi says, shoveling eggs into her open mouth. "Certainly no one *in the family*, no one who really cared about *Arianna*, would have wanted to make her questionable final wishes public in such a tawdry manner."

"No." As Helen lifts her teacup from its saucer, her jaw makes a clicking sound. "Well. Nothing to be done about that now."

"Nothing?" Colin asks. Is he having a hard time looking at Maya as she retakes her seat, or is Maya having a hard time looking at him? She's not sure. Maybe she's afraid for him to really see what's behind her eyes. "I know a lot of influential people read *Parler*, but it doesn't have *that* much reach; surely we can keep the story from spreading—"

"Not likely." Marcus cuts Colin off. As he speaks, Marcus's hand drifts toward his jacket pocket, ready to pull out his phone and start tapping away, strategizing a plan to deal with this latest PR crisis. "Has anyone seen my—"

At that moment, a pretty maid refilling the sugar lifts Marcus's BlackBerry in the air. "It was on the breakfast buffet," she says as she brings it over, places it in his hand.

Maya feels like an idiot, and she's not sure Marcus quite believes he set his phone down as he was getting his plate, especially as his eyes stray her way. He knows he didn't bring it to breakfast. But then, is he really going to share that?

"I must have dropped it," Marcus says, taking the phone from her outstretched hand. Then he waves his arm, moving on seamlessly as if he hasn't just realized that a dirty little thief stole his phone and had it all night.

"Let's not make this a bigger story than it already is by clumsily throwing our weight around," Marcus says. It's disarming how calm he is. Colin winces, but nods at his cousin's command. "Let the story play out and give it a chance to die a natural death."

Marcus eyes Maya for a moment—perhaps a moment too long—and her face reddens. She wonders if this is exactly what he said behind her back while she was being flown to Portas Brancas and the tabloids were profiting mightily off her pain. *Let it play out.* She feels smacked by the easy cruelty.

"Yes," says Gigi aridly. "Let us all pray for a natural death."

———

Back in the nursery suite, Colin finally looks Maya full in the face. "What the fuck, Maya."

"I'm sorry." The words come easily, because they're true. "I never should've gone out. Your sister is a lot more persuasive than I gave her credit for." As long as the scandal getting out is Gigi's fault, Maya figures she may as well blame her for everything else too.

Colin sighs. "You're a mother now; you can't keep doing this."

Angry heat rises through her chest. She wants to remind him how he went out partying in Puerto Vallarta, wrathfully spit out, *And you're not a* father *now?* But she manages to temper her tone. "Is this really about what people are going to say?"

"No! That's not what I mean." He pushes his hair off his forehead. She notices the skin under his eyes is creased and pink. There's a fresh bit of stubble on his jaw. He opens and closes his mouth, searching for words. "I *worry*, okay? I want you to be safe. Becca and I need you."

She softens, remorse parting her lips. "Of course. I know. I really am sorry. Those photos are misleading—the night was actually very tame."

Does he sense there's more? That the real guilt has nothing to do with what happened at the club but what happened *after*?

"Just please don't get caught up in this game." He pulls her to him, tightens his arms around her, kisses her hair. "You know how I feel about the press."

Maya should be relieved, she knows, that Colin isn't angry anymore—that he's protective of her, not asking questions, not blundering toward the truth.

She's a traitor. A liar. It would break him. And then he'd take Becca away forever.

The dread is a constant throbbing in her gut.

———

By afternoon, the shitstorm comes raging over Sterling Park.

The London Standard is printing a special evening edition with the image of Maya dancing in the club. Gigi's been cut out, which makes Maya look even worse and, ironically, infuriates her sister-in-law further. Headline: *What Do We Really Know about Maya Sterling?* Tomorrow, all the London papers will be running debriefs on Maya—her humble beginnings, her tawdry introduction to the public sphere, her suspect arrival into the realms of the power elite.

So far, the public seems to be divided on the implications of Maya inheriting everything from the murdered heiress. The blogs and gossip sites speculate: Is she a conniving gold digger who wrapped herself around a great fortune like a snake? Or is she an everygirl who found herself living a fairy tale?

Rory has a more robust team, suddenly: lawyers, consultants, public relations specialists. Early drafts of tomorrow's top news stories have been procured and are being analyzed from every angle.

A war room progresses through assorted parlors and salons. As the CEO, Marcus is hustled from room to room, the strategy teams seeking his input on suggested maneuvers. Which means Maya has exactly zero chance to get him alone and ask about Portas Brancas—about how much he really knew about why Arianna was sent away, and what happened to her after she escaped.

Despite the PR disaster this presents for the family, all this commotion feels bizarrely comforting. It almost reminds her of an earlier phase of fame, when it was still novel, a fun game she was playing. And she's reminded, too, of the days she reclined naked in hotel rooms, listening to Marcus belittle politicians, concierges, the editors of rival papers. She has that old instinct— with chaos, comes opportunity.

The PR people put word out about an upcoming board meeting, an effort to show that the family isn't being secretive. The shareholders will be informed of the possible changes in company ownership in due course. Marcus, apparently deciding that tamping down the media vitriol toward Maya is in the best interest of the company after all, gets flattering counternarratives about Maya placed in a few papers. She takes a phone interview with a folksy and beloved gossip columnist, plays up her humble beginnings. Maya finds it easy to summon all her charm, put on a fascinating performance. The online sites eat it up.

By afternoon tea, the atmosphere has reached a high turbulence. The paparazzi have figured out where Maya is, and they've descended on the perimeter of the property. In another time and place, Maya would have been gratified to find herself the beating heart of the whole operation, would've been turned on by those people clambering at the gates for her story, readers demanding more Maya.

But now, as she stirs sugar into her Darjeeling, she feels like her mind has gotten caught up in the swirl too. What dangers are arising that she hasn't noticed yet? Who's a threat; who's a friend?

Was this how Arianna felt in her final days at Sterling Park— her suspicions mounting, not knowing who to trust, not even her own mind?

Helen rises from the corner of the room where she's been conducting a hushed phone conversation and hangs up abruptly, startling everyone as she tosses her mobile on the table and roughly clears her throat.

"Well," she says.

The discussions around the room break off. Everyone shifts. The room reorients toward Helen. Maya has a deep instinct to roll her eyes.

Helen, crossing her arms tightly across her chest, puts her attention on Maya. "Now you've done it," she says.

Is Helen shaking? Is that anger flushing her face pink? Or fear? "The headlines have reached Harry. He's raging, says he's going to have to fix this disaster personally. He's arriving tonight."

Maya freezes.

Marcus pushes his shoulders against his chairback.

Colin massages his temples.

The corners of Gigi's mouth flex in amusement.

"Oh dear," says Julian.

Harry, the man conspicuously absent from his own estate in the wake of his daughter's murder. The golden boy. The loner. The man who everyone says follows his own rules.

Harry, who, Maya believes, is a killer, maybe twice over.

A slow, painful swallow moves down Helen's white neck. She braces herself against the table. Helen's power intimidates Maya, but it's even more disturbing to see her quivering at the thought of someone else.

To Barrow, in a voice low with significance, Helen says: "Prepare the staff. Mr. Sterling will be returning to Silver House."

30

This morning I woke up feeling something I haven't felt in a long time. Maybe ever. It's the most wild feeling, truly—as though I could fly, see through walls, read a book in seconds without even opening the cover.

This feeling—it's freedom.

Not to be confused with real, practical freedom. No. It's the kind of freedom I imagine a person feels when they glance away from the road for a moment and, whoopsie, their car sails off a cliff and they see suddenly for sure that it's the end, but at least they don't have to go back to that dead-end job and that nasty marriage. At least they are feeling something *real* for once. Even if it's just blood gushing, heart beating with terror.

Because, here's the thing, I finally get it. *Nothing matters.*

I stay here, I'm going to die alone.

I go out there, and I will die alone. Perhaps a little sooner.

I tell the truth, I get zapped all over again.

I hide the truth, and I slowly let myself die inside.

But the outcome is the same. For everyone in all the world.

Death, the great inevitable. Lord Equalizer. All that matters is my readiness, my willingness to do what is right, no matter the consequences. I'm free of caring, free of the false belief that any of it matters a whit.

What shall I do with this freedom?

The only person who makes me feel a little bit not alone is Dr. Caro.

So I went to dear Dr. Caro for our two o'clock session and began thusly: "I remember."

I remember not just my lusty man hunk of a teenage boyfriend Lyman, but what he taught me—about fake IDs and how to look for the squiggly lines to know if they're real. I remember what I heard—how I couldn't erase the words from my mind, couldn't cover over them mentally the way I covered over so many cassette tapes in those years, when I was trying to record songs from the radio.

I remember how, right before I came here to Portas Brancas, I found proof. Hard evidence of what my father had done.

Or at least, the man I thought was my father. Now I don't know *what* he was. The only words that come to mind are *monster, liar, murderer, thief.* He stole it all, everything. He stole my life.

And the craziest part is that when I told Dr. Caro, she had the gall to look at me and say, "Good."

"Good?" I must have looked like a madwoman—slack mouthed, bug-eyed, etc. "How is any of this *good?*"

"Now that you remember, you're ready."

"Ready for what?"

Her dark eyes changed, the empathy burned off by some more intense emotion. Anger, maybe.

"To get out of here," she said.

Which is why I'm writing in here now, at the dead of night. Waiting for her to come, as promised, to take me away.

PART V

31

Colin takes Maya's arm to lead her into the east drawing room, where the family has gathered before the supper hour to wait for the latest arrival. This room boasts a massive fireplace, tall enough for a man to stand inside. Maya feels the warmth, the solidness of Colin's arm laced with hers. It's good, she thinks. Possibly the only good thing about this day, but she'll take it. They *look* unified (even if that's not entirely how it feels). Like the power couple they are, and a very sharply dressed one at that. But there's an ever-widening distance between them that physical proximity can do nothing to close.

Maya's eyes drift across the room to where Marcus is chatting with his father, both sitting cross-legged in stuffed chairs, the border collies in a heap at Julian's feet. Eva hovers nearby, a whiskey in hand, boredom immobilizing her face. She must feel Maya's gaze, because suddenly Eva gives Maya a knowing glare. For a moment, Maya sees the woman who, once upon a time, managed to captivate Marcus Sterling. She slides her hand down her husband's arm with easy intimacy and sends a pointed glance

Maya's way before erupting into laughter at whatever joke Julian's just told. *You may have gotten your dirty hands on the Sterling fortune,* her gestures seem to say, *but this is mine.*

Looks like Maya will not be getting a chance to pull Marcus aside tonight to demand information about Portas Brancas.

"You want your usual?"

Colin's voice at her elbow brings Maya's attention back. She's grateful to find nothing like Eva's aggression in his soft hazel eyes and braces herself for another swell of self-loathing. How could she risk something so pure? This kind, fiercely loyal man, so sincere that his own grandfather used to joke he must be a changeling because he showed none of the toxic guile the rest of his family possessed.

"Thanks, I think I'll just stick to water tonight."

Colin nods, a small smile forming. And in that moment, their partnership feels real, and she's confident that she can put Marcus behind her, bury last night's mistake, let the wound heal over.

But Colin's approval isn't the only reason to stay sober this evening. Harry Sterling is due around seven, just in time for dinner.

Between PR strategy sessions, Maya observed the household staff preparing for the master's arrival under Barrow's meticulous supervision. Maya wonders if the maids were instructed to dust Harry's long-abandoned office, the one with Arianna's little nook and the Blackburne artifacts hidden beneath the floorboards.

At the bar cart, Helen engages Colin in conversation. Their discussion seems benign but Maya decides to make her way to the other side of the room to avoid her wrath. She'll just park on one of the brocaded sofas and stay out of trouble for once.

But trouble finds her anyway in the form of Gigi plopping down beside her.

"Hello, Nancy Drew."

"Fuck you, Gigi," Maya whispers. "I know you used Willy to leak the story about me to the press. What's the point? Do you really think you can frame me as some kind of murderous gold digger and ascend the family hierarchy in my place?"

"Christ, Maya, you sound fucking insane." Gigi sinks into the sofa and fishes a cherry from her highball glass. "You want to know why people keep calling you crazy? Because you *say crazy shit*. You think I don't know I'm never going to be on top in this family? I'm never going to get handed the top spot, or even fun jobs like Marcus and Colin. That's why I have to crawl my own way up."

"What does that mean?" Maya asks. Before she gets an answer, she's distracted by a disturbance out in the hall. Voices, feet running, a fleet of staff on the move. She glances at the ornate clock on the mantelpiece; the skin of her arms prickles. It's 6:52 p.m.

"It *means*," Gigi says—paying no mind to the sounds from the hallway, tilting her glass and draining the last of its liquid— "that if I play my cards right, I'll be the next editor in chief of *Parler*."

Maya's attention whips from the noises in the hall back to Gigi. "*Parler*?"

"Celebrity news, big ideas, lifestyle," Gigi rattles off, as though Maya's surprise is just unfamiliarity with the publication. Then she heaves a sigh and lowers her voice. "*Parler*'s editor in chief is retiring soon, and she's going to recommend me to fill her seat. I mean, I have the sensibility, and I've been quite helpful in providing her leads. You know, all those stories my family's publications won't print."

"Oh." So, all this drama was just a side effect of Gigi's extracurricular ambitions. It makes sense. Maya remembers that feeling she had in the club, that Gigi is smarter than anyone gives her credit for. She'd have to do something with all that frustrated ambition and intelligence. Maya just wishes that thing wasn't at her expense and is about to tell Gigi to fuck off and find somebody else to gossip about, when the agitated sounds out in the hallway become undeniable and draw her attention fully toward the door.

The dogs at Julian's feet have become alert. A lifted head, a muted growl. One darts through the door and the other follows.

"What's this?" Julian says, launching himself off the chair.

Out in the hall, in a voice deep and loud: "Where the fuck *is* she?"

There's more scuffling, doors banging open, the dogs begin to bark vociferously, their snarls in the great cavern of the entry hall. "Get those damn dogs away from me!" the man in the hall—Harry, who else could it be?—cries, and there follows an earsplitting blast that can only be a gunshot, followed by an explosive crashing of metal and glass.

Maya is on her feet. She whirls, searching for Colin, but he's already at her side.

Travis, who must have been hovering at the room's perimeter, tells everyone to stay put and quick-steps to the door, hand on his holster.

The shouting in the hall grows louder. Then they hear Travis call out, "All clear," and the Sterling family hurries into the foyer.

Maya grips Colin's hand as they approach the grand entrance. One of the chandeliers has burst spectacularly upon the polished wood floor. The dogs have been leashed and are being pulled away from the shards sprayed across the floor. Numerous servants in uniform circle the wreckage, trying to figure out how best to proceed. In a moment, Maya understands their hesitation.

Helen is swanning forward, approaching a man wearing a tan duster and an enormous fur hat. Maya thinks of the portrait of Harry in the second-floor west wing hall—that long fine face. He's made a real hash of it. The nose is pinched, the cheekbones angular. The way the rich indulge in plastic surgery is, to Maya, a true mystery. There's something ghoulish in his appearance now, after what appears to be successive shavings, lifts. But despite the ravages of time and the knife, Maya recognizes him from the portrait, his handsome features, unmistakably similar to those of the woman Maya met in the Iguana Bar. Arianna.

"Harry dear." Helen's voice is round with faux warmth.

Harry gestures with the pistol, which Maya sees is still in his hand. Helen sees it too. She stops moving toward him, and they regard each other at a remove.

The servants are watching Helen and Harry, more wary than fearful, probably trying to determine who's really in charge.

Helen sings out a laugh. "Harry, you bad boy, what a needless fuss."

"Oh I think a fuss is quite needed." Harry also laughs, not in a way that puts anyone at ease. "You said you had everything here under control. But clearly not. Now—*where* is she? Where's the scheming little slapper who stole everything? Where is Maya Miller?"

Maya hovers. Searching for help, her gaze falls on Marcus, grim-faced and uncharacteristically rooted in place. Her anxiety billows, her mind thrums with trying to identify the nearest escape route. But before she can take a step, Colin pulls her back, maneuvers his body protectively between his wife and his uncle. "Hello, Harry. I'm thrilled to introduce you to my wife. But I believe the supper hour is upon us, and I imagine you want to wash up first."

Harry sneers, his mouth puckering around some argument, or insult. But before he can speak, Colin issues a stern, "Get this cleaned up, will you?" to the staff before drawing Maya back into the parlor, out of the high beam of Harry's glare.

———

The walls of Silver House's formal dining room are covered in burgundy velvet, decorated with antique muskets and the heads of long-dead beasts. Down the center of an oblong cherrywood table, a line of taper candles has been lit.

Waiters circulate with bottles of red and bottles of white. The conversation moves from luxury luggage to liquid diets. Harry is performing the worldly host, the man with the definitive line on everything—word on the street in Moscow, mining in Congo, factories in Shenzhen.

Maya accepts a refill and experiences that hot tingle of being scrutinized. Glancing up, she sees Harry staring at her from his perch at the head of the table. When she meets his eye, he lifts his glass in a sort of salute.

Is he toasting a worthy adversary?

Or wordlessly saying:

You had a good run, girl, but it's all over now.

Once everyone's been served, Harry, at the head of the table, stands and clinks a butter knife to his glass. "First of all," he begins, blessedly not looking in Maya's direction, "I hope you'll all forgive my rather theatrical arrival."

"You always did put on a good show, Uncle Harry." Gigi grins and lifts her glass.

Harry gives a little bow of the head. "A toast to our dear Arianna. To my daughter." He lowers his eyes. The room murmurs Arianna's name, drinks to her memory. "My sweet girl," he says, face contorting. "My only heir."

There's a venomous note in this final bit that makes Maya's stomach tighten.

Does Helen hear it too? "To my brother," she says. She touches her glass to Harry's and archly adds, "In his time of need."

"Oh yes." Harry's sardonic words travel through gritted teeth. "You've really been ringing me up nonstop, asking what you can do, what I might need."

"Well," Helen replies, matching his sarcasm, "I'm just tremendously pleased you managed to leave that bordello of yours and join your loved ones at last."

If Maya weren't so on edge with Harry's arrival, she might find this amusing—the tartness and venom, this business about a bordello. Helen can't mean that literally, can she? Maya glances around the room, wondering if the rest of the Sterlings will turn away from this sibling spat.

No one does.

Harry sneers. "Is that what you hoped for? That I would be in mourning, and you could manipulate everything while I grieved?"

"Grief." Helen spits out the word. "This has nothing to do with your *grief*. If you were really mourning, you would have been here four days ago. This is about business."

"Yes." Harry fixes his eyes on Helen. His upper lip curls. He seems to have taken her measure, decided he has the edge. "This *is* about business. It's about my legacy. For the record it is not a *bordello*," Harry adds. "And we all grieve in different ways."

Helen's expression tightens. She puts her glass down on the table with too much force, shattering the crystal base. Maya hears the breakage as though it were happening inside her own head, as though the jagged pieces were terrifyingly close to her own neck. What was the meaning of the expression that flicked across

Helen's face? It reminds Maya of that side of Helen she glimpsed briefly, the first night she arrived, in Arianna's room.

But it's gone in the next instant, and Helen curses, brushing away the wetness of the wine on the table. She must catch a shard, because she gasps and cherry red droplets spring from her fingertips. A waiter rushes to blot and press a cloth against the wound, but Helen scarcely acknowledges this. With irritated self-justification, she says, "We felt very tenderly toward Arianna."

Harry savagely quotes: "'How tender 'tis the babe that milks me…'"

"Harry, don't," Helen warns with icy exasperation, examining her fresh cuts.

Gigi leans toward Colin and whispers, "Christ, are they really going to do this? *Now?*"

But Harry persists, chewing and spitting out the words: "'I would, while it was smiling in my face/ Have pluck'd my nipple from his boneless gums, and dashed the brains out, had I so sworn as you have done to this.'"

"Jesus," Helen mutters.

"Shakespeare, actually," Harry says in a correcting tone. "Lady Macbeth. By *it* she means *baby*. Some scholars interpret those lines as signifying that the Macbeths lost a child in infancy, as was of course common in medieval Scotland." Harry breaks off. His gaze sweeps over his family members. Then he smiles, as if at a private bit of rude humor, stands, begins to pace around the table.

With alarm, Maya realizes he's advancing in her direction. He rounds one end of the table, pauses just outside her peripheral vision. Maya feels what he must want her to feel—vulnerable to attack, like prey. But she summons her grit, the resolve of the little girl who's saved herself from worse. She pushes her chair back, faces him, unwilling to appear afraid.

He pauses, arms crossed over his chest like a professor in thought. "What do you think, Maya? Or do you Americans not read Shakespeare in school?"

In fact, Maya has read *Macbeth*, along with all the other plays in that beautiful, pilfered volume her father deemed worthless. There's this one line she thinks of all the time. She wrote it over and over on the inside cover of her spiral-bound notebook, illustrated it with a ballpoint doodle of a rose. During her years playing the femme fatale on *The Springs*, that line was a kind of mantra. Maya sips her wine with as much nonchalance as she can muster, then meets Harry's gaze. "'Look like the innocent flower, but be the serpent under it.'"

"Oh ho!" says Harry. "Colin, you didn't tell us your little wife was a *scholar*."

Colin grimaces at Harry but says nothing. Maya's insides are at a snapping boil, and she presses her lips together, trying to contain her anger.

Harry rests one hand on the table next to Maya's fork, his massive gold cuff link, ornately carved with an ancient insignia, glinting in the candlelight. "That's exactly what you are, isn't it? A snake. I've known people like you. People always scheming for a free lunch. Frauds in expensive clothes. Trust me, people like that always get what's coming to them in the end."

Maya remembers Julian's description of Mikey Blackburne—always on the wrong side of the law, until fate caught up to him and he perished in that fire.

Not fate, Maya thinks. *Harry Sterling.*

He's leaning closer now, his breath hot on the shell of Maya's ear. "I see it in you, Maya. You're nothing but a common thief. Just like your father." Maya goes rigid, wills her body to show no sign of intimidation, though a mighty effort is necessary to keep her hands from shaking. *Who is this man to judge her?*

"That's enough," Colin says, and Maya is grateful, even if she hates the reedy voice in which he speaks.

"Nothing is official yet," Helen says. One servant is tweezing glass shards from her hand; another attends to the red splatters on the carpet, collects the red-stained rags. In a lighter tone of recitation she concludes: "'Blood will have blood.' As I was saying, the lawyers are reviewing Arianna's will. Due diligence—it's to be expected."

"'Oh, the lawyers! The lawyers!'" chirps Harry in a girlish tone. In his own, deep growl: "To hell with lawyers. To hell with the chair*woman* of the board."

"If you didn't like the way I've been running things," Helen says hotly, "you could've come back at any time. Instead of hiding God knows where all these years. Instead of leaving me to clean up your messes, as usual."

This rebuke seems to smack Harry. He pauses, absorbing it.

Then he shifts into a lower gear. No less prancing and intense, but quieter. He's completed the circle, returned to the head of the table, to Helen's side.

"I think we both know, duck, that that is not entirely true." With jarring gentleness, he shoos away the servants and performs the final wrappings of her bandage.

Helen sucks in breath—surprised either at his touch or some vile subtext.

When he finishes taping her up, Helen speaks in a wondering tone. "'In what distant deeps or skies, burnt the fire of thine eyes?'"

She's quoting something new, Maya can hear it in her voice, but she doesn't think this is Shakespeare. Too singsongy and mystical.

As Harry puts an old-fashioned kiss on Helen's knuckles, she continues in the same tone, "'On what wings dare he aspire/ What the hand, dare seize the fire?'"

Maya glances at Colin, hoping for some guidance. But he's staring at the hearth, the roaring flame just beyond the head of the table. He appears dazed and transported to the past. They all do. In the next moment, the Sterlings are quoting, with feeling, the poetry Maya recognizes from the walls of the nursery suite:

"'Tyger, Tyger, burning bright/ in the forests of the night/ What immortal hand or eye/ Dare frame thy fearful symmetry?'"

The words, spoken in unison, have the sound of an incantation. Maya feels cast under a powerful spell, under the sway of ancient, invisible forces. And echoing against the walls is Arianna's version, a child's frightful reinterpretation. Maya wants to scream. Wants to interrupt this strange, fucked-up interlude. Wants to flip the long table on its end and shut up every Sterling, with their stupid formalities and their creepy poems.

"Know that one, Maya?" Harry asks.

Maya is jolted from the moment and tries not to appear as unsettled as she is by the chanting. "Yes, it's on the wallpaper in our room. Blake."

Harry's smiles glints and spreads. "Indeed, Blake from the wallpaper. Very good, Maya the Scholar."

Colin's gaze finally does rise to meet Maya's, and for a moment she glimpses him as a little boy, a stranger among his fearsome family.

"Why do you all know it?" Maya asks. "What's so special about that poem that you each got told it like a bedtime story?"

"Oh, they just thought it had a nice rhyme scheme," Harry says dismissively, at the same time as Helen says, "It's about the duality of Man."

Julian, who had risen to refresh his drink at the bar cart, breaks the tension, softly quoting: "'The small gilded fly does lecher in my sight.'" The room's attention swings toward him. His mouth purses around the words as he continues to quote. "'Let copulation thrive.'"

"What's that about a fly?" Harry asks.

And what's that about copulation? Maya thinks.

"*Lear*," Gigi says, as though this is all very tiresome, as though

341

she's the bored brightest student in the class. "You know, the play about the king whose daughters tried to kill him."

Helen's eyes blaze in her husband's direction. "Julian, do shut up."

"I was only talking about Harry's bordello," Julian replies defensively.

"Enough!" Helen roars. She seems to be emerging from a trance, shaking away the previous moment. "Come on, let's have another round." With a languid toss of her fingers through the air, she sends the waiters back around the room refilling empty glasses.

Harry gives Helen's hand one last pat, then turns to address the rest of the table. "I regret I *have* been away from Sterling Park too long. But I'm back now. This is a time of sorrow, but we must find ways to be together, enjoy what we have. What say we have a little fun tomorrow for once? It looks like the pond has frozen solid. We're long overdue for a skating party. We'll put a good face on things. The Sterling family in top form."

Colin leans toward Maya and quickly explains the tradition Harry is referring to, a tradition Colin's grandfather started decades ago. When the pond freezes, the gates of Sterling Park are thrown open and the local villagers invited to come and skate.

It sounds lovely enough, but Maya doesn't want any part of it—she doesn't want to be in the same place as Harry any more than she must.

"We'll invite some press, all friendlies, of course. Marcus, I'll let you sort that out," Harry says. "We'll do it tomorrow.

Let's show the world that Harry Sterling is back. That our family is ancient and noble and we won't be brought down." He looks right at Maya, before adding, "I, for one, *never* go down without a fight."

32

Next day, a blanket of ice crystals glimmers on the lawns and statues and paths of Sterling Park, as if even the weather has bent to Harry Sterling's command. The pond, situated on a picturesque plot on the far side of the greenhouse, is a hard metallic oval. The air is astonishingly cold and dry. Maya, layered in borrowed Sterling clothes, feeling shaky, steps out onto the snow.

Look calm, she tells herself.

Look like you suspect nothing. Look like "the innocent flower"—or at the very least, an idiot American.

The staff have set up a white tent for guests, white tables laden with refreshments, and built fires in iron braziers for warmth. The cold has a way of effacing all the modern updates of the place. If Maya had a picture of this tableaux, cropped in the right way, it might seem a hundred years old.

A member of the staff appears, drapes Maya in a fur coat. Colin steps away from Marcus, gestures for her to join him, filling Maya with relief and shame. As Maya approaches, she notes Harry's position in the group. He's swathed in head-to-toe sable, topped with a hat worthy of a Muscovite. The fur coats are part of the tradition, Colin explains. There's enough for all the commoner guests. A great display of Sterling largesse.

Maya is amazed at this. One or two days a year of being treated like royals was apparently enough for the nearby villagers to tolerate pauperism the rest of the year. That's the kind of compromise Maya has never been able to accept. Yet the scene at the pond *is* cheerful. The local people are delighted to be wearing these extravagant furs, to be gliding across the smooth surface of the pond on borrowed skates, laughing and red-cheeked, excited to be close to the glamour of money and scandal.

A few photographers have been let in and are being given the same treatment as the other guests. Fur coats, hot beverages, a heaping platter of scones and fat berries freshly airlifted from some faraway place. Harry is playing host, buzzing from the journalists to the local butcher to the farmers' children, asking if everyone is warm enough, has what they need, if they are enjoying themselves.

It would be heartwarming, if Maya didn't feel compelled to see it all through Arianna's eyes. Sterling Park, a very impressive and lethal mirage.

As one of the servants helps Maya into skates, her eyes track Harry, marking where he goes in the crowd. She doesn't want him out of her sight line—doesn't want him to sneak into her peripheral vision and disappear. The presence of cameras, his performance of bonhomie—she doesn't trust any of it.

Harry approaches Helen, does an elegant bow. Then they

glide onto the ice together hand in hand, just as they probably did as children: brother and sister, the local aristocrats showing their lowly neighbors how the *haves* live.

Helen's eyes are sparkling, but also wary. Harry's hand is low on her back, steering. There is something between them that Maya can only characterize as *knowing*. It reminds her of how she used to be with her father—more co-conspirator than daughter.

Aligned, but mistrusting.

What do you know, Helen?

Maya surveys the rest of the scene. There's Gigi, jokingly encouraging everyone to put rum in their tea. Lance and Ian are running in circles, manic, unsure what to do with other kids their own age.

Eva corrals the boys and leads them onto the frozen pond. She looks impressive in ermine. Those handsome features framed in a pouf of white fur.

"Will you be all right for a minute?" Colin asks, handing her—bless him—a warm cup of coffee. "There's a reporter from *The Observer* I've been hoping to connect with. I want to pitch a feature on our CDMTech deal."

"Go ahead, I'll be fine."

What else can she say? *Don't leave me alone with your uncle out here—he's probably a murderer, and he's leering at me like he'd very much like to do me in.*

Maya watches Colin trudge across the snow-covered lawn, then becomes aware of a presence beside her, where Colin had been moments before.

"Hello." Marcus doesn't look bad in fur, either. There's something of the oligarch in his appearance this afternoon. Powerful, handsome, a little outside the law.

They stand side by side, looking out onto the frozen pond, not making eye contact. Maya knows what it would betray if they did. Even without looking at him, even in the early swirls of falling snow tingling against her bare face, she feels the heat off him. But any stray photographer who captured an image of them now would see two cordial distant relatives politely enjoying the spectacle together. Effortfully maintaining this illusion, Maya says, "You knew Arianna was at Portas Brancas."

A wintry gust blows between them, lifting flurries of fallen snow. Marcus sips from his own mug, says nothing.

"Did you know that's where they sent me too? After Miami?"

When Marcus answers, he keeps his eyes trained on the ice, where his boys are now chasing their mother around the rink. "I suspected after the fact. The fixers, they have their usual places, their contacts. But I didn't *know* that's what they were going to do. I wouldn't have—" He breaks off, and Maya senses how much he wants to turn and look her full in the face. "If I had known, I wouldn't have let you be sent somewhere like that. You weren't crazy, you were just…lost. *I* was lost. I'd just barely become CEO and I was worried that Eva suspected us, that the affair would come out and everything would be ruined."

"Did Eva know?"

Marcus pauses. "Yes, she figured it out. She was a good investigative reporter herself once—she knew how to track that kind of information down. It's all right. She isn't sentimental—she just used the information to renegotiate our terms."

The realization digs into Maya's belly. All those years ago, when he seemed to abandon her, really his hand was forced. "Of your marriage?"

"What she gets, if we divorce. You should be glad—it means she can't tell anyone, not even *Colin*; she'd lose everything if she did."

Maya winces at the mention of the husband she's betrayed, though she's relieved too. Eva knows. But she can't tell. "And that's why you ran that headline about me," she murmurs. "To prove that it was over."

"Yes. I'm sorry. It was a mistake. Maya, I can't stop thinking about you," he says. "The terms with Eva, after she found out about us—they aren't great, but they aren't bad, and now, with your holdings…" Marcus's grin hitches up at Maya, and she knows that if anyone captured a photo of them now, it would be obvious, the whole sordid history written on their faces. "Let's do it. You and me. We could rule everything, together."

She wonders if he can even separate what he feels for her and what he feels for his family's business, the whole manic pursuit of power and profit, or if for him conquest is all one mad impulse.

Maybe he guesses her thoughts, because he adds, "I love you, you know."

Does she love him? She's never really asked herself. She's only wondered if he loved her, like a little girl pulling petals off a daisy.

Her heartbeat is expectant, her skin is yearning for his touch. She loves him, why deny it?

But what kind of girl would she be if she gave in to that?

And where would it leave Becca?

Maya's own mother wasn't much of a mom, and she caused Maya as much pain as anything else. But she taught her daughter one valuable lesson. She, Maya's mother, didn't want a dead-end life as the long-suffering helpmate of a gambler thief, a petty crook, with his colorful, overbearing sister and ruinous schemes. She had a vision for herself that didn't include her oldest child. And she went out, made that life a reality. In so doing she showed Maya that Maya's life was her own too, to do with as she pleased.

But Maya can't think about that now. She moves a little away from Marcus, forces him toward the other questions she needs answered, away from the impossible romantic situation she's created for herself. "What about Arianna? What about the things she claimed to know about this family? Crimes she said she had proof of—is any of that true?"

At this, Marcus does turn to meet Maya's eye. His brow goes taut, then smooths in recognition. "Arianna was troubled. She was crazy, okay? I mean, you've seen Harry now for yourself— can you imagine growing up with a father like that?"

Maya hates to admit that she can. Her father was never prone to violence (and he *never* would have ruined such an expensive chandelier), but he could be erratic.

"Arianna witnessed a tragedy at a very young age, and it drove her insane," Marcus continues. "We looked into her theories—they were nuts, the rantings of a deranged woman. And if there was any 'proof' of such conspiracies, we would have found them. SterlingCo doesn't leave anything to chance."

Maya's not sure if this is the whole truth—but she's fairly certain that *Marcus* believes it's the truth. She can hear this break of pain in his voice, an effort to earnestly tell her what he knows.

She wants to say more—about what happened two nights ago in the library. About what he just said. About what it does to her—this shattering attention.

But suddenly, Colin is at Maya's elbow. He playfully comments, "Marcus, stop trying to flirt with my wife," which skewers her. Then he's linked arms with Maya, drawing her along with him toward the ice. His cheeks are bright and pink, and he moves with happy ease. Maya allows herself to be pulled away from Marcus and things unsaid about the mystery of Arianna Sterling and the dark mass of her own heartbreak.

Colin is skating backward now, showing off. He's so boyish and delighted she almost catches his joy. But then she realizes that in the sea of faces surrounding the pond and under the tent, there is one that is now glaringly absent. Harry's gone. He must have slipped away sometime while she was speaking to Marcus. Was that his plan all along? Set up the spectacle of the skating party and then use it as a cover to have the house to himself? Is he in there right now, searching for the proof that Marcus has just dismissed as fiction?

Proof that Arianna, when she last lived here, vociferously claimed was in her possession.

Colin is farther from her now, and locals skate in the space that's opened between them. Then Maya sees a face that stops her breath.

Everything in her field of vision—the skaters, the journalists, this family she's married into—slows. Sounds are echoey and far-off. And there, a little bit ahead on the ice, is the woman.

She wears a fur coat like the others but appears not of this world. Maya can see in that fathomless gaze that this woman is not enchanted by the display of wintry spirit. She looks alert, almost soldierly.

But Maya has seen her before. That's what really has her heart hammering.

It's the dark-haired woman hovering in the mirror's reflection in the club bathroom, that night Maya and Gigi snuck out. The one with the scar.

Maya had convinced herself that woman was a hallucination. Yet, here she is, plain as day.

Maya, now shivery with dread, takes an awkward turn on the ice. Has the woman been stalking her all this time, waiting for a chance to get close again?

Then, in the next moment, the woman has come away from the observers on the side of the pond and is skating alongside Maya, saying in a thick country accent, "Maya! I am such an enormous fan!"

The woman's voice is loud with cheer, but Maya hears the erratic undertones as she whispers, "Don't panic or this will all get very, very messy."

Maya smiles thinly, tamping her fear down as best she can. Where are the security people who followed her all the way to club? Why aren't they watching out for the dangers right here?

Before Maya can think how best to play this, the woman speaks, so quietly that Maya wonders if she's hallucinating her words too: "Harry isn't who he says he is."

"What?"

"She knew. She told me. The proof is in the house."

She knew.

Realization sinks in. *She.* As in…Arianna? This woman—the woman with the scar—she *knew* Arianna.

Maya looks at the woman's face, the puckering white curve along the line of her cheekbone, remembering again the phone call with Sarah-Jane. This woman didn't just know Arianna. She's the doctor who broke Arianna out of the asylum.

"Who are you, what do you want?" Maya whispers, trying to keep her voice calm.

"No time for all that," the woman whispers. "We are going to find it together."

"Find what?"

"The tape."

Maya forces a fake smile onto her face even though her pulse is wild.

"Tape? What tape? The ones in Harry's—"

"You're not listening," the woman says. "Harry *isn't Harry*; he's—"

"Maya?" Her name is being called from across the pond. Julian.

Maya glances over her shoulder and sees him skating toward her. The whole episode is so surreal that she isn't even immediately surprised to find the woman has gracefully skated off into the crowd. In the next moment, she's completely disappeared.

"Maya," Julian is saying in an insistent tone. She has the sense that he's been trying to get her attention awhile. He has her by the arm, guiding her across the ice. "There's been a security breach—probably nothing, but they want family members off the ice for now."

"What?" Has she been hallucinating again? The temperature seems to have dropped. The mood has shifted abruptly. A moment ago, all the faces were smiling, but now they're drawn, wary. Or is that her projection? Maya blinks, notices the security team making moves. It feels presumptuous, an overreaction like at the club. Except there *is* an intruder. Maya was just talking to her.

"Are you all right?" Julian is asking. "Was that person harassing you?"

Maya shakes her head. So, Julian saw that dark-haired woman—she wasn't imaginary.

"I—she," Maya begins. "She said she was a friend of Arianna's."

Julian's brows knit together; his voice has a thin urgency she hasn't heard before. "What did she want?"

"She seemed to know something..." Maya trails off. What did that woman mean, *Harry isn't Harry*? "But how could he *not* be Harry?" she murmurs to herself.

"Where is she now?" The blunt sound of Julian's voice jolts

Maya's focus back to the present, to him. To the security team ushering the Sterlings away from the scene, toward the protected house, even as Barrow assures the crowd, telling them to drink up and continue their fun.

"Maya, if that woman knew something about Arianna's death, we need to bring her to speak to the authorities. Which way did she go?"

But Maya has no answer. Icy wind roughs her hair and chaps her face. The woman is gone. Maya can't locate her in the crowd. No figure darts away across the lawn. Nor does she see Harry, who has already been gone awhile.

Perhaps he's inside searching for what the woman just whispered urgently about in Maya's ear—Arianna's proof. *The insurance policy.*

The tape.

33

The chill is on the tip of Maya's nose as she and the other Sterlings are led out of the driving snow and back into Silver House. The hazy romance of the morning has been dashed by the sudden panic. Maya is glad of this excuse to withdraw, but she fears it might be more than it seems. The extravagant ice skating scene, the abrupt interruption—it's all too contrived.

They enter through the great front door and are welcomed by the staff, at the ready in a two-column formation, promising hot toddies and a warm fire.

As the family is funneled in the direction of the nearest parlor, Maya feels an arm interlace with her own.

"What a relief to be back in good old Silver House!" Julian says. "What'll you have? I've been dreaming of a whiskey neat, myself."

But Maya is distracted. There, at the bottom of one of the house's grand staircases, having already shed his fur coat and hat, is Harry. What has he been up to while everyone else was distracted outside? He has a slick, pleased-with-himself, vulpine air.

Maya removes her arm from Julian's and gives him a playful pat. "Do I look a wreck?" she asks.

"Darling, none of us look our best," Julian replies. "The northern climate is unforgiving."

"For some of us more than others. I'll be right in—I'm going to ask that my makeup bag be fetched from my room. Fix me a gin and tonic, will you?"

Julian appraises her. "Are you sure you're all right? Not still shaken up over that girl on the ice?"

Maya forces a grin. She's afraid now that she divulged too much and wishes she could retract her earlier babbling. "I'm fine, I'm fine. I thought she said something ominous, but I must have misheard her—that wind was really something!"

Julian appraises Maya a moment before making a gentlemanly flourish of his hand. "Don't be long," he says.

As soon as she's down the hall, out of view of the others, she hangs a right and begins to run. As she ascends the servants' stairways, her mind churns around a few phrases:

Harry isn't Harry.

The proof is in the house.

The tape.

That email from the Portas Brancas doctor to Marcus, relaying Arianna's "delusions." Sarah-Jane telling Maya how Arianna ranted about liars and frauds and murders.

In Arianna's secret closet, among the treasures she kept under the floorboards, was Mikey Blackburne's watch. His wallet. His brass knuckles. His knife. There were cassettes, too, weren't there? That old Dictaphone on the desk, the drawers full of unspooled tape.

How much time does Maya have? She's moving swiftly down the path to Harry's office. Praying the staff hasn't tidied those items up—or that Harry didn't lock the office upon his return.

Maya finds herself in a more remote area of the house. The air has that heavy, slick chill—a night creature's trail lingering in the atmosphere. Here is the hall with the buckled wallpaper. Sleek navy, embossed with a paisley pattern. Masculine, outdated, water damaged. She has to grip the wall for balance as she throws herself around the corner, entering through the still-open door to Harry's office.

The office has the same harsh energy as when Maya first saw it a few days ago. The Dictaphone is still centered on the massive desk, still coated in dust. It's Maya who's different, whose heart is pounding in her throat, who can scarcely keep her thoughts from hurtling to a thousand conclusions. She grabs the side of the desk, crouches to the drawers. Only then does it occur to her what a monumental task this will be. There are so many tapes, which one is the one that Arianna considered proof?

And Arianna was insane—at least, unstable enough to be committed. A nut, Gigi called her. And was, in any case, just a girl the last time she lived here.

In the next moment, Maya sees that her worries hardly matter. In the drawer where a mess of tapes had been, now there's nothing. She opens every drawer of the desk, all empty. Then she crawls to the little girlish door, the hideaway. The shoe boxes are still there, still ordered in the same way, but they are all empty.

Harry. As she feared, he must've come in and removed the evidence. She feels like an idiot for not following her instincts sooner.

With trembling fingers, she pulls back the floorboard that covered the secret compartment.

Maya exhales. This hiding place hasn't been touched. It's the same collection of objects—an empty wallet, a set of brass knuckles, a watch.

A knife—pewter handle, little dagger blade, protected by a worn bit of leather.

Maya's not sure if these things will be useful, but she doesn't want them to disappear like the tapes. She straps the watch on her wrist, tucks the knife into her waistband.

The watch grabs her attention. She turns it over, runs her thumb over the engraved *Michael Blackburne.* There is an insignia too, of the Blackburnes.

She has seen it recently, but where?

That's when it hits her. The cuff links. The ones Harry had been wearing at dinner last night, when he stalked the table and sneered Shakespeare lines.

Maya has an eye for the expensive. Her father taught her that young. He used to say, "You've got the million-dollar eye, girl." That was back when they both thought a million dollars was an impossible, set-for-life amount of money.

The cuff links Harry wore last night match Mikey's old

watch. But why would Harry have Mikey Blackburne's cuff links after all these years, much less continue wearing them? Were they just another token he took off his dead friend? Or...

Harry is not Harry.

The windowpanes shudder under the force of a brutal wind.

The rattling glass brings back a memory from her first night at Sterling Park, of Barrow stooping to sweep up the broken shards of her shattered highball. Barrow, the silent sentinel who has been in service to the Sterlings his whole life. Who said that Harry came back from La Digue *a different man.*

It's insane, this notion that's crept its way into her head. And yet... *The staff knows everything. They see everything.*

Maya searches her brain, thinks of all she knows about Harry Sterling's early days, the man he was before the fire, before Mikey and Jessica Blackburne met their horrific ends, their bodies burned beyond recognition... In the archive, she read that note from Harry claiming he had no head for Shakespeare—but that Mikey had been an expert.

Maya stands up, blood rushing to her head.

Outside the room, she hears an animal's call. Or is that coming from outside the window? From the grounds? Perhaps there's still a crowd out there, enjoying the Sterling spread by the pond.

The window is closed. She doesn't want to go near it. She has a presentiment of being pushed, of falling and falling and breaking on the pavement.

The story writes itself—the untimely death of an unlikely

heiress. Broken childhood, broken neck. The tragic Sterlings (of whom it is whispered that every loss is an inside job).

She adjusts the knife, making sure the leather is around the blade, not wanting to nick herself, then moves into the hall.

There's the sound once more—but it's just beyond understanding. Not animal, not exactly human, either. She follows it, placing her feet carefully now. Then suddenly she's face-to-face with a little stone-faced girl.

The portrait of young Arianna—no more than four or five years old, the same age she was when the fire raged on La Digue—but posed here, against the yew tree, her gaze opaque, her mouth hard. Those dark eyes so hollow and haunted. The image is close to Harry's heavy office door.

Barrow said: *He came back a changed man.*

When Arianna lived here, there must have been so little separation between them. Perhaps he could even hear her in his office—if she slipped out of bed, maybe the floorboards above his office creaked; if he was on the phone late, perhaps the echo was audible through the ceiling plaster.

You have to think like a teenager, Maya thinks, ascending the little stairs to the garret room. *A very privileged, very trapped teenager. Where would she put this proof? Someone else is looking... but they weren't thinking like her... They were looking where the other tapes were...not where a melodramatic magpie hid her treasures...*

The room is empty when Maya enters, but she can already imagine footsteps pounding up after her. She forces her breath to slow. She's alone; she has a little time. She can find it.

Her feet take her to the bookshelf, to the hidden Blake. She pushes the other books aside, and finds it in the same place.

She spreads the binding, holds it upside down, shakes. Out fall the little folded notes—to Jessica, the dead daughter of Mikey Blackburne.

The girlish homage to Blake's "The Tyger."

A crayon drawing of two girls, holding hands. Both with yellow hair, in gray dresses, one with green eyes, one with brown. Jessica and Arianna, the girls are labeled. Maya touches the picture, wondering at the depth of this obsession. Arianna's only "friend," her dead playmate.

If what Maya has begun to suspect is true, then Arianna was not simply raised in isolation with a volatile and sometimes cruel father. She was raised by her own father's murderer.

Harry is not Harry.

He's *Michael Blackburne.*

Harry's friend turned enemy. Always jealous of Harry, the raging and mercurial man who wanted what his best friend had.

How horrifying must it have been for Arianna—to be parented by someone who was willing to let his own child die by fire so that he could be reborn, assume another man's identity, inherit another man's fortune.

On the other side of the crayon picture, the handwriting— girlish, but no longer a child's—has recorded song lyrics. The same lyrics, several times over, as though she were testing her memory. As though she were learning the refrain by heart.

The eye of the tiger.

The eye of the tiger.

The eye of the tiger.

Again and again and again.

Now, why would that song have been in her head, and why would Arianna have written it over and over again? Just because of the fucking wallpaper?

Then Maya remembers. That night in the Iguana Bar, Arianna humming a song Maya recognized. Had she been trying to tell Maya about the tapes?

Was it Arianna's little memory device? Maya lurches off the floor, into the main space of the bedroom. She moves along the wall, following the patterns of jungle trees, the tigers, feeling in between the tigers' eyes, searching out weak spots. She feels a little deranged, but also deadly certain.

It's a big room, the walls are high. There are so many repetitions of the pattern. So many places for another secret compartment. So many eyes.

Is Maya's theory insane; is she going mad? There would have been so many witnesses to this impossible switch.

And yet Mikey had a criminal's mind and an appetite for lying. He would've figured a workaround—hiding away in Sterling Park alone for almost a decade, letting the image of Harry Sterling as a young man fade from the collective memory. Conducting all his important business over the phone. Having the plastic surgery done in secret, flying the doctors into the regional hospital. Letting his new face settle. Traveling from country to country, never staying in one place long. And all this, years before the internet would make photos of Harry Sterling accessible, just a click away. Could he really have pulled it off?

Not without help, Maya thinks. He must have had co-conspirators. Who else knew, all these years? Who benefited from Mikey stealing Harry's crown?

And then, just there—*is she making it up, or is it real?*—Maya's hand has landed on a softness in the wall, not far from a fringed standing lamp. As if it wants to give. Wild with conviction, she yanks the knife from her waistband, ready to tear into the tiger's face.

"Careful there," says a man.

First she thinks it's Marcus. She slips the knife back, turns to him.

But the figure hovering in the doorway is older than Marcus.

Her pulse spikes at the thought that Harry has her cornered. Then he moves into the light.

"Oh," she says with relief. "Julian."

"You thought I was Harry, didn't you?"

I thought you were Michael Blackburne, she wants to say. She manages a smile. "Yes. I mean, he can't like me very much."

"Well, you're in good company on that score, dear."

"Yeah, well..." Maya glances around. Her heart is pounding. She needs Julian to go away so she can keep searching. She's close, so very close now. But she can't tell him what she's put together, what she's looking for. He might tell Helen, or Marcus. She needs to find this supposed proof, get it away from Sterling Park as soon as possible. She tries to appear cool. "What's up?"

"What's up?" Julian echoes, doing a very bad imitation of Maya's American accent—a vapid Valley girl—and chortling.

I'm from New York, Maya wants to snap back, stuck by his casual cruelty. He's usually so flattering and warm. "I only meant, everything okay down there?"

"Oh yes, everyone relaxing with a nice bevvie. *What's up* with you?" he persists, drawing closer.

"I just keep thinking about Arianna, you know. Nothing particular. Just wishing I understood her better."

"Yes, I understand that. Here—" He moves to pull out the arm tucked behind his back, and Maya instinctively presses herself against the wall. In a moment, he's placed a cool highball in her hand. "I brought you this. Your drink?"

She lets out a breath. "Right. Thanks!"

"You know, my dear, you are looking a little out of sorts..."

"I'm fine, Julian, really. "

"Have a seat, enjoy your drink. Harry is carousing; we have a little time."

"Good idea." Maya takes an anxious gulp of the gin and tonic and finds her way to the mauve chair that Helen had been sitting in, the first night Maya saw this room. As soon as she feels the softness take the weight of her body, she realizes how tired she is. "It's been a hell of a week," she says.

"I know. So much to process, as you Americans say." Julian clinks his own drink to Maya's, perches on the chair's arm, sips.

He's a little *too* close—but of course, Maya is abnormally jumpy, and Julian's never had a strong sense of personal space. "One deserves a nice drink, don't you think?"

"Yeah." Maya nods enthusiastically, robotically takes another sip. But there's something else on the horizon of her consciousness, something not quite right that she's trying to bring into focus.

"You know—when I came in, you were a mite jumpy."

"Really?" Maya has that weightless tingling sensation, as though she's moving through a dream. She knows Julian's body is very close, but his voice sounds a long way off. She has a dim, fearful thought that something is about to go very wrong.

"You were feeling up the walls."

"Oh." Maya takes another gulp of her drink, chews the ice, trying to wake up.

"You know who it reminded me of, Maya?" Julian is asking.

"Who?" There's a dull throbbing in Maya's head.

"Her."

34

Maya's mouth is desert dry. Gin and tonic, she needs more gin and tonic. She forces a long swallow, then says, "Her? You mean Arianna…"

"You're both so wild. Unpredictable. Out of control." Julian's voice has an odd, almost echoey quality to it. "This family does seem to have a problem with women with loose tongues…"

"I don't…" It feels like there's cotton in her ears.

The corners of Julian's mouth dart downward. "You all right there, Maya? You look a bit peaky."

"I'm fine, I'm just…tired." Maybe that *is* all it is. It's true she's barely slept these past few nights. She's been going going going. Fatigue's come over Maya like a thick wool blanket. Keeping her eyes open suddenly seems an impossible ask.

"You know," Julian says, tilting his head and giving Maya an appraising look. "I've always found you a rather fascinating creature. You're wild, but clever. Far too clever for Colin." Maya's having trouble following the thread of the conversation. She wants to snap to action, shoo Julian away, and get back to searching for the tape. But her limbs feel leaden, her mind dim. "But I will admit, I wasn't happy when I found out what was going on between you and my son. It was a real pain, helping him out of that mess he got himself into."

"Wait." Maya struggles through the sludge that is her mind to grasp what Julian is saying. "You? You knew about us? *You* sent me to Portas Brancas?"

"Like I told you, Maya, when you marry into this family you have to do everything you can to preserve the family name. At that time, you posed a liability. Little did I know how far you'd advance within our ranks. Maybe I would have taken a stronger tack."

Maya tries to move her hand and can't. Something is definitely not right. If she tried to push herself up from the chair and flee the room, her legs would give out beneath her. "What do you want from me?"

"The woman out there on the ice today. I need to know who she was, what she said."

"I told you, I don't know. Why do you care so much?" But somewhere, in the recesses of her consciousness, the answer is clear. *Mikey must have had co-conspirators...*

Julian ignores her question, just presses on. "So she told you nothing? What about Arianna when you met with her? Did Arianna tell you if she'd seen anyone in Mexico? Anyone from the family, I mean? What did she want you to know?"

Maya tries to think it through, but thinking has become a challenge. "She *did* want to warn me about...all of you, I guess. But that's it, that's all it was."

Maya opens her mouth. She's so very, very tired. She feels a cold wet puddle in her lap, smells the floral odor of the Sterlings' house gin. Her drink. She's spilled it.

Her heart squeezes, the fear transmogrifying into a quicksilver, molten anger that burns off her brain fog.

"You put something in my glass."

The feeling that's come over her, it's exactly how she felt when she entered the ocean waves in Miami, a big nothing heavying her consciousness.

"You were there too, weren't you? In Miami. Did you come to the W? Did you drug me there? To get me out of Marcus's life?"

Julian says nothing. He makes a face, a little chagrined, a whole lot pleased with himself. Proud to be the one who does the dirty work. "It wasn't *me*..." he says. "We have people for that sort of thing. I just gave the order."

"You *motherfucker*. You're *insane*." She remembers coming to in Miami, the photographer who knew her name, how for a moment all she knew, all she'd ever known, was rage.

"Maya, calm down now. There's no need to get so upset. Besides, do you really think anyone will believe you? You don't have a marvelous track record in this area, I'm afraid. Poor little Miss Mayhem—"

She lurches upward, shoves, and Julian goes tumbling off the armchair. "You sick fuck."

Julian sneers, humiliated at being knocked down and sprawled across the floor. Glaring at Maya, he begins to right himself.

Maya's vision is blurring, but she blinks hard, trying to keep herself awake, to keep herself here, alive. "Did you kill her? Is that why you're so desperate to figure out what I know?"

He lunges, grabbing for her. "I warned you to settle down," he spits. "But look at you; you're the same crazy as ever. The girl I had to get locked up in Miami. I remember seeing you, you know—very pretty, definitely mental—and I remember thinking, my son and I, we have the same taste in women." Julian gets a fistful of Maya's hair and begins dragging her across the room.

Maya struggles, screams, curses. Julian is so much bigger than she is. She has the gasoline of anger, but he does too. She hadn't noticed that before. But then she remembers—the knife, tucked into her pocket. She squirms around, trying to get at it while underneath his weight. She jerks up her knee, tilting him off balance before scrambling away, pulling the knife out. She gestures with the weapon, keeping it as steady as she can.

"Back off." Her voice is low and weak.

He pounces, easily ripping the knife from her hand. Smiles, *tsk*s. The sound awakens in Maya a sobering fear. Enough to spike her adrenaline.

With everything she has, she wrenches her elbow hard across his jaw, hurls herself against his chest, pushing with sufficient force to send him crashing backward. His head hits, she can hear it break the plaster beneath the wallpaper. He swats at her, grunting. She scratches his face, trying to keep him away from her, but also trying to land some blow. Weaken him, even their power, get the knife back.

But she can feel her energy draining—water through a sieve.

Whatever he put in her drink, it's growing stronger, sending a enervating gray fog over everything. Desperately she presses her fingers into his cheeks, trying to claw at his eyes, while he swats and pushes, trying to subdue her. She gets his face in her grip, thrusts his head back. Against the wall. Again and again. Hard. Hears the impact. Skull against plaster.

The knife clatters to the floor.

She bends to grab it, and once again he has her by the hair. Just as she swivels with the point, he steps away. And they both see it.

The tear in the wallpaper.

They pause, panting.

Through that tear—right down the face of a stalking tiger—a carved-out pocket in the plaster.

Inside, there's a Dictaphone. Not the big black important looking one on Harry's desk. A little plastic Fisher-Price tape-recorder. And inside that, she's sure of it, is the proof. The insurance policy. What Arianna told the people at Portas Brancas she had on tape.

Julian reaches for it.

"No!" Maya shrieks, grabbing at his arm.

"You dumb bitch." He turns on her, and there's absolutely nothing in his eyes. His big hands fly forward, push Maya with the all the power he has. She careens backward, hitting the floor with force.

"Don't," she says, but it's hard to even breathe. Her lungs feel desiccated; they ache.

She watches, helpless and weak—too weak to get up now—as he seizes the cassette player. But as he's turning back on Maya, a shadow crosses him, and his eyes open in surprise.

Soundlessly, someone else has entered the room behind Maya, but she can't see who.

Her vision blurs, eyes drifting shut. *Oh my god,* she thinks, *I'm never going to see my daughter again. He's going to kill me.* He can't let her live, now that she knows the truth.

And that's when she hears a stomach-curdling moan of surprise. An angry gurgle. And then an atmospheric disturbance as he goes down, heavy as a felled oak.

She forces open her eyes. Sees Julian, awkwardly splayed on the floor beside her.

"He's gone," a woman says. "We have to go, now." It's the woman with the dark hair, the dark eyes, the white scar curving along her face. The woman from the club, from the skating rink, the one who has been following her.

Blood pools, surrounding Julian's body.

"Who are you?" Maya manages to say.

"You can call me Caro."

"What have you done?" she gasps.

"He could have killed you." The woman, Caro, says this very evenly, as though she's flatly observing the weather. "He's done it before."

A heavy, heavy feeling is pinning Maya to the ground.

Then Caro repeats: "We have to go. Now."

Maya is aware of only a few things. A woman, Caro, watching

371

her. The smooth, hard plastic of the child's Dictaphone in her grip.

"I can't move," Maya murmurs, her voice so weak it's barely audible. Caro kneels down, assessing. Maya tries to lift herself up, pushing against the floor.

Her hand touches on something—what is that? A piece of paper maybe...

On the floor, about a foot from the pool of blood, Maya sees the picture that had been hidden in the Blake book, scrawled with song lyrics. A child's drawing. Two girls, hair of yellow, labeled Jessica and Arianna. One with green eyes, one with brown.

Same brown as in the portrait that hangs in the hall, a child whose life was about to be stolen.

Brown-eyed girl, labeled *Arianna*.

Maya reaches for the drawing. Her fingers grasp it, get it a little closer. It's not right—there's something not right about it. Her mind gropes through the fog to comprehend the picture, the truth of Arianna, who she was, and why she had to die. Maya blinks, trying to understand, but she's beyond understanding now, and the best she can do is tuck the picture in her pocket, thinking, *Tomorrow, I'll figure it all out tomorrow.*

Caro lifts Maya to her feet. She's so strong, it's like she's been training for something a long time.

Training for this.

That's the last real thought Maya has before the room fades and the gray nothing sets in.

35

Maya drifts up and above the known world. A part of her mind can see herself stumbling, dragged through the dark underground tunnels of Sterling Park. Trudging limply through falling snow, shoes drenched, body shaking as she clings to the woman. But her consciousness is flickering. What she mostly sees is him.

Harry the murderer, perched on the edge of little Arianna's childhood bed. He's telling her an old saying about the Sterlings, ominous as the warning of a dark faerie:

To be born a Sterling is to be born with death in the blood.

"When I die," he says, "this shall all be yours."

In her dreamlike state, Maya walks alongside Arianna on the last night of her life. For the first time she really gets it, understands how her birthright might feel like a curse. All the grandeur and responsibility of an illustrious family name, the spectacle and tragedy of great wealth, the bequeathal of treasure and superhuman importance.

An abundance of attention, little of it nice.

Maya is with Arianna, traversing a noisy street. Out in the

world, free but at risk, going by the name of her ill-fated friend Jessica. Someone follows her through the streets of a foreign city, at that hour when the light plays tricks on the eyes. A car backfiring one street over, a cobblestone wobbly under foot—these sounds make her jumpy, though she has no reason to think they have anything to do with her.

The lobby of the building is empty, but she sees a man dressed in black in the elevator. Maybe he's just a driver, waiting to be summoned by his employer. Still, she takes the stairs. Her rented room is only on the second floor. She no longer likes being very high up. On the stairs, she hears a noise below. But when she reaches the door, no one is trailing her. She's all alone. She sighs, relieved.

This is a mistake, though probably not the fatal one.

Whatever the fatal mistake was, she's already committed it. She knows this for sure when she unlocks the door, pushes it open. He's inside, waiting for her, and she understands that her father's warning was inadequate, could never have prepared her for this.

This is her inheritance. It would be foolish to run. In the end, she cannot escape the role in which she was cast—the noble heiress of a storied family.

But, in her last moments—Maya knows this in the deepest sinews of her brain—Arianna rose up—seething, mighty, entirely herself.

Doomed, maybe. But unwilling to go down without a fight.

36

The world is bigger, bigger than I ever knew. Almost overwhelmingly big.

In the past weeks I've been in it, all over it, and haven't had any time to write. From Portas Brancas (an elite and very secret facility for the unwell daughters of prominent families, located on Bermuda—so I have since learned) we fled in a fisherman's boat, from island to island, switching boats frequently, sleeping on concrete floors. With Caro, my savior, my guide.

She's not actually a doctor, she says. Just call her Caro.

After the Bahamas, we were in Cuba.

From Cuba, we were on a commercial ship to Mexico.

In my whole life, I think I've only really encountered about a hundred people.

In these last few weeks, I've passed thousands in the streets. I mean there are *just so many people*. And *cities*. And *things*. I want to touch everything, taste it all.

Caro is very patient with me. She's very smart too. She says they're not on our trail yet and she indulges me, like a child learning to walk, trying out sounds. Saying: "No one knows where we are; we can do whatever we want!"

Although when we arrived in Mexico, and I ordered a margarita, she said to the waitress, "Let's have that virgin," and I didn't know what that meant until I tasted it.

I think she understands it's all very tenuous for me.

The world is thrillingly big, but it's also very small.

How small?

I've been afraid to write it down. I haven't wanted to allow it to be so.

But I feel the steady gaze of Caro's dark eyes. She knows the truth, and she sees it as her duty to help me accept it. She has this rather mad dossier on the Sterlings—their affairs, their crooked dealings, etc.—which she's been showing me little by little. Even a picture of Maya Miller and Marcus, which I think she thought would please me, knowing I'm a fan. And it did, a little—I remember thinking Marcus was handsome; it follows Maya would too. But that was just a small piece of the evidence she's collected about them.

Caro thinks the truth will make me free. I'm not sure about all that, but I guess I owe it to her to try. She was the one after all who came for me at Portas Brancas, broke me out. Made it her life's mission, really.

After we left, for about forty-eight hours, we were on the move.

Then I slept a long time in a tent.

When I awoke, I came outside and found Caro sitting at a fire she'd made. It looked very much like *Survivor*, which was maybe my second- or third-favorite show, after *The Springs.* "How'd you sleep?" she asked.

I told her I slept well, which I had, but I still felt like I could sleep for several years more.

"Before we left, you said you found proof," Caro said. "Can you tell me what that proof is?"

My eyelids were very heavy. I closed my eyes and tried to taste the sea on my tongue, to be nowhere but this moment.

But I felt Caro waiting, wanting to know.

So I began to talk:

This was before they hauled me off to Portas Brancas, I was maybe fifteen, Harry away on business. The usual house arrest— not especially strict, but every member of the staff had been warned that I was a flight risk. About the tunnels and how much I liked to use them to sneak out into the night.

So, I was dreaming of some boy or other, some local boy and the songs he liked and wanting to feel him with me. I was listening to the radio and recording him songs that I thought he might like. I had run out of new cassette tapes and so I went to Harry's office, went through his old tapes, but they were all a bit roughed up. I went digging, and way down at the bottom of the drawer, I found a cassette that was still in a box.

New, I figured, though it had no plastic shrink-wrap.

So, I was back in my room; I was again listening to the radio.

I recorded Pulp and was listening for a Cranberries song that had recently been released, but I accidentally snagged a commercial, so I rewound—I thought—to begin fresh. But I must have fast-forwarded accidentally, because when I pressed play and began to listen, there was Harry's voice…and Helen's…and they were saying they were so sorry about what had happened to me.

So, I'm thinking, sorry about *what?* And why *why WHY* is Harry talking about himself in the third person? He can be grandiose, but he'd find that too, *too* American, the third person thing. But they keep talking, saying things, Harry insisting quite forcefully that they did what they had to do. That they had no other choice.

And Helen saying it was wrong, this wasn't the plan. "You know she was never meant to die. That's not what we agreed. It was only Harry we wanted out."

And Harry, my father, or the man who called himself that, said to her, "And we succeeded. He's dead, Hel. It's over. And I know we lost one girl in all this—but you have to think of *her.*"

And there I was, alone in a great house, which still I feel I shall never escape. Because of what they did. They conspired to kill my real father.

It was unthinkable. Murderers, liars, thieves, all of them.

At first, I was too sick, too scared to confront him. Instead, I went to all of those treasures I'd been hiding—all of those little items like the watch and the dagger that once belonged to Jessica's father. Little mementos. And then I remembered Lyman and what he taught me, and that's when I went looking for Harry's passport and ID, and how I knew, as soon as I held them to the light, that they were counterfeit.

That my suspicions were correct. The man who raised me,

kept me locked up so many years in that terrible big house where no one could see me, he had never been my father.

He'd been my captor.

On the beach, Caro was nodding. The light had changed. The sun going down already. It was warm but I felt cold.

She wrapped me in her arms, quieted me. "And where is the tape now? You know what a blow this would be to them, if it got out."

I nodded. "I don't want anything to do with that family anymore."

"You don't want them brought to justice?" Her dark eyes burned in the light of the fire.

"I don't know; they always seem to win, no matter what."

For a moment, I felt afraid of her.

"Why are you helping me?" I asked after a long silence. I'd been wanting to ask that a long time, ever since she helped me escape, told me she wasn't a doctor. But I was afraid to know the answer.

"Do you really not recognize me?" she asked, then. The sun was on her face. Her dark hair was wet from a swim, pushed back from her face, revealing her scar, the patch of white blistered skin across her cheek.

"You mean...from the facility?" I was afraid she thought my memory was damaged. That maybe it was.

But she said, "No, from before. Way before."

I shook my head, and I must have looked as afraid as I felt, because she said, with a little sadness I think, "I'll explain in time."

"But I want to know now. Why won't you just tell me now?" I asked her, my voice a weak tiny thing. Scared because I was starting to guess the truth.

"Because, Jessie," she said. "It's going to be hard to hear."

Jessie.

She called me Jessie.

The world around me vibrated, then came into razor-sharp focus. She meant Jessica.

"Jessica died in the fire." Though I said it confidently, I wasn't sure anymore, gazing at that peculiarly familiar face. "I'm not her."

"Yes, you are," Caro said. "You are Jessie. And I'm—"

She didn't have to say her name. *My* name. Or the name I'd worn all my life, a name that had been thrust on me, but had never felt right. They told me that I was crazy. But I knew. I knew, and now I was crying so hard I thought I might break into pieces.

But we didn't have time to talk anymore about it more, because for a while all I could do was sob, and soon after that, we had to get moving again. Later that day we learned that the Sterlings, or their people, had picked up our scent.

37

In a one-room cabin, a woman feeds magazine pages into the fiery belly of an iron stove. Caro, that is what she called herself after she...

Maya, laid out on a cot, squeezes her eyes shut at the memory of Julian roughly dragging her by the hair, the knife flying from her hand, that final awful gasping sound, his pooling blood, a gleaming pomegranate red encircling his body. How the whole room shuddered when he crashed to the floor. Maya tightens all over remembering the cache of secrets she unearthed last night. How Julian aided Mikey Blackburne in his scheme to take over Harry Sterling's identity, then killed Arianna before she could tell the world.

How Mikey let his own daughter die in order to pull off the con.

But no—that's not quite it.

Something urgent is plucking at the back of her mind. Something she was trying to put together last night in Arianna's room before she lost consciousness.

Maya pulls out the child's drawing, still folded in her pocket. Two blond girls, one with brown eyes, one with green. In the picture, the green-eyed girl is labeled "Jessica." Realization washes over Maya. Harry isn't Harry—that much was clear. But now she understands. Arianna wasn't Arianna, either.

The "Arianna" Maya met in the Iguana Bar, the one with the piercing green eyes who emailed from the handle *j_oncemoore*... She wasn't borrowing her dead friend's name. She was using her *own name*. She was *Jessie once more*. Before she died, she learned the truth, who she really was.

She was Jessica Blackburne. A pawn in her father's plot, raised to believe she was the true Sterling heiress.

No wonder she was so fucked up, so deranged by an incomprehensible violence. It wasn't *just* the murderous secret she'd discovered. It was a lifetime of brainwashing, being told she wasn't who she thought she was, she was wrong about herself. Knowing, on some level, that a girl had died so she could be named heir.

Maya's thoughts whir. Her limbs are useless and leaden as she tries to sit upright on the cot. Where is she? The light hurts her eyes, but she does her best to take in her surroundings.

Logs are stacked against the stone wall. A collection of moss and twigs is laid out under the iron stove to dry. A shelf is lined with canned foods. So, Maya thinks, this woman has been here awhile. Long enough to get comfortable. Through the window, Maya glimpses the snow-blanketed world. A predawn light. She remembers Julian on that long-ago tour mentioning that there were hunting lodges scattered in the woods that surround Sterling Park. This must be one of those.

But how far are they from the estate? Its protections, and its dangers.

Of course, who can say what dangers are present here, in this little hut. What does Maya even know about Caro? Only that she kills quickly when she wants to.

Across the room, Caro crouches at the fire. She holds her palms out to absorb the heat, then presses them over her eye sockets.

"I see it now," Caro says without turning.

Maya flushes, realizing that Caro knows she is awake. "See what?"

"What the public saw. The TV producers and magazine people, whatever. You really are breathtaking." She stares at Maya, and though Maya is usually the victor in staring contests, that gaze is too steady. "You have your own power. Not everybody does, you know. Anyway, *she* saw that in you, before I did."

It seems silly to confirm who is meant by *she*. "When we were both at Portas Brancas?"

"Yes, but she liked watching you on television, even before that."

"And she saw your power too?"

Caro's gaze drifts toward the ceiling. "Something like that."

"Did you drag me all the way through those tunnels last night by yourself?" Maya asks.

"I had to. Whatever he gave you, it really messed you up. Do you remember what happened?"

"I remember that you killed him." The words leave a strange metallic flavor in Maya's mouth. If Caro killed Julian, if she carried Maya a mile or more underground, through the night, to a secret location she's obviously occupied for some time already, then what else is she capable of? Trying to smooth her expression, Maya says, "But you had to. To get the tape."

"To get *justice*, yes. And he would've hurt you. That I was sure of. And I was already too late to stop him from hurting her..." Caro flinches. The impassive veneer is broken by a momentary flash of anger. "I wasn't about to make the same mistake again."

"What's on the tape?" Maya asks.

"I'm not sure yet. I thought we'd listen together." Caro relaxes her shoulders, catching her eye. "I want you to know you can trust me, Maya."

Of course you do, Maya thinks.

Caro lifts one of the floorboards and removes the Fisher-Price player from a little subterranean cubby. From a small tool bag, she removes a pair of batteries, slots them into place.

Maya nods. Caro holds Maya's gaze another moment. Then she hits play.

The first sound is a crescendo rock song, a man singing, "Ooh la la," over a synthy outro. Then it ends, and a man's voice abruptly takes stage midsentence. The voice Maya has come to recognize as Harry Sterling's. "And it's done. We can't undo it."

A posh female voice, precise and nasal, replies: "Not as we planned, it wasn't."

Maya shifts on her cot, says: "That's Helen."

"I know," says Caro.

"The man isn't Harry though, right?" Maya asks. "He's Mikey Blackburne."

"Maybe she was right about you," Caro replies, seeming a little impressed that Maya has figured this out on her own.

On the recording, Mikey is saying, "Could not have been avoided. It was the perfect method. Harry's paranoia was well-documented, his worry about unrest in the area. The house fire—it was the only way."

"I never thought so."

"Well, it's men's business. I understand that with our method, it was difficult to prevent collateral damage…"

"Did you try? To prevent that?"

"What I didn't count on was that Everett person—Harry's nanny. She did not behave predictably. It's almost as if… Anyway, nothing to be done now, but that's where it went screwy."

"You promised," Helen sobs. "You promised no children would be harmed."

"Duck," says Mikey, laying on a saccharine persuasion, "it was an accident. She wasn't supposed to be inside the house. But maybe…it's fate."

"Fate?" Helen sounds inconsolable. Her voice is raw and loud. "How can you say that?"

"Shush, duck, I just mean, maybe it's for the best. We can't have two little girls running around, vying to be heiress, figuring out their true identities."

The phrase *two little girls* lingers in the space.

"My god," Helen says eventually. "You *wanted* it to go this way. You wanted to make sure everything goes to *her*. I never should have trusted you."

Mikey laughs. "Too late for that now."

Helen sounds like she might be hyperventilating. "Oh my god."

"I know how you feel, duck. But we have our own sweet girl, and she can live out in the open now with what she deserves—"

The legs of a chair screech across a floor; someone walks away from the recording device and comes back.

Maya observes Caro, sees a hardening of her jaw. Her muscles are taut; she seems almost braced for an attack.

Then Mikey mentions complications with Helen's other brother, Dickie, but Helen icily declares that Dickie won't be a problem. He's usually drunk by noon.

They discuss the legal wrangling that she will soon face—declaring old Richard Sterling non compos mentis—he *has* been in decline—leaving "Harry" as the sole official heir, but in fact giving Helen half control. "Harry" will make Helen the chairwoman of the board, and they'll choose some neutral MBA type for CEO. Then there's another awkward moment when Mikey demands to know whether Helen plans to have more children, and she begins to cry.

"Duck," he says, returning to the sickly-sweet register. "I only want to know that our daughter is set up in life. That she is the heir to your father's fortune, just as you should have been."

In quite another voice, Helen says: "She will have all this and more."

Maya turns to Caro as the tape sputters out. "They said *our* daughter. Jessica Blackburne was Helen's daughter, the product of an affair with Mikey?"

The disturbed feeling inside Maya is nothing compared to what is written on Caro's face. "Yes."

"So..." Maya feels like the truth just lay down on top of her. "So that's why they did it. Switched Harrys, and switched Ariannas too."

Caro nods.

"And do you think Mikey ever meant to let her live, like they're saying on the tape?" Maya asks. "The real Arianna, I mean."

"I *know* he didn't," Caro says bitterly. "Helen is a little bit human. She may have had a soft spot for her niece. It was Mikey that wanted her gone completely. However." Caro's brown eyes reflect the rising sun, glint with triumph. "There was a nanny, like he says. Nanny Everett. She suspected something was wrong when Mikey and Jessica snuck out of the house on La Digue in the middle of the night. Harry and Arianna had only just arrived that morning, and it seemed strange that the Blackburnes would abandon their hosts so quickly...and so she picked up the sleeping child, Arianna, who she had cared for since birth, and brought her to safety. She figured she had more time to help Harry, but she was wrong. The bomb went off almost immediately. The nanny and her charge barely made it out of the house alive."

"How do you know?"

Caro closes her eyes, runs a hand down the white puckered skin of her cheek. When her eyes open on Maya again, they have a dark burn, and Maya sees it at last. The hard gaze of that portrait of Arianna as a child, the one that hung by her room. It must have been painted before the girls were switched. She sees the dishwater-blond roots showing against the dark of Caro's dye job.

Maya's lips part. "You're the real—"

"Yes," Caro says quickly, as though she doesn't want Maya to say that ill-starred name. "Nanny Everett was the only mother I ever knew. Caroline 'Caro' Everett. When she died, I started calling myself Caro, in her honor. She's the only family I remember, really, except for a handful of images of my father, by the yew tree at Sterling Park, at the beach on La Digue. And of course, memories of me and Jessica." Caro's face is wrenched with emotion. "Nanny took me far away, shielded me from my blood relations. My father, killed by his own sister and her lover, Mikey—my dad's former best friend. Nanny saved my life. She died, some years ago. And just before she died, she told me everything. She had wanted me to live as much of a normal life as possible before she told me. But she kept tabs on them, a kind of dossier, for my protection. Once I learned the truth, that's when I went to look for her."

"For Jessie," Maya whispers.

Caro nods. "For Jessica. My old friend. She was one thing I never forgot from those years."

Maya thinks of all those letters in Arianna's—no, Jessie's— room. "She never forgot you, either," she says now.

Caro seems to be gazing out the window on another world. "I know."

"The Sterlings, they murdered your father, they stole what's yours—" Maya breaks off. She feels sick. "Is that why you've been following me? Jessica gave it all to me and now you want to take it back?"

"No—"

"Please don't hurt me. I have a daughter—"

"Stop. That's not it at all. As far as I'm concerned, Jessica deserved every penny of that fortune. She suffered enough for it. It was hers to do with what she wanted. After they killed my father—and me, or so they thought—they brought her back to Sterling Park and locked her up. They brainwashed her. They told her she was Arianna, that there was no Jessica, that her father was Harry, that Mikey had died. What they did to her, it destroyed her, really. And then when she was older, when she remembered, they sent her to that place—"

"The place where you found her," Maya interrupts.

Caro nods. "I tracked her down, learned that she had been committed to an institution. It was like she was a part of me, and I wouldn't be whole until I saw her with my own eyes. To make sure she knew the truth. I owed her that, at least. And I wanted to make sure she was okay."

"But she wasn't," Maya says.

"No. They'd drugged her pretty good; she underwent these treatments. It took a while for her to regain her memories. As they came back, she told me about the evidence. The tape. She never wanted to come back here. She was too afraid, which I understand. But it seemed so wrong to let the truth die. And anyway, we knew she'd never be safe from them. Not if they knew she remembered. We had to do *something*." Caro sighs, rubs her eyes again. "And that's where you came in. She thought we could trust you. When I found out about you, she had already signed over everything ages ago. I thought she was kidding, I begged her to change it back, to leave you out of it. But she couldn't be convinced—said she knew this was only going to end one way, and she needed to make sure the power went somewhere else. Somewhere *not them*. She had this idea that maybe you'd help us. And look—you have."

Maya is not sure about that. "She was so scattered in our meeting in Mexico. I didn't realize what she was trying to tell me—"

"She was drinking again by then," Caro says, expression shuttering. "She might have been high when you met. The constant running, when we discovered they were onto us, it was a lot for her to handle."

Maya murmurs in understanding. Arianna—*Jessica*—was a tragic heroine *and* a chaos agent. If Maya's life has shown her anything, it's that both can be true at once. She knows the press feeds on her, yet she craves the attention, the power that comes from the churning center of a scandal, even as she also yearns for safety. She has chaos in her soul too.

"Jessie realized that we could approach you in Mexico," Caro is saying, "and she took my file and found a way to contact you, to lure you out. And there was no telling her no once she heard news of your wedding plans.

"Of course, I underestimated the Sterlings. They were onto

us. By the time we arrived in Puerto Vallarta, they knew we were there; they'd tried to contact her. Wanted to meet. Made threats. I saw men in black lurking in doorways, I heard them breathing on the phone lines. I told her to be careful. But she was so elated after she spoke to you, so reckless. It was like she was just, I don't know, *ready*. She said, 'Oh, it's just *Julian*, he's always been such a lackey, I'll be fine.' And because he didn't yet know that I had survived the fire, she insisted I hide. She thrust her little notebook into my arms, the one thing she cared about more than anything, and she met with him. I was on the roof the whole time, holding her words in my arms, while Julian tried to persuade her to come home, or so we thought…

"Apparently, he had another idea, and it all went wrong somehow. I don't know. When I found her… I could have stopped him if only—" Then Caro breaks off, and Maya suddenly sees the helpless, frightened child within.

"Are you okay?" Maya asks.

Caro opens her mouth to say yes, but her head wags no.

"Here," Maya says. "Come sit."

Caro approaches, sinks down onto the cot, and Maya absorbs her weight. "You smell nice," Caro says. "Isn't that funny? It's all blood money; I don't want any of it. But those little luxuries, like nice shampoo and perfume and a hot bath, I still want those, even after everything. You must think I'm weak." She lays her head on Maya's shoulder, closes her eyes. "Don't worry, I'll be all right in a minute."

"You're fine, okay? Those motherfuckers, they are *not* going to be okay. We have *proof*…"

Caro murmurs, her eyes sinking closed, "You'll help, right? We'll make the story public, and then the whole house of lies will fall. Jessica thought you'd be great at that, you know, the public relations game, and I think she was right."

Maya gently rubs Caro's cheek, the way she does for Becca. They lean back against the wall, and Maya pulls the army surplus wool blanket over them. "Rest; we can figure it all out later…"

Caro's body is growing heavy against Maya. "Just don't let me sleep too long."

———

A beating wind whips against the walls of the hunting cabin. Not a natural wind. Even half-conscious, Maya knows that's the sound of the cavalry closing in. Beyond the sounds of the helicopter, she can hear men shouting, dogs barking in the distance.

Beside her, Caro is sleeping—perhaps the first true rest of her life.

There isn't much time, Maya knows. The Sterlings will find the cottage soon.

What will they do to Caro if they discover her?

And what will they conclude about Maya, if she and Caro are found together?

Maya bolts from the warm bed. She's still wearing the jeans and the layered sweaters she put on nearly twenty-four hours ago, for the photo op on the frozen pond. She's also still wearing the old Seiko.

Mikey's watch, the one that was hidden in the little compartment in Harry's office.

Maya couldn't help herself. Maybe she is what they say. A common thief. Or maybe she just wanted to feel it on her skin.

Outside, she hears the blades whirring against the bitter morning.

She presses her face to the window, trying to see what's coming for them.

A helicopter swoops close overhead, and either doesn't see the cabin, or can't find a place to land.

The dogs are farther off, but it can't be long until they come upon the two women hiding out. She and Caro have got to move. Caro is clever, and so is Maya. They can escape; they can survive until they break the story.

But the moment Maya has that thought, she knows it's not going to play out that way. She can't leave her own daughter surrounded by them. The kind of people who will end the lives of young women to secure their fortune.

Maya removes the watch from her wrist. She presses the buttons, trying to remember how the Seiko works. How she used to set her father's alarm after his rough nights, to make sure he was up to drive her to school on time. She sets it for ten minutes from now, then changes her mind. Three minutes. Once the alarm is set, she tightens it around Caro's wrist.

As she crosses toward the door, her eye falls on the Fisher-Price Dictaphone on the floor.

She thinks of what Harry—Mikey—said to her over dinner.

That he refuses to go down without a fight, refuses to let Maya win the inheritance his daughter granted her.

Maya tells herself the tape is not safe here. That if the security team arrives before Caro can escape, they'll destroy it.

Maybe that's the reason she does it.

Or maybe it's because she's gathering ammunition for her own fight.

Anyway, it's an old habit.

Her movements are almost automatic. She presses the eject button, slips the tape in her jacket pocket, silently crosses the threshold, steels herself against the cold. Then she begins to run toward the sound of barking. Once she's put some distance between herself and the cabin, she cries for help. Throws her arms over her head, screams, "Can anyone hear me?" as loudly as possible, hoping she'll draw their attention, hoping that it will give Caro—no, hoping it will give *Arianna*—enough time to get free.

EPILOGUE

The day of Julian's burial is unseasonably bright. A gray London sky penetrated by a fine, steadily increasing sunshine. Nice light for the photographers, Maya thinks. Already they line the path of the funeral cortège.

The route was shared with the press, of course. From Sterling headquarters, to Saint John's Cathedral, to the Sterling Plot at Kensal Green. The whole thing has been planned and orchestrated to put an attractive spin on the Sterlings' recent tragedies. The botched robbery in Mexico that felled the heiress, the drunken tumble with an heirloom blade that took the chairwoman's consort. Or so the official story goes.

So far, no one has questioned this version. Either the most recent loss has stunned the press into reverence, or it all sounds too preposterous to have been invented by a flack. The realm of Sterling is apparently understood as a one-of-a-kind supernova, its density drawing to it every variety of fortune—good, bad, incomprehensible, perverse. The bizarre and sudden.

It's a sad day, but for Maya, the flattering light feels

appropriate. As the motorcade exits the basement parking lot of headquarters, she is taken by a rising optimism. She glimpses the SterlingCo building through the limousine's window and thinks of her future. It's one of those showy modern constructions that people love to hate. A massive glass and steel temple on an up-and-coming bit of real estate. Maya hadn't wanted any part of that building, what it represents. But maybe, she thinks as she adjusts the lay of her crisp black blazer—lifting her pickaxe necklace from beneath the high collar of her dress, letting it fall where anyone can see it—maybe she was thinking too small.

When she was growing up on the wrong side of the Hamptons, when she was trying to build her brand up from the basest form of stardom, New York had seemed the only goal that mattered. And Maya, hell-bent on Manhattan, forgot about the wide world.

As they travel up the road, Maya catches sight of the Thames and the Tower where, half a millennium ago, two boys with a claim to the throne were murdered. Or where they were last seen before departing their old lives to assume new names. Seems appropriate, Maya thinks, that the Sterling corporate offices come with a picturesque view of a bloody history.

Bloody history. As if there is any other kind.

Dynasties are maintained by such cruel acts. She has an intimate understanding of that now.

Across from Maya sits Gigi, wearing a high-necked black lace concoction with a cutout over the décolletage that's sure to get her in all the magazines' outfit-of-the-week roundups.

"Ready?" Gigi says as they arrive at the cathedral.

Maya smooths her hair, center-parted and slicked into a low bun, and lowers the black veil over her eyes. Then she follows Gigi onto the sidewalk, into a phalanx of Sterling family members, headed by Helen, with Marcus and Colin at her heels. Behind them are Lance and Ian. Eva, Gigi, and Maya making up the rear.

The formidable Harry Sterling is absent from the solemn occasion. No one seems to find it odd. It's known he never got along very well with his sister's husband, which is close enough to the truth Maya's uncovered. He must have figured he'd do better waiting out the coming months in a country with no extradition agreement with the UK. Just before he left, she stood over him while he signed official documents validating Arianna's will on behalf of himself, her closest relative, and the entire SterlingCo board.

"How's your *Lear*?" he muttered to no one in particular as he signed the papers. "'Tigers, not daughters. What have you performed?'"

He wasn't asking for a reply. Smiling, Maya said, "Nice cuff links."

"Helen was right about you," he growled as Marcus and Colin escorted him from the room. And then he was gone.

With a brave squaring of her shoulders, Helen leads the family through the photographers crowding the cathedral steps. Helen's little black veil is similar to Maya's. It only covers her eyes, leaving those plump lips and sculpted cheekbones visible for the cameras.

Once Helen is seated, the service begins. Rory gives the

eulogy: Julian Maxwell Lambert, great father, sportsman, writer, wit. Descended from the royal lines of Europe. Rory doesn't mention that Julian married into a notably patriarchal dynasty, whose own son is nevertheless known by his maternal grandfather's surname.

Colin—good Colin, the family conscience, handsome as ever in his own black suit—speaks of Julian as the dashing figure he remembers from childhood, athletic and urbane. He speaks, too, of Julian in his final days. How hard he took the loss of his niece, and how, while the family holed up in Sterling Park, he spun wonderful yarns about her life even as he drank heavily to mute the pain. Julian and Arianna had a special connection, Colin explains—both writers, both great tellers of tales. It was perhaps inevitable that he'd cope by self-medicating. And that when there were reports of an intruder on the estate—which proved false—he became protective of his family, started acting like a vigilante and carrying a knife.

As Maya sits in the pew, she reflects how true this is. Arianna—or at least, the girl he knew by that name—had a tale to tell. And Julian, who strove terrifically all his life to be something he was not, tried to smother her story, and in so doing, silenced her forever.

In the days since Julian's death, Maya's had to spin some of her own stories.

After Maya's "escape" from her mysterious abductor in the woods, she was questioned for several hours. She told the authorities all she remembered, but of course, that wasn't much. After all, she had been drugged—the tox screen confirmed it.

Agent Cetin proved a true friend to the Sterlings. She's convinced the various investigating authorities that it's better to publicly go along with the story of Julian's "accidental" death, while performing a cursory review of the evidence that an intruder—caught on security cameras entering Sterling Park during the ice skating—killed Julian. They have no name for her. And the authorities, pressured by Sterlings' people and not wanting to look like fools, kept this intruder, and Julian's precise cause of death, to themselves.

No one knows that the intruder was in fact the one who saved Maya's life. Nor do they know her real identity.

After several hours of interviews, Maya was allowed to clean up. Shower off her ordeal. Against Colin's wishes—by then he wanted to get the hell out of there, bring his family home to Manhattan—she demanded an audience with Helen, who was steely as ever but asked no hard questions. She did not, for instance, inquire about Maya and Julian being alone together in Arianna's room. The ripped wallpaper, the empty hiding place. Was she being tactful, Maya wondered? Or did she already, on some level, know the reason why?

What Helen wanted to know, she said, was the nature of Julian's final moments. His mood, what he was thinking about. And Maya told her that they had discussed the poetry of William Blake, and the nature of madness, and that they had shared a drink. That the drinks were probably a little too strong. She suggested to Helen that Julian had attempted to protect Maya when the intruder attacked. With punched precision, Maya added that she knew Julian would do *anything* for the Sterlings. That he had, in the past, done certain deeds in their interest, which could not be mentioned in any official report.

To protect the family, Maya emphasized. And its secrets.

Having said all that, Maya simply leveled her gaze at Helen, so Helen would understand what Maya meant by *secrets*, what she meant by *protect*. That Maya knew the truth and would tell the world, if necessary.

Helen had lifted her chin, then glanced away in apparent acceptance of these terms.

For Julian was the one who did the dirty work—he knew it, and she knew it. He did things to keep secrets that could not be told, and with his passing, many of those secrets would disappear forever. A blood sacrifice had been made, order restored.

And Maya, thinking back to Helen's unmade face that first night in Arianna's bedroom, knew that Helen felt the sting of that sacrifice more than anyone.

"Did Julian know?" Maya had asked. "That Jessica was your daughter?"

"He knew that I had an old connection with Mikey, though not the details. I'd loved Mikey since I was a kid. He was so charming, so exciting. My father forbade it, of course. For all their business together, he never trusted the Blackburnes. He said they were pirates, and I suppose that's the literal truth if you go far back enough. The first time I was pregnant by Mikey, Richard forced me to have an abortion—it wasn't even legal then, and they did a bad job of it, that's why it was so hard, later. I thought Marcus would be my only child but then, on a trip to La Digue... And I wasn't about to give it up, that time. We decided it would be safer for her to be raised with him in Seychelles— invented a story about a local woman, sent her away once the baby arrived, told everyone the mother had died in childbirth. I wanted to bring our baby home, pass her off as Julian's, but Mikey insisted. And Mikey... Well, it was always Mikey, even when I wanted to kill him."

"Did Julian? Want to kill him?"

"He tried once."

"That fight in the bar," Maya recalled. "The one that made the papers."

"Julian was never much of a strategist; he never could see very far up the road. Going to Mexico to confront Jessica like he did... It was ill-advised, to say the least. He'd always been resentful of the arrangement. He understood it was good for us, that it gave us control we'd never have otherwise. But I think deep down he knew the truth. Why I'd been so willing to cast out my niece in favor of the little Blackburne girl. He just convinced himself of what he wanted to believe. He was always a great fabulist, my Julian. He so *wanted* to be a Sterling."

Maya feels a brief burst of compassion for Julian. Didn't she have a similar dream as a little girl holding an out-of-date *Vanity Fair* in an empty beach house?

"He buried his anger—mostly. When it appeared, it was terrifying."

After that they had nothing further to discuss. Maya left Helen and returned to her room, to her own precious daughter, cradled the baby to her chest, too relieved to cry.

———

Once the service is concluded, the coffin is ferried back down the aisle, the cathedral steps, into the hearse, so that the cortège can proceed to Kensal Green. When Marcus moves to take his seat in the lead limousine, Maya steps in his path. She's been avoiding him, whatever conversations he'll try to force her into, but she responds to his searching expression with a firm, "Go with your wife," and pushes past him into the back seat of the car, where she sits beside Colin, opposite Helen.

They ride in silence, London streets passing through tinted windows.

As they approach the cemetery's gated entrance, Colin adjusts his black coat. Clears his throat. "I'm going to say this to you now, Helen, and then I'm never going to say it to you again. If you ever, ever put my family—my wife, my child—at risk, I will destroy what's left of your terrible line. The world will know—immediately—what you and Mikey did. What Julian did to Arianna. But you—you won't be around for the fallout. Because, Helen, I will murder you myself if I have so much as an inkling of you threatening what's mine."

Helen's pale eyes widen. They flash at Maya—is she shocked Maya told Colin everything she's learned about his family? But she shouldn't be surprised, really. Maya and Colin have always made a good team. She saw his potential, even when his family failed to. She went to him as soon as she left Helen, that terrible day in Silver House after Maya returned from the cabin in the woods. The way he stood by her, when Harry returned and shot up his own chandelier, she knew she could go to him for anything. And now he knows who to put his trust in. Maya grips Colin's hand and smiles defiantly at Helen. They've arrived at the family plot. Everyone is waiting for the widow to emerge, throw dirt upon her husband's coffin.

After a pause, Helen's avid gaze moves off Maya, to the graveyard beyond. She elbows open the door, saying, "All right then, Colin."

———

Once Julian's coffin has been lowered into the earth and the bagpipes begin their doleful wail, Helen drifts off to put flowers on the new headstone that reads *ARIANNA STERLING*. Colin and Gigi go to pay their respects to their parents' graves. Marcus walks away from Eva and his boys, lighting a cigarette as he approaches Maya.

"Want one?" he asks.

"Sure."

"Thank god that's over," Marcus says. He's been trying to get close to her these past few days, but she's successfully sidestepped him until now.

"Yeah." Maya exhales a cloud of smoke, puts her arms tightly around her own middle. "I'm really sorry for your loss."

"Thank you. He was my father, and I will miss him. But all the same, I never knew him really. He was a stranger to the end."

Maya wants to believe this—that Marcus doesn't know his father well enough to think him capable of killing Arianna. Or his mother well enough to know that the girl he called Arianna wasn't really his cousin at all, but rather his half sister.

And having known her own father—a man who fancied himself an outlaw—a little too well, Maya thinks Marcus may be lucky to regard Julian as a bit of a mystery. She exhales, and says, "You better get back to your wife. She'll start to wonder."

Eva and the boys are walking between graves now. She's not looking their way, but she must be aware that Marcus and Maya are talking. She knows what happened between them in the past—at least the events leading up to Miami. Will she suspect a more recent trespass? "Let her wonder," Marcus says.

"Marcus, don't—"

"Maya. You have to talk to me. I meant what I said in the library. It's always been you."

Her hand shakes, the cigarette emitting a tremble of smoke in the air between them. "I don't want to have this conversation."

"But you're in charge now," he says with eager force. "You can do whatever you want. And I'll show you how. I know how it all works. You don't need Colin. You can be at the helm, and I'll be your loyal second-in-command. Let's do it, Maya. It always should have been us."

"Should it have been?" It's not that Maya doesn't feel it—the buzzy madness that rises at the first sign of Marcus's attention. But it doesn't have the same power anymore. "I don't think you understand."

"Understand what? Your ridiculous loyalty to my sweet fool of a cousin? Just because he's Becca's father? *Is* he Becca's father, Maya?"

Maya flicks ash from the end of the cigarette and risks looking him in the eye. "You still don't get it, do you? What you did. I'm not talking about the fucking tabloid covers. I'm talking about—" She breaks off, searching for the words. "You know, Marcus, I'm just like any other girl. I don't want anything insane. I want to be happy and loved. Does that sound boring? Used to sound boring to me too. Same old story. My dad was a rogue, so I loved rogues. That was a pattern you fit into perfectly. I mean, you weren't the first; don't think you were. But you will be the last."

Maya drops her cigarette, puts it out with her toe. She gazes up at Marcus, his broad handsome face, thinks of the deals they'd make if she took his offer, the conversations they'd have, the hundreds of hotel rooms they'd occupy together over a lifetime. He has those pugilist's hands, a pugilist's nose. There is so much raw energy in him, and she wants to drink it up. But when she looks at his face now, she sees something she didn't before. He looks like his father, and she can see his father in his features, the low simmer of violence that erupted when threatened. It's not that she thinks Marcus would harm her, not exactly. But he has chaos in his soul, and so does she. Together, they would destroy.

"I love you. And you love me," Marcus says. "I know you do."

The woman Maya was two years ago would happily trade everything she owned, her very future, to hear those words. To live out of a suitcase with Marcus anywhere in the world. Her heartbeat is expectant, her skin is yearning for his touch. She loves him, why deny it?

But it's only one kind of love. The desperate kind. And why choose that, when she has something better?

"Not like that I don't." She controls her facial features. Offers a gloved hand for Marcus to shake. After a moment, he does. Eva is walking back in their direction now. Maya makes a show of taking a big step away from Marcus and remembers what Eva said that night outside Harry's office. That you don't need to tell all your secrets—there's more power in letting people wonder. "I am very much looking forward to working productively on furthering SterlingCo's interests with you." She inhales sharply and adds, "Let's have our assistants set up a working lunch in New York next time you're there."

As she walks away, she spots Colin approaching from the other direction. They reach each other, he puts an easy arm around her waist, and together they move toward the limousine. The ceremony is over; they can travel to the airfield where their daughter is already on board the private jet, protected by their security detail and Maya's aunt Rebecca, who flew to England as soon as she heard about the intruder and Maya's ordeal in the woods. From now on, she'll travel with Maya, go where Maya goes, and take care of the baby.

The world is full of threats, and Maya only trusts her own people with her daughter.

As she stands beside Colin, posing for a few photos—wearing a sad, supportive smile, not letting the pain of her pinched toes show on her face—it comes to her, one of her favorite memories of her own father. It was after another funeral, the oldest of his uncles. Maya's dad hadn't shown up for the service, but he arrived at the cemetery to accept his sister Rebecca's loving exasperation for missing the whole thing. She wasn't really annoyed. She knew what he'd done—he'd taken the few hundred dollars their uncle had left him in his will and gone to the casino. And for once he won big. Everyone could see by the way he swaggered up, took his daughter's hand, and said, "Life is for the living. Let's go get ice cream, kid."

As they walked along the beach in Amagansett, licking their mint chip cones, letting the waves surge over their toes, her father said, "You want to know the secret to winning?"

Little Maya had said yes, she most definitely did. And her dad showed her his empty palm. Then, with a shake of the wrist, an ace of hearts was in his fingertips. "Always keep an ace up your sleeve."

"Daddy," Maya said. "You're not a cheat, are you?"

"The card up the sleeve, it's not so much that you're *going* to play it. It's more that you play better, knowing you have it there."

Right now, back at Sterling Park, new portraits are being installed. In memory of Arianna and Julian, and to celebrate the newest additions to the Sterling family, Maya and Becca. Each of these has a special silver plaque engraved by a silversmith in New York. These are Maya's gift to the family—she's ordered them special.

And behind each silver plaque is a thumb drive—a recording of the tape, of Mikey admitting he had Harry killed and assumed his identity, of Helen saying she knew all about it—so even if there is another protocol 202, and Maya can't get to a safety deposit box, she'll still have access to her ace, glinting under those heroic depictions of Sterlings, some still breathing, some dead and gone.

———

The last of the day's sun breaks through the clouds as Colin and Maya's limousine departs the cemetery for the airport. The sky overhead is shudderingly huge, a reminder that there is no such thing as total safety from the threats of this world. Maya gazes across the police barrier, the crowds gathered on the patchy fields beyond the cemetery gates, as though she'll see her there.

But no. If she was there, she wouldn't allow Maya a glimpse; that would be too much of a risk. And somehow, Maya thinks that if Caro were close by, she'd know. She has this connection with Caro she can't explain. Almost a sixth sense. Improbable as it is, she thinks they have some things in common. Like Maya, like Jessie, Caro is a survivor. Solitary at heart and very hard to cage.

As the limousine moves through the city, Maya thinks about the true heiress. The real Arianna. Out there, forever on the run.

She saved Maya's life, and Maya gave her enough time to get away. If she wanted to come forward, she could. Even without the tape, she could tell her story. Plenty of people would believe her. Maya doesn't think she will, though. Caro wanted some kind of justice, but above all, she seemed to want to get free from the curse of the Sterlings.

Jessica and Arianna both have the blood of the Sterling family in their veins. They were marked from birth with a formidable destiny. But Maya is a different species. Her life is her own, to do with as she pleases. A nobody from nowhere, with no past and no predetermined future. A little thief who learned early that if you want something, you just have to take it, and that it's easier to run the table when you hold a secret ace.

Now Maya has her ace. And if she needs to play it, she will.

She's just that kind of girl.

READING GROUP
GUIDE

1. What qualities does Maya have that make her a successful reality TV star? How do those qualities transfer over to being a Sterling?

2. What do you make of the Sterling family? Would you want to be part of their empire? What are the pros and cons?

3. Imagine you received a pickaxe necklace from your in-laws. How would you react? If you were in Helen's shoes, how would you go about handling the "Maya situation"?

4. Compare and contrast Colin and Marcus. How are they similar? How are they different? Who do you think is right for Maya?

5. Silver House is a grand estate with a storied history. Would you live at Silver House? Why or why not? What part of the estate would you be most excited about? Least excited?

6. How would you describe Arianna? Do you think there are marked similarities between her and Maya?

7. Which Sterling family member do you most relate to? Why?

8. What do you make of Maya's final decision at the end of the novel? What would you do if you were in her shoes?

A CONVERSATION
WITH THE AUTHOR

The Sterling lifestyle is one of extreme wealth and power. How did you go about bringing this lavish and corrupt family to life?

All good writing is in the specific well-observed detail, so I hope I have made the Sterlings real—and their lifestyle and status believable—by showing what they love, covet, and obsess over, what they believe themselves entitled to, and how they treat other people. Upstairs/downstairs stories are threaded through some of my favorite movies and novels, and I think the lesson of those, at least craft-wise, is that the comparison is what reveals the individual, what reveals the other—that you know who people are by how they treat the less powerful people around them.

Which character was the most fun to write? The most difficult?

I loved writing Maya! To me, she's easy to root for and fun, and she has a nose for BS. She has access to a lot of remarkable experiences, but she's also frank and at times insecure and relatable in any number of ways.

Julian was probably the toughest—he was the character who

I knew what he had to do plot-wise, but I didn't initially under-stand *him*. The thing about him being a writer started out as just a little quirky texture, but it ultimately felt like the key to his motivations—he's a fabulist, he's committed to a somewhat delusional version of life, and he can convince himself of anything.

Maya sure does go through all the twists of turns of Sterling-land throughout the novel. What does your thriller-writing process look like?

In my experience, the process is a bit harrowing too! I was figuring out how it all fit together late in the process, which is probably good on some level—I was still able to surprise myself! But sometimes I did feel a bit like Arianna—confused, fright-ened, lost in a scary house, just trying to get out.

What do you want readers to take away from this thriller?

I hope they are entertained and infuriated and nostalgic for a time twenty years ago, which was honestly kind of a horror show, but it was the horror show of my earliest adulthood and thus a period I find rich for revisiting. And also something of a roller coaster.

There are so many fun aspects to the book—the locked-room estate, the devious family, the extreme luxury. How did you balance that all across the novel?

I never really thought of any of those as separate—the luxury is part of the Sterlings' power, and part of the way they maintain their power is control. And the estate itself is an expression of the family—an intentional symbol to the world of their stature, but also unintentionally, as with many people, the house reflects the buried and twisted parts of their personal histories and psyches.

You previously have written young adult novels. Why the switch into adult thrillers? What do you love most about the category?

I love writing young adult books because the characters and readers are living in the automatic intensity of teenagerhood, that all-or-nothing age. I heard someone say once that coming-of-age novels are often novels of entrapment—they are about people who don't yet have autonomy—so I see a kind of through line there. But I like a little edge in what I read and what I write, so doing a thriller for grown-ups appealed to me as an opportunity to really find that edge in myself.

What are you reading now?

It's hurricane season, and I guess for that reason I just dug into Jesmyn Ward's *Salvage the Bones*, a stunning novel set during Hurricane Katrina that has been on my TBR pile for ages. It actually just occurred to me that that's the era of *A Girl Like Us*—and it reminded me that I was bartending the night before Katrina hit, and a customer came in and said, "After tomorrow, there won't be a New Orleans." I remember standing there, not believing what I'd heard. Perhaps that was an overstatement on the part of that person—but not really, not in the long view. I hope we are closer to believing it now.

ACKNOWLEDGMENTS

What good fortune to get to make books in such good company! Thank you, Lexa Hillyer and Jenna Brickley, for being such fun and brilliant collaborators. Thank you, MJ Johnston, for believing in this project and for being such a solid gold editor and always pushing it to be the best version of itself. Thank you, Stephen Barbara and everyone at Inkwell, and Celia Johnson and Maria Gagliano at Pub Pros, for early, sure-handed shepherding. Thank you, Anna Venckus, Cristina Arreola, and Liv Turner, for getting *A Girl Like Us* all dressed up to meet the world with the most pitch-perfect Y2K inspo ever. Thank you, Erin Fitzsimmons for the breathtaking cover. Gratitude to Alyssa Reuben, Darin Strauss, and most especially to Martin McLoughlin, who knows where all the bodies are buried.

ABOUT THE AUTHOR

Anna Sophia McLoughlin lives in Litchfield County with her family, where she teaches creative writing and profiles artists and designers for various publications.